for Felix

C.F.

Yes We Can!

Text copyright © 2006 by Sam McBratney

Illustrations copyright © 2006 by Charles Fuge

Manufactured in China.

For information address HarperCollins Children's Books, a division of HarperCollins Publishers,
1350 Avenue of the Americas, New York, NY 10019.

Library of Congress Catalog Card Number: 2006929497

ISBN 10: 0-06-121515-5 - ISBN-13: 978-0-06-121515-5

1 2 3 4 5 6 7 8 9 10

Originally published in Great Britain by Puffin Books

First U.S Edition, HarperCollins Publishers, 2007

Yes We Can!

Sam McBratney & Charles Fuge

![] HarperCollins*Publishers*

Little Roo was chasing leaves one windy day.
Roo's friends, Country Mouse
and Quacker Duck, were waiting
to play with him.

"Let's make a big pile of leaves," said Roo.
"A mountain of leaves," said Country Mouse.
"The biggest ever seen!" quacked Duck.

They began to collect up all the leaves they could find
but making a leaf mountain is hard work,
so after a while they stopped for a rest.

While they were resting, Little Roo
said to his friend Quacker Duck,
"I know something you can't do.
You can't jump over a big, big log."

"Yes I can,"

said Quacker Duck.

Quacker Duck tried as hard
as she could,
  but little ducks aren't
  made to jump over
  big, big logs.

Country Mouse thought it was
so funny when Quacker Duck
  fell over the fallen-down tree.

"Don't you **laugh** at me!" said Quacker Duck
to Country Mouse. "I know something you
can't do. You can't **float** on a **puddle**."

"**Yes I can,**"

said Country Mouse.

So Country Mouse tried to float on the puddle . . .

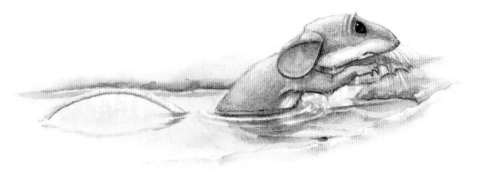

but a little mouse isn't really made for f l o a t i n g.

Little Roo thought it was **so** funny when Country Mouse crawled out of the water, soaking wet and dripping.

"Don't you **laugh** at me!"
said Country Mouse.
"I know something **you** can't do.
You can't **catch** your own tail."

"Yes I can,"

said Roo.

Roo tried as hard as he could
to catch his own tail,
but his tail would not
be caught.

It was too far away.

Country Mouse
and Quacker Duck
laughed and laughed
as Roo ran around
in circles.

"Don't you dare laugh at me!" cried Roo.
"Well, you laughed at me!" said Mouse.
"And you laughed at me!" said Duck.

No one
was
happy.

No one was happy because each
had made fun of someone else
and someone else had made fun of them.

Instead of making the biggest mountain
of leaves that anyone had ever seen, they
looked as if they might all go home in a

bad mood.

Little Roo's mother came over
   to see what the fuss was about.
"I'm not surprised the three of
   you look so grumpy," she said.
"Nobody likes to be
   laughed at!"

It was true.
No one likes to be laughed at.
"Why don't you show each other
what you **can** do?" said Roo's mom.

Roo cried, "I can jump over a big, big log!"

He hopped up and over the fallen-down tree.

"That's **really** good **jumping**,"
the others said.

"I can float on a puddle," said Quacker Duck, taking to the water with ease.

"That's **really** excellent floating!" the others agreed.

And when Country Mouse caught his own tail,
Little Roo and Quacker Duck
thought that his
tail-catching was
the best they had
ever seen.

"There now," said Roo's mother,
"can we all be friends again?"
Little Roo, Country Mouse, and
Quacker Duck looked at one another.
They were all thinking the same thing . . .

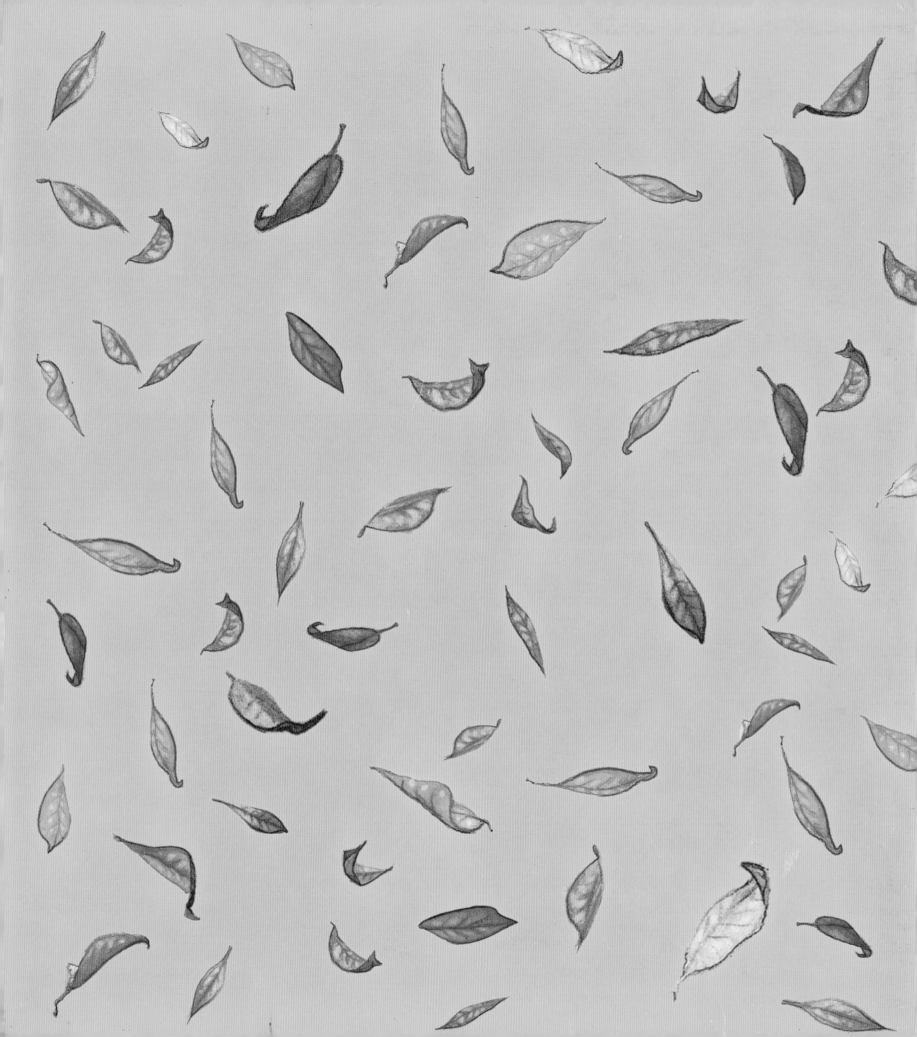

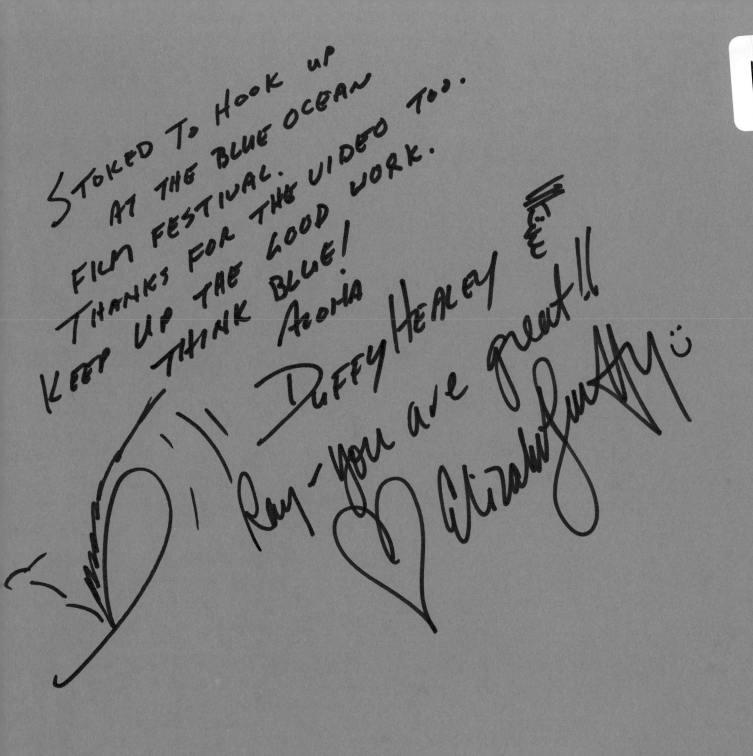

Stoked to hook up
at the blue ocean
film festival.
Thanks for the video too.
Keep up the good work.
Think blue!
Aloha

Duffy Healey

Ray - you are great!!
Elizabeth Murphy

Dedication

We would like to dedicate this book to

our children

Lilianna & Thiesen Healey

and to our niece and nephew

Jane & Peter Healey

and to all the children around the world.

The Front Cover - Top Row: Alexandra Cousteau, David de Rothschild, Dr. Jane Goodall and Dr. Supraja Dharini, Isabel Lucas, Kelly Slater, Robert Kennedy, Jr., Ziggy Marley

Lower Row: Dr. Sylvia Earle, Jack Johnson, Karina Petroni, Wallace J. Nichols, Ted Danson, Daryl Hannah & Captain Paul Watson

The Back Cover - Top Row: Greg McCormack, Stephan Lessard, Joel Harper, Amy Tan, Terry Tamminen & Arnold Schwarzenegger, Wyland

Middle Row: Ray Huff, Sea Turtle, Pierce Brosnan & Jeff Pantukhoff, Slater Jewell-Kemker & Jean Michel Cousteau, Ahmed Pérez, Greg MacGillivray

Lower Row: Scarlet Rivera, Louie Psihoyos, Bonnie Monteleone, Garrett Dutton (G Love), Turtle & Diver, Joanne Tawfilis

Healey
Publishing,
Inc.

Published by Healey Publishing, Inc.

(949) 498-5114

www.SeaVoices.com • www.Facebook.com/SeaVoices

ISBN 978-0-578-06033-0

Library of Congress Control Number: Copyright Pending 2010

Built and created with passion in San Clemente, California, U.S.A

Printed in Canada

Working toward a sea change

Table of Contents

1 .... Dedication

2-3 .... Copyright & Company Information

4-7 .... Table of Contents

8-9 .... Introduction

10-11 .... Daryl Hannah

12-13 .... Prince Khaled bin Sultan

14-16 ...... Dr. Sylvia Earle

17 .... Terry Tamminen

18-19 ...... Alexandra Cousteau

20-21 ...... Ted Danson

22 .... Robert Sulnick

23 .... Sam Waterston

24 .... Robert Ballard, Ph.D.

25 .... Lt. Don Walsh

26-27 ...... Jason Mraz

28-29 ...... Supraja Dharini, Ph.D.

30-32 .... David de Rothschild

33 .... Shepard Fairey

34-35 .... Robert Kennedy, Jr.

36-37 .... Ray Huff

38-39 .... David Guggenheim, Ph.D.

40-41 ...... Jack Johnson

42-43 ...... Roz Savage

44-45 ...... Pierce & Keely Brosnan

46-47 ...... Isabel Lucas

48 .... Serge Dedina, Ph.D.

49 .... Paul Naudé

50-51 .... Amy Tan

52 .... Anne Earhart

53 .... Stefan Lessard/Dave Matthews Band

54-55 .... Julie Packard

56-58 ...... Jeffrey Short, Ph.D.

59 .... Prince Jigbenu Bolaji Akran

60 .... Kate Walsh

61 .... Garrett Dutton/G. Love

62-63 ...... Kelly Slater

64 .... Yoko Ono

65 .... Ed Begley, Jr.

66 .... David Chokachi

67 .... Shaun Tomson

68 .... Pierre André Senizergues

69 .... Tanna Frederick

70 .... Gregor Hodgson

71 .... Derek Sabori

72-73 .... Paul Kelway

74-75 .... María José González

76-77 .... Luke Tipple

78-79 .... Mati Waiya

80 .... Scarlet Rivera

81 .... Ziggy Marley

82-83 ...... Joanne & Fouad Tawfilis

84-86 ...... Dr. Wallace J. Nichols

87 .... Dr. David Jenkins

88-89 ...... Chris del Moro

90 .... James Pribram

91 .... Holly Beck

92 .... Grif Alker

93 .... John John Florence

94-95 ...... Zoltán "Zoli" Téglás/Ignite

95 .... Nick Hernandez/Common Sense

96 .... Wang Niandong

97 .... Izzy & Danielle Paskowitz

98-99 ...... Christopher Gavigan

100-101 ... Jo Ruxton

102 .... Ross Thomas

103 .... Conrad Humphreys

104 .... Dr. Stephen Leatherman

105 .... Frank Scura

106-107 ... Atossa Soltani

108-110 ... Captain Paul Watson

111 .... Steve Roest

111 .... Laurens de Groot

112 .... Anna Cummins & Marcus Erikson

113 .... Stephan Soechtig

114-115 ... Gary Petersen

116-117 ... Louie Psihoyos

118 .... Jean Beasley

119 .... Carl Safina

120-121 ... Jackie Savitz

122-123 ... James Balog

124 .... Frances Beinecke

125 .... Wyland

126-127 ... Fabien Cousteau

128-129 .. Debbie Levin

130 .... Kathleen Frith

131 .... Michael Muller

132-133 .... Tristan Bayer

134-135 ... Boris Worm

136-137 .... Jerry Schubel

138-139 ... Manuel Maqueda

140 .... Malloy Brothers

141 .... Emmett Malloy

142-143 .. Doug Tompkins

144-145 .. Ahmed Perez

146 .... Bob McKnight

147 .... Joey Santley

148 .... Dianna Cohen

149 .... Captain Charles Moore

150 .... Adam Gardner

151 .... Joel Harper

152-153 ... Andrew Sharpless

154 .... Dan Stetson

155 .... Monika Steinberg

156 .... María Celeste Arrarás

157 .... Gregory Harrison

158 .... John Picard

159 .... Kama Dean

160 .... Shannon Mann

160-161 ... Charles Hambleton

162 .... Daniela Sea

163 .... William J. Cooper, Ph.D.

164 .... Coco Nogales

164 .... Timmy Curran

164 .... Raimana Van Bastolaer

165 .... Tom Servais

165 .... Peter "PT" Townend

166 .... Fernando Aguerre

167 .... Karina Petroni

168 .... Greg MacGillivray

169 .... Donovan Frankenreiter

170-171 ... Slater Jewell-Kemker

172-173 ... Chris Jordan

174-175 ... Q'orianka Kilcher

176 .... Ric O'Barry

177 .... Lincoln O'Barry

177 .... Ramon Cardena & Judith Pascual

178 .... Captain Kurt Lieber

179 .... Captain Brett McBride

180-181 ... Greg McCormack

182-183 ... Thomas Peschak

184 .... Tony Hawk

185 .... Ken Jordan/The Crystal Method

186-188 .. Jeff Pantukhoff

188 .... Garry Brown

189 .... Bonnie Monteleone

190-191 ... Acknowledgements

192 .... Closing

Introduction

If you were to ask most people to shut their eyes and visualize the ocean, and then ask them to describe their thoughts of what first came to their minds, most of them would describe a beautifully magical place filled with happy visions, a vast edgeless sea of blue green beauty conjuring up memories or dreams of swimming in the sparkling water, and diving under to a serene place where there are no worries. The ocean has given us a place of peace, and it gives us joy. Some of us enjoy sailing or boating, while others surf, dive, snorkel, water-ski, fish, or simply relax and sunbathe. The beach is a place where all of our senses are reborn from the sound of the waves, the smell of suntan lotion, the taste of the salt water on our lips, and the sight of all its majesty. The ocean has given us life, and we actually owe nearly two out of every three breaths we take to the ocean. We are also fed and employed from the ocean. When we think of vacations, it is the number one place people dream of going. The ocean has given us so much.

It is hard to believe a place that seems so huge and infinite could actually be hurting. The ocean has sustained us for nutrition for tens of thousands of years, and it has provided us with jobs and pleasure. Nearly one billion people rely on fish as their main source of protein and sustenance everyday, and hundreds of millions of others depend on the ocean as their way of life, and a way to make ends meet. There are fishermen, the people who make and mend their nets, eco tourism, water sports, restaurant owners, and surfboard makers to beach ware, hoteliers to boat makers, the list goes on.

The ocean has given us so much, and we have taken so much from the ocean, and it's time to give back because what we have thought for so many years, that the ocean is an infinite inexhaustible resource, we are finding out is untrue. The ocean is suffering from a wide variety of issues from over-fishing, ocean acidification, sea-level rise, shark finning, global warming, plastic pollution, detrimental fishing techniques, coral bleaching and coral reef destruction from dynamiting and other factors, toxic waste, and more. The good news and the bad news of what the ocean ails from is the exact same thing . . . it suffers from human beings not treating it right. The bad news is the ocean needs a lot of help; the good news is we can actually help the ocean, and as Ted Danson would say "It's not to late to turn the tide and create a sea change."

Most of us over a certain age have memories of going to the ocean as young people and having the most carefree time of our lives. Then there are others that dream of doing just that. Some of the best times of my life have been surrounded by going to the beach or swimming in the ocean, or sailing with my brother and my father. I remember collecting thousands of sea shells with my mother, especially sand dollars and abalones, and diving under the crystal clear waves with all of the schools of fish. To me there is nothing better than taking a long swim and then letting the sun dry the salt water on my skin. The ocean was and always will be my place of solitude, yet the smashing of the large waves can give you a positive charge, if the waves are too big it can create fear, but no matter what the sea is always a place I respect. I was lucky enough to grow up mostly in Laguna Beach, California on the Pacific Ocean, and the ocean has always been a part of my life.

Duffy on the other hand grew up in Brooklyn, New York, and also had some of the best memories of his life swimming in the ocean, on the East Coast in the Atlantic Ocean. Only he vividly remembers how dirty the water was on a semi-regular basis. He says that before they would go in the ocean they would ask the others how it was on that particular day first. If they said it was good, they were in luck as long as there were not too many jellyfish, if they said it was rough or dirty on the beach, they would swim on the bay side, or vice versa. He recalls sometimes not even caring and getting in to cool off anyway; he says they would move their arms in swanlike motions to skim away the trash or dirty foam. When he was in junior high school he moved to La Jolla, California and he was amazed at how clean and wonderful the water was there.

Several things happened along the way that changed the way we both felt about the ocean, and that is what lead us to create this book. It was really a combination of events that took place over a couple decades, and then a wake up call that summoned us both at the same time. One of the events that started me off questioning if the ocean was as clean and safe as it was made out to be was when I was in my twenties, and I went to the beach in Newport Beach, California not far from my home and ended up getting a severe staff infection. I had shaved my underarms just before I went to the beach and the water was polluted although the beach was not closed, and my skin had not healed from shaving, and I got extremely sick as a result. Staff can be very dangerous if you don't take care of it. In fact, my grandfather stubbed his toe while fishing in the water on a rock, and he too got staff. Only he did not take care of it, and he ended up losing his entire leg from an infection that started in his toe. Then Duffy recalls moving to Manhattan Beach, a part of Los Angeles, in California when he was just out of college. He says the water there was different than it was in La Jolla years before. His favorite sport is surfing, only surfing in what they call the Santa Monica Bay can be a real hazard. He had flashbacks of the dirty foam he remembered as a kid, and lots of his friends would get upper respiratory infections and chronic bronchitis.

Fast-forward to several years ago, Duffy and I had began to recount the different stories of our memories that we both had of the ocean, and we realized that the baseline for what the ocean was like when we were both kids growing up had changed to what it is now like for our own children. This worried us. I started to wonder when was the last time I had actually seen a sand dollar or an abalone shell, and I realized it had been many years. Now rather than seeing schools of fish in the waves, there are only a few. I remembered diving down 20 feet as a kid and seeing the ocean floor from even higher up than that. Now when we are in waist high water we consider it clear if we can see our feet. How can this be?

Then we were referred to an ocean conservation organization called Oceana by our friend Valarie Whiting, and we started to learn about the over-fishing of the world's oceans, and a number of other issues we had never even heard of like ocean acidification. We both knew that if we wanted our children to have a healthy ocean again, we had better act quickly. The good news is we were told that the ocean is resilient, and if given a chance, it can recover.

This is when we decided to get more involved in a number of ocean organizations to learn all that we could to protect the place that we loved the most. We went to a lot of functions, and we met some of the most brilliant ocean people there are, we also met a lot of celebrities and we were impressed that they would take their fame and direct it in a positive way to help create change. Recounting all that we were able to learn in just a few years we decided that we wanted to share the same information with as many people as possible. This is when we decided that we must compose a book with all of our publishing experience to share with the world. We have chosen people through invitation to be in our book. People we feel have all done great things, and that all have one main thing in common, they all love and respect the ocean! They may not all agree or disagree with each other, but they all have passion to help save our world's most valuable treasure!

We hope that everyone who finds this book will be able to relate to a person or two inside its pages, and we hope that they will then decide that they too would like to make a difference and help save the ocean and its creatures. There are many great ocean organizations mentioned in this book, and they all care. It is our greatest hope that if you learn something, that you will put that info to a positive test, and pass it around.

We thank each and every one of you for even reading a page, for that we are honored!

For the future health of our shared global oceans!

Saludos,

Elizabeth & Duffy Healey

Photo Jen Johnson

Daryl Hannah

Q. Whether interviewing notable fellow ocean defenders on *DH Love Life*, starring as a Mermaid in the hit movie *Splash*, or supporting various ocean charities, your name is synonymous with being a dedicated ocean activist. Can you please explain what specifically makes the ocean so special to you and why you feel so compelled to protect it?

A. I grew up swimming and scuba diving as a kid. They used to make these mini scuba tanks before it was decided that you had to be 13 years old. What magic the underwater world holds! There are creatures that are speckled, spotted, see through,and those that glow in the dark. It can be so wondrously amazing! I love flying weightless in the water and seeing that gorgeous, strange and fascinating world under the sea. I've played games for hours with wild dolphins, hugged a manatee and been followed around all day by a Napoleon Wrasse. Less than 1% of the human species have ever spent time under the water, and I think that makes us unaware of our lifestyle's damaging effect. I never thought I'd see so much devastation and destruction in my lifetime.

Q. What are your largest concerns for the oceans and do you have a particular "ocean hot spot?" If so, can you please elaborate and please explain what people can do to help overcome these issues?

A. As Dr. Sylvia Earle told me, 90% of the big fish in the ocean are gone in the last 50 years! 90%!!! I've witnessed this tragedy myself in just the years I've been diving. The places I could count on to have abundant sea life now look like ghost towns. It's so frightening! In some areas there is more plastic than plankton and dead zones are expanding exponentially. We really need to take urgent action.

Q. Do you have a favorite quote or words to live by that you would like to pass along to others?

A. Let common sense be your guiding force. Common sense taught me that all life is interdependent and that what we are doing to our environment, we're doing to ourselves, our children, and all other life on this planet. Try to make thoroughly informed choices. Speak up for the voiceless and for an ethical world and don't be afraid to take action!

Q. Is there anything else that you would like to add, any thoughts, ideas, recommendations regarding your personal experience with the ocean?

A. We spend billions to explore space yet we still don't know what mysteries our oceans hold. I just joined Dr. Sylvia Earle's Deep Search Foundation which I believe will help to re-invigorate the interest in our own planet and is dedicated to exploring and protecting earth's ocean, the cornerstone of our planet's life support system.

Daryl Hannah is an American award winning film actress and environmentalist. She has starred in many Hollywood movies including Blade Runner, Splash, Wall Street, Roxanne *and more. She drives a biodiesel car and is a passionate humanitarian and a heartfelt environmental activist. Her DHlovelife website is filled with short eco-videos.*

www.dhlovelife.com

Photo Jan Baldwin

His Royal Highness Prince Khaled bin Sultan

Q. What propelled you to dive so deeply into ocean conservation and preservation?

A. In the late 1990s, I was certified as a scuba diver. The experience of diving among the beautiful coral reefs opened my eyes to what has been described as "nature's richest realm." The colors of the corals and the vibrant fish life were in stark contrast to what I had observed growing up in a desert environment. The Kingdom of Saudi Arabia is very fortunate to have abundant coral reefs along all of our coastlines, including the Gulf of Aqaba, the Arabian Gulf and of course the Red Sea. With the good fortune of having this incredible natural resource comes the responsibility to conserve it for future generations.

Coral reefs are often compared with tropical rainforests due to their abundance of species and great ecological complexity. However, to see many of the animals in the jungle, you must be in the right place at the right time. This is not so among the coral reefs. Even a first time snorkeler will be amazed by the multitudes of exotic life forms that appear everywhere before your eyes on a coral reef. As I began exploring the coral reefs, I also realized a change was happening in the short time I had been diving. Some reefs I had previously visited had become less colorful with fewer fish. This affected me on a personal level and I asked questions of the experts to understand why this is happening. Upon learning that unsustainable fishing and land-based pollution are major contributors to the decline in coral reef health, I was inspired to do whatever I could to conserve life in the ocean. To this end, I established the *Khaled bin Sultan Living Oceans Foundation* in the year 2000.

Q. Can you explain what you do at the *Living Oceans Foundation*?

A. The *Living Oceans Foundation* is a public benefit, non-profit foundation headquartered in the USA. We have a global mission and are primarily focused on coral reef research. We are classified as a "Private Operating Foundation." Therefore, the majority of our resources are applied to scientific studies of ocean environments for the purpose of promoting conservation. We also emphasize education and public outreach to expose people to the importance of our natural resources in our seas so that more people will become passionate about conserving ocean life. The *Living Oceans Foundation* operates under the guiding principle of Science Without Borders®, which states that life in our seas does not respect man-made territorial borders, and that man's impact on the seas crosses all borders. Ocean conservation is a global concern. The common objective to conserve ocean resources can be a powerful unifying force. Through collaboration between leading experts in marine science and local scientists, we hope to build scientific and management capacity and provide resource managers with tools and information that will enhance their ability to effectively manage coral reef resources around the world.

Q. What do you see as the biggest threat to our oceans, and what do you suggest people do to help?

A. The harsh reality is that man is the biggest threat to the health of our oceans. Many years ago, human civilization made a very poor judgment of our oceans by thinking that the oceans natural resources

His Royal Highness General Khaled bin Sultan is a leading member of the Royal House of Saudi Arabia, commander of the the royal Saudi Air Defense Forces, and an accomplished scuba diver. Becuase of seeing the rapid deterioration of the world's coral reefs, due to anthropogenic causes (human impacts) particularly in the Red Sea, he started the Living Oceans Foundation.

www.livingoceansfoundation.org

were inexhaustible, and that the oceans are a bottomless pit for the waste products of an industrial civilization. Man is an unnatural predator of life in the sea.

Our hunger and greed has resulted in the exploitation of entire stocks of some fish and many commercially important fish populations today are on the brink of collapse. For hundreds of years, man's technology was no match for the vast oceans but industrial technologies changed that. Now, no life in the sea can hide from our sonar, deep water trawling gear, and floating processing facilities. We must realize the short-sightedness of habitat destruction and the risk of destroying the natural ability of fish populations to be self-sustaining. Science has given us the technology to deplete our ocean resources and now science must give us the knowledge to sustain and manage these resources responsibly.

The ocean is the last frontier on earth, but that frontier is shrinking and we must curb our appetite for endangered species and better regulate our fishing practices. We must develop ecologically responsible aquaculture systems to augment wild-caught fish resources. We must also develop better waste management systems to stop polluting our rivers and seas. Coral reefs are at the same time robust and fragile ecosystems. They have existed in the ocean for millions of years but are extremely vulnerable to exploitation and pollution. Because they occupy such a small footprint of our ocean area, we have the potential to conserve and manage these valuable resources responsibly. Coral reefs are also a bellwether of ocean health and the degradation of the corals is a harbinger of things to come for our oceans as a whole. Climate change is also of serious concern to the coral reefs. Our oceans are warming to the point which exceeds the temperature tolerance of coral reefs, resulting in "coral bleaching" and a progressive decline in their health.

Q. Are there any last thoughts you would like to share about our global oceans?

A. The vastness of our oceans and the magnitude of the threats upon the health of our oceans require the cooperation of people and societies from around the world. Establishing marine protected areas without the infrastructure and resources needed to monitor and enforce regulations will not be successful. In addition, international agencies must become more active in stopping illegal, unreported and unregulated fishing on the high seas. My final message is that we should be hopeful in our quest to preserve our natural resources of the oceans for the benefit of future generations. Man has incredible technological capabilities and I am optimistic that we can reverse the decline in ocean health and put our planet on a better path for the future.

Photo Annelise Hagan

Photo Kip Evans

Dr. Sylvia Earle

Q. Can you explain what "Hope Spots" are?

A. A Hope Spot is a code name for marine protected areas in the sea. When protected we help restore what has been lost, and safeguard what remains of the natural systems which maintain the integrity the way the world works, not only for the ocean, and not only for the fish, but for us as well. One thing that has become clear since the middle of the 20th century is the ocean governs the way the world works. Without the ocean, Earth would be a lot like Mars with an atmosphere that is not very congenial to support human life, or the rest of life, as we know it. Mars is an atmosphere of CO_2. There is some CO_2, of course, in our atmosphere here on planet Earth because it is necessary for photosynthesis. And photosynthesis is necessary for life support, which we depend on not only for generating food, but also for turning our oxygen both for creatures of the land and creatures of the sea. In fact, most of the oxygen in the atmosphere comes from the ocean mostly from small creatures we can barely see or cannot see at all without high-powered magnification.

Another major fact we have discovered since the latter part of the 20th century is how vulnerable the ocean is. Many have thought, until recently (some still do) that the ocean is infinite and it has the capacity to recover no matter what we put into it, or whatever we take out of it. But now we know in fact that we can, and have, removed 90% of the big fish species in the ocean. Big fish like tunas, sharks, swordfish, groupers, snappers, and in many parts of the world the herring are down to historic lows. All of this is disrupting the way the ocean works. About half the coral reefs are either gone or in a state of cataclysmic decline. About 400 dead zones have developed in the coastal waters around the world in the last 50 years. People say, "Well, nothing ever happens until you are in a state of emergency then people take notice," but we are in a state of emergency. People simply have not noticed yet. Most people figure if we can breath, there is no problem. You can still find great diversity of marine life when you go to a restaurant or supermarket, wildlife that would be equivalent to seeing leopards and eagles and owls at the counter. We take carnivores, top of the food chain creatures, out of the sea to eat. We also take creatures out of the sea that are low on the food chain like the herring, and the anchovies. We are indiscriminate and comprehensive about what we take out of the sea. More than a hundred million tons a year are extracted which means a hundred million carbon based units are being essentially allowed to discharge their carbon dioxide back into the atmosphere as we consume them or turn them into fertilizer or products of various sorts. They are not doing what they do best, which is live their lives while maintaining the integrity of the planet upon which we are all dependent and most of us tend to take for granted.

Q. How can an ordinary person help with our current situation in the ocean?

A. First thing is to become aware of the issues. I can forgive those from 50, 100 or 1000 years ago who did what they did to the natural world, to the land, to the air, to the waters, to the wildlife because these actions were done in ignorance. But there is no excuse anymore for ignorance. The information is all around us. It is on the Internet, it is in books and magazine articles, it is something even a ten year old can see in his or her eyes. The changes are taking place around us every day. Changes that really should be of concern to things we really care about like our economy, our health, our security but most importantly, life itself. So that is number one. Number two is to pick up a mirror and ask yourself, what are you good at? Whatever it is, it will be useful in applying that talent, that interest, that love, that capacity to making a difference in one way or another. If you are good with numbers, use numbers as a way to make a difference to turn things around, to understand what is happening. If you are good with words, write a letter, write a poem, or write a song because it communicates to a wider audience what you know that they should know. If you are a grown up or a parent, a teacher, big brother, or a big sister, take a child to some wild place. People are increasingly detached from nature, especially the youngsters. It is hard for youngsters to experience or to know what the natural world is all about unless they have a chance, unless somebody makes it possible for them to have that kind of experience. And it shouldn't be just a now and then outing. It should be incorporated into everyday thinking not only for kids but also for all of us. We learn our ABCs, we learn our numbers at an early age but some never learn that we are dependent on the natural world for every breath we take, every drop of water we drink and the ocean gives us these things and much more. We should also use our power as consumers, we vote with our choices, we also should vote people in office who reflect a sense of caring about the natural world. Vote with your pocket book, don't buy endangered ocean wildlife. Really, the time has come to give tunas, swordfish, sharks, grouper, snapper, flounders, shrimp, lobsters, clams, crabs, you name it, give them a break! Let them recover! We have indulged ourselves wantonly, gluttonously, in terms of taking ocean wildlife as if they had no limit . . . but they do have limits. We discovered that, finally to our dismay, there are some who will say, "well, we just need to cut back," but we already cut the numbers down to 10% or maybe 20% or possible 30% of what they were 50 years ago, but how many years before we take them all? Or take so many that the capacity of the ocean to work as a functioning system is simply destroyed. We are perilously close to that happening in many areas where damage is concentrated. Like Chesapeake Bay, for example, maybe if we just stop killing the oysters, clams and crabs, and stop dredging the bottoms so the sponges have a chance to recover, we'll see some recovery in Chesapeake Bay, too.

Q. You've clocked more than 7,000 hours underwater, can you explain what that has done for you to encourage people to know more about the ocean?

A. Almost anybody has the ability to dive or at least snorkel. My mother waited until she was 81 years old to try. The excuse I hear from some people is that they have ear problems or others say they are claustrophobic. Many who say they are claustrophobic but if they use a proper face mask they discover they are not claustrophobic at all. In fact it is another world which they find totally intoxicating, thrilling, and enlightening. To encourage people to go see for themselves is of paramount importance. For instance, *National Geographic* says one picture is worth a thousand words, and certainly pictures are wonderful, but a real experience has got to be worth at least thousand pictures. Take your children, yourself, your family, and go for it! The wonderful thing is that almost anybody can dive and you can dive all your life. Treat yourself to an opportunity to go to a place where the water is clear, warm and blue. It is worth it! If you don't want to dive, hop into a passenger submarine. There are more than two dozen of them in strategic places around the world where it is like getting on a bus. Buy a ticket and go down 100-150 feet. There is one in the Cayman Islands that can go down 1,000 feet, and another one in the Caribbean near Honduras, or off Cocos Island off of Costa Rica. Check it out, go find it and explore! Find a place that might be appropriate to you and your whole board of directors, your family, or whomever to go down for a cruise.

Q. What is the importance of mapping the oceans?

A. It does seem somewhat pathetic, ironic and unbelievable that we have better maps of the moon, Mars, Jupiter and Mercury than we do of Earth, yet most of the earth's surface is under that mantle of blue. We have invested so enthusiastically in our search for new frontiers skyward, and yet we have been neglecting the ocean. So presently, only about 5% of the ocean has been mapped in the same kind of detail we have for the land that is the floor of the ocean. Even with that map, it is just the beginning because the ocean after all, is the juicy part that extends from sea floor back up to the surface. The ocean is filled with life yet we know less about it than any part of the planet. It is amazing that we, with such a cavalier attitude take from the ocean, and put things into the ocean when the level of ignorance about the ocean is so vast. We know enough to know that the ocean keeps us alive, and we know our fate and the ocean are inextricably linked, yet we treat it

Photo Kip Evans

as if it is infinitely able to recover, no matter what we do to it. As with many things, it really helps to have a map to start with, to know where the mountains and valleys are, to know something about the way the currents run, to get a feel for the distribution of temperature throughout all the ocean and how it changes over time, to know what the migration routes are of many of the big creatures that are in the sea, to know where their breeding and feeding areas are, to know what creatures tend to be home bodies, and don't travel widely. We need to know before we start tearing it all apart.

Q. Does it worry you to know that we have technologies, like satellites and GPS that can hone in on such large bodies of fish and go swoop them up? It seems the more fish they know of, the more fish they will take. Does that worry you?

Photo Kip Evans

A. That is an issue, but knowing is better than not knowing. At the same time, we learn about where the fish are but we have to learn to understand that we can't blatantly go out and kill. As Charles Clover who authored the book and later the film, called *End of the Line* says, "We have allowed the industrial fisherman to steal the ocean." If anybody has a claim on the fish and the sea, all of us have a claim, I want my claim alive. Those who want them dead should have a voice too, but they shouldn't have the only voice, but right now they clearly have the dominant voice.

Q. What are your top concerns for the ocean that we all should think about?

A. We need to think about what is outside the ocean, too, but also what it is we are putting into the ocean, like the plastics of course, and other noxious materials. Back to the point of what people can do with personal choices and what they buy, it is also how they choose to dispose of things that they acquire and to move away from one-time use things. Use it once and throw it away? What kind of economy is that to base and squander our resources like that? It may appear to be good for the economy for the short term because you can get people to buy, buy, buy and throw, throw away but we've reached a point where the throw away part is overwhelming. We need to think in terms of how to have a much lighter footprint on the planet as a whole. It is our only home, and to treat it as if we are increasingly living in a garbage heap, we are forcing ourselves to live that way, we are crowding out the healthy parts of the planet as we distribute our debris and our toxins everywhere.

Q. Do you have any last words you would like to share with the people?

A. People should feel empowered that as never before, we have the insight and knowledge that can guide us to a prosperous and enduring future. We have learned more in the last 50 years than in all the preceding history. Information is vital to understanding how we can fit within the natural systems that sustain us. We may never again have such a good opportunity to fix things. If we continue doing what we're doing, we'll loose the chance that we now have to get it right.

Dr. Sylvia Earle (a.k.a "Her Deepness") has been the most famous female oceanographer for four decades. She has led more than 400 expeditions worldwide involving more than 7,000 hours underwater along with setting the women's depth record of 1250 ft (381m). She was the Chief Scientist for National Oceanic Atmoshperic Administration (NOAA) *and serves as Explorer in Residence at the* National Geographic Society.

www.missionblue.org • www.deepsearch.org

Terry Tamminen

Q. What are your thoughts on off shore drilling now that we have had this new spill April, 2010 in the Gulf of Mexico?

A. The disaster in the Gulf plays out every day in Nigeria, Ecuador, Kazakhstan, and a dozen other countries around the world - - the oil from these places often comes to America, but the images of these impacts never makes it to our evening news. As long as we use oil, we should accept responsibility for its impacts. I'm certainly not in favor of offshore oil drilling - - anywhere - - but hopefully the lesson learned this time is that there is no free lunch (or free driving of our SUVs to get to lunch!) and the only way to avoid these catastrophes in the future is to rapidly transition off of oil and onto sustainable, clean forms of transportation.

Q. If you could add one more chapter to your book *Lives Per Gallon - The True Cost of our Oil Addiction*, what would you speak about?

A. I would show the increasing lengths to which our societies will go to get the next fix of oil. Since writing Lives Per Gallon, we see devastation of vast tracts of land and rivers in Canada to get oil from tar sands; agreement by the highest officials in the Bush administration that the Iraq war - - and the thousands of lives lost and a trillion US dollars wasted - - was entirely about getting oil; and of course the latest disaster in the Gulf. By highlighting this desperation and extrapolating its inevitable outcome - - we will soon run out of oil at any price - - I would use it as an even louder call to action to transition to clean fuels as described in the book. I would also offer a hopeful note - - since the book was published, I have driven a hydrogen-powered car using hydrogen created from sunlight and wastewater, something we could all be doing and ending our oil addiction within a decade while creating vast new industries and jobs.

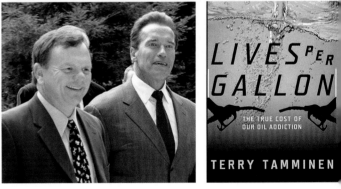

Q. People tend to feel helpless when there is an oil spill, especially in the United States because there is so much red tape, can you make any recommendations as to how people can help in the US, and is it any different in your opinion in other countries?

A. Each of us should first accept responsibility for our role in the spill - - how much oil do we waste every day? Could we drive less, use more efficient transportation, throw away less plastic (which is also made from oil), and take other steps to lessen our use of oil in the first place. Europe has done a much better job of this than the US and even China has tougher vehicle efficiency standards than we do, so there's a lot to learn from other nations.

Q. Knowing you care so much about whales too, is there something you would like to say about them?

Terry was appointed as Secretary of California E.P.A. Terry is an accomplished author, lecturer, and strategist on energy and the environment who works as an advisor to the Governor Schwarzenegger.

www.terrytamminen.com

A. My heart ached when I heard about the first dead whale floating in the midst of the oil spill about a month into the tragedy. Eleven humans died the night the rig exploded and many more will die from disease related to exposure to toxic fumes from the spill. How many more living creatures will we sacrifice for this addiction before we are all prepared to make changes?

Alexandra Cousteau

Photo Blue Legacy International

Q. As an environmental leader, and water advocate, can you explain the necessity of keeping our water clean and safe?

A. When you look at images of our planet from space, it's pretty obvious that we live on a "blue planet"—Earth is roughly 70% covered by water. Our wealth of water is key to the balance of life and is at the very core of nearly every system on which we depend. But if you could put all of Earth's water into a gallon jug, the water we would have available for drinking would only fill a teaspoon. It's this tiny teaspoon that makes life and health as we know them today possible. The quality and quantity of the water in that teaspoon is connected to and kept in a fragile state of balance by the full water cycle. Water is never "destroyed" or goes away, but when we throw any part of the cycle off by polluting air and water, altering our climate, or destroying water-shaping ecosystems, we shrink the teaspoon—we alter the tiny amount of water available for life. When you consider that today, nearly one billion people face life-threatening water shortages and that a lack of safe drinking water is one of the principal killers of children worldwide, you begin to realize how dramatically important it is to work toward balance and sustainability. And that's just the "people" side of things. Our hydrosphere does more than just connect us to each other, it connects us to the Earth's ecosystems and the myriad forms of life that share our planet home. The water cycle is one of the principle ways that our "footprint meets the sea," that our patterns of consumption and waste impact the balance of systems, and that in so many ways, we shape the flora and fauna of the world our children and grandchildren will call home.

Q. Can you explain what a dead zone is, and how it is caused?

A. Oxygen is just as critical for life in our oceans as it is here on land. To put it simply, when chemical nutrient levels in a concentrated area spike to unusually high levels (a condition called eutrophication), the single-celled organisms at the bottom of the food chain have a feeding frenzy and multiply at dramatic and unnatural rates, consuming oxygen both day and night. This chemical-fed explosion of demand throws things way out of balance, literally exhausting the area's oxygen supplies and basically suffocating all life. Scientists first started recording this devastation in the 1970s as significant amounts of chemical fertilizers added by large-scale agricultural practices and industrial run-off were being washed into watersheds and concentrated at the mouths of rivers and in gulfs, bays, lakes, and other areas. The dead zone we studied in the Gulf of Mexico during Expedition Blue Planet 2009 is more than 8,500 square miles. This area, polluted by the chemicals carried from farms and factories along the Mississippi River, represents an area void of life that is larger than the state of New Jersey.

Q. What are some tips you can offer people to help in regards to water and ocean conservation?

A. I'm a firm believer that each of us has a responsibility to learn all that we can about our own footprint. Every single one of us ought to start by doing a little bit of research on four things: 1) Where does the water you consume at home, school or work come from? In other words: What watershed(s) are you drawing resources from and what can you do to keep them healthy and reduce your demands? 2) Where does the water you send on down the drain go? Or, what watershed(s) does the water you put back into the system affect and what should you be doing to reduce your impact on it? When you start considering the toxic cleaning products and things like paint and other fluids many people wash down their sinks when cleaning either end up in a local watershed or cause the city to have to add a lot of processing and treatment to

the waste water before releasing it, you can't help but consider switching to safer products or changing your practices. 3) Where does the water in your yard or street end up? The rain and irrigation water that falls on many yards or that runs from driveways and pools usually ends up in a local river, stream or groundwater system carrying the pollutants it picked up along the way. Things like fertilizers, motor oil, pet waste, and pool chemicals can be just as toxic when concentrated in a local watershed as the chemicals coming from industrial farms and factories. and finally; 4) What are your demands on the global water cycle? Reducing your impact on climate change through managing your carbon footprint and getting to know more about the water impacts of the products you buy—especially when it comes to food—really matters.

Q. What are some of the most important things you learned from your grandfather Jacques Cousteau?

A. Even though I was just four months old when I went on my first expedition with my family, I was always pestering my grandfather to tell me stories about the places he'd been and answer questions about the incredible things we'd see. He was so great to feed my curiosity with amazing stories, but he would inevitably say, "Alexandra, you just have to go and see." Those words say a lot. Environmentalists have for too long asked people to protect things they've never experienced. There is nothing that can replace the power of spending time in nature. I try every day to do that with my work—to create opportunities and interactive experiences that help people experience the incredible ways in which water connects us all. It's a challenge I give every group of people I have the chance to visit: "Go and see." For some, it's as simple as setting aside time to just be quiet and soak in the sites and sounds of a nearby seashore or river, for others it's saving up and taking that trip of a lifetime to experience an undersea world or a far away culture. Whatever the case, nothing inspires one to live responsibly more than simply "going and seeing" the treasures of our "blue planet."

Q. Do you have any particular stories you would like to share, or would you like to offer any last thoughts?

A. My life is shaped every day by the stories people share with me and the places and cultures I experience in my work. It's almost impossible to choose a "favorite." One thing that is consistent though is that regardless of where I go to talk about water issues, people tell me, "water is life." From spiritual leaders in India and government leaders in Africa to farmers in Jordan and Missouri; from Saudi royals to fishermen in Louisiana, all people say the same thing, "Water is life," they always say, "water is life."

Alexandra Cousteau is the Founder of Blue Legacy, *a Washington, D.C. based nonprofit dedicated to exploring how humans relate to our water-based planet. Honored as a National Geographic's "Emerging Explorers." The granddaughter of legendary French explorer Jacques-Yves Cousteau campaigns to raise awareness of world water issues. "I believe water will be the defining crisis of our century — from droughts, storms, and floods to degrading water quality. We'll see major conflicts over water and the proliferation of water refugees. We inhabit a water planet, and unless we protect, manage and restore that resource, the future will be a very different place from the one we imagine today."*

www.alexandracousteau.org

Alexandra in Uganda with her father, Philippe Cousteau

Photo Cory Wilson

OCEANA.ORG

Ted Danson

Q. How did you first get into ocean conservation, and what drives you to be such an ocean activist?

A. I grew up in Arizona in the desert. We took vacations to the beach and our whole family always had fun there, and we always loved the ocean. I loved playing in the water and even sitting there on the beach looking at the ocean.

But there were two other things that really got me involved.

One was when my children Kate and Alexis and I were walking on the beach and there was a big sign there that said "Water Polluted – No Swimming." They asked me why and I couldn't answer. So, it got me thinking and asking questions.

The other big thing was when I met Robert Sulnick. Bob was the president of *No Oil, Inc.* and we were living in the same neighborhood at the time. Bob was fighting for about 15 years to keep Occidental Petroleum from digging about 60 oil wells and drilling into the ocean near us. I started to help him and we ended up winning that fight together. And, out of that relationship, we decided to see if we could make a difference by focusing all of our time and energy in one area: ocean activism.

Also the *Cheers* television show was paying me a lot of money, and I realized that if money and celebrity are used wisely and responsibly, you can get things done. So Bob and I started *American Oceans Campaign* and we were off and running. I've been around incredibly bright scientists, lawyers, policy makers, ever since, and it's one of the reasons why I've been here doing this for over 20 years.

I've learned a lot over the last two decades. We have to deal with petroleum and our reliance on oil. We will never be able to be self reliant when it comes to oil; we only have 2-3% of the world's oil, so we will never be able to drill ourselves out of this. We will always be dependent on foreign oil if we do not handle this in some way like using alternate sources of energy, like offshore wind energy, which has great potential.

Carbon dioxide emissions from burning fossil fuels, like oil, are turning our oceans acidic, changing the pH balance of the entire ocean. The oceans can't absorb the amounts of carbon dioxide that we are pouring into the atmosphere.

When carbon dissolves from the atmosphere into the ocean it causes a phenomenon known as ocean acidification. When this happens, and it is happening, it takes away the ability of corals to make reefs, and tiny little sea creatures, like pteropods and krill, to make their shells. These little tiny sea creatures form the base of the ocean food chain.

Q. Is there one ocean issue that you would like to discuss i.e.: a problem/solution idea?

A. Yes, I would like to talk about overfishing. If we don't address this issue, we could be in big trouble. The good news is we *can* solve this problem, we just need to act soon. This is one of the most achievable environmental challenges in the world today.

In order to cure overfishing, we need to fish responsibly. And, we need to understand that we need to be friends of the fishermen, not anti-fishermen. I enjoy eating fish. Nearly one-third of the world's population depends on fish for its primary source of protein. We just need to make sure we fish responsibly, in other words, sustainably.

Industrial-scale commercial fishing is ruining our oceans by taking out fish faster than they can reproduce. The U.N. reports that at least 75% of the world's seafood species are overexploited, fully exploited or recovering from depletion. Industrial fishing ships throw away 16 billion pounds of unwanted fish and sea creatures every year, because they were caught and killed accidentally, or were not commercially valuable enough. We use bottom trawls, heavily weighted nets that destroy the ocean floor habitat, including coral reefs, which are the nurseries of the sea and vital to ocean health. Thanks to massive government subsidies, about $20 billion a year, scientists say we have twice the amount of boats out in the ocean that we should have to fish sustainably.

Most of the boats that are causing these problems are part of the large industrial, deep water fleets. The smaller fishermen around the world have been fishing the oceans for generations and know how to do it the right way, how to fish selectively rather than indiscriminately. The huge industrial fishing ships employ the fewest people, by the way. In Santiago, Chile, for example, they have 18-20 foot wooden boats with nets that they use to catch their fish the old-fashioned way. Each boat employs a number of people, mending nets or selling the fish etc. When I was growing up in the 50s, there were 90% more of the big fish out there. Now one out of ten are surviving. The big tuna, the sharks the marlin are disappearing, all due to overfishing and a few other factors.

In our lifetime, our grandchildren will be asking us what did you do to stop overfishing? Why didn't you do anything? To me it's all about stewardship. Overfishing is one of the biggest crises facing our world and our oceans, but we can solve it! These issues are fixable – this is the good news. That's exciting to me . . . to know there is a problem, and to know how to fix it, and then, go and do something about it!

The ocean is resilient. It just needs to be given a break. If we manage our fisheries and oceans responsibly, they can come back. We just need to do the right thing.

Q. Are there any last thoughts you would like to offer?

A. Become involved. Become an activist. There has never been a time before where it has been so critical to participate in a solution. Do not be cynical. Do not rock back on your heels, and do nothing. Be critical, absolutely. Be informed. Let science guide you, but you have to become involved. No one has the luxury anymore, to sit back and do nothing. Give money if you can to a good ocean organization or become an activist and help to change policy. You can do this from your computer right from home. It's easy to get involved. You can also be mindful about the products you use, the fish you eat, and try not to eat the endangered fish. Get a seafood card, there are lot of great ones out there (you can find one at oceana.org) and find out about what fish are sustainable. You can also find out for public health reasons, and for your own health, what fish are contaminated with high levels of mercury and heavy metals. And, you should also ask your supermarket to post FDA warnings about what fish to avoid.

I really encourage everyone to look and find an organization they like and get to work. In my case, I support *Oceana*, look them up, they are doing great things. Just remember to ask yourself one question: Am I going to be part of the problem? Or am I going to be part of the solution?

Actor Ted Danson is best known for his role as Sam Malone in the TV series Cheers. *Ted was the co-founder of American Oceans Campaign which has merged with* Oceana *where he sits on the board of directors. He is very active in the fight to save the ocean and recently hosted the award winning documentary on fish population called* End of the Line.

www.oceana.org

Robert Sulnick

Q. As a leading environmental lawyer, and a co-founder of *American Oceans Campaign*, what is one of the top preventable, or rather fixable ocean issues that really bothers you the most; and what needs to be done in order to do so?

A. There are two: coastal pollution and offshore drilling. The Outer Continental Shelf, the first three miles out from shore, is home to most of the ocean's biodiversity. This "eco-system" is of course the most heavily impacted by coastal pollution. It is absolutely essential that the educational process ensure that people understand that all of the storm drain and watershed runoff inevitably ends up in coastal waters. This kind of runoff includes pesticides, fertilizers, toxic chemicals, such as oil and anti-freeze leaking from vehicles, and hormones just to name a few of the toxicants which are the ingredients of coastal pollution. This toxic cocktail spreads throughout the Continental Shelf destroying habitats and threatening the health and viability of species. This kind of pollution is, at this point in history, ubiquitous and in a very real sense, perpetual. On the positive side, it can be stopped through better management of watershed and storm drain runoff assuming the political will can be developed ensuring adequate funding for public education and the installation of state-of-the-art anti-pollution control technologies.

Offshore oil drilling is something AOC worked hard to prevent and I had thought that the debate was settled; it is simply too much to risk to drill a mile down into the ocean and release forces that are super human. With the recent spill in the Gulf of Mexico and the Obama Administration's attempt to lift the offshore oil drilling ban off of the east coast that debate is once again front and center in American political life. The debate however, is not just about oil spills and the devastation they cause, it is about energy..

Obviously we need energy. Equally obvious, we need to break our addiction to oil. America does not have enough oil to satisfy its energy needs even if we were to drill every square mile of our oceans. As long as we remain addicted to oil, we will remain addicted to foreign oil which has become a national security issue. The tragedy of the Gulf oil spill goes beyond the harm done to the ocean ecosystem and the economic well being of the Gulf Coast. It is a harsh, stark reminder that America needs a sane energy policy which starts with conservation and includes domestic renewable energy.

Q. If you could offer people words to live by, what would you say to them?

A. Remember, the oceans are the lungs of the planet. They regulate our climate and ensure a stable environment. If we damage the Earth's lungs, we have placed future generations of the myriad of species which populate our planet in jeopardy.

Robert Sulnick is an environmental lawyer ad co-founder (with Ted Danson) American Oceans Campaign (AOC). The (AOC) worked to address issues of coastal pollution, offshore oil and energy production, habitat preservation and marine biodiversity. The (AOC) is now merged with Oceana.

www.environmentalproblemsolving.com

Sam Waterston

Q. Having grown up in New England and doing many interviews on behalf of our environment, you have made mention that you have witnessed fisheries collapse in the seaside towns near you. For the benefit of those not living on the Eastern Seaboard can you elaborate on what you have experienced, and give your thoughts on it?

A. What I've said is that, growing up in the world of sea-food plenty that prevailed all up and down the East Coast when I was a child growing up after WW II, it conditioned me to expect abundance to continue. I read the papers, and kept up with local events, though, and thought of myself as being up-to-date on what was going on around me. I heard very little to alarm me until it was very late in the day. I knew from reading that the cod that gave Cape Cod its name, and attracted Europeans to the East Coast of North America from the start, needed attention, because their numbers were declining. But I also thought I knew the problem was being carefully taken care of.

It was the discovery that neither was the case, that the collapse was catastrophic, that the parties directly responsible and with the largest interest in preserving the fishery, the state, the fishing industry itself, even the scientific community, had allowed the crash to happen and failed to raise an alarm about it sufficient to prevent the worst from happening. The media also failed to do their job of investigation and notification. It was learning about all this, and more than a little suspecting that this was how the oceans were being treated generally, as inexhaustible, and in good hands, as nothing. In Twain's great phrase, for 'intelligent and human people to be concerned about,' when the opposite was true, that got me mad enough to do something.

The plight of the fishermen, insofar as it was reported, was largely described as a fight between the regulators and the regulated, with sympathy to the regulated. What this left out, of course, was the fish! That without fish, there would be no fishermen, was a point largely overlooked, and where mentioned, most often, it was only to pooh-pooh the idea that there was a real problem. The fishermen themselves, in other words, were suffering from the same lack of information, and misinformation, that I was, and their lives, and the life of their home ports, depended on them knowing what was going on.

To this day, incredibly, the available information that could double the size and worth of the fishing industry in the northeast under only a few years of reasonable husbandry is not known to, or denied by, the people who could most directly benefit. It's really shameful. On land, the visible result is in the fish shops and in the landings our fishermen make. Scallops are a good business still, but bottom fish, populations of flounder, cod, and so on, are a shadow of their former numbers. New England, fishing, and the sea, are one in our minds. But not in fact. We could have the old way back. WW II is just my own lifetime back. It's not too late.

Q. Do you have any last thoughts you would like to say to the people around the world with regard to our world oceans?

A. Shame on us if we didn't make a noise for our grandchildren's sake. The lesson of the last 50 years? Don't leave it up to the 'experts'. Get involved, it's not yet too late!

Photo Institute for Malcolm Ludgate

Robert Ballard, Ph.D.

Q. As the Director of the *Center for Ocean Exploration and Archaeological Oceanography*, can you please explain the need to explore our oceans and preserve its cultural heritage?

A. Our oceans, which cover 72% of the planet's surface and average 4,000 meters in depth, are largely unexplored. It is hard to create a plan to protect the oceans when we do not know what is there. When it comes to cultural material that has been lost in the sea, there is perhaps more history in the sea than all of the world's museums combined but most is at risk. Bottom trawling activity by commercial fishermen have destroyed much of the cultural material lost in water depths down to 500 meters or more.

Q. Over the years you have discovered so much that is new to us about the oceans aside from the discovery of *The Titanic*, and other shipwrecks. What is one of the other most fascinating things you have found in the deep seas?

A. Clearly, our most important discovery in the sea was our 1977 discovery of hydrothermal vents in a segment of the mid-ocean ridge known as the Galapagos Rift. There in total darkness at a depth of 2,500 meters, we discovered exotic life forms living around warm water vents that thrived in waters laden with hydrogen sulfide through a process known as chemosynthesis. This discovery revolutionized our understanding of the origin of life on the planet and the high probability of finding life not only elsewhere within the Universe but within our own Solar System. We made a related discovery in 1979 of high temperature "Black Smokers" that helped to explain the chemistry of the world's oceans as well as the existence of commercially value ore deposits of copper, lead, zinc, silver and gold.

Q. If you could send one message to the people of the world in regard to our oceans, what would you say to them?

A. Remember that our planet is small, embedded in a black velvet void of nothingness. I do not believe the human race will leave earth to populate other planets, so it is important that we understand how the earth works, what it has to offer the human race, and how to live in harmony with it.

Former commander, U.S.Navy, oceanographer, Robert Ballard has reached depths of 20,000 feet in submersibles then developed deep sea robots which enabled him to discover Titanic *and* Bismarck, *and the wreck of* John F. Kennedy's PT-109.

www.mysticaquarium.org

Photo Institute for Malcolm Ludgate

Photo Institute for Exploration

Lt. Don Walsh

Q. In 1960 you and Jacques Picard took the deepest human dive in ocean history to well over 35,700 ft. below the sea level, a remarkable record that you still hold today, over 50 years later. What are your thoughts on ocean exploration since then?

A. In brief we are simply not doing enough of it. By "we" I mean all the nations who have programs in ocean research. None, including the U.S., are making sufficient national investments that will help us better understand our world and the ocean that covers 70% of it. This manned spacecraft that we call "Planet Earth" is our home and we just do not know much about it.

Q. What are your most honest thoughts on the overall health of the ocean today?

A. We are running out of time to take better care of the World Ocean. Things happen there very subtly but inexorably. Once a negative situation becomes a serious problem, it may be too late to take remedial measures. There are so many 'health' issues such as plastic wastes, acidification, warming, coastal pollution, dying off of the coral reefs, over fishing, etc. Things in the sea are linked so that a negative effect with one will have a cascading effect on many.

Q. Do you have any words of wisdom that you would like to pass on for future generations in regard to the ocean?

A. Be concerned about and take care of the World Ocean. Ocean awareness needs to be formed at the earliest stages of a person's education. And it should be a lifetime habit. Whether you live in St. Louis or San Francisco, the oceans critically affect all of us. For too many people, the sea is only an abstraction and not real part of their existence. So most of all . . . participate! Make sure you are informed and see that your elected representatives pay attention to ocean issues.

Dr. Don Walsh and Jacques Picard hold the record for going to the deepest part of the ocean on the Trieste in 1960, going more than 35,700+ feet under the sea to its deepest trenches (that's over seven miles)! Dr. Walsh is also named on of the World's Great Explorers by Life magazine. He even dived on the Titanic, and the German battleship Bismarck.

www.explorers.org/about/walsh.php

Photo Jen Rosenstein

RESTAREA

Jason Mraz

Q. Can you explain your relationship with the ocean and what the ocean means to you, have you had any experiences in the water as a surfer that have caused you to think differently in your approach to life?

A. When I was kid, I used to love having an adult pick me up and fling me through the air, high over the surface of the water. With flailing limbs I'd contort all my fears and excitement together as I'd come colliding with my reflection. Now that I'm a grown up (sort of) the only force in my life strong enough to toss me across the water is the water itself. This is why I love surfing. People are quick to mention the peace and tranquility of sitting out past the break and others go on about synchronicity, those perfect views sliding along the face of a wave. Some are all about the rush of tucking into a tight barrel. While I am in no disagreement with anyone's reason to surf, my most favorite aspect continues to be the beat down. In my non-laborious line of work, there's nothing like being pitched over the falls of an 8-foot wave, taking a deep breath and then letting your body go limp in the wash. My search for mind, body and soul balance brims at the bottom of the ocean, for once you arrive there, the only other place you can go is up.

The ocean is my mentor, my master and my friend. I've had my share of close calls. I've been caught inside on a head high day standing ankle deep on a reef with a snapped leashed. I've tread sharky waters with bloody knees, been run over countless times and kissed my own rail and fins more than once doing my own inventive radically uncontrolled maneuvers. I believe it's the respect I have for the pacifist sea that keeps me floating safely back to shore without harm to my self or others. I learned early on to say a prayer of thanks and to bless everyone and everything in the water before shuffling out to begin another session. Spirited, I remain humble no matter how high the swell.

Since becoming a waterman in the 2004, I take more notice of the weather. After a heavy rain, many beaches in my San Diego community become toxic from chemical run-off, especially near river mouths. Unless my immune system is willing to work overtime, I heed the signs posted about the beach being unsuitable for surfing and swimming. This really turns me off because I've been to other places like Peru, Costa Rica and parts of Indonesia where there is no immediate (apparent) threat of pollution on the coast. The beaches are pristine. Besides, it's after a rain that's usually the best time to surf!

Surfing was my first major connection to nature. It's thanks to surfing that I now monitor more closely how I care for my own land, which I consider an extension of my body as my senses have the ability to embrace it and nurture it. On an avocado farm about ten miles from the coast, we have a solar-efficient home that shelters our artful community. We are meticulous re-users and recyclers, savers and storers. We auto-share a hybrid car to the beach everyday singing songs as we go.

We're learning how to grow our own food, and are in the process of converting our 30-year-old avocado trees to organic fruit bearers. Our goal throughout the complex is to be completely self-sufficient and no-impact by 2012. I doubt I would have ever considered such a task had I not been properly introduced to the sea.

Taking action like this at home also translates on tour. Our mission on the road is to have as little impact as possible, other than leaving the world looking better than we found it.

Q. What is your largest concern for our oceans, and what do you think people can do to help the situation?

A. My main concern for our oceans is pollution, namely plastics. There's more than enough evidence that shows how man-made garbage is changing the way the ocean and its many inhabitants operate. Some coasts are finding more plastic polymers than bits of sand. Some believe the only way to actually get rid of the plastics in the ocean is to wait for an organism to evolve that can actually ingest the material and use it as food. Should we advance about 10,000 years into the future, there may not be many humans, but there will probably be a few plastic crustaceans.

I encourage everyone to bring home organics, not plastics. Refuse plastic bags and one time use containers. Insist that your grocer no longer offer plastic over paper. Choose glass or easily recyclable aluminum over plastic when purchasing soda or snacks. And always drink from the tap. Everything you buy is a vote for more of it. If you want to taste cleaner water and swim in safer seas, put your dollar on products and organizations that are doing something about it. If we're not part of the solution, we're part of the problem.

Q. Do you have any words to live by, or any particular quotes that you love that you would like to share?

A. You don't have to live near the ocean for it to have an impact on you. And you don't have to live near the ocean for you to have an impact on it.

Jason Mraz is a critically acclaimed, Virginia-born, live performer known for making very large sold-out shows seem intimate. His recent Atlantic Records album, We Sing. We Dance. We Steal Things. *has multi-platinum certifications all over the world. Songs from the album set lots of records and garnered many awards; Grammy win for his song* Make It Mine, *Grammy win for the song* Lucky, *plus two other nominations and two Teen Choice Awards. Jason wrote a song called* I'm Yours *for this album that set the record last year as the longest-running song, EVER, on Billboard's Hot 100 chart. Jason Mraz is a passionate advocate for our environment and received an Environmental Media Association Award for his efforts alongside Sir Richard Branson. He is a spirited proponent of equal rights for all, and does a lot for charity. Mraz is also an avid surfer, and lives on an active avocado farm north of San Diego.*

www.jasonmraz.com

Photo Jen Rosenstein

Supraja Dharini Ph.D.
TREE Foundation
Roots and Shoots India

Dr. Jane Goodall and Dr. Supraja Dharini

Q. Can you please explain a little bit about the *TREE Foundation*, and some of the things you?

A. *TREE Foundation* inspired by Dr. Jane Goodall DBE., primarily started by working with the fishing communities to prevent illegal poaching of olive ridley sea turtles and their eggs and to reduce by-catch deaths of the same. It has grown, using community engagement programs, to include the study of marine wildlife, the protection of turtle nests and the release of hatchlings, improving environmental literacy, health and hygiene among the fishing community, and developing skills for current and future generations to act as stewards of this invaluable resource: The ocean. *TREE Foundation* uses the sea turtle community based conservation program to reach out to coastal communities, students, the general public and government to enable them to understand the land/ocean connection and ensure a sustainable marine conservation program.

Q. What types of sea turtles do you have in India, and what is their plight?

A. All sea turtles are listed as endangered. We have four species of turtles nesting on the Indian coasts and a fifth species, the Loggerhead turtle (Caretta caretta), swimming across the Arabian Sea. The olive ridley (Lepidochelys olivacea) nests along the east and west coasts of mainland India and the coasts of Andaman and Nicobar Islands, juvenile hawksbill turtles (Eretmochelys imbricata) and green turtles (Chelonia mydas), forage in southern coasts and the adult turtles nest on the Islands, the Gulf of Kutch, the Gulf of Mannar and the northwestern coast. The leatherback turtle (Dermochelys coriacea) nest only on the beaches of Andaman and Nicobar islands.

The local coastal communities are unaware of the protection laws and importance of the turtles in the coastal marine ecosystems so rampant poaching of turtle eggs and in a few areas poaching of the adult turtle still continues. The major threat to all sea turtles in the India waters are injuries and death caused due to indiscriminate fishery related activities. The need of the hour is extensive outreach and awareness to fishermen and the general public, since scientists believe that only one out of 1,000 hatchlings that reach the ocean reaches adulthood. Since turtles are long lived and slow maturing species, they need to be protected during every stage of their life cycle. They are good indicators of the health and the wealth of the ocean as they swim across oceans and nest on beaches bridging the gap between land and sea. They are a flagship species indeed. Only when people understand the importance of turtles will they care. Only when people care can turtles be protected. So we at *TREE Foundation* tailor our outreach programs to suit different audiences. We use a variety of methods which include visual art, street theatre, music and dance to reach to as many as we can.

Q. Do you have any inspirational environmental stories about the people in your community that you would like to share?

A. There are many, many stories which are gentle reminders to me that I am truly blessed to be God's tool, as those are times, I strongly experience the Divine presence around. Yet I wish to share this powerful statement of the first time I visited and interacted with the Periya Neelankarai fishing village youth, and explained the ecological role of the sea turtles and the need for the turtles to be protected by the fishing community. One of the young men (named Pugalarasu) in the group stood up and told me "I have been a fisherman for the past 13 years and have been only taking from the ocean; I will involve myself in the sea turtle conservation. Protecting the nesting turtles and guiding the hatchlings back to sea will be my way of thanking the ocean." He has been with *TREE Foundation* volunteering as the *Sea Turtle Protection Force*, from that day on and continues to inspire others to give back to the sea. Also, when I visit the fishing villages during the turtle's nesting season, many times one or the other fishermen would walk up to me and narrate his story on how he and his team cut their net and released the turtle that had got entangled in their fishing net during the season. They would tell me that it took 10-15 minutes, but yet they cut the net and when the turtle swam away they were happy to see her take a deep breath and swim away. Otherwise, they always make sure the information reaches me through the *Sea Turtle Protection Force Youth*. It is this information that gives us the strength to carry on in spite of all the hurdles one needs to cross in community based conservation.

Q. If you could offer people from around the world words of advice in regards to our oceans, and our environment, what would you say?

A. I believe that people are not uncaring; it is just that they are unaware. Extensive outreach and awareness is the need of the hour. We need to rediscover the compassion within ourselves and make simple life style changes toward environment care. It is our responsibility to take action now, to protect the ocean and its wildlife for generations to come. It is possible: Each and every individual can make a difference.

Dr. Supraja Dharini is the Founder of the TREE Foundation *which engages in environment education, sea turtle conservation and community development.* TREE Foundation *is inspired and guided by the world famous environmentalist Dr. Jane Goodall and is a member of* Roots and Shoots International Network. *She was awarded for the extension of community based sea turtle conservation and marine mammal study in the Kancheepuram District, India.*

www.treefoundationindia.org

David de Rothschild

Photo Luca Babini

Q. What was the motivation for you to get involved with the green revolution, and take on such large projects?

A. Most information we are being presented with in the green movement is about being exclusive, not inclusive, and guilt mongering. So when I started to look at this, I started realizing a lot of the information I wanted, I could not find. I wanted to change that, but I did not want to start another non-profit organization or green group, that was focusing on only one issue.

I wanted to create a platform for curiosity and take new environmental and social issues. I like to tell stories that are compelling, engaging and hopefully create enough curiosity for people so they can find one or two areas of interest that they find inspiring. I hope people are inspired by what we are choosing to do because it is a great adventure. I like to push the boundaries, and get people to look outside the system. Once *Plastiki* is completed, hopefully we will have captured people's attention in various ways of reuse, new ways of building things, and designing things.

With the projects I am working on like the *Plastiki*, we are trying to position ourselves to come up with new innovative ideas, new ways to engage people. You should always continue to nurture your own curiosity... that's what keeps me going, and hopefully a lot of other people. I'd like to inspire people to get outdoors more and to learn about their surroundings too. We need to encourage people to explore more, and also live more naturally, and to realize that not only the fact that we are what we eat, but we are what we breathe.

Q. What kind of environmental message are you trying to convey to the public by building the *Plastiki*?

A. Fundamentally, we are trying to showcase the fact that waste is a design flaw, and to show people how do be smarter about the products we use and produce. We are also trying to change the perception that plastics are simply single use items or short term items. Plastics are ubiquitous, and they are only going to become more present in our everyday lives. So we have to start looking at creating ostensive values around materials we are making. We need to start engaging in the plastic material so it has longer life spans and different life-cycles. The *Plastiki* is demonstrating the most basic level of understanding by showing people that we can reuse waste, and explaining why we need to.

The *Plastiki* is a one of kind 60' catamaran that is made out of 12,500 reclaimed plastic bottles, and recyclable srPET plastic waste products. The goal is to take a voyage on the boat and demonstrate the human finger print on our planet. It is so large that it's out of control, especially when you look at areas like the great garbage patch. Ninety percent of

David de Rothschild is a British international eco adventurer, environmentalist who has built the Plastiki *made of 12,000 reused plastic bottles to draw attention to the amount of plastic in our oceans and our absurd dependence on bottle water The vessel visits the Eastern Pacific Garbage Patch. He is the Founder of* Adventure Ecology, *a non profit based in London that runs expeditions to environmentally sensitive places to raise awareness of global warming.*

www.theplastiki.com • www.adventureecology.com

the marine debris is plastic. Can you imagine one billion dollars worth of plastic is going into our landfills every single year . . . and what are we still doing with styrofoam? . . . That should have ended in the 80s! We can do better now by manufacturing the plastic in a new way. We need to learn more about the engineering of the plastic, and we need to showcase different ways of doing things.

Q. What are your largest hopes and concerns for the ocean?

A. It is important to look at the ocean from a different perspective, like a view from 60,000 feet up. If you relate the ocean to the body, like a cardiovascular system, and really look at it like, a hydrological cycle drive like our planet, there are obviously immediate threats that need to be looked at. What we really need to do is look how much the ocean supports the life on our planet. My fear is the total disregard for the ocean. A majority of the world's population don't get to see the ocean simply because it is out of sight. Like the saying goes: Out of sight, out of mind. Also, people must think the ocean is an inexhaustible resource. There seems to be a big disconnect between humans and the ocean. People should know that we all have an impact on the ocean whether we live near it or not.

I look at the world like it has two oceans. The ocean around us, and the ocean of sky above, the two Big Blue Oceans! The blue ocean around us is just as important as the blue ocean above us, yet we pay more attention to the blue ocean above us, because we are in contact with it daily.

It is very hard for people to contemplate the fact that they can have an impact on a body of water so large and so infinite. For instance, if you put a bottle in the wrong bin it's hard to see the impact. But if you leave a bottle on the beach, it's easy to see because it is actually there.

Our biggest challenge is trying to connect people to why they should care about the ocean. My largest fear for the ocean, is the over saturation of carbon our ocean absorbs. I am deeply concerned about things that lead to decalcifying of crustaceans, and also concerned about the changes that we will have on our beaches and coral reefs. Once you reach that point of saturation, it becomes the largest acceleration of carbon which can expedite our warming planet. It then becomes a runaway system. That in itself to me is a frightening thought because there is no second

Photo Luca Babini

chance, there is no going back once you reach that point.

This is an ominous situation and difficult to figure out, and that worries me. However, on a more optimistic note, our oceans are resilient. And the ocean has the ability to rejuvenate and replenish itself if given the space to breath and time to do so. We actually have the ability to bring the oceans back, have more marine protected areas, set proper limits on fishing regulations and quotas. We need more marine protected areas, and we can legislate for that. We need to write letters and have our voices be heard. We need to act like the gate keepers for the next generation. We need to set stiff, rigid regulations around fishing quotas and enforce them. It's shocking that only 1% of our oceans are actually marine protected areas. In this day that is beyond comprehension.

I was thinking about the fact that our ocean would have a completely different storyline if the ocean was made up of fresh water, and it was drinkable. We would have much tougher regulations and people would say there is no way we can dump our chemicals and throw our trash in it. Although we depend on the ocean for life, we still dump our trash in it. Could you imagine if people would go dump in their local dams? People would say "Go hang that guy!"

We don't have a sense of value at all with the ocean because it seems so infinite, which makes it so easy to disconnect. We need to take action, and we have the ability to make change! We need to change our mentality, our mind set and our living habits.

Q. If you had one last message to send to people what would you say?

A. I always go back to this native Indian proverb that is one of my favorite sayings, "We do not own this earth, we are borrowing it from future generations." We need to act like gate keepers for future generations, and act like we are returning the earth back to its original state of being.

Without nature we are nothing. We need to reconnect to the web of life. It does not matter if you have money, what religious views you have, without nature we are nothing, and it is as simple as that. We also need to turn our life into a great adventure and get outdoors, where we can observe what we are trying to protect, and love it!

Photo Luca Babin

Photo Luca Babin

Photo Glen E. Friedman

Shepard Fairey

Q. You are a well known artist with global recognition, especially with your Obama HOPE poster. If you could do one poster with a message about the ocean that got that same kind of attention, what would your message be?

A. The fates of not only sea-dwellers but also land-dwellers depend on the oceans, and if you have any sense of self-preservation you should understand the importance of preserving the oceans. With that said, the ocean means so many things to so many people, from those who occasionally hang out on the beach to those who see it as a source of spirituality. It's hard to put one word on something like that.

Q. You have a ton of followers, and a lot of people look up to you, but who are your heroes, and why?

A. I grew up skateboarding and listening to punk rock and hip-hop, and I looked up to people like Chuck D, Henry Rollins and Joe Strummer for being iconoclasts, questioning the system and doing things their own way—and showing me that I could do things my own way too. Some of my other heroes include Andy Warhol, Jasper Johns, Woody Guthrie, and Cornel West.

Q. If you could list three suggestions for all people to do, to make this a better planet, what would they be?

A. Turn your lights off when you're not using them, don't drive a gas-guzzler and vote for politicians who want to invest in clean energy and green technology.

Q. Do you have any last thoughts about the ocean you would like to share?

A. Everywhere I've lived in my life (South Carolina, Rhode Island, and Southern California), I've always been near the ocean. In a lot of ways, I think people who have grown up around the ocean take it for granted, but when you haven't been in front of the ocean for a while and you go to the beach, it's easy to understand why the image of a sunset over the ocean has become such a powerful cliché for peaceful escapism. There's something indescribably beautiful about it.

Shepard Fairey is one of the most influential "street artists" and creator of "Obey" Giant Series. He is a leading artist who also created iconic "Hope" poster for the Obama presidential campaign. His work is shown at the Smithsonian, LA County Museum of Art and the Museum of Modern Art in New York.

www.obeygiant.com

Original photograph by Tom Servais

Robert F. Kennedy, Jr.

Q. What is mountain top removal and how does it affect our oceans and waterways?

A. Mountain removal is the worst ongoing environmental tragedy our country has ever endured. It is a catastrophically destructive form of strip mining where large companies like Massey Coal are using giant machines called drag lines, that stand 22 stories high and cost over a half billion dollars, to blow the tops off of large mountains in Appalachia to get at the coal seams that lay below. They use approximately 2,500 tons of explosives (ammonia nitrate explosives) that are detonated everyday in West Virginia, which is the equivalent to the power of a Hiroshima bomb once a week.

After they use the explosives to get at the coal seams that lay below they take the rock and debris and scrape it into the adjacent river valleys. They've already blown off 500 of the tallest mountains in West Virginia. They have flattened an area of 1.4 million acres that is an area the size of Delaware. They have also buried over 2,000 miles of streams and rivers that are mainly headwater rivers of the Ohio River. Headwater streams are critical to the health of river ecosystems; they control/regulate the hydrology of our rivers to make them friendly and stable for aquatic communities. The poisons associated with coal mining, like arsenic and mercury, travel thousands of miles downstream affecting the quality and health of fish in our global oceans, and human health as well.

The Appalachian Mountains are the richest ecosystems in North America because it is the oldest forest. Most deep forest systems have 2-3 tree species, the Appalachia have 80 tree species. There is more diversity per cubic meter than any other ecosystem in the Northern hemisphere. During the Pleistocene Ice Age, the glaciers extended as far south as New York, which was buried a mile and a half under ice. The rest of North America became tundra. The only place where the forest survived was a small area in the area of what is now the Appalachian Mountains of eastern Kentucky and southern West Virginia. When the Pleistocene ended and the glaciers went through, all of North America was reseeded from those mother forests of Appalachia. Today, companies like Massey Coal are accomplishing what the glaciers could not which is to destroy the rivers, flattening the mountain ranges, and leveling the forest. In doing that, they are destroying terrestrial and ecosystems, as well as impacting aquatic and marine ecology all the way down to the Gulf of Mexico.

Coal may be part of our foreseeable energy future, but that doesn't mean we should let mining companies destroy biologically diverse forests and fill our rivers and streams with debris.

Q. What are your thoughts on the BP Oil spill?

A. The BP oil spill in the Gulf of Mexico is the single greatest damaging environmental incident in modern American history and arguably the greatest theft ever perpetrated against the American people. The Exxon Valdez spill affected 1,300 miles of shoreline. Most all the fisheries have never recovered fully including the salmon and herring. But the BP Gulf spill will impact 9,000 miles of American shoreline, which serves 40% of American seafood, 60% of the oysters, and 85% of the shrimp, and will hinder recreation areas, and property values for millions and millions of American citizens.

Those shorelines do not belong to British Petroleum Corporation. They belong to the American public, that is what the law says. There is an ancient law called the Public

Mountaintop removal destroys ecosystems

Trust Doctrine since the probligation of the Code of Jestinium in ancient Rome, it's also in the Magna Carta, and in the Constitution of every state. The Public Trust Document has protected the public right to shoreline, fisheries, and waterways, and are the same rights which are also guaranteed by the Magna Carta since the dawn of constitutional democracy.

It was the fountainhead of constitutional democracy, and these laws are enshrined in the Constitution for each of our states, including the Constitutions for each of the Gulf States. They mandate that waterways, beaches, shorelines, and the fisheries belong to the public. They do not belong to the governor, the legislators, or the conservation departments of any of those respective states, and they certainly do not belong to the oil companies or other corporations. They belong to the people. Every citizen has a right to use them. No one has a right to

Oiled washed up on beach in Louisiana   Deepwater Horizon explosion   Oil and crude in the Gulf of Mexico

use them, to injure or diminish their use as enjoyment by others. When BP dumps or causes oil to be dumped on a public beach, there is no difference.

Legally speaking, if someone pulled a tanker up to your front lawn, and dumped the contents and all the oil residues into your yard they would be trespassing and stealing from you which you would not tolerate. You would tell the company to take it all away, down to the very last molecule. This is our property and for every citizen in Alabama, Louisiana, Texas, Florida, and Mississippi, the Gulf of Mexico is the people's property, and for most of them it is the single biggest thing they will ever own. So we need to fight, we need to punish BP the same way you punish any other thief.

The only way our environment will be saved is by the people who love it, who are willing to give their lives and passions to protect it, not by corporations driven by greed.

Mr. Kennedy serves as Chief Prosecuting Attorney for the Hudson Riverkeeper *and President of* Waterkeeper Alliance*. He is also a Clinical Professor and Supervising Attorney at* Pace University School of Law's Environmental Litigation Clinic *and Senior Attorney for the* National Resource Defense Council*. Earlier in his career he served as Assistant District Attorney in New York City. Mr. Kennedy was named one of* Time *magazine's* Heroes for the Planet *for his success in helping* Riverkeeper *lead the fight to restore the Hudson River. The group's achievement helped spawn more than 130 Waterkeeper organizations across the globe. Robert F. Kennedy, Jr. is the son to Robert F. Kennedy and nephew of President John F. Kennedy and Senator Edward M. Kennedy. Among Mr. Kennedy's published books are the New York Times' bestseller* Crimes Against Nature *(2004),* St. Francis of Assisi: A Life of Joy *(2005),* The Riverkeepers *(1997), and* Judge Frank M. Johnson, Jr.: A Biography *(1977). He is a licensed master Falconer, and as often as possible he pursues a life-long enthusiasm for white-water paddling.*

www.robertfkennedyjr.com • www.waterkeeper.org

Ray Huff

Q. As an architect, and living near the coast, you said you have some concerns about the way people build in regard to the ocean, and where they build. Can you elaborate on that subject?

A. Living in a delta plain, it is apparent that building patterns of the recent past have been irresponsible at best. I live in the South Carolina Low Country, which is a watershed and consists of a rich maritime environment of marshes and barrier islands. These features have immense importance to the coastal ecosystem. The marshes are beautiful vistas of spartina grasses that are some of the most fertile ecosystems on the planet. Barrier islands are essentially sand bars formed over many years that provide natural protection to the mainland during storm events. Both the marshes and the barriers are under threat. Over development on the islands have contributed to various degradations such as accelerated erosion and loss of natural flora including species that minimized erosion due to tides and wind.

Traditionally, people who either worked the land or subsisted on maritime occupations inhabited the islands. Today, new development has been occurring at an alarming rate, as it is in other similar areas around the world. The natural environment cannot sustain this level of development so we see familiar patterns of degradation. These patterns of coastal development occur up and down the eastern seaboard and show no sign of abatement. The imbalances in the environment itself constitute a major concern but when rising ocean levels are factored in, the situation becomes calamitous.

Now, society will be saddled with effectively undoing these developments at tremendous expenditures of public and private funding and resulting in dramatic changes in settlement patterns. And, the condition I've described relates primarily to non-urban environments. Urban developments like my home, Charleston, South Carolina, portend even more serious considerations. Not unlike what the country faced with the Katrina catastrophe, the question must be asked at what cost does a society decides to value a community? Charleston, like New Orleans, is an historic city with an important history. It, too, is a low-lying urban village with parts of the city no more that 5 feet above mean level. As sea level increases occur what can or should be done to protect this city? Or any other for that matter? This 350-year-old plus city developed as a major shipping port because of its naturally protected harbor. In the beginning, development occurred only on 'high ground' and densified on the peninsula. More recently, development has abandoned this original pattern resulting in sprawl like virtually every other American city and now constitutes a community imperiled by the consequences of climate change.

These two conditions represent but some of the difficult choices societies face with regard to the nature of the type of retrenchment that prognosticators suggests will be required as sea level changes and settlement patterns are inalterably affected.

Q. As one of the few people that have been fortunate enough to visit the North Pole, can you talk about your trip and share what you learned by actually being there?

A. Visiting the northern most territories of Baffin Bay is an eye opener for anyone that has made that voyage. Imagine flying out of Ottawa Canada for six hours and 2,200 nautical miles due north before you arrive at one of the last settlements to the north. When you experience the utter vastness of this still not entirely charted region do you begin to really comprehend the reality of global climate change. Talking with local Inuit people about how their lives have been affected and how they have observed firsthand the accelerated changes in the Polar Ice

Cap, brings home in blunt fashion the immediacy of the issue. Most of us understand the new global society we live in but when visiting settlements like Resolute in Nanavut Territory, this situation is revealed in high relief. Resolute is one of the most northern settlements in the world. Immediately upon arrival young Inuit boys dressed in urban street threads and listening to hip-hop on their iPods greeted us. The interdependence of global societies was brought home loud and clear. But nevertheless these young people understand the changes that are occurring with the melting of the ice cap as their villages' traditions have had to adapt to these changes even within their young lifetime. With traveling through this enormous territory and listening to the locals tell you of the vanishing polar bear and the diminution of traditional hunting grounds, this crisis is exposed in stark reality to vagaries of the lower world's indecision about this pending calamity.

Q. What are your thoughts on sea level rise, as you mentioned that is also a concern of yours?

A. Absolutely. As I've described, I live on the coast in a delta plain. My urban home sits on land that is only nine feet above mean sea level. In addition to my design practice, I teach graduate architecture at the *Clemson Architecture Center* in Charleston. Recently, the students examined the effect of sea rise on Charleston using several climate models. Their approach was graphical to illustrate the immediate risks that a coastal location likes Charleston must confront. The study first demonstrated what would happen to the city, which has a median high tide of seven feet above mean level, if the sea rose one meter. The effect was alarming and would have significant impact on the city. But at three meters, the dynamic changed demonstratively. Much of the low-lying areas would be submerged and the city would return to its historic form that had been defined by its high land. This was precisely the circumstance in New Orleans wherein the historic city core, the high land, managed to escape much of the flooding that beseeched other parts of the city.

At six meters, the city all but disappears. The students worked with university scientists to arrive at their projections and if recent accounts prove to be true and the Greenland ice cap does melt, then cities such as Charleston throughout the world would either cease to exists or be dramatically changed.

Such an event will mean a sea change in settlement patterns throughout the world. One might argue that such changes are perhaps needed as cultures have exploited the sea edge in more recent periods unwisely and this pending phenomenon is the price for irresponsible development. Charleston and New Orleans, perhaps among many coastal cities, will have to learn to retreat to a development pattern that is more resourceful and respectful.

Q. If you had another particular ocean issue that you could focus on what would it be, and how can people help the situation?

A. The oceans are a vast resource not to be solely exploited but to be better understood. It continues to amaze me how little we understand of our oceanic bodies. It has been said that we know more about celestial development than we do about the oceans at our feet. While sea rise has garnered much of the attention of late and for good reason, we must prioritize efforts to protect the quality of our oceans and its resources. Over fishing, pollution, contamination, and essentially general disregard have marked our recent past. This must change if we are to survive beyond the rigors of climate change and the deterioration of our oceans.

Q. Do you have any last thoughts you would like to share?

A. The debate around climate change has been thoroughly politicized, either for ideological or economic reasons. I have often wondered why there should be objection to the very idea of climate change if one removes the prevailing polemic and simply ask the question: What is the right thing to do regardless if man is or is not responsible for this situation? Put aside the debate and simply ask the fundamental question, why not be good stewards of the environment and our future regardless of whether is it facing impending collapse or whether this is a naturally occurring phenomena? Isn't this simply the right thing to do?

Ray Huff's architectural firm has been selected by the City of New York for Mayor Michael Bloomberg's design and construction excellence program. In addition to teaching at Clemson Architecture Center, *Ray held the distinguished Bishop Chair at* Yale.

www.huffgooden.com

Photo Shari Sant Plummer

David Guggenheim, Ph.D.

Q. Can you explain what a submersible is and a little about its technology?

A. A submersible is a submarine, though usually smaller and designed to operate underwater for shorter periods of time than the larger military submarines. I've been lucky enough to live out my childhood dream of being a sub pilot, beginning more than a decade ago. I'm now proficient on two subs, the *DeepWorker* and *DeepRover*, both manufactured by Nuytco, Ltd. in Vancouver. Both hold only one person and have no tether to the surface, so you're free to move about the ocean! The *DeepWorker* will take you to 2,000 feet, the *DeepRover* to 3,000 feet, and both will keep you there for up to three days, though the average dive is usually 4-6 hours. These submersibles are powered by electricity and use air recirculation systems just like spacecraft, removing the carbon dioxide from the air with special CO_2 scrubbers. Essentially, it's a rebreather, except instead of strapping it to your back, you're strapped inside. The most important thing about this technology is that inside the cabin you are always at one atmosphere of pressure, so you experience no pressure change from the surface, even though outside the sub is experiencing tremendous pressures at depth. Pressure is the biggest danger to divers, resulting in all sorts of maladies, including the bends, nitrogen narcosis and oxygen toxicity. Using conventional scuba, divers are typically limited to a depth of little more than 100 feet and can only stay for 20 minutes or so. Using special "mixed gases" or rebreathers, divers can go more than 200 feet, but again, not for long, and they must take great care to ascend slowly to allow nitrogen, which has dissolved in their blood under pressure, to escape, lest bubbles form and decompression sickness – the bends – ensue. With a mini-sub, you can stay at depth as long as you like, move up and down, and never worry about pressure effects. It's truly revolutionary technology.

Q. What have been some of the biggest surprises you've experienced underwater both positive and otherwise?

A. Over the past decade I've spent more time as a submersible pilot with the opportunity to go deep and explore areas no other humans have ever seen. Most of us have an abstract vision of the bottom of the deep ocean as dark and lifeless. The dark part is correct, but "lifeless?" Not hardly. During an expedition to the Bering Sea in Alaska with *Greenpeace*, I went deeper than I ever had before, to close to 2,000 feet, and found it dark, cold, under incredible pressure, yet absolutely teeming with life. I love to see such rich diversity in such a hostile environment, including absolutely beautiful deepwater corals, in remarkably brilliant shades of pink, orange and white in stark contrast to the brown-gray mud and sand around them.

On one dive at about 1,000 feet, I thought I had found some sort of geologic feature until I realized I had landed my sub in the swath of where a huge fishing trawl had passed. I was shocked by the scale of what I was seeing. It was like an airport runway, wider than an 8-lane highway and undoubtedly miles long. Nothing was left in the trawl's path – the fish, corals, even the rocks were gone. Bottom trawling is horrific, and it was surely the worst thing I've ever laid eyes on underwater.

I think the biggest underwater surprise of my life – and fortunately the most pleasant one – came during some of my field work in Cuba. I recently visited an area near Cayo Levisa, I was absolutely stunned to see massive stands of healthy elkhorn coral, the poster child for the demise of corals in the Caribbean, a species that *NOAA* estimates has been reduced by 95 percent in the Florida Keys, and much of the Caribbean. A few weeks later, off Cuba's southern coast in Jardines de la Reina, I was even more stunned to experience what can best be described as a journey back through time to see what the oceans looked like when Columbus first plied these waters centuries ago, and what the oceans should look like today. Surrounded by large numbers of large, friendly groupers and sharks on virtually all of their dives, we even found plentiful numbers of the endangered Nassau Grouper along with healthy corals and other invertebrates, including the long-absent black

David Guggenheim is known as the "Ocean Doctor." He is an ocean explorer, scientist, submarine operator as well as a consultant for ocean policy in Washington D.C. With a Ph.D. in Environmental Science and Public Policy and a Masters in Population and Aquatic Biology, David members the Advisory Council of the Harte Research Institute for Gulf of Mexico Studies. *He also serves as Cuba's programs manager.*

www.1ocean1planet.org • www.oceandoctor.org

spiny sea urchin. I found profound hope in the fact that places like this still exist. And I found more hope knowing that this was an example of what is possible when human beings find the courage to do no less than what it takes to take care of our oceans.

Q. You were kind of joking that you spend half your time in a "wool suit," and half of your time in a "wet suit." Can you explain what your actual job is for those who don't know, and explain about how you are working together with Cuba, the United States, and Mexico?

A. I pursued a career as a marine scientist, envisioning myself as an academic scientist. However, as my career evolved, I came to realize that science alone wasn't enough to change the world. Someone had to take the science, interpret it, translate it, and bring those insights to the public and governmental leaders. I began to realize that if I wanted to achieve this I needed to be part scientist, part science manager and part science communicator. I moved to Washington, D.C. and completed a Ph.D. in Environmental Science and Public Policy, essentially a marriage of science and policy – one that I've come to realize isn't always such a happy marriage. I have suits that I wear to conservation policy meetings around D.C., and hanging next to them are a couple of wetsuits that I wear to my more interesting meetings with my "clients," the fish and corals. The work of conservation requires both work in the field and work in the countless windowless conference rooms and I think it helps me to have a foot in both the science and policy worlds. It also helps to be a diplomat. Over the past few years I've been leading an effort to elevate collaboration in marine science and conservation among Cuba, Mexico and the U.S. to a new level. I enjoy international work immensely, perhaps for the same reason I enjoy exploring the oceans. It's a great gift to be able to travel the world and learn about new cultures, build new partnerships and form new friendships. Though working in Cuba and other exotic places may sound glamorous, the sad truth is that there are many windowless conference rooms involved. Still, it's a blast.

Q. You have been traveling around the country with the goal of donating speeches about the oceans to schools in all 50 states. What is the message that you are trying to convey to these kids and what do you see for their future?

Photo Todd Warshaw

Photo Abel Valdivia

A. Since I began this journey – Ocean Doctor's 50 Years - 50 States - 50 Speeches Expedition – I've been on the road constantly and have delivered dozens of speeches to tens of thousands of students. What began as a deeply personal quest to celebrate my 50th birthday, and honor the memory of my father, has evolved into something much more. I try to get kids excited about careers in science and the oceans, and I'm always reminding them that 95 percent of the oceans remain unexplored, so it's their generation that will have the best opportunity yet to explore this vast frontier. Young people still know very little about the oceans, and in many parts of the country, are increasingly living lives devoid of any contact with nature. Many of the students I've met had no idea about the critical issues facing the oceans, such as over fishing, pollution and the devastating impacts of climate change. In a small community in Georgia, many students in the local high school have never traveled more than a few miles from home and have had virtually no experience with Mother Nature, and school budget cuts are not helping. I was especially inspired by a sixth grader near Atlanta named Shelby, who started a petition against shark finning, the cruel and unsustainable practice of slicing off a shark's dorsal fin for shark fin soup, a practice that kills the animal. Her petition made its way all the way to the U.S. Senate in Washington, and earlier this year the Senate passed the Shark Conservation Act of 2009, banning the practice in the U.S. We have to engage the next generation like never before, and make sure they engage the generation that follows, and so on. I'm inspired by the students I've met around the country. They want to do the right thing. With a little encouragement from us, they will.

Jack Johnson

Q. What is your favorite thing about the ocean?

A. One of my favorite things about the ocean is my memories of spending time with my dad exploring the Hawaiian Islands. We would camp, fish, snorkel, surf, and check out the islands. We would spend the entire day on the ocean investigating the rocks, and the shorelines and we would go on hikes in the valleys. Those are some of the most fun times I had as a kid, and my best memories growing up. It was so nice because we were on a little boat with very few material things, yet we were having the time of our lives. Looking back as I get older, I believe it was those significant experiences that have shaped me for who I am today. I feel so lucky to have been able to have had those experiences being in nature like that.

The ocean is a soulful thing, too. Whether it is surfing and telling stories to friends, or simply gazing at the sea. The ocean is a place that I enjoy myself, and on the other end of the spectrum, it is a place where I can balance myself. The ocean grounds me, it fulfills me and it gives me a good perspective so I feel connected with myself and all the people around me. The ocean is like my church because I connect to it spiritually, and it is my place to go for solitude.

Q. Which of the many ocean issues concerns you the most?

Photo Emmett Malloy

A. Growing up in Hawaii, it is quite apparent we have a major plastic pollution issue. On the windward side, or the eastern sides of the island you will see that the Hawaiian Islands act as a filter for the Pacific Ocean. It catches all the debris and there are walls of plastic along the east shore. Seeing all this debris at such a young age gets you to wonder how could there be so much of it? You then realize that this is only a small fraction of it all.

Reducing the amount of single use plastics in the world, and in my community, is an issue close to my heart. When we go on tour, my band and I like to acknowledge to the people that we need to consider using less plastic bottles and bags, and other single use plastics. This is an arena we feel comes with a certain amount of responsibility. We enjoy playing music night after night, and also promoting people to be more conscious of making little changes. We feel the messaging is an important part of our job. We like to use the stage for entertainment, and playing music and singing songs, but we like to provide other areas for people to learn about both local, and national, non-profit environmental groups. For instance, *Surfrider Foundation* was able to deliver a strong campaign about using less single use plastics on our past tour. I believe that kids between 15 years old, to their early 20s, are the years that kids figure out which way they're going to approach the world. Lots of these people are learning with us, and from the groups that are at our concerts, and that gives me a certain sense of satisfaction. It is not like I have all the perfect answers, or I am living the perfect life, but I do have the chance to direct people to these groups that have tons of great information. It is nice to know that we can teach, as well as learn, while we are on the road.

Q. You've been a great role model as a musician and an environmental advocate. What are some of the things you can recommend to people to be more environmentally conscious and to help our oceans?

A. The key is to listen to your kids, and if you don't have kids then listen to the younger generation. They are the ones that are going to be the leaders with great ideas. I know for me, when I try to look at the world through the eyes of my kids, I get really inspired to keep learning, and to keep an open mind, and for me, that's what I think it is all about. There are a lot of little baby steps we have taken in our personal life from recycling garbage, vermicasting, installing solar panels around the house, to building little water catching rain barrels with the kids for irrigation. We need to refrain the definition of an environmentalist, and what it means to be one. I would think anybody who cares about the world would naturally be an environmentalist. If you consider humans to be part of nature, which I hope that everybody does, then nature and the environment are the same thing because we are connected to all the things around us.

Everything is part of the environment, like humans and the things that we make, everything . . . including the most environmentally taxing structures we've built such as oil rigs. All the things we have made become our environment, the same way a bird builds a nest. Even if it is something we need to move away from, and more toward alternative fuel, or renewable energy; these are all natural steps along the way. Rather than finger pointing and claiming, "That guy is an environmentalist," we need to take a different approach and reframe that word, and understand that this is a fun way to live. It is not just a scary thing like some people do, and some people don't. It's all about taking little steps in changing living habits, like reducing and recycling. These are little things we can all do around the house, and they are fun little projects, and an inspiring way to live.

Q. What are your thoughts on offshore drilling, especially with the recent oil spill in the Gulf of Mexico?

A. It is such a complex issue, but of course I would wish we would never have to drill offshore at all. But then you have to realize how much of our current infrastructure is set up on oil right now. I'd much rather see all our energy, and our money, go toward renewable energy. Especially living in Hawaii you can see how it could be the leading place in the world for renewable energy since we have so much wind, solar ability, and waves. There are plenty of ways we can tap into this natural energy here and around the world.

Q. If you could send a message to all the people around the world what would it be?

A. Work with the kids. The best ideas anyone may have should focus on a plan toward kids, and planting seeds with them. With all the work we do, we like to focus on environmental education toward the younger generation because we really enjoy seeing them grow. I like to go to the classrooms and sing songs to elementary schools about reduce, reuse, and recycle. It's cool to engage with the kids and tell them about how to vermicast. It's cool to let them put their fingers in the dirt to touch the worms, and plant seeds and gardens around their schools. It's quite rewarding to see the kids you've met with over the years graduate from high school, that end up studying environmental law, or starting a club on campus at high school or becoming a leader to recycle in their school. Everything grows exponentially when working with kids and seeing their personal growth is one of my favorite things.

Photo Emmett Malloy

Jack Johnson is a singer, songwriter, filmmaker, surfer, and record label owner. He was born and raised in Hawaii. His organization hosts the "Kokua Festival" where all the money earned goes back to the community. Jack encourages kids to interact with nature and to reduce, reuse and recycle.

www.jackjohnsonmusic.com
www.kokuahawaiifoundation.org

Roz Savage

Q. You once said that you envisioned fast-forwarding your life and saw two completely different scenarios. Can you please elaborate on this?

A. I was in my mid-thirties, and still doing the job I had taken as a stop-gap at the age of 21. I seemed to be living somebody else's life, not my own, and the main clue my life had fallen off track was a subtle but pervasive unhappiness, a hollow, empty feeling deep inside. I had always done what I thought other people expected me to do, following my head rather than my heart. And now I was too bound up in my day to day life, too attached to the things I'd come to rely on like my need for "success" and security to think freely and figure out what I really wanted out of life. In order to liberate my dreams, I had to step outside myself and pretend to be the kind of person whose obituary I enjoyed reading, a colorful, vibrant, vividly alive kind of person. I remember that as I wrote that obituary I felt excited, happy and fulfilled. Then I tried to write the obituary that I was actually heading for. My emotional state totally changed. I felt faintly depressed, bored and an overwhelming sense of wasted opportunity. I was shocked at the contrast between the emotions aroused by two conflicting obituaries and scared of the changes that now seemed necessary. But now, several years later, and having made those changes, I have a strong sense of integrity and happiness, and I am so grateful for that moment of insight.

Q. In 2006 you rowed solo across the Atlantic, and now you have completed two stages of a three-stage solo row across the Pacific. Why did you do this, and what is the message you hope to convey by doing so?

A. Ocean rowing appealed to me because I wanted to grow as a person, and find out what I was capable of, and the ocean has certainly enabled me to do that. My three long voyages, each involving spending around 100 days completely alone, thousands of miles from land, have given me plenty of time to think and figure things out. There were so many times on the Atlantic when I thought I had hit my absolute limit – of boredom, pain, discomfort, or impatience, and I just had to figure out how to deal with it without going crazy. It's amazing what you can handle when you have no choice. I hope I'm showing what an ordinary person can achieve, given enough determination. It was also essential to me that my adventures be environmentally low-impact. Just after I had my obituary epiphany, I also had an environmental epiphany, inspired by reading about the Hopi tribe of North America and their ethos that we have to look after the planet if we want it to look after us. This made absolute sense, and I was suddenly horrified by how blind I'd been to the obvious fact that we are on an unsustainable path of over-consumption and pollution. So although I'm still far from perfect, I'm doing my best to reduce my

environmental impact, and through my rowing adventures I hope to inspire other people to live more consciously too.

Q. What is your number one concern for the environment, specifically for the ocean?

A. Rather than expressing something bad, I'd like to express a wish for something good. I wish that humankind would stop for a moment and look at where we're heading, just as I did when I wrote my two obituaries. If we carry on living as we are now, where are we going to be in 50 or 100 years? Is that where we want to be? And if not, then what changes do we need to make to get back on track for a sustainable future? It's not rocket science. You don't need to be an environmental expert to see that we can't carry on taking good stuff out of the earth, turning it into trash, and throwing it back into a landfill or into the oceans. On a finite planet, you can't carry on pumping toxins and pesticides into the environment and hope that they will just go away. The ocean has taught me that we are, ultimately, just another animal, and as

Photo Mrs. Rita Savage

subject to the laws of nature as any other creature. If a population gets out of control and places too heavy a demand on its environment, eventually there will be an adjustment. It would be better for humans if we succeed in regulating ourselves before nature does it for us.

Q. If you could offer people around the world words to live by, what would they be?

A. My father used to say to me, "Whatever you do, put your whole heart into it," and those are words I try to live by. It sums up so many things: the power of enthusiasm, the importance of being passionate about what you do, and the idea that you know you're on track when both head and heart agree on which way to go.

Roz Savage is a British ocean rower, author, motivational speaker and environmental campaigner. She has rowed solo across the Atlantic Ocean and is attempting to become the first woman to row solo across the Pacific. Roz is a United Nations Climate Hero, a trained presenter for the Climate Project, and an Athlete Ambassador for 350.org. Her Pacific row is a project of the Blue Frontier Campaign and she is an Ambassador for the BLUE Project.

www.rozsavage.com

Keely and Pierce Brosnan

Photo Mark Liddell

Q. You two have been working to protect whales for many years and have had some significant successes, including helping to stop Mitsubishi from building the world's largest industrial salt plant on the shores of Laguna San Ignacio, Mexico which is a vital breeding ground of the grey whale; and stopping a proposed liquefied natural gas (LNG) terminal from being built off the coast of Oxnard and Malibu in a marine sanctuary. What other concerns do you have for the whales now?

A. Surprisingly, whales face more threats today than ever before . . . from entanglement in marine debris and fishing gear, to ship strikes, noise pollution, ozone depletion, global warming, ocean acidification, and whaling. However, the biggest threat whales face today is pollution and contaminates--particularly toxic metals. Roger Payne's institute, Ocean Alliance, has just released a report from their 5-year voyage around the world measuring baseline levels of toxic metals and POPs (persistent organic pollutants--substances like DDT, PCBs and fire retardants) in the skin and blubber of sperm whales. They brought back 955 sperm whale biopsy samples from all the world's oceans.

Marine toxicologists John Wise at the University of Southern Maine and Maria Cristina Fossi at Italy's Sienna University analyzed these samples. They concluded that sperm whales are contaminated wherever they are found--even in ocean regions that lie far from major industry and corporate agriculture. Research indicates the worst problem is chromium. It's a major carcinogen—a cancer-causing agent. (The film "Erin Brockavich" is about chromium pollution.) Some of the sperm whales biopsied had chromium levels equal to those found in the lungs of human workers who had worked for decades in factories producing chromium compounds and who had died of lung cancer triggered by such exposure.

These results from Ocean Alliance's work indicate that ocean life is polluted to a shocking degree. Roger chose to study sperm whales because they live at the top of the ocean food chain. Humans also live at the top of ocean food chains, which means that what is happening to sperm whales may also probably happening to us.

As for whaling, concerned individuals, animal lovers, and environmental groups worldwide recently fought a major battle to maintain the 1982 global moratorium on commercial whaling. Against all odds, we prevailed. After several years of closed-door negotiations, the Obama Administration and other conservation-minded governments wisely rejected an appalling proposal designed to legalize commercial whaling for Japan, Iceland and Norway and to allow the slaughter of whales in the international whale sanctuary in the Southern Ocean.

The moratorium on commercial whaling (which has saved tens of thousands of whales worldwide) and the creation of the Southern Ocean Whale Sanctuary in 1994 were both attained with high level, bi-partisan support from the United States. That same level of leadership and commitment is needed again now, following the International Whaling Commission meeting in Morocco to secure previous gains, end illegal/commercial whaling, and to put the International Whaling Commission on course for a sustainable, conservation-based future.

Our current administration must implement a new agreement and pass legislation (H.R.2455 the International Whale Conservation and Protection Act of 2009) that will guarantee both the conservation and the rehabilitation of whale populations for generations to come. The health of the oceans and the ocean ecosystem will be greatly diminished if we do not protect these majestic creatures (some of the most endangered species in the world).

Q. What needs to be done in order to better protect the whales worldwide?

A. The vast majority of Americans support whale conservation. They recognize that whales are of great aesthetic and scientific interest to mankind and are a vital part of the marine ecosystem. Thus, we need to influence, persuade and sometimes pressure our government to:

- Encourage Japan, Iceland and Norway, the last three countries killing whales to halt the international trade in whale products and to join the global movement for whale conservation. As whales migrate throughout the world's oceans, international cooperation is essential to successfully protect them.

- Join Australia, New Zealand and other nations in funding world-class, non-lethal research on whales and their habitats.

- Work through the IWC Conservation Committee to advance state-of-the art conservation plans that safeguard threatened whale species and populations.

- Reform and recast the IWC as a more transparent and accountable "International Whale Commission" with a clear and compelling conservation mandate for the 21st century.
- Restore the primacy of the IWC Scientific Committee as the recognized international authority on whale conservation science and engage its expertise to improve human understanding of whales and the numerous threats they face.
- Consider environmental issues related to climate change as well as the possible adverse effects from high intensity anthropogenic sound, and new offshore industrial developments for energy projects.

Naturally, this is a rather ambitious agenda, but one that may be possible to achieve if we put heart and soul into protecting whales. Rather than facilitating protracted negotiations to define terms under which commercial whaling will be permitted to continue, the time has come for the United States to lead the effort to protect whales and end whaling. We must reassert global leadership to ensure that commercial, scientific, or any other type of lethal whaling for non-aboriginal subsistence purposes does not occur. In that sense, our most important work has just begun.

Q. How can people help?

A. The answer is simple: use your voice. Stand up for what you believe is right. Ask our President and your state representatives to pass legislation to protect whales and their habitat. Everything begins with education. The most important thing anyone can do is to align themselves with an environmental organization that is committed to issues they believe in. We work with the International Fund for Animal Welfare, the Natural Resources Defense Council and Ocean Alliance because of their interest in protecting marine mammals and the oceans.

Q. LNG seems to be making news headlines, as more and more people protest facilities being built in their hometowns. What are your views on liquid nitrogen gas?

A. As the planet begins to run out of oil, the largest oil and mining corporations are hinging their hopes on a global market in Liquefied Natural Gas (or LNG) to replace an anticipated decline in oil revenues. It is critical to remember that LNG is a (polluting) fossil fuel, which is extracted in its gaseous form, super-chilled to a liquid state, then shipped on supertankers to markets across the globe, where it must be converted back into a gaseous state; only then can it be delivered to homes in the form of natural gas. It is during the liquefaction and regasification process that the potential for a catastrophic event can occur. To date, several fatal accidents related to LNG have taken place in the US and abroad. Given that LNG poses a serious hazard of explosion or fire, a U.S. Congressional Research Report stated that LNG terminals and tankers are vulnerable to terrorist attacks.

In addition to safety and security concerns, LNG and its life cycle from extraction through combustion is just one more highly polluting way station that blocks our path to a clean, renewable energy future in the 21st century. The massive 971 foot floating terminal that was potentially to be anchored off the coast of Oxnard and Malibu (and curiously sited near the Channel Islands in a marine sanctuary), was estimated to produce 200 tons of smog pollutants and 25 million tons of greenhouse gas emissions each year. Left unchecked, the potential proliferation of LNG terminals and tankers will significantly increase our contribution to global warming and climate change. Finally, these terminals are often proposed in ecologically sensitive areas, over the objections of local residents, and carry the potential for devastating impacts to our ocean, marine life and land-based ecosystems.

Q. Do you have any last thoughts you would like to share?

A. We believe in the power of one and the power of many. When we work together, we are stronger, our voices louder and the synergy of our actions more powerful. Protecting the environment is a bi-partisan issue and a global issue. Pollution knows no boundaries. Protecting the environment should be at the forefront of all our actions and United States policies, because the health of our bodies (and our children's bodies) is inextricably linked to the health of our environment. The one crime for which our children and grandchildren will not forgive us is the destruction of unique life (species) and the impoverishment of our environment.

Isabel Lucas

Q. What is your direct and intimate relationship to the ocean? (i.e. did you grow up near the ocean; did you have an experience at a young age that bonded you to the ocean?)

A. I grew up predominantly in Melbourne and then Cairns, Australia, both are coastal cities. When I was a child we spent a lot of time on the beaches in Melbourne playing and looking for shells and washed-up treasures, and later in Cairns I discovered the wondrous world of the Great Barrier Reef with its colorful fish and coral. I'm truly in awe of the sea and its amazing creatures from whales to dolphins to sea horses.

Q. What is the most important issue for you surrounding ocean preservation, and do you have any ocean heros?

A. The ocean is an amazing eco-system that is threatened because of global warming, acidification, over-fishing, pollution, and other unbalancing factors. The preservation of its creatures and their food sources through creating large-scale sanctuaries and protected zones is equally important as preventing pollution and exploitation. We should focus on eco-tourism as a means of income rather than killing whales and marine life. As far as heros, Captain Paul Watson (and *Sea Shepherd*), is an uncompromising and determined warrior who has saved

Photo Peter Carrette   Photo Peter Carrette   Photo Peter Carrette   Photo Mark Squires   Photo Peter Carrette

many whales. I also deeply respect Dave Rastovich (a surfer friend who organized the ceremony in Taiji), Ric O'Barry (*The Cove*), and Jeff Pantukhoff (*Whaleman Foundation*). They dedicate so much of their time, energy and resources to creating awareness of the importance of the oceans preservation and protecting the amazing sea creatures.

Q. What feelings and emotions did the Taiji action evoke and would you do it again if given the opportunity?

A. Yes, I would do it again. This cause and trip to Taiji was a deeply emotional and personal experience. We wanted to create our own small ceremony to honor the lives of the dolphins and whales that had been slaughtered. Each of us who paddled into the killing cove were overwhelmed by the sadness and absurdity of what was happening in front of our eyes. We've all seen our share of animal rights films, and documentary footage in slaughter houses etc, but to actually be witnessing these events, this cruelty, firsthand, was life-altering. Reflecting back now, before I went on the trip I was an idealist and I now consider myself a realist. But whether you're realist, idealist, pessimist, optimist, it's blatantly clear and glaring us in the face how wrong this it is to barbarically slaughter intelligent life. I came to see that these sentient beings are not that different from our kind. The main difference is they are living peacefully with one another.

Q. Do you have any advice you would like to offer?

A. Join and support environmental organizations, educate yourself about the issues and discuss them with friends. Recycle whenever you can, write letters to politicians and the media to express your thoughts that the oceans need to be protected for our children and future generations. Also appreciate and enjoy the ocean and beaches, and show your respect through living more sustainably and thoughtfully.

Isabel Lucas is an Australian actor who was featured in the American film Transformers. *She has dedicated much of her life to various environmental campaigns from whaling to protesting against Japanese dolphin slaughtering in Taiji.*

www.whaleman.org • www.protectourcoralsea.org.au

Serge Dedina, Ph.D.

Q. You were only seven years old when you first began doing environmental work. What inspired you to make a difference and why?

A. I grew up near the Tijuana Estuary in Imperial Beach, California, just north of the U.S.-Mexico border. One day I heard that there was going to be a marina and high-rise buildings built there. Since the Estuary was my backyard playground and the favorite beach spot for my family, at seven I wrote my first letter to the editor of our local newspaper stating my opposition to the project. Later at the age of 16, I sat in front of bulldozers to stop the destruction of the estuary. We stopped the marina project and the Tijuana Estuary was later declared a National Wildlife Refuge. Today, it is so satisfying to surf just outside the Tijuana Estuary with my two sons and bird watch there with my wife Emily, knowing that I helped save what is now one of the largest remaining coastal wetlands in Southern California.

Q. What does *WiLDCOAST* do, and what areas in Baja California, Mexico are most important to protect?

A. *WiLDCOAST* conserves coastal and marine ecosystems and wildlife. We are conserving large coastal areas in Baja California where you have a combination of island, salt marsh, mangrove, marine and desert ecosystems. Priority coastal and marine conservation areas for conservation in Baja include Bahia de los Angeles, Bahia Concepcion, the Upper Sea of Cortez, Loreto to La Paz coastal corridor, Cabo Pulmo, Bahia Magdalena, Laguna San Ignacio, Los Cirios Central Pacific Coast, and the critically important Sea of Cortez and Pacific Islands.

Q. Why is the coastline of Baja such a magical place to you?

A. The coast of Baja California is everything a wild seascape is supposed to be and what California once was: endless untrammeled beaches with a vast ocean and desert surrounding them. I have had the most memorable experiences along the coast of Baja including surfing perfect waves with bottlenose dolphins, kayaking around breaching gray whales, swimming with whale sharks and observing the stunning beauty of rare Peninsular pronghorn prancing in the desert near Scammon's Lagoon. One time in Laguna San Ignacio, I surprised an adult bobcat that had fallen asleep next to a recently dead baby whale. I'll never forget the look of surprise on the cat's face and how it sauntered away into the desert.

Q. What campaign(s) are you most proud of that *WiLDCOAST* worked at? What did you accomplish and why?

A. At *WiLDCOAST* we have had great success with our efforts to stop the slaughter of sharks and sea turtles, but I co-founded *WiLDCOAST* to make sure we could conserve what was remaining of the peninsula's wild coastline. So I am exceptionally proud of our role in helping stop the Mitsubishi Corporation from building an industrial salt facility in Laguna San Ignacio. We then subsequently worked with our conservation partners, local landowners and the

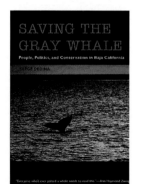

Serge Dedina is the Executive Director and co-founder of WiLDCOAST. The author of Saving the Gray Whale *and the forthcoming* Eco-Wars *and* Surf Stories from the Coast of the Californias, *Serge received the* San Diego Zoological Society's *Conservation Medal,* Surf Industry Manufacturer's Association (SIMA) *Environmental Award, and the California Coastal Hero Award for his role in helping to conserve the coastline of the Californias.*

www.wildcoast.net • www.costasalvaje.com

Mexican National Protected Area Commission to protect over 200,000 acres of pristine lagoon habitat in a way that both benefitted local wildlife and residents. That success gave us the boost to be able to protect an additional 30 miles of wild coastline so far in the Los Cirios Wildlife Refuge in Central Pacific Baja.

Q. Do you have any last thoughts you would like to share?

A. There is something so great about seeing and interacting with wild coastal and marine places. Giving the chance of future generations to have the opportunity to witness and be in nature as it is meant to be is so important. Who would not want the opportunity to make sure that our children and grandchildren can swim with sea lions, explore empty coves on a stunning island, or pet a baby gray whale in Laguna San Ignacio.

Paul Naudé

Q. What does the ocean mean to you?

A. Since the age of 12, the ocean has been an integral part of my life. I have had some of my most spiritual moments in the ocean, and swimming with her dolphins. The ocean is the platform from which stems my sports, lifestyle, and livelihood. She's a wonderful mother. I could not exist without her.

Q. What suggestions can you offer to people that would like to help, or the ocean in general?

A. Get involved! Conduct research in your area as to which ocean related environmental groups are active and lend assistance where you can. The power of ordinary people coming together to get behind a worthwhile cause is not to be underestimated.

Q. What is the largest problem you foresee regarding the ocean and what do you think can be done about it?

A. Lack of education as to the threat the ocean faces primarily due to human impact. Western countries have improved awareness and legislation over the past decade particularly, but if one looks at a map of the world and considers the large swaths of emerging and third world countries where very little, if any, ocean environmentalism exists, then you realize the threat at hand. Governments and environmental groups in leading nations need to urgently accelerate environmental education efforts worldwide.

Photo Gary Ward

Paul Naudé, an ex-pro surfer from South Africa is the Executive Director, President of Billabong American operations. In 1976, Naudé was the South African Surfing Champion. He also finished 3rd overall at the Pipe Masters that same year. Naude is the president of the Surf Industry Manufacturers Association (SIMA) Environmental Fund.

www.billabong.com

Amy Tan

Q. It is known that you love the water, and you live near the bay and ocean, can you please explain what the ocean means to you?

A. As a child, I did not see the ocean as one entity. There was the ocean an hour away, which we could drive to, where we could make footprints in the sand, where we dared ourselves to walk down with the receding waves and race back up before they grabbed our ankles. Another ocean was also an immense watery barrier, one that separated my mother and father from the past, which was China. It was an expanse that hid secrets, that separated people in terms of numbers of years and not just numbers of miles. Our relatives lived on the other side of the ocean and were unknown to me. Another ocean grew the fish and crabs that were held captive in tanks in Chinatown. Under the waves, the creatures were slimy and ugly. Another ocean was a fairy tale place, where immortals played cards. Another ocean was a dangerous place where I could drown. And one day, the ocean became for me a world of unimaginable beauty. It was the day I finally overcame my fear of drowning and donned a snorkel and mask to see what was beneath the waves.

Today, I live in a house that overlooks water. When I wake up, what I see out my window is water. It is the same and it is always different. Each day, it reveals a different mood and personality. I have seen it dotted with sailboats, speckled with birds, and twice darkened by oil.

There is a Chinese concept called Feng Shui, and it has to do with where nature is placed relative to where we are placed. This position has to do with what might affect us. Where I live is one of the luckiest of positions, facing water, an island and a mountain. And just as I am conscious everyday of how I am affected by these elements, I am also aware of how I affect those elements. What water runs out of my house that pollutes the water? I am bothered by that, and it is good to be bothered in that way. It is the reason I am building a sustainable house, with a green roof and water catchment, with elements that will not harm the other elements.

Q. Nearly two billion people worldwide depend on the ocean as a source of food everyday or for their living. Human impact is drastically affecting our beautiful oceans from pollution to expansive over-fishing. You have a worldwide audience yourself as an author and a leader in education, can you please explain to our audience why it is so important to take good care of our oceans and land?

International Best selling novelist, Amy Tan's books have already been translated in over 23 languages, Some titles include: The Joy Luck Club, The Bonesetter's Daughter *and* Save a Fish from Drowning. *Amy resides in Sausalito, California, both her parents were Chinese immigrants.*

www.amytan.net

A. Like many, I once believed the ocean could absorb anything and provide anything. It was infinite in its powers. Anything that you put in the ocean was no greater than "spit in the ocean." Any fish you took out of the ocean was one of millions just like it. But in the last ten years, I learned that fish from the sea had led to my having dangerously high mercury levels. People say fish is brain food. Now we hear of cases of people whose brains were permanently damaged by eating mercury-laden fish. If I continued to eat the fish I loved, I risked becoming cognitively and physically impaired. I cut out the big prey fish: swordfish, marlin, Chilean sea bass, Ahi tuna. Later, as pollutant levels steadied increased, I had to eliminate more fish. Just two weeks ago, my doctor said that for someone with my condition, I could not assume that any species of fish was safe to eat. And there are more toxins out there than just mercury. I now have a personal relationship with the ocean. We share an illness. The fish and sea mammals share an illness. The spit we put in the ocean is poison.

Q. Do you have any environmental or ocean heros that you would like to tell us about?

A. Most people would not think of Charles Darwin as an ocean hero. But his oceanic voyage led to a major rethinking of the influences of the environment on the development of the species. That influence was not something that took place in the past. What we are doing to the ocean changes its environment, and that changed environment influences the ongoing development of the species, or its extinction. Darwin's story is not just about a theory of evolution. It is about what is evolving now and why some of that evolution is very bad indeed.

AMY TAN

A NOVEL

SAVING FISH
from DROWNING

Anne Earhart

Q. As an environmentalist, and someone who really understands chemicals and toxins, can you explain how the chemicals we use on land actually affect the ocean?

A. We think of the ocean as a pristine place. Yet vast rafts of plastic, pooling in the great ocean gyres, exist. And every chemical and toxin we use on land, eventually makes its way to the sea. We think the ocean is limitless in its capacity to dilute anything we put in it. But these chemicals don't go anywhere. They end up in the plants and animals and in the ocean. The higher you are on the food chain, the more you accumulate. Whales, tunas and other top predators carry particularly large loads of toxins. Sperm whales that have never been in sight of land are highly polluted. You might want to think twice about that tuna you eat. These toxins affect the sea in ways that we can't see and certainly don't understand yet.

We need to have a rational and safe chemical policy and laws in this country. These animals are the canaries in the coal mine. What is happening to them is happening to us. As go the sea creatures, so go we.

Q. Being a long time avid diver as well, what are your favorite things about diving, and also have you noticed any significant changes over the years in your diving experiences?

A. I've been lucky to dive in some amazing parts of the world, and few of these places are truly untouched by man's hand. The reefs in Indonesia were gorgeous but there was not a shark to be found, they had all been finned. I have heard dynamite fishing while underwater and wondered how long it would be until the beauteous reef I was looking at would be decimated.

Thirty years ago in Southern California, the kelp was thick and abundant with a myriad of species. This year the kelp has come back and I hope to see a Marine Protected Area here and all around the globe really. I think these protected areas would give us a good start in restoring the health of the ocean and all its creatures.

Q. What advice can you offer to people who want to help the ocean but don't really know where to start or what to do?

A. There are lots of great ways to help the ocean. We need to think about every chemical we use at home or work. Reduce, recycle, and reuse to keep plastic out of the ocean so we won't be eating plasticized fish one day. Write your elected officials. Tell them you want a healthy ocean with vibrant fish stocks.

And, I would love to see more people picking up trash at the beach. It is a small thing but if everyone picked up a few pieces of trash, imagine how much we could take off the beach. Why walk by when you could help care for Mother Ocean, who gives us so, so much.

Anne Earhart has worked for decades to defend coastlines and the marine environment throughout the world. As Founder and President of the Marisla Foundation*, she has become a mainstay of environmental advocacy along the Pacific Coast and throughout the Pacific Rim. The* Marisla Foundation *has supported a broad range of groups, from community to international, that support ocean health, including sustainable fisheries and marine areas protection, to water quality and environmental health.*

Stefan Lessard

Dave Matthews Band

C. Taylor Crothers

Q. What are some of your favorite things about the ocean?

A. Being in the ocean is a very spiritual experience, and yet it is cleansing too, and it brings out a feeling inside of me that is also very physical that means so much. I have had some of my most profound moments in the ocean while kayaking and also while surfing. Once on my kayak, and once on my stand up paddle board, I encountered a whale that was within a few yards of me, and I have also been close to pods of dolphin. On the one hand, when I was so close to the whale, and I felt its enormity, I felt immense fear simply because of its size next to me. It looked as big as a submarine, but at the same time it was magical and spiritual all at once. It's hard to explain the way the ocean can make you feel, but I gravitate toward it and miss it if its been too long since I've seen it.

Someone once said to me that the waves in the ocean are started many thousands of miles out to sea, and each wave is an energy source that slowly progresses closer to land, and as a surfer each time you are lucky enough to catch a wave, you get the chance to share that last source of energy before it hits the ground. I always remember that and I feel that I share the oceans energy and it stays with me.

Q. Is there a particular ocean issue that bothers you the most, and if so what is it?

A. I would have to say people I guess, the earth is infested with humans and we have polluted the earth and our global oceans with cigarette butts and trash. Having said that, we are also an intelligent species, and we can do better. We need to do better while there is still a chance to reverse the damage we have done. I have been to some beautiful places where the beaches are clean and pristine, and I have been to poverty stricken places where it is literally a health hazard just to go into the ocean. That is sad to me, I think that we should concentrate on educating people that every single piece of trash, and every cigarette makes a difference. I also think that we should all try harder to push for more recycling centers, and disposal containers for recycling worldwide, even in the place where I live now. The earth really is our playground, and we need to take care of it from the mountains, cities, and oceans, it's all connected.

Q. Being in one of the top U.S. touring bands, the Dave Matthews Band, and a band that also really encourages being more eco conscious, do you have any words of advice you would like to share?

A. Well that is a double edged sword too, on one hand we know a lot of great tips to offer people, but at the same time we don't want to come across as preaching or being hypocritical, and also the music industry generates a lot of energy so we do our best to curb that. Again, I don't want to be a finger pointer but some of the things I personally try to do are to eat as sustainably and as locally as I can, and I try to always buy water that comes from the country I am actually in and preferably the state I am in. When I drink water I try to use a filter first, or I try to buy water in a glass bottle. Water is a very critical issue worldwide, and we should always respect our water, and do our best to be as mindful of that as possible. I also try to support local farmers markets, and I do my best to keep my own footprint as small as I can, and I think everyone should at least be conscious of their own impact so they can make their own good choices. Our earth and our oceans deserve that.

Bassist Stefan Lessard is the youngest founding member of the Dave Matthews Band. He was just 16 when the band formed . The DMB frequently sells out amphitheaters, arenas and stadiums around the world. Lessard is also the Founder of the IZSTYLE Project which presents DMB's greening efforts on tour and beyond, and he is the founding member of the band Yukon Kornelius which gets together for charitable purposes. Lessard enjoys his down time living by the beach with his family. Surfing and snowboarding are two of his passions. His love of playing in the waves and on the snow has fueled his passion to fight against pollution and trash and to promote clean water and a clean planet.

www.davematthewsband.com

Photo Monterey Bay Aquarium

Julie Packard
Monterey Bay Aquarium

Q. Can you please explain what the *Monterey Bay Aquarium Seafood Watch Guide* is, and explain why it is so important that many other non-profit organizations take the lead from you in regards to this program?

A. The mission of the Monterey Bay Aquarium is to inspire conservation of the oceans. We hope that this inspiration will lead to action, and one simple way to help the oceans is to choose seafood that's caught or farmed in ways that contribute to healthy oceans. More than most anything else people do, seafood choices have a real impact on ocean wildlife. Our Seafood Watch program helps consumers and businesses make ocean-friendly choices by providing them with the science-based recommendations listed on our pocket guides: "Best Choices," "Good Alternatives," or species that we should "avoid" due to concerns with the way they're fished or farmed. Since we began our Seafood Watch program in 1999, grass roots consumer interest has caught the attention of major seafood buyers. Those buyers are now asking their suppliers for seafood from sustainable sources. And that's beginning to result in real change in the way fish are caught and farmed. We're part of a larger movement that's helping make sustainable seafood the norm rather than the exception. As more organizations join the movement, I believe we'll see even faster progress.

Q. Monterey Bay Aquarium is very special for several reasons, one being the location and the natural habitat right in your back yard. Can you tell us some interesting facts about sea otters since there are so many where you are?

A. Monterey Bay Aquarium exhibits reflect the varied ecosystems and habitats of Monterey Bay. We are fortunate that the bay has been designated as a National Marine Sanctuary, with additional areas protected as state marine reserves. One of the most important species to the productive kelp forest habitat of Monterey Bay is the California sea otter. The sea otter is known as a keystone species, because it's the top predator of grazing animals like sea urchins and abalone. By keeping the grazers' populations in check, sea otters allow the kelp to flourish. And the kelp forest supports a rich diversity of life. When sea otters were hunted almost to extinction due to their luxurious fur – the densest of any animal on the planet – kelp forests disappeared in Monterey Bay. Now protected by law, otter numbers have increased and kelp forests are thriving. But the California population struggles to recover to historic numbers of around 18,000 animals, with less than 3,000 sea otters in the wild today. The Monterey Bay Aquarium is home to the only rehabilitation center for the California population and works hard to return sick, injured and stranded animals back to the wild where possible. Our research contributes to the understanding of why this population continues to struggle, and we work with state and federal agencies to help uncover the causes so sea otters can recover once again.

Q. You also have a few other special exhibits including the kelp forest, the jelly fish exhibit, and also a very special area for seahorses. Can you explain one or two special things about each of these that most regular people are probably not aware of?

A. The Monterey Bay Aquarium was the first in the world to exhibit a living kelp forest outside the wild. Many people thought it couldn't be done, and that no one would want to see a kelp

Julie Packard is the Executive Director of the Monterey Bay Aquarium, Commissioner for the Joint Ocean Commission Initiative, a member of Pew Oceans Commission and recipient of the Audobon medal for conservation.

www.montereybayaquarium.org

forest if we could grow one in an exhibit. In fact, our three-story living kelp forest is our signature exhibit and has been a visitor favorite since we opened in 1984. The rhythmic motion of the kelp and the gentle sway of the rockfishes fascinate young and old alike. The swaying motion created by pumps that move nutrient-rich water over the kelp, and the fact that the exhibit is open to the sunlight, are both essential components that allow the kelp forest exhibit to thrive. The Monterey Bay Aquarium was also one of the first aquariums to display jellyfish and has been a leader in husbandry techniques and jellyfish culture since. Many of the jellies on exhibit have been raised behind the scenes at the Aquarium, which means we are able to display year-round some species of jellies that appear only seasonally in the bay. We also share animals and husbandry techniques with other aquariums. Seahorses are always a visitor favorite and we often exhibit them in our permanent galleries, as well as featuring them in special exhibitions. One of the fascinating things about seahorses is that it's the male that broods the young in his pouch and then gives birth!

Q. Not everyone will be fortunate enough to be able to visit Monterey Bay Aquarium in California, but can you explain the importance of people going to aquariums in general all over the world?

A. For most people, the underwater world is a mystery – out of sight and too often out of mind. Yet the oceans are vital to the survival of all life on earth – a source of much of the oxygen we breathe and the food we eat. Aquariums bring people face-to-face with extraordinary animals and plants from this unique habitat. We have learned that putting people in touch with nature in this way is a life-changing experience. By helping people fall in love with ocean life, they care more about the threats facing the oceans today and become inspired to do something to make a difference. We have the potential to create new generations of ocean stewards through the experiences they have at the Monterey Bay Aquarium and other aquariums around the world.

Q. If you could share any last thoughts with the people of the world in regard to the ocean, regardless if they live hundreds of miles from it, what would you tell them?

A. We are all connected to the ocean. It controls our weather, provides us with protein and the oxygen we breathe. Even if we don't live near the ocean, our rivers and streams are connected to it. What we do in our neighborhoods and communities will ultimately affect the oceans. There are things we can do in our everyday lives to make a difference: We can choose seafood from sustainable sources, recycle and reduce the volume of chemicals we use in our homes and gardens. The industrial scale of global fishing has profound effects, which we can address through our seafood choices. Global climate change may prove to be the biggest threat to the health of our oceans. There are so many ways to get involved, to be informed and to make meaningful changes each day. These small steps we take as individuals, and together with our neighbors and communities, can ultimately improve our own way of life as it helps safeguard the wildlife we all care about in our oceans.

Photo Monterey Bay Aquarium

Jeffrey Short, Ph.D.

Q. Can you explain in layman's terms what ocean acidification is?

A. Some of the carbon dioxide added to the atmosphere from cars, factories and other human activities has dissolved into the ocean, where it reacts with seawater to form carbonic acid. This process is exactly the same as that used to make carbonated water, which is produced by mixing carbon dioxide gas with water, which makes the water quite acidic. Natural seawater is mildly alkaline, meaning it tends to neutralize acids, but as acid is added it weakens this neutralizing ability. This weakening results from depletion of chemicals in seawater that react with the acid. The most important of these chemicals is called carbonate ion, which are also important building blocks for shelled and reef-building organisms in the sea. Within the last 20 years, scientists have discovered that over the course of the Industrial Revolution, enough carbonic acid has been added to decrease carbonate ions in seawater by about 17% on average in the surface layer of the ocean worldwide. Scientists estimate that if carbon dioxide continues to be added to the atmosphere at the current rate, carbonate ions could fall another 20% from the current level by the end of this century, with serious consequences for marine life.

Q. What are the effects of ocean acidification, and why are so many people worried about it?

A. The most obvious effects of ocean acidification are on reef-building corals and on organisms that make shells out of calcium carbonate, including lobsters, crab, shrimp, oysters, clams, mussels, and a host of other animals. Depletion of carbonate ions makes it more difficult for these organisms to build reefs or shells. The most vulnerable period is during the embryonic stage, when organisms need shells most for protection but have little energy to spare to build them under more difficult conditions. Experiments with coral reef-building organisms indicate that they will not be able to keep up with natural erosion by about the middle of this century, when coral reefs will begin to irreversibly die out.

But ocean acidification has many other more subtle effects on how the ocean functions too. It changes some of the forms of nitrogen available to nourish marine plants, which affects their growth and distribution. It affects the potency of marine toxins, making plants and animals more or less able to defend themselves. It increases the toxicity of many pollutants discharged into coastal marine waters. It alters the ability of at least some fish to orient themselves in the water column and to release their metabolically produced carbon dioxide (i.e. "exhale"), which may make them more vulnerable to predation. It even increases the efficiency of sound transmission in seawater, making the ocean noisier for sound-sensitive marine mammals.

Moreover, these changes are happening simultaneously and fast, making it difficult for marine life to adapt. The last time the ocean acidified was anywhere near as fast as it is today was at the end of the Paleocene era 54 million years ago, and it caused a biological mass extinction in the ocean then. That is why scientists are so concerned today about ocean acidification, because it has been known to fundamentally transform the character of the ocean by killing a large proportion of the species that live in it.

Dr. Jeffrey Short recently retired from a 31-year career as a research chemist at NOAA, where he worked primarily on oil pollution and other contaminant issues. He was the leading chemist for the governments of Alaska and the United States for the natural resource damage assessment and restoration of Exxon Valdez oil spill, and guided numerous studies on the distribution, persistence and effects of the oil. Dr. Short is the author of more than 60 scientific publications and has contributed to 3 books. Dr. Short is now Pacific Science Director with Oceana.

www.oceana.org

Q. What needs to be done to help the problem globally, and what can the individual person do to help?

A. The cause of ocean acidification is clear; it results from the carbon dioxide that humans are adding to the atmosphere. Since the Industrial Revolution began, we have added enough carbon dioxide to increase the level in the atmosphere by 40%, and most of this rise occurred within the last 50 years. If it continues, atmospheric concentrations could more than double by the end of this century, with a corresponding increase of carbonic acid added to the ocean. The only way to avert this is to dramatically reduce emissions of carbon dioxide. Geoengineering schemes to neutralize the acid are impractical, primarily because of the difficulty of mining, transporting and distributing neutralizing chemicals effectively across the surface of the entire ocean.

The average person can do two things that will not only help, but could turn the tide. First, try to reduce fossil fuel and other energy use by avoiding unnecessary travel and walking or bicycling whenever you can, make your house or apartment more energy efficient, use less heating and air conditioning, and consume less meat. Just these simple steps could reduce our national carbon dioxide emissions by more than 25%, enough to make an immediate difference. Second, urge political leaders to support steps to transform our national economy from one based on fossil fuel consumption to one based mainly on alternative energy. Studies show there are enough wind resources alone to satisfy most of the energy needs of the United States.

According to most economists, the most efficient way to accomplish a transition from fossil fuels to alternative energy sources is by imposing a surcharge on fossil fuels, and distributing the revenues back to individuals as income tax credits so that every person gets an equal share of the revenues. This would reassure investors in alternative energy that their investments won't undercut fossil fuel prices when conservation efforts increase their supply causing prices to fall. At the same time, it would reward people for not using fossil fuels and ease the burden of the transition on the poor. Coupled with an energy policy favoring development of alternative energy sources and a more efficient electrical transmission system, these policies could not only dramatically reduce our emissions of carbon dioxide, but reduce our dependence on foreign oil, create jobs and ultimately lower the cost of living for everyone.

Q. The possible "loss of sea ice" has also been a major concern, what are the consequences from loss of sea ice?

A. The loss of sea ice during summer in the Arctic has the potential to dramatically accelerate global warming. The minimum size of the Arctic ice cap during summer is only about half as large as it was 50 years ago and appears to be declining at an accelerating pace. The more rapidly receding ice during the period of greatest sunshine allows more of the light and heat from the sun to be trapped by Arctic seawater instead of reflected back into outer space by the ice. This makes the whole Arctic warmer, including the land surrounding the Arctic Ocean to nearly 800 miles to the south. This land contains enormous stores of methane that could be released to the atmosphere as the permafrost melts, and as the Arctic seawater warms over the continental shelf, huge deposits of methane that are now trapped on the sea floor by cold temperatures may also be released. Just slight increases of seawater temperature, on the order of a couple of degrees or so, may be enough to de-stabilize these methane deposits in the Arctic Ocean, and the rapidly warming land mass surrounding the Arctic Ocean

is already causing accelerating releases of methane from the melting permafrost. Because methane is a powerful greenhouse gas, more that 20 times as effective as carbon dioxide, these releases could dramatically accelerate global warming.

Methane released as a result of Arctic sea ice loss will also accelerate ocean acidification. Methane oxidizes into carbon dioxide in the atmosphere within a couple of decades, and some of this will dissolve into seawater increasing ocean acidification. The combined effects of the relatively rapid rise of seawater temperature and increase of acidification will make it even more difficult for marine life to adapt.

Q. Do you have any examples, or stories that actually gave you hope for how people can change their behaviors in order to help, without too much effort on their part?

A. I first became aware that ocean acidification is a serious environmental threat in 2005, when I began reading the scientific literature on global warming. I did that to see for myself whether the arguments advanced in support of the view that global warming is caused by humans had a strong scientific basis. The upshot was that it seemed to me that most of the arguments that had been put forward to deny the human cause of global warming were either misleading or downright dishonest, and the ones that weren't, posed questions that helped to refine the picture but did not change the fundamental conclusions. But where the physical mechanisms of climate science are very intricate and complex, ocean acidification is simple, and no less alarming. As a result, I began giving public presentations in Alaska to help educate people about the threats posed by ocean acidification. When I gave these presentations, I made sure I was well informed to address concerns raised by people who didn't want to believe what I had to say. I often wondered whether these presentations were worthwhile, because most of the people who came seemed predisposed to "believe in global warming," but I really wanted to speak to people who were either undecided or had doubts. At one of my presentations, a minister attended who listened intently and asked a number of probing questions afterward. I later learned that he had been convinced by my presentation, and had decided then and there to incorporate the concerns raised into his ministry to his congregation. It really made a difference in his life. This reassured me that when people pay attention and evaluate the evidence with an open mind, instead of relying on someone else's opinion on their favorite TV program, they can make an informed and intelligent assessment.

It all boils down to people realizing that what they do has consequences, and then trying to make a difference. Fixing climate and ocean acidification is part and parcel to fixing oneself: eating sensibly, getting exercise, saving money (it turns out that conservation pays), spending more time with family and friends. More and more people, and especially young people, are realizing this, and when people pay attention and then try, great changes are possible.

Prince Jigbenu Bolaji Akran

Q. What are the largest concerns regarding the ocean for the country of Nigeria, the country you are from?

A. The largest concerns regarding the ocean for the country of Nigeria are: a) the slow poisoning of the waters of the country and the destruction of vegetation and agricultural land by oil spills which occur during petroleum operations, b) the over-fishing that happens in her territorial waters within the Gulf of Guinea.

Q. How has over-fishing affected the people of Nigeria, or how has fishing changed there over the years?

A. The fishing industry is an essential part of Nigeria's sustainability; it is the primary source of protein within the context of her populace diet and nutrients in general. The higher demand on fishing has resulted in fish populations declining as they are being depleted faster than they are able to restore their number. The local fishermen are not able to fish their traditional waters as they used to because of the presence of larger fishing vessels that operate within these waters that overfish without any consideration or within any guidelines as to the preservation of fish stock etc. Nigeria, now imports almost 80% of fish eaten by her populace at astronomical prices, this has resulted in a loss of livelihood for the local fishing villagers. At this moment, eating fish is a delicacy that most people cannot afford. At the present time, there are almost 200 Spanish fishing trawlers along the coast of Western Africa.

Q. What role has the government played in the protection of the ocean, and also how have the oil companies affected the environment there, especially as they relate to the ocean?

A. The oil industry in Nigeria is more than 25-years-old and there has been no effective effort on the part of the government, let alone the oil operators, to control environmental problems associated with the industry. There has been widespread spills that could match if not surpass the size of the present spills on the coast of the United States. These spills have been in populated areas, destroying crops and aquacultures through contamination of the groundwater and soils. The agricultural communities along the delta and oceans have been wiped out, due to the careless nature of oil operations in the Delta Region. The environment is now uninhabitable, resulting in a drastic increase of migration to Lagos, a city that is already over populated.

Q. What needs to be done, and how can people help?

A. The most important first step will be to impose catch fees; this would help by bringing attention and educate the stakeholders on the importance of preserving fish stock. The countries of West Africa have to join forces in order to fight the powerful European countries whose fishing entities are guilty of overfishing her waters. It's a known fact that 77% of the world consumption of fish comes from developing countries, and most of these countries don't have adequate laws in place to protect the oceans that surround them.

Q. Do you have any last thoughts you would like to share?

A. To conclude, we are destroying the oceans daily, we live as if it doesn't have anything to do with our lives. We are wrong. Everyone believes the oceans contain inexhaustible resources, which is not true and a signal that we have to start laying a proper foundation for the education of the people of the world as a whole regarding the oceans. The facts are out there; the oceans CANNOT support a worldwide fishing fleet of over 4 million ships (which have increased by 75% in the last 30 years) that feed our forever increasing human population, presently at almost 7 billion. Our attitudes toward the ocean have to change NOW or the result of our ignorance and arrogance will be irreversible.

Jigbenu Bolaji Akran, grandson of Oba C.D. Akran, is the late ruler of the historic town of Badagry and a former Minister of Economic Planning and Community Development-Finance, Western Nigeria (1961). Bolaji Akran, like his grandfather, has dedicated his life to the preservation of the traditions and heritage of the people of Badagry a coastal town on the gulf of Guinea. He is the Founder of the Badagry Institute of Economimc Development and Culture Preservation, *a film producer, and an avid polo player who resides in Los Angeles, California.*

www.obacdakrancommission.org • www.badagrymedia.com

Kate Walsh

Photo Tim Calver

Q. What are some of your favorite things about the ocean?

A. I spent my formative years on the beach every weekend with my family, trolling the tide pools, touching sea anemones, finding sand dollars, building sand castles, swimming, and body surfing. I've always loved the ocean, the waves always made me feel like it was a living entity, even before I got to experience the joys of snorkeling and diving. I also love that there is basically an entire universe under water to be explored. There are so many creatures big and small, and it fascinates me to think that we are still discovering new sea species all the time.

Q. What made you want to get into ocean conservation, and why do you think others should consider doing the same?

A. Getting involved in ocean conservation was a no-brainer for me, since I have such an affinity for the water and all the creatures and plant life in it. I love bringing awareness to others who didn't grow up at the beach, and I enjoy educating people about what's endangered, what's sustainable, and how we can keep the oceans alive and well for generations to come. With carbon emissions and commercial fishing, there are serious risks to the ocean's short term and long term viability, so I believe education and outreach are paramount.

Q. Being involved with *Oceana* and their Sea Turtle Campaign, what are some of the fun facts you have learned about sea turtles, and what tips can you offer to people that also want to protect them like you do?

A. When I went on an expedition with *Oceana*, I got to see baby leatherbacks hatch and try and get to the sea. They're so tiny, and they work so hard to be born and there are so many natural environmental things working against them, yet when they do finally hatch out of the eggs and they do their long walk to the ocean, it's just incredible. The sea turtles life is an arduous journey, that unfortunately has a lot to do with humans and our sometimes reckless fishing practices. Because of this, and the fact that most sea turtles are currently endangered species, I feel the desire to do whatever I can to help. I want the sea turtles to be around for many generations to come, and if we all pull together and take action, then they will be.

Q. Do you have any favorite quotes, or words to live by that you would like to share with people in regards to our environment, and/or our precious oceans?

A. "There is one knows not what sweet mystery about this sea, whose gently awful stirrings seem to speak of some hidden soul beneath," Herman Mellville.

Photo Tim Cal

Actress Kate Walsh is an established television star, best known as the driven neo-natal surgeon Dr. Addison Montgomery on the hit shows Grey's Anatomy *and* Private Practice*. But when the actress wanted to lend her fame to the greater good, she came to Oceana. It was a perfect fit: Kate, a native Californian, has a natural affinity for sea turtles, and the character that made her famous, Dr. Montgomery, could perhaps relate to the staggering odds that face just-hatched sea turtles as they struggle toward the sea.*

www.katewalsh.com

Garrett Dutton/G. Love

Q. Is there one particular ocean issue that speaks to you most, that motivates you to want to help, and if so what is it?

A. I would have to say it's general pollution and garbage in the ocean. On a local level, I try to remove as much beach trash as possible. Simple things like fishing line, plastic bags and beach toys can tangle up and choke fish, birds and turtles. Of course, there are bigger problems like sewage, illegal dumping, oil spills, and runoff. I'm very concerned about our sick oceans.

Q. Do you have any particular ocean experiences that have driven you to become an ocean advocate?

A. I've grown up my whole life surfing, fishing and enjoying the ocean. In Stone Harbor, NJ, as a child, I went to the *Wetlands Center*. They had many educational day camps for kids and I learned a lot about the ecosystems of the marshes and the ocean. I think those educational programs really made a lasting impression on me to be in touch with the nature of the beach and really care about our oceans.

Q. What does the ocean mean to you?

A. The ocean means life, motion, endless possibilities and sustenance.

Q. What is the largest problem you see regarding the ocean, and what do you think can be done about it?

A. There are many concerns. The problems in the Gulf of Mexico where shrimp and fish populations are being decimated by the jellyfish which are flourishing from fertilizer in the runoff. Other problems include the oil spills, climate change, over fishing, fish management, the pros and cons of farming fish, pollution and trash. We have to take care of our oceans and rivers. We need stronger global legislation and coalitions to defend our fisheries and oceans from over fishing and pollution. This is a world problem.

G. Love and Special Sauce *is an alternative hip hop band from Philadelphia. Garret Dutton loves to surf. He is a supporter of ocean conservation.*

www.philadelphonic.com

Kelly Slater

Q. What can people anticipate learning from your new movie *The Ultimate Wave Tahiti 3D*?

A. Along with wonderful visuals of how waves are formed and sequencing how the ocean and waves relate to each other, the movie portrays the science involving waves, the development of the wave, how deep water waves need to break in, how islands and reefs are formed, especially the volcanic islands of Tahiti, and the life cycle of a mountain forming. The visual effects also make you feel like you are actually there.

Q. When you first started surfing did you really understand the swell action and science of the waves, or did this movie introduce you to the science of a wave?

A. I always sort of knew that when the wind blows strong for a long period of time waves would form, but I really didn't understand the real math of it all. Now, I really understand forecasting better. If the wind blows 35 knots, over 500 miles then waves will be so big, etc. Especially through "Surfline" and Sean Collins, I have learned a lot. Sean and I recently took a long drive down to Baja together, and he was teaching me, how based on the interval between waves, how deep that energy will reach down, the longer the interval and the deeper the energy reaches down to the ocean. I'm not exactly sure but for example, in a 13 second interval the energy will reach down 300-400 feet, in a 16-18 second interval, it will reach down to 600-800 feet, etc.   So then if you have that mass of energy on the bottom, it can alter the swell based on the energy and interval of the wave.

Q. As a nine time World Champion you have thousands of followers that will listen to what you have to say, some celebrities have simply lent their name to causes which is wonderful, but you have actually started your own charity. Can you explain a little about the premise of your charity and what is all about?

A. I have the *Kelly Slater Foundation* which is difficult to sum up in a nutshell, but I am geared toward environmental causes, and people who help out with kids. A good friend of mine has a skin cancer foundation who we support, as well as the *Quiksilver Foundation*, *LA Surf Bus*, *MiOcean*, the *Surfrider Foundation*, *Pipeline to a Cure*, the Paskowitz family and *Surfer's Healing*, which helps kids with Autism. We divide up the funds appropriately to those in need over time. We have had the foundation for about three years now.

Q. If you could focus on an ocean issue, and ask that all your friends and fans do the same, what would that be?

A. The plastic issue is a big one to me. We really could get by without all the single use plastics, especially plastic bags. Even if I can't carry everything in my arms out of the grocery story, I still never use a plastic bag. If I really, really have to use a paper bag, I'll return the bag back to the store, or just use the cart only. I also don't really understand why people would want to kill dolphins and whales, however, having said that, if you're going to point the finger on things like that, you really need to be really clean with your own life. The problem for me is I occasionally eat meat, and those are mammals. I do eat more sustainable fish, than I eat meat, but I do eat red meat every now and then. That is why it is hard for me to point the finger. How do you decide which animal is better than the other? If people would be more conscious about what they eat, and cut back on what is less sustainable, we would all be better off. I really think we have this fascination with whales, and dolphins that goes on beyond a sheep or a cow, but that does not make it right, or better to kill those animals. I really think we all could be much healthier if we did not eat meat products at all. Another really big issue that concerns me is pollution run off. I have an issue with the use of pesticides, as there are indications throughout the world that we can farm without pesticides. Although it can make things easier for farmers, pesticides are a mess, and they are dangerous for our environment. It seems it is all driven by companies wanting to make more money, and people not looking into the ramifications. I think it comes down to corporations worry more about their bottom line, rather than the health of people, and the horrible pollution issues that occur from pesticides.

Q. Lastly, do you have any words to live by, or sayings you've heard that have seemed to stick with you over the years?

A. There are so many good sayings, and quotes I have heard, but what seems to make the most sense to me is to always go with the results whatever you do in life. Go with the results on your actions, see what happens after you do something. If it makes a positive change in your life, or someone else's, than stick to it!

As a nine time World Champion, Kelly Slater is considered on of the best surfers of all time. He is a surf icon and an advocate to ocean conservation.

www.KellySlaterFoundation.org

Yoko Ono

YOKO ONO NYC Photo by Tom Haller©

Q. It is said that your name translates to "Ocean Child" - that is very powerful. What does the ocean mean to you personally, and what are your reasons for wanting to protect it?

A. Ocean is where we've come from. Now we are all ocean carriers with the powerful energy of the ocean within us. When the ocean shines, we dance the dance of life. When the ocean suffers, our blood smells the smell of death. And when the ocean dies, we die.

Q. Is there a particular ocean issue that bothers you the most, and if so what is it, and what can you recommend people do to help the problem?

A. Thank the ocean for the powerful energy you have as an ocean carrier.

Q. What is your favorite thing about the ocean?

A. That it is in constant motion of its own.

Q. Do you have any words to live by you would like to share?

A. I live by counting my blessings, and knowing that everything is a blessing . . . for somebody!

Yoko Ono is an artist, singer, songwriter, musician, filmmaker and peace activist who lives and works in New York City.

www.imaginepeace.com

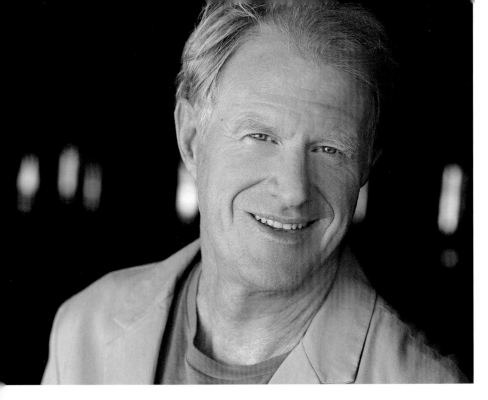

Ed Begley Jr.

Q. You are often referred to as Hollywood's "Greenest" actor. Can you explain the premise and goal of your show *Living With Ed* so people will understand why?

A. My goal is to get folks to become aware and active on environmental matters, and to do it exactly the way I did when I started in 1970. That is to say, to pick the low-hanging fruit first. To do the cheap and easy things that we can all do TODAY that will make a difference in our oceans and on land.

Q. Can you please explain how being "Green" at home can help our ocean?

A. Since nearly all of us in this world live above sea level, all of our actions uphill are soon felt somewhere downhill. And, downhill usually means in our groundwater or our oceans. The motor oil, the lawn chemicals, the plastics have an uncanny way of finding their way in our oceans and other unfortunate places we never intended.

Q. What are five important things people can do to help to become more "green," and what will help us all become more "blue"?

A. To get single use plastic out of your life, as much as possible.
- To stop using pesticides, herbicides and fungicides on your lawn or garden.
- To change out your light bulbs to more efficient ones.
- To ride a bike when weather and fitness permit
- To take public transportation, if it's available near you.

All those things I mentioned are cheap and easy. Start there, and you might just want to do more once you get a taste for the savings and the positive effect that you're having on our world.

Q. Do you have any thoughts, or words to live by you would like to share?

A. Live simply, so that others may simply live.

Ed Begley Jr. is an actor that has received six Emmy *nominations for the long-running TV series* St. Elsewhere*, and has appeared in many other television shows and movies. He is also well known for his TV show with his wife Rachelle Carson called* Living With Ed*. Additionally he has an eco-friendly natural home cleaner www.begleysbest.com He is also an award winning environmental activist that never quits advocating for our planet.*

www.edbegley.com

David Chokachi

Q. As a surfer yourself you also spend a lot of time in the ocean, can you explain to us why you have spent so much of your time dedicated to helping the ocean and our rivers, and what the ocean means to you?

A. I have been fortunate enough to have spent most of my life, on or near the ocean. Growing up in a house where my mom was an avid sailor and loves the beach and ocean, and my dad loved to fish, go clamming, and was equally passionate about the water. They passed those traditions on to me and my two siblings. As a kid, when we were at the beach, my mom would look for me and I would constantly be underwater, exploring. I started sailing and racing sailboats at a very young age and went to the Junior Nationals three times, once for windsurfing, and twice in a class of boat called the 420. I became head sailing instructor at The Plymouth Yacht Club and sailed to Bermuda and back from Massachusetts, which was an event that really left a mark on me. After moving to the West Coast, I went to work on two television series that revolved around the ocean; *Baywatch* and *Beyond The Break*. One shot in Los Angeles and the other in Hawaii.

I have always been drawn, in a very powerful way to the ocean. In a sense, I am most comfortable there. When I'm sailing, surfing, scuba diving, I have this sense of being where I am supposed to be. This sense of belonging. That does not happen that often to me. The amount of joy I get from the ocean is something I want to be able to pass on to future generations, the way my parents passed it on to me. The only way this will be possible is if we encourage people to respect and protect these valuable resources.

Being a working actor who was lucky enough to be on a couple hit TV shows, I realize one of the greatest perks of my job is to have a voice and to be able to have a positive influence on people. I started to support ocean and water-based charities like *Surfrider* and *Oceana* out of personal interest, but it was also clear that people paid attention and that this brought more awareness to these causes. It was a chance to give something back to the ocean, that has given so much to me. *Water Keeper Alliance* is equally as important, because these guys (Bobby Kennedy Jr, and the rest) are going after the people and companies who dump and pollute our rivers and waterways. Not only is that very dangerous to the habitat in and around these waters, but we all know, most rivers eventually flow to an ocean. So whatever goes into the rivers, ultimately will affect the oceans. The two are directly related, and both are worthy of everything we can do to protect them.

Q. Can you explain what the most important ocean problem is to you, and tell us what people can do to try to help alleviate the problem?

A. I think one of the most important problems is that we have this feeling that the ocean is infinite, in its supply of resources, and its ability to recover from damages that we, as human beings, do to it. That could not be more false. I surf all the time, and I see first hand the effects of people throwing trash out the windows of theirs cars, not cleaning up after themselves when they go to

Born, raised and educated in New England, David Chokachi holds a degree in Political Science. He became best known for his role in the TV series Baywatch. *Awarded Environmentalist of the Year by* Surfrider Foundation, *he also is actively involved with* Waterkeeper Alliance, Unicef *and others. As an avid surfer and stand up paddler, David continues to raise coastal awareness amongst friends, family and the public.*

www.waterkeeper.org

the beach, dumping things into sewer drains miles and miles inland. It all ends up in the ocean. We have to be smarter than this. The lack of understanding about how each one of us and our actions has an impact on the oceans is just mind blowing. The ocean's resources and its ability to recover is FINITE. We can, and I mean everyone, do our part. Everything from not littering, to picking up a piece of trash at the beach or at the park, that is where people can start. Just by educating themselves a little bit, and understanding the impact. People can also get involved with organizations like *Surfrider Foundation, Oceana, Water Keeper Alliance*. It's important for people to understand that each individual really can make a difference. I think a big problem with environmental issues is that people are overwhelmed, and they don't feel like alone they can have an impact. This is the very reason why it's so important to get people involved in ocean-related charities.

Shaun Tomson

Q. You have been an environmentalist of sorts since at least 1987, being one of the most vocal voices for the *Surfrider Foundation*, saying that we all have a responsibility to the ocean, can you elaborate on that?

A. Surfing has given me so much, a lifestyle built around the ocean and I have a personal responsibility to give something back. Whenever I paddle out I take waves and each wave is something special, a gift, so for me, it is only right that I try, in my own small way, to give back and being involved with Surfrider is the primary way I do so.

Q. Can you state a few simple environmental lessons you have learned in relation to the ocean that you would like to share?

A. Never turn your back on the ocean is a lesson that speaks to an awareness of the dangers one can face in the ocean and the necessity for taking care of the ocean and giving back. All surfers are joined by one ocean. The community of surfers around the world are interconnected and how an environmental problem in the ocean is a problem faced by surfers everywhere. Problems and solutions are global rather than local in nature.

Q. What ocean issue concerns you the most and what can people do to help?

A. The ocean has become a dumping ground and the primary source of life on this planet is being destroyed by abuse and over-consumption. Join an environmental group and get active locally and globally.

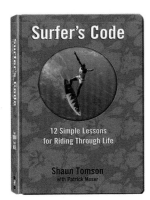

As a native South African, Shaun Tomson began his surfing career at age ten. As the 1977 World Champion, Shaun is still considered the finest tube rider in the world. He is an author of the book, Surfers Code *and co-produced film* Bustin Down The Door. *He is a spokesperson for The Surfrider Foundation.*

www.surferscode.com

Photo Dan Merkel

Pierre André Senizergues

Q. How did you get involved in the film *The 11th Hour*, and what could you say you learned from doing it; what message would you like to portray from the movie?

A. I was put in touch with the filmmakers through my involvement with *Global Green*. I became involved because it supports my commitment to the environment by creating awareness and continues in the process of educating our future leaders on the possible solutions to reduce our impact, to lighten our footprint. I learned a lot during the process since it was my first time involved in a film. I became more versed on the many important issues the film addresses such as deforestation, water conservation and pollution and very importantly - over consumption. For me, the film is more than just an eco documentary, it is an eco movement to educate and inspire people to make positive changes, however big or small, in their everyday lives. My hope is that it will continue to be used as an educational tool to reach new audiences and keep the movement going.

Q. Ocean acidification is an enormous issue that is a direct cause of humans emitting too much carbon into the atmosphere. You have set aggressive environmental standards and goals for your companies, including your Etnies Building being carbon neutral by 2020 and have much stricter guidelines that you adhere to than are even asked for by the government. Can you please explain your practices to set an example of what other companies could be doing with their own proper political will?

A. From the beginning I wanted to build a company that took responsibility for its actions and always gave back. My passion for the environment has always been with me so it was only natural to introduce these beliefs into my company. Some of Sole Technology's early initiatives were installing an extensive solar panel system, company wide recycling efforts and creating the Blue Bin Brigade-an internal committee whose goal it is to increase industrial awareness about waste and find more environmentally friendly means of conducting business in all aspects of the company. Since then we have expanded ever further with an Energy and Waste Management Task Force, expanded our environmental affairs department, implemented a carpool program, started an eco-learning center for employees and incorporated more recycled materials throughout our entire product line. We believe in transparency and understand the process of going green is a journey. In order to get to your destination you have to know where to start, asking these questions, however daunting they may seem, is the first step. The next step is finding solutions to put them into action.

Q. You were quoted as saying "Going Green equals Green." Can you explain that as well?

A. Green equals green means that each of us as consumers has the power to vote with our dollar. Every time we buy green products and support companies that take action to become more sustainable, we are voting to protect and preserve our planet's future. To see that today's consumers can enjoy a sustainable lifestyle without sacrificing on quality or style and that they are willing to do so, proves that everyone must evolve, as our planet will, in the future.

Q. Do you have any thoughts you would like to share about why going Green is good for the ocean?

A. Going green is good for our ocean, our planet and humanity. I want people to see the connection of how lightening our footprint translates into our oceans, mountains and our future. As a surfer myself and a new father, I want my son to be able to enjoy and share in the beauty that our oceans provide to us. We are each privileged in being more than spectators, but active participants in our environment. Let's take the steps for the next generation to enjoy.

Photo Atiba Jefferson

> *Former World Champion, Pierre André Senizergues began his skateboarding career at age 15 in his hometown of L'Hay Les Roses, France. His personal commitment to the environment and ecologically conscious lifestyle has made him a trailblazer in the industry winning numerous awards such as Microsoft's Customer Excellence in environmental sustainability. Sol Technology is working to become carbon neutral by 2020. Senizergues was also the executive producer of The 11th Hour hosted by Leonardo Di Caprio.*
>
> www.soletechnology.com

Tanna Frederick

Q. You are an actor, a surfer, and an activist, and you've worked hard on various events including hosting Project Save Our Surf. What is the most pressing ocean issue for you related to surfing in particular?

A. Storm sewer run-off in Santa Monica directly affects me, and I would say is the most pressing issue because of the illnesses that come along with surfing in the Bay even after waiting to go in the water a week after a rain . . . and it affects not just humans, but Santa Monica sea life. There are numbers of contaminated species of fish in the Santa Monica Bay that were found to have DDT and PCB's in their bodies. Those are the issues that are blaringly obvious being a surfer in the Bay. However, it is hard to say what is the most pressing issue as every part of the ocean's ecosystem is in trouble and one part of the ecosystem being out of whack throws the whole environment out of whack.

We need to keep pressing forward bills like Oceans-21, rally against offshore drilling on our coasts, and protect our freshwater sources as well, such as Balonna Wetlands, and reduce our own wastewater at home. There are a ton, and I mean a ton, of organizations working to preserve our oceans that need volunteers, and sometimes even the most miniscule daily task, like signing up with one of those organizations, and checking out daily updates on their sites, or signing a petition via email, can make a huge difference.

Q. Can you name a couple of your role models environmentally and tell us why they inspire you?

A. My parents. They've raised me to appreciate everything – from daddy longlegs to twisters . . . not to be afraid of things, even frightening things nature creates, but to be mystified and feel privileged by all of the universe's quirks that we get to be a part of. They taught me to take charge and if something isn't right, do something about it. Don't wait around for others to do it for you. I started becoming environmentally and politically active as a kid because they never diminished my interest or potential at any age to alter the world around me and to become a better individual.

> *Tanna is an avid surfer, actress, writer, producer and environmentalist who founded Project Save Our Surf and the Iowa Film Festival. She works tirelessly to bring the entertainment and surfing industries together in support of clean oceans.*
>
> www.tannafredrick.com

Gregor Hodgson

Q. What is *Reef Check*, and what is its reach?

A. *Reef Check* is an international non-profit organization with a mission of empowering local communities to improve the health of their reefs through research, education and conservation. Our core EcoDiver program involves training citizen-scientists of all ages and walks of life to learn how to collect reliable scientific data on the health of coral reefs and rocky reef ecosystems. Each year, in over 90 countries around the world, thousands of *Reef Check* volunteer citizen scientists collect data so that we can track reef health and improve management at the local and national levels. *Reef Check* carried out the first global survey of coral reefs in 1997 and the first survey of California rocky reefs in 2005. Through this process we build up a constituency of ocean supporters who often become directly involved in conservation activities such as establishing marine parks.

Q. What is the overall status of our world's coral reefs? Some scientists have predicted that coral reefs may soon be a thing of the past. Is there a broad or best case scenario?

A. On a global basis, we have lost about 25% of our coral reefs over the past 30 years. If we had lost 25% of the Redwood forests people would be very upset. But because coral reefs are underwater and most losses have occurred slowly, this tragedy is not well known. Overfishing and global warming are the two most serious threats to reefs today. We lost 10% of the worlds reefs in 1997/98 when the oceans overheated. If the reefs are in trouble, the oceans are in trouble, and if the oceans are in trouble, the human species is in trouble. If climate change is allowed to continue we are likely to lose most existing coral reefs within 50 years. However, due to the fact that there are over 800 species of corals, and they have been around for 150 million years, I believe that some will adapt and survive climate change. But the one human species may not make it if we don't take better care of our planet.

Q. What is the importance of coral reefs?

A. Coral reefs are the second most diverse ecosystem after rain forests. This genetic cornucopia is a source for drugs from the sea. Cytaradine is one of the most powerful anti-cancer drugs. The original source of this drug is Crytotethya crypta a Caribbean sponge. Tourism is the biggest industry in the world and millions flock to white sand beaches, the product of ground up coral, not to mention the millions of snorkelers and divers who enjoy a closer look. Coral reefs protect the coast from storm waves that could damage coastal structures and about half a billion people rely on coral reefs for their daily protein.

Dr. Gregor Hodgson is the Founder and Executive Director of Reef Check Foundation*, an international non-profit organization dedicated to improving the health of coral reefs and rocky reef ecosystems throughout the world.*

"Community involvement is the cornerstone of environmental protection. I support Reef Check *because it helps local communities protect their own reefs through education and involvement in Reef Check Surveys" -Leornardo DiCaprio, Honorary Chairman.*

www.reefcheck.org

Q. Why do people dynamite the reefs and what does that mean?

A. Since WWII, blast fishing using explosives became common in SE Asia and then spread to other parts of the world. When using a beer bottle filled with fertilizer to make a bomb, it is an extremely efficient although very dangerous method of killing schools of fish. As reefs are overfished, and the effort to catch a meal increases, blast fishing is a short-term solution to find dinner. Unfortunately, there is a lot of waste and the reef itself is damaged, ultimately leading to fewer fish. The good news is that *Reef Check* has shown that by creating marine protected areas, it is possible to allow reefs and fish populations damaged by poison and blast fishing to recover in as little as two to three years.

Q. For people who want to help the reefs of the world, what suggestions can you provide them in order to help?

A. Help educate others about the value of coral reefs and threats to their existence. Get involved directly by becoming trained as a Reef Check EcoDiver. Support organizations that are fighting to stop global warming and those like Reef Check that are working to conserve coral reef and rocky reef ecosystems.

Derek Sabori

Q. Tell me about the earth bugs from your book *Lu and the Earth Bug Crew* and their mission?

A. *Lu and the Earth Bug Crew* are a modern day set of eco-action (sports) heros that are calling kids to action. The concept is this: Lu, the captain of the crew, came to planet Earth after his home planet was destroyed by the Un-Greens: The Litter Bugs, the Water Hogs, the Energy Spikes, the O-Zoners and yes, the Oil Slicks. Upon his arrival, Lu went surfing in Fiji, snowboarding in Mammoth and hiking and skateboarding in Canada and Yosemite. Just like you and me, Lu fell in love with all the amazing things we have here and then made it his mission to protect the planet and to spread the word about "Greener Living." That's what makes him an Earth Bug. While studying at the fictional Greener University, Lu met Rock, Fern and then Kordy, each of whom have an eco-specialty, and a passion for taking action and being a good friend. Together, traveling around in the Bio-D, their very cool, bio-diesel powered, all terrain action van, the Earth Bugs have become the coolest, smartest, healthiest, and most fun adventurers you've ever met in a kids book! They rock & roll. They surf, they skate, they snowboard, they go to Earth Day rallies, and most importantly, when they see something happening that's just not right (usually the Un-Greens trying to crash the party), they go straight into action - Earth Bug Action! and all of them do their part to save the day! The mission of the Earth Bugs? Simple: Be a good friend, take care of the planet and all its resources and of course, have fun doing it!

Q. What are your thoughts for the kids of today, and their future?

A. Do I believe, kids are our best chance for true and lasting change? Of course. The kids of today are amazing, they always are. We will always say they're smarter, they're more informed, they're more capable and they're equipped with more resources than we have ever had. However, they can't do it alone. They need role models, and leaders that challenge them to rise up to their fullest potential and to question the status quo and look to a smarter, more sustainable future. Together, I know that we will create real, and significant change, and I'm a firm believer that it can start with a simple act like reading a book together.

Derek Sabori has made it his own mission to live up to the standards that the Earth Bugs have set. In real life, Derek is the Director of Sustainability and Corporate Social Responsibility at Volcom, Inc. and loves spending as much time as humanly possible outdoors, on planet Earth, with his family and friends.

www.earthbugcrew.com

LU EARTH BUG and the CREW
ZAP the Energy Spikes

"They're trying to CRASH the party!"

an Eco-Action Adventure
written by
Derek Sabori
illustrations by Steve Riley & Mark Adams

Paul Kelway

Q. When there is an oil spill what is the main concern for the birds you rescue?

A. There are many variables: time of year, location, climate, species affected and type of oil, but the most immediate concern for birds is how oil affects them externally. Seabirds rely on their feathers to keep them warm and dry while in the water. The feathers interlock, stopping cold water from getting in and trapping warm air in the soft down feathers next to the skin. Oil affects the integrity of this barrier. Water seeps through and, depending on the climate, hypothermia can set in fast. It's like trying to surf or dive in a torn wetsuit. The colder the water, the more immediate the problem. From there it's a downward spiral. The birds can't regulate their own body temperature; they lose buoyancy and the ability to feed. They become weak and dehydrated. The lucky ones head to land. Many don't make it that far and are lost at sea. It's for these reasons that *International Bird Rescue Research Center (IBRRC)* puts so much emphasis on pro-active rescue and has developed methods and expertise to capture birds from the shoreline as well as by boat. There is only a small window of opportunity for these animals.

Q. What are the most important things you do when you are alerted of another oil spill/disaster?

A. Firstly, we have to determine if we can help. There are many elements involved in mounting an oiled wildlife response. The location, climate, local environment and politics, all have a significant impact on how we respond. Outside of the U.S. it is sometimes as simple as whether or not we are invited to assist. We will often say that we are not 'spill chasers' and it doesn't work to force our help on governments and communities who don't want it. We need their support to make any response a success. Once we are activated the team moves quickly. Often our senior response team will be in the air within hours. Only when they are on the ground at the spill can they begin to determine our strategy and the resources and expertise that will be needed. After that, it's all about maintaining a sense of calm amid the chaos so we can make good decisions fast.

Q. What is the most important thing you do for an oiled bird, and how do you attempt to let the birds back into the wild after they are rehabilitated if the oil spill is still present in order to prevent the same thing from happening to them again?

A. When people think of oiled birds they think about bird washing, but the first thing we do is stabilize the animals. This means getting them warm and dry and giving them first aid. We also need to get them rehydrated and their body weight back up to a normal level. Only then will they be strong enough to be washed, one of the most stressful parts of the rescue process. When oil is still present we rely on the best knowledge available on the situation: movement of oil, species, habitats, time of year and the expertise of local biologists and wildlife agencies. We don't want to hold animals in captivity longer than necessary so we will try and find appropriate habitat in areas away from the oil. With migratory birds we'll try and get them beyond the oil in the direction they're heading. If they're resident year-round or likely to return to nests, our main goal might be to get them out of the firing line to buy time for the clean-up crews. In South Africa, 20,000 African Penguins were evacuated after an oil spill hit their breeding islands. They were released hundreds of miles away and, although they made a beeline back to their nesting sites, it was enough time to clean up the area and prevent a much larger problem.

Q. What can ordinary people do to help when there is a major oil spill?

A. It is a question we get asked a lot. On many spills we will often rely on local volunteers to work with our rescue team. However, oil spills are quite different than natural disasters and are often highly politicized with complex regulations governing the response. Often there are already plans in place and groups identified to play a lead role. International Bird Rescue is a named wildlife response organization in many of these spill plans around the world.

The best way to help is to start volunteering for your local wildlife rehabilitation organization on a regular basis. That way you will already have some experience should you have an opportunity to help during a larger event.

Q. Do you have any other thoughts you would like to share?

A. I have been very lucky to work with some of the most experienced oiled wildlife responders in the world. When I first met Jay Holcomb and *International Bird Rescue's* response team many years ago I was so inspired by their practical and positive approach to situations that, to so

Jay Holcomb and Paul Kelway   Cleaned pelicans awaiting release   Oiled pelican   RRBC bird clean up

many, seem hopeless and devastating. They have taught me that whatever we can do, no matter how overwhelming the circumstances, can make a positive difference, not just to marine wildlife but also to the communities affected by oil spills. Our goal at *International Bird Rescue* is to match this philosophy with sound science and practical expertise so that our efforts can be both felt and measured.

Paul Kelway is Associate Director for International Bird Rescue Research Center (IBRRC). *He first connected with* IBRRC *in 2000 at the Erika Oil Spill in France while working for* EarthKind, *a marine wildlife rescue organization. He was also part of the* International Fund for Animal Welfare (IFAW) Oiled Wildlife Team *in Cape Town, South Africa, which cared for 20,000 oiled African penguins following the Treasure Oil Spill in June of the same year. This team was a partnership between* IFAW *and* IBRRC. *After working with* EarthKind *he become* IFAW's *Emergency Relief Manager for the Oiled Wildlife Division and* IFAW's *primary contact with* International Bird Rescue Research Center. *He has responded to and been involved in the coordination of a number of oil spills around the world including the Prestige spill in Spain and France, the Rocknes spill in Norway, the Pemex pipeline spill in Mexico and, more recently, the Deepwater Horizon oil spill in the Gulf of Mexico. Kelway is originally from Cornwall in the South-West of England and also served as a Press Officer for the* Royal National Lifeboat Institution, *one of the UK's oldest and largest charities.*

www.ibrrc.org

María José González

Q. Where is the Mesoamerican Reef, and what is its significance?

A. The Mesoamerican Reef (MAR) has the largest coral reef in the western Atlantic and is part of a larger interconnected system of coastal habitats and currents that stretch throughout the Caribbean basin and beyond. It spans 1,000 km across the four sovereign boundaries of Mexico, Belize, Guatemala and Honduras, stretching from the tip of the Yucatán Peninsula in the north, to the Bay Islands of Honduras in the south. The watersheds of the four countries that drain into the Caribbean are an integral part of the region. It is a massive natural structure formed by different types of reefs, including long barrier reefs, near shore fringing reefs, offshore atolls, and patch reefs and is considered one of the biodiversity hotpots of the Atlantic. It is home to over 500 species of fish, including the whale shark, the largest fish in the seas; some of the largest remaining populations of manatees and sea turtles, and valuable concentrations of mangroves, sea grass beds, and corals (over 66 species of spiny coral alone) live there. Depending on the source, between one and two million people live along the coasts and the islands of the MAR region, and depend on the health of the reef to carry on sustainable livelihoods. The Mesoamerican Reef is also culturally diverse, including the following ethnic groups: Miskito, Garifuna, Caribbean Creole, K'ekchi, Mopan, Yucatec Maya, and Mestizo. The region's stunning coastline and vibrant waters make it a prime tourist destination; the availability of natural resources attracts the presence of industry and agriculture; and the abundance of commercially valuable species fuels both artisanal and industrial fisheries.

Q. What are the major threats to the Mesoamerican Reef? Is it in good shape?

A. There are several important threats to the reef, many of which are shared by reefs in other parts of the world. The major threats include the following:

- Habitat loss, due to change in land use and unplanned coastal development.
- Contamination of aquatic and terrestrial systems by sedimentation, urban and industrial waste, and agriculture runoff.
- Over fishing, through unsustainable, and sometimes damaging fishing practices and lack of control and enforcement of fishing regulations. The fact that fishing norms are not standardized throughout the region is another negative factor.
- Unsustainable tourism practices have a big impact as they degrade natural resources in the region. This can be due to lack of territorial planning, disorganized development, lack of adequate zoning in protected areas, and replication of mass tourism models in small areas.
- Climate change is possibly the single most important threat to the reef in the mid to long term. Its effects include coral bleaching and more frequent and severe storms and hurricanes.
- Lack of adequate funding to support the protection and management of the region puts the whole system at risk. In addition, local inhabitants are affected by reduced income due to the reduction and degradation of natural resources.

The Healthy Reefs Initiative (Healthy Reefs for Healthy People) is an international multi-institutional effort that tracks the health of the Mesoamerican Reef. It produced the first report card on the health of the MAR in 2008. Seven core indicators of reef health were measured, including herbivorous and commercial fish abundance. The results are sobering. Overall, only 41% of the MAR reefs are in fair condition, and 47% are in poor condition. The indicators for fish abundance are a particular cause for worry, as they are in poorer condition compared to the Caribbean average. However, it is not cause for despair. On the contrary, it is a clear and loud call to action. This is the moment to take the right measures toward recovering the reefs and the natural systems and resources in the region. As a result of the first report card (the second one will come out this year), several recommendations have been made for different sectors of society, and some are

under development. For example, the government of Belize has enacted important legislation to protect key reef species, and many local and regional organizations are working hard to reduce and mitigate the threats.

Q. What is the MAR Fund and its objectives?

A. The Mesoamerican Reef Fund (MAR Fund) is a regional environmental fund established to support conservation and sustainable use of resources in the MAR region. It operates as a participatory, privately managed fund that raises and allocates funds, while relying on the preexisting technical, administrative, and financial capabilities of its four founding funds: Protected Areas Conservation Trust (Belize), Fundación para la Conservación de los Recursos Naturales y Ambiente en Guatemala, Fundación Biosfera (Honduras), and Fondo Mexicano para la Conservación de la Naturaleza. It thus builds on existing structures looking for the most efficient and effective arrangement to attain its objectives and truly operates at a regional level.

The founding funds comprise the MAR Fund's Board of Directors, in addition to a representative of the regional Central American Commission on Environment and Development, notable conservation experts from each participating country and international donors. The mission of the MAR Fund is to inspire innovative, transnational solutions to critical Mesoamerican reef issues through providing meaningful, long-term financial support and trustworthy reef management advice so that future generations can enjoy and benefit from a thriving reef system.

The goals of the MAR Fund are (1) to provide long-term financial sustainability for natural resources management and conservation initiatives in the MAR ecoregion, (2) to strengthen the alliance among the four participating funds, and (3) to consolidate and allocate donor contributions to common and strategic objectives in the ecoregion.

The MAR Fund raises funds for the following initial program areas:
- Saving our Sanctuaries: A legacy of caring. This program supports the establishment and protection of an interconnected network of the coastal and marine protected areas in the region.
- Fishing for the Future: Sustainable fisheries for a thriving reef. Community participation in co-management of their fisheries is supported through this initiative.

Q. Do you have any further thoughts about the reef or oceans in general?

A. The resources provided by the Mesoamerican Reef are intricately linked to the well being and the future of the people that live along the reef.   But this is also a region of global importance. We must continue to support the four countries that share the reef and the many organizations that work tirelessly to maintain a thriving reef, but also to generate awareness, at a larger scale, on the wealth of this region in terms of biological and cultural diversity and the importance of sustaining these ecosystems for generations to come. Besides, the economic importance of this region to the four countries that share the reef, it provides valuable services that extend beyond the limits of the region. We must work to ensure that these environmental services and processes are maintained.

María José González was born and raised in Guatemala, where she studied Biology, then obtained a Master's Degree in Wildlife Management in Costa Rica. She has worked worked with many international NGOs on different research topics including vertebrate population analyses, baseline studies for the establishment of private reserves, and development of criteria for certifying sustainable coffee.

www.marfund.org

Martin Goebel, Bill Reilly, María José González, Beverly Castillo, Lorenzo Rosenzweig, Rod Fujita, and Valdemar Andrade

Luke Tipple

Turtle survives shark attack - Photo Alex Thornton

Q. As a marine biologist and shark specialist can you please explain why sharks in general are critical to our oceans?

A. Great white sharks, just like all species of shark, are critical components of a healthy and diverse oceanic ecosystem. Over the last 40 million years sharks have evolved to inhabit most, if not all, of the niche environments in the ocean. In fact you can pretty much point to any place in the ocean, be it a shallow coral reef, the deep abyssal trenches, brackish fresh water mangroves or blue open oceans, and you will find a species of shark that has adapted to the particular challenges of that environment. As Apex predators, sharks are at the top, or near top, of the food chain. This position is extremely important as they are responsible for keeping the numbers of many of their subordinates in check. Without this population control we would see an over-abundance of animals which, having no predators, would quickly overrun the natural balance of the area causing instability in the food web and ultimately a potential crash in biodiversity and hence productivity of the ocean.

What most people don't realize is that sharks have natural mechanisms for their own population control and thus need no unnatural population control. They can take up to 15 years to reach sexual maturity, require direct sexual contact to reproduce and exhibit low fecundity when they do succeed in mating. Add to this the challenges of finding a mate and surviving the gauntlet of cannibalism in their juvenile years, and it's amazing that they are even able to reach the numbers necessary for their survival! In contrast, their prey are usually characterized by high fecundity and broadcast spawning where literally millions of juveniles can be made by only a few individuals. Without sharks we would have a very different ocean that most likely would be characterized by much smaller species of animals that probably would gain much of their energy from sunlight, plankton or other broadcast spawners. It is unknown exactly where the trophic web would balance out, but it is fairly safe to say that without sharks in the ocean, the food web would collapse from the top down, resulting in an ocean depleted of fish and human nourishment. In a very real sense, the measure of a healthy ocean is the presence of sharks.

Q. Will you explain your initiative for shark free marinas?

A. The *Shark Free Marina Initiative* is a fairly simple concept with a singular purpose: to reduce worldwide shark mortality. After extensive conversations Patric and I came up with an idea: "What if the marina simply did not allow a caught shark to be brought to the dock?" The idea grew and started to make sense, by supporting catch and release fishing we could still allow fishermen to have their sport but we would save the animals from a useless death. We believe that this is an acceptable middle ground and supported the idea of sustainable use of the oceans resources rather than the traditional 'ethical' use argument purported by most environmental groups. There is another reason for Shark-Free Marinas, setting a global principle. It is all too easy to point the finger at Asian countries for shark depletion but we seem to ignore the regular news features of the man who 'caught the monster' and the bloody pictures of an endangered species of shark hung up for proud display before being thrown in the dumpster. Currently, almost every species of fish which is caught for commercial and/or recreational purposes is fished beyond a sustainable level, and commercial fishing fleets currently remove around 40-60 million sharks per year. Many shark species have declined in numbers by 90% and there are currently over 150 species of shark listed on the IUCN's red list as near threatened or worse. The realistic goal is to save millions of sharks per year while also setting a new global standard for responsible management of our ocean's resources.

Q. Do you have any tips for people who encounter sharks while they are diving?

A. There is a much higher chance of an encounter when swimming in river mouths, morning or dusk hours or in any area where there is a large amount of food such as bait fish or seals. Also try to avoid areas where there is a sharp drop-off such as a ledge or sand bank as sharks often patrol the deeper water hoping to catch something by surprise. Avoid wearing sparkly jewelry or bright colors, as a visual predator anything that grabs their attention is likely to be investigated. 2. If you see a shark and are either snorkeling or scuba diving you have a big advantage, you can see the animal. Sharks are predators and like to take their prey by surprise. By simply keeping your eyes on the shark, they are less likely to be curious and think about an attack. Never turn your back and frantically swim away, that's what food does. In fact if a shark is acting aggressive (look for erratic swimming, a hunched posture or eyes rolling in the head) you are better off swimming directly at it. They will take this as an offensive maneuver and are likely to leave the area. 3. If the shark comes too close for comfort a swift kick or punch to the snout or eye area will usually be enough to deter them from further investigation. A shark is not used to being touched and will probably be quite startled by the unfamiliar aggression. 4. In the worst case scenario a shark will try to bite. In this situation, you have no option but to leave the water. Swim back to the boat or shore making sure to never turn your back on the animal. Keep your eyes trained on the aggressor and be ready to fight should it decide to bite.

Q. If you had one message to relay to people about our oceans what would it be?

A. The ocean is the most important resource on the planet. I don't care if you are a believer in evolution and science or a higher creationary power such as God, every theory or theology gives credit to the ocean as being the source of all life. As this is the case, it is senseless to believe that we can continue to thrive as a species without addressing the very serious issues our ocean is facing. The ocean today is at a crisis point; global warming, pollution and land reclamation are already destroying the fragile balance of the sea. When we add to that the destructive effects of over fishing and mismanagement of fish stocks the scientific community agree, we may well witness the total collapse of the oceans ecosystem within our lifetime. Within our current generation we will see severe changes from sporadic and unpredictable weather patterns to eradication of species and worldwide hunger. We are in a fight that ultimately will determine the quality of life as we know it. When deciding on where to allocate resources I would urge our decision makers to lean toward working on developing sustainable practices of ocean resource use . . . if the cost of saving an ecosystem is the loss of one cuddly species then as a scientist I find that acceptable. However, as a human I am disappointed in our species and that we have squandered and destroyed our evolutionary home to such a point that we have to pick and choose what we save. We can do better and we must!

Luke Tipple is an Australian marine biologist and is the director of the Shark Free Marinas Organization. Luke works as a travel guide, instructor and operations manager with many dive operations throughout Australia and Baja California.

www.luketipple.com • www.sharkfreemarinas.com

Photo 089 Design

Photo Frank Lamonea

Mati Waiya

Q. Will you explain a little bit about the Chumash Indians and also about the basic laws of the Chumash people?

A. In our culture we have to recognize the balance and the lessons of our natural, spiritual and physical world. We believe in the upper world (the sky), the lower world (the ocean), and the middle world (the land). As we are growing up both physically and spiritually, we learn from our elders about understanding the three basic laws: the laws of limitations, moderation and compensation.

Limitation: We realize that we are only going to live so long, then we are going to die. We only can be so strong and do so much. The more we can understand about what we can do and our abilities, the more we can accept who we are as human beings.

Moderation: If we go harvest from the ocean or the land, we take only what we need and we give before we take because we realize what we take is a gift. We leave some for tomorrow, for the future and for someone else.

Compensation: If you want to do something for your children, for the land, or for another person, do it because it's inside your heart and don't expect anything in return. Compensation can come in many forms; it can be a child, or happiness, or health, or wealth. It often comes when you need it most, and you least expect it.

We apply these three laws mentally and physically, and we live by them. We also believe in awakening one's spirit by teaching the values of Respect, Honor, Humility, and Awareness of our natural surroundings. We believe in living as sustainably as possible, and we respect our plants, our ocean, and our wildlife. Another thing about the Chumash is we honor our women. Our women, our mothers, our daughters, our sisters, and our wives. They bring us into the world, and they give us life. Chumash people have recognized that since long ago, and many were our leaders. Men have a tendency to take a life. Our mothers teach us about love and how to care. They nurture us. The world is as fragile, and we respect the wisdom of our elders, and our women.

Q. What advice can you offer to people about what they could do to help our world environment and ocean?

A. I think we have forgotten the simplicity of life. We have gotten very comfortable and accustomed to the luxuries of modern life. There was a time when we harvested our waters from the springs and creeks, and we would appreciate each drop because there was an effort to go get it. There was a time you would appreciate the food and plants you would harvest because there was an effort. Today, we turn on the faucet to get water, or turn on the switch to get light. We don't even have to pray for the creatures we consume and the meat that we eat. We go to the store and it is all packaged. We've lost our respect and appreciation for those things that are part of every day life. It is going to take all of us together to protect and heal the pains that we have caused in this world, to the oceans, to the habitat and the things that we depend on. When people start praying, and dancing, and practice giving thanks again into their life, they can have a better understanding of life itself. If we would pay attention, and not be so greedy and be more mindful about the impacts that we have, the sensitive life around us that we continue to tread on like polluting our air, contaminating our fish,

Mati Waiya is a Chumash Native American and he is a native to Ventura County, California. He is a Chumash Ceremonial Priest and the Director of the Wishtoyo Foundation, *and also the Chumash Village in Malibu, CA. Mati is additionally the Ventura Coastkeeper for the* Waterkeeper Alliance, *created and headed by Robert F. Kennedy, Jr. (www.waterkeeper.org)*

www.wishtoyo.org

and disrespecting the history, then people can live in peace and harmony.   There is peace when you see whales migrating, speaking their ancient language that they have exchanged with one another for thousands, possibly millions of years. Mankind, on the other hand, is never satisfied, were insatiable, we always want more. We are rarely content, we are always changing what we think we need. If we could invest in a future that we will never see, then we will be on the right track. Our children, and their children deserve what our ancient ancestors had. If we all thought like that, we would be fine.

Q. What does it mean to you to be a coastkeeper for the *Waterkeeper Alliance*?

A. We became the 54th Keeper, and I am the first Native American to be part of this international alliance. It is very encouraging to see people in this group who actually care so much about the water and our environment. It wasn't too long ago that we relearned how to hug a tree. It concerns me that some of the environmentalists, and experts, may have turned their duties into a business; however, I can see the role that it takes, and the efforts that it takes to enforce laws. To see people care about this environment and commit themselves for something they believe in gives me hope. I think it is about time that more people open their eyes to this type of commitment.

When we look around and see the threat to the environment, and the health of our waters, it has an impact to our resources. People are getting cancers from our native community, from the reeds and the materials they use for our cultural values. If you look at the species that are disappearing, and find the contamination that we are discharging into our oceans through our rivers, you have to learn the laws in order to bring change. We could go in a court room and bring our sacred materials, but they don't understand that in court. They only understand the biology, the science and the laws. So people that are counting on their leadership, whether its local, state, or federal government, are wrong.   Each and everyone of us has to step up, and step forward to protect the health of our waters.

The Waterkeepers allow protection, and we can all share international resources with each other. It is a network of eco-warriors that fight for the health of our waterways. There are not a lot of groups out there that step up like this. It is an honor to see the different groups out there fighting for our true right, and that is our true freedom, not a document that our government imposed on us that tells us about our freedoms. Our freedom is the health of those oceans and rivers. That's our true freedom, our birthright that we have and our obligation to protect, to respect, and to steward. We need more people to help, and we all need to realize that water is the bloodline of the world and of our very existence!

Q. Do you have any last thoughts you would like to share?

A. We may have been separated by race, religion, creed, wealth, or whatever has caused wars in the world, but there is only one world and one people. We need to be engage together. It is a responsibility, and something we should never forget.
If we stay connected, and true to this life, then we could have sense of the environment, and its suffering. We need to continue to send out the positive vibration of that spiritual world. When you send, you receive, it could be negative or positive. Right now, we are all suffering along with our environment. We have to make a conscious effort to work toward faith, and trust, and strength and hope. We are deteriorating our own core because we are destroying our own world, and that is not healthy. We need to live, and appreciate our lives, moment to moment. We need to get back to living more natural, more sustainable lives, and to take care of our Mother better, our Mother Nature.

Scarlet Rivera

Q. You have been an advocate for endangered species for years. Why is animal advocacy so important to you?

A. I believe that all life is sacred and that is the foundation of why being an animal advocate is so important to me. All creatures on land and sea are integral members in the family of life on Earth. Each one is possessing immense grace, intelligence and purpose and are deserving of respect.

Q. What was your response to the BP oil spill?

A. When the BP oil spill began, I was filled with a sense of dread. I feel we are witnessing an atomic bomb in slow motion. Corporate destroyers are an example of humans using 'Dominion Over' the natural world they view only as a resource. We are now witnessing the callousness of this system of thought, as the oil silently kills innocent ocean creatures and birds in its path. My passion in life is to be an artist, musician, composer, but I feel an equal passion to raise my voice against the forces of destruction and ecological imbalance, and to express a message of urgent action. If we do not protect the oceans with a sense of urgency, the consequences will not be insignificant.

Q. You have worked with many famous musicians including Bob Dylan, Keb Mo, Tracy Chapman, Indigo Girls, and many more, but you also wrote a CD and book, 'Voice of the Animals', and a song about Dolphin. Can you tell us about it?

A. 'Voice of the Animals' CD and book, is about animals in myths, legends, and cultures of the world. Each chapter speaks of cultures throughout history that lived in peaceful co-existence with animals, even lifting them up to a position of gods, ie: Horus, the falcon god of Egypt, and as divine messengers. I composed original music for a World Society for the Protection of Animals (WSPA) documentary, with footage of the rescue of two dolphins from a swimming pool in Mexico, to their release in the wild. I tried to capture the etherial essence of the dolphins, and the joy of their successful release into the ocean in my musical score.

Q. Do you have any meaningful or favorite quotes you think are relevant to share?

A. Yes, it is by Mahatma Gandhi. "The greatness of a nation and its moral progress can be judged by the way its animals are treated. Only when we commit ourselves and others to act upon the principles of compassion and respect for all living things can we be truly great." What would the world be without the ancient wisdom of the ocean, the joy of dolphins, and majesty of whales.

Q. Do you have any other thoughts you would like to express?

A. It is my greatest hope that humanity will soon shift to a deep awareness that all life on earth is sacred. The voices of the dolphins, sea turtles, and whales of the Gulf of Mexico are crying to be heard. Let us be their voices.

Scarlet Rivera is one of the most prominent, active and versatile violinists. She is also known for her contributions to influential artists like Bob Dylan, Indigo Girls, Tracy Chapman, Keb Mo, and David Johansen.

www.scarletrivera.com

Photo Johnnie Black

Photo Wonder Knack

Ziggy Marley

Q. Do you have any inspirational thoughts about the ocean you would like to share?

A. Two nights ago I had a vision. My father visited me. He told about a journey he was on. It seems he was travelling from pole to pole. He looked weathered, as any adventurer who spent lots of time outside in nature would. He gave me some beet juice, and told me about his adventure. He said it is good to sometimes listen to the ocean speak. I believe his words were "it is good to listen to the ocean talk to you." He seemed to have really enjoyed that particular aspect of his adventure.

When I was starting my spiritual journey many years ago, I spent hours by myself in my small zodiac off the coast of Nassau. I would paddle out and just stop and float for hours reading, meditating, listening to the ocean talk, as my father said in the dream. It was a great source of peace and a perfect place for learning about oneself. The ocean is a great facilitator of spiritual experiences, including faith. One day the ocean decided to get rough. I was far from the home we were staying at, but I made it there, paddling all the way with a great sense of respect for the ocean and what it had taught me about myself that day. I was tested, and I felt proud that I had passed that test.

Those times I spent on the ocean have played a significant part in who I am today. Without that, I would be a different man, a different human being. I have not listened to the ocean talk for a while now, I mean really listened. Maybe that was what my father was reminding me about. Maybe we all need to take some time to really listen to what the ocean has to say. We could learn a lot. I certainly have.

Jamaican musician, Ziggy Marley is a five-time Grammy award winner and founder of Unlimited Resources Giving Enlightment *charity which works to help children.*

www.ziggymarley.com

Joanne and Fouad Tawfilis

Photo E. Laul Healey

Q. We believe the *Art MIles Mural Project* is one of the most important art collections in the world with thousands of people worldwide participating in the painting and promotion of peace and education. Can you please explain what you hope to share with the world about your environmental and ocean miles of murals in particular?

A. The collection of ocean murals is a visual documentation and a testimonial by the thousands of people who have painted them, voicing their concerns about the degradation of the seas and all related and connected within them. Young children and people of all ages have expressed their concerns about survival of life forms, be they sea animals and fish, to the garbage that now fills the waters, over fishing, endangered species, etc. It is evident that they are paying attention to an issue that literally covers 3/4 of our earth. They paint what they SEE and how they feel. If one country (Philippines) paints 4.5 miles of murals about the sea and fish, there is more than just awareness, there is concern and they have come up with solutions and recommendations to fix problems by bringing this incredible 4.5 mile stretch of canvas to the world to see and hear their voices. The creation of the murals is like taking a snapshot of a time in history, hopefully inspiring and motivating each of us to take on individual responsibility to DO SOMETHING. *Art Miles* is not just an educational project, but an ARTIVIST project that serves as a springboard for action. It is art that is the language that transcends all language, religious, political and social barriers.

Q. By painting murals about the ocean, love, peace, music, and the environment, etc. you have literally brought together tens of thousands of people from countries that don't necessarily share a lot in common, but you have found common ground. Can you explain how or why you think your project has been so effective in spreading its message so you can give others ideas and hope of doing something good for love, peace and our common ocean?

A. *Art Miles* has been and is organic and that is what has made it so effective. We do not depend on huge corporate sponsors or famous names to keep the project going. We reach out to the masses, to the people on the ground. Each of the layers that work on saving our seas are sea voices. *Art Miles* has fostered the grass roots movement that it will take to make changes at the "ground zero" of change makers. It has grown from a seedling of an emotional idea from a war zone in Bosnia, to a "movement," where the art forms and themes of the mural miles has grown on its own through the minds and hearts of the many volunteers who

Joanne Tawfilis' Art Miles Mural Project *is a passionate and colorful 12 year movement combining the efforts of children and adults worldwide to promote global peace and harmony through mural art. The "Environmental Mile" of murals was birthed as a result of Joanne's participation in the* United Nations Environmental Program Millennium International Children's Conference. *The murals are dedicated to Philippe and Alexandra Cousteau.*

www.artmiles.org

facilitate this project. We are likely one of the very few projects that is totally 100% volunteer (140+ of us worldwide), and has no funding for operational overhead costs because it is done from the heart. *Art Miles* is living proof that the effectiveness of what and how we do what we do works because it is a sincere and heartfelt commitment that has left its footprint in history because it has that element of common ground. It is the common ground that illuminates the common problems and when you see ocean murals, you can't differentiate if they are from the Pacific or Atlantic or an island nation. Water and life within it represents the life blood of humanity and the fact that if we continue to destroy the life and environment that provides us nourishment, then our planet and all forms of life will simply die. The murals have captured those feelings and emotions.

Q. Do you have any favorite quotes that you would like to share with others?

A. "If I were to wish for anything, I should not wish for wealth and power, but for the passionate sense of what can be, for the eye, which, ever young and ardent, sees the possible." -Soren Kierkegaard

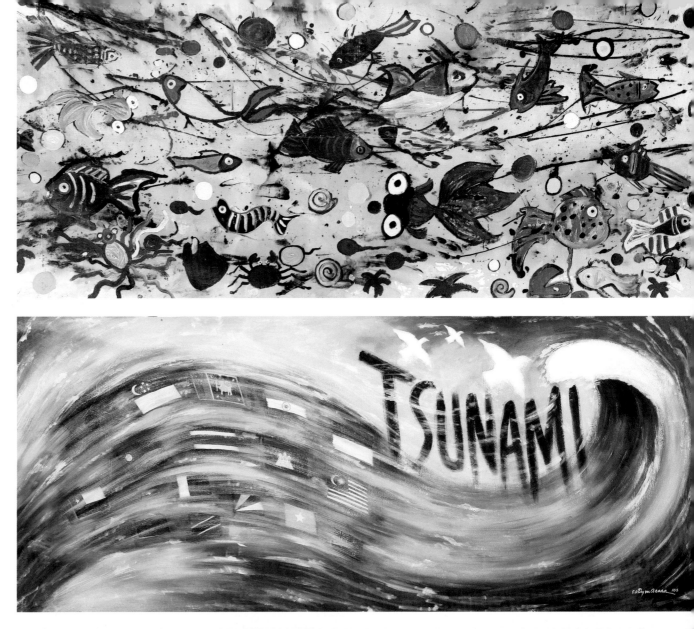

Dr. Wallace "J." Nichols

Q. What does the ocean mean to you?

A. As marine biologists we know that the ocean equals life. Intellectually and scientifically we know that it's true and each year it becomes more and more clear as we explore more of the ocean's ecology. But emotionally, the ocean holds an important place in our lives as well. The sounds, smells and sights of the ocean sooth us and remind us that we're small. We need to be reminded of how small we are.

Q. What are some of the problems we are facing, in particular with the turtles?

A. Generally, we've put too much IN to the ocean, taken too much OUT of the ocean and we are destroying the EDGE of the ocean. As a result, our ocean is full of pollution in many places, our fisheries are collapsing and fishing communities are having a hard time. Coastal areas have lost biodiversity and productivity. For sea turtles, this is particularly problematic, as they are sentinels of ocean health. They eat the plastic in the ocean and are sickened by pollution. They get caught in our fishing gear and are hunted for their meat. Their nesting and feeding habitats have been transformed. As a result, all seven sea turtle species are considered endangered or threatened.

Q. Can you give a little bit of background on the turtles in danger? (perhaps a quick comparison of how they are and how they should be)

A. Long ago sea turtles were one hundred times more abundant in our ocean. What we see now is a remnant of their former populations. They used to be one of the principal bioengineers on the beaches, reefs and sea grass beds of the world, and their presence was the keystone of ocean and coastal ecosystems.

Q. Can you explain what it is that you do to help . . . and what can the ordinary person do to help?

A. Our work essentially focuses on removing the gravest threats to sea turtles and restoring their natural roles in the ocean. We do this by working closely with people: fishermen, other scientists, coastal residents, travelers, government folks, business people and anyone who expresses interest. By building a diverse network of people with this shared goal, and by sharing our new knowledge in creative and useful ways, we build local sea turtle "movements." While it's a sea turtle on the flag, the bigger goal is healthy oceans and coastal communities.

Q. What are some of the other dilemmas we are facing in the ocean that are of major concern to you, and again what needs to be done about them? . . . Are you at all optimistic that if we act quickly we can change our current situation in the ocean? How fast do we need to act if at all?

Photo Neil Osborne

A. Global warming is essentially ocean warming. The ocean has always been our buffer against drastic changes in climate. But when it warms quickly, becomes more acidic and sea level rises, those changes are disastrous. In front of us right now is a huge opportunity to change the way we relate to the ocean, recognize

Dr. Wallace "J." Nichols works with several universities and organizations to advance ocean protection. He is also spearheading the Ocean Revolution, a program that inspires, involves and mentors the next generation of ocean conservation leaders. Dr. Nichols is also a regular contributor to the Huffington Post.

www.wallacejnichols.org

that the status quo doesn't work and seize the range of ways we can reinvent virtually everything we do. It's not an exaggeration to say that we need an Ocean Revolution. We have the knowledge, much of the technology is "off-the-shelf." We just need the personal and political will to make it happen.

Q. Can you tell us more about the "shrimp issue"?

A. In my lifetime, shrimp has gone from being a special, rare food to something that seems to be everywhere. Shrimp is now cheap, fast food. For a few dollars you can get all you can eat shrimp. The reason is that the scale of global bottom-trawling went way up and fuel costs were subsidized. Some nations have required shrimp trawlers to use Turtle Excluder Devices so that they catch and harm fewer sea turtles. But bycatch of everything else remains a serious problem. Dragging huge nets on the seafloor is considered the worst way to fish, but that's how most wild shrimp are caught. Then shrimp farms began to pop up around the world, also subsidized and made possible by sparse regulation of environmental and social standards. Taking out a mangrove forest and replacing it with a temporary shrimp farm is a quick way to make money. The U.S. market has been flooded with cheap Asian shrimp, forcing shrimpers here to cut costs or close down. It's been a race to the bottom of the ocean. This is what happens when there is no value put on mangrove forests or on bycatch, which includes sea turtles, baby sharks, a wide variety of fish and invertebrates, and the consumer has no idea how their food is caught. The sustainable seafood movement has helped a little, but because the shrimp industry is so enormous and the margins on shrimp are so large, most groups are compromised. The result is that the #1 seafood in the U.S., which is also by far the most destructive, largely gets a pass. Spend a few days and nights on a shrimp trawler, or visit an Indonesian shrimp farm. Or do a google search for the words shrimp and bycatch. It will open your eyes to the real world of seafood. If you must eat shrimp for some reason, support the fishermen and farmers who are doing it right. You'll pay more, but your money will go where it belongs.

Q. Your work with sea turtles seems to connect you with many ocean issues?

A. Sea turtles have been my "window" into a wide range of topics. Work organizing coastal communities to protect coastal lands and create Marine Protected Areas and collaborating with indigenous groups on restoring sea turtles. Raising awareness about the global shrimp industry. In the US shrimp is our #1 seafood, and it has gone from a special meal to food you can buy at Dairy Queen. But few people know about the sea-floor destruction and high bycatch caused by bottom trawling for wild shrimp or about the pollution by shrimp farms built on top of former mangrove forests (shrimpsuck.org). Unfortunately sea turtles have also been my window into the problem of plastic pollution. In 1996 we tracked Adelita, a loggerhead sea turtle, across the entire Pacific Ocean. She went straight through an area people now call the "Garbage Patch." While we followed her migration, I became more interested in that vast area of the ocean and started collaborating with oceanographers like Curt Ebbesmeyer and Jim Ingraham. I learned about all the garbage, mostly plastic, floating around out there and vowed to help stem its flow here on land. Sea turtles have it hard enough without having to swim through plastic in the ocean and dig through it on beaches (pluckfastic.org)

Q. What new projects are you working on?

A. I'm excited about our Oceanophilia.org project. In a way, I've been working on it all my life. And in a way, it's what we all work on. I'm digging deep into the Mind-Ocean connection, learning a lot about cognitive neuroscience and thinking about how we can better reach people about the ocean. It's fascinating to consider how the ocean affects us emotionally, how it stimulates all of our senses and to explore the revolution in neuroscience that is underway from an ocean perspective. The human brain is the most highly developed organ on the planet as far as we know!) and the ocean is the biggest feature of our planet. Put the two together, and things get pretty interesting. If you look in the index of most books about the ocean, you won't find the words neuroscience, brain, mind, emotion or psychology. The reverse is true for the books on neuroscience: nothing about the ocean. We plan to change that.

Q. What books, movies, websites, and organizations are your favorites?

A. Books: *Here Comes Everybody: The Power of Organizing Without Organizations* by Clay Shirky and *The Man Who Planted Trees* aka *L'homme qui plantait des arbres* by Jean Giono. Films: *Voyage of the Lonely Turtle* (PBS-Nature) and *The 11th Hour* (Leo DiCaprio.) Organizations: *Grupo Tortuguero* (grassroots sea turtle conservation group in Baja), *SEEturtles.org* (helps people see, connect with and help sea turtles.)

Q. Do you have a favorite quote?

A. One simple quote I seem to come back to and share with the young people we work with is: "Don't stop. Never, ever stop." The work we do can be thankless at times. Sometimes our adversaries seem unstoppable, better funded. But we can't stop. We've made some progress, just read the news. But still, we have a long way to go. And when we are done with our work, we'll pass the baton to the next generation of ocean revolutionaries to continue.

Photo Neil Osbor

Dr. Dave Jenkins

Q. You created *Surf Aid International Emergency Preparedness Program* that is a community based disaster risk management program, funded by the Australian Government through AusAid's Australian-Indonesian partnership in order to improve disaster management from tropical storms, cyclones, floods, landslides, tidal surges, and health epidemics. Clearly Surf Aid provides many services, including providing life saving mosquito nets to help prevent malaria, among other things, can you please explain what specifically *Surf Aid* teaches people about the ocean?

A. Our disaster preparedness program teaches communities about Tsunamis, their causes and the warning signs that include closely observing the ocean's movements. This helps us all to understand the key fact that we are all interdependent, sea and land and all life. If we are to save this planet, I believe it starts with all of us understanding this fact. We must wise up. The key opportunity to help the planets, oceans, lands, and people is to reduce population growth. The world's population has tripled in the last 50 years putting unsustainable pressure on the world's ecosystems and oceans. The single most powerful way to reduce population growth is to reduce poverty and child mortality. As parents learn to keep their children alive, they choose to have two not six children and seek to invest what little resources they have in fewer children. This is now well proven from research in all continents.

Q. What are some of your major concerns related to the ocean for Indonesia, and its surrounding areas, and how can people help?

A. Indonesia used to have some of the largest collections of virgin coral forests and pristine oceans. Now, Indo has lost most of them from bombing, cyanide fishing and climatic oscillations such as bleaching and toxic run off from poisoned rivers. Again reducing poverty gives people an alternative to destroying their environment.

Q. What are your hopes for the Indonesian people, and for the future of *Surf Aid*?

A. My hope for Indonesia is that it continues the strong progress it is making toward a vibrant and tolerant democracy where corruption gives way to a truly unique and successful society that celebrates its diversity. I hope the Indonesian people take this chance to develop without the usual influence of the politically motivated or resource grabbing outsiders. In other words, I hope for Indonesians to be free. For *Surf Aid* we will continue to be uncompromising in our determination to help people control their own destinies and improve their own lives using their own skills and self motivations. Specifically, I hope we can prove that this strategy can be the most cost effective use of donor dollar enabling us to scale the work and hence join others in improving the overarching results from the AID sector. As a result, the world focuses in on the grass-roots poverty reduction work that is not only desperately needed to save us all, but do-able, as we are showing.

In 1999, Australian physician and surfer Dr. Dave Jenkins went on a surf charter to the Mentawai Islands with one goal in mind: to find perfect waves. The surf proved to be everything he hoped for, but he also found the Mentawai people, mostly women and children, suffering and dying from the ravages of malaria and other preventable diseases. Dave found that he was unable to just walk away. It was a defining life moment. Dr. Dave co-founded Surf Aid International, *a non-profit organization dedicated to the alleviation of human suffering through community-based health programs.*

www.surfaidinternational.org

Photo Todd Glaser

Chris del Moro

Q. Did you grow up around the ocean and if so, how did that experience impact you from an early age? (Any particular experience or story you wish to share, please include)

A. My family history is very much tied into a long line of ocean lovers. I was raised between Florence Italy and the South Bay of Los Angeles. I was very fortunate to have been raised at the waters edge in both cultures. Salt water has been in my veins since before I could walk and in many ways has shaped the very life I live today. When I moved back from Italy at five years old I was often pawned off to my older cousins who lived a stones throw to the sea. They taught me to surf so I didn't cut down on their time in the sea. They gave me an old board, tattered wet suit, and just like that I was given the best gift of my life, a 20 year plus love affair with the vast blue waterway that has brought me infinite joys. Through this awareness, I have been moved and inspired to channel my energies to help cetaceans and overall well being of the ocean.

Q. Is there one particular ocean issue that speaks to you the most, and if so can you please explain a bit?

A. Pollution and beach debris are a constant reminder of the footprint large amounts of people have on their local environment. We definitely have a long way to go to educate and spread awareness about consumer purchasing habits, and general care taken with disposal of waste, i.e. cigarette butts, food packaging, car oil, city run off and the infinite amount of plastic water bottles people go through. These issues speak to the general health of the sea. I am also highly motivated on protecting the future of the incredible amount of sea life we share the seas with. I've always had a strong connection with porpoise/whales and see it is my duty to help serve and protect their existence as long as I am able. The negative issues surrounding the slaughter of whales and dolphins are much, and the same, the same plight faced throughout the fishing industry. Until humans as a whole can make the connection between what's on their plate, and the diminishing levels of sea creatures around the world, we are heading for disaster.

Q. Any key influences and or fellow surfers, artists, organizations that you particularly resonate with you?

A. Paul Watson is a hero. I believe that the Sea Shepherd Society plays a crucial role in spreading awareness to the issues I've mentioned. It does so in a manner that is potent enough to stand up against the horrible injustices the sea currently faces. Unfortunately, the sea is at war, and fortunately Paul is a master strategist. In many ways, Dave Rastovich opened my mind and heart to the incredible Taiji slaughtering a few years back. It was at that moment that I went from a passive environmentalist, to one who felt their blood boiling. It was my quest to help in any way possible and through fate I fell right into working with Surfers 4 Cetaceans. To this day, I am constantly inspired by Dave's drive, giving and overall kinetic spirit he brings to these issues. I am constantly learning the dedication and commitment it takes to make lasting change from incredible activists like Howie Cooke, Shannon Mann, Ric O'Barry and many others. Their hard work is reinforced through shows like Whale Wars and films like The Cove.

Q. What does "Respect for the Ocean" mean to you and do you have any advice or suggestions for younger surfers on how to make a difference in protecting the homeland?

A. For me it means treating the sea as you would treat your family. Realizing that although the oceans are large, they can no longer act as society's waste dumps or sole food source. It seems we are at a tipping point where humans and society need to stop taking and start giving. So if you are inspired by issues regarding the sea, try hooking up with a local non-profit or start your own with some friends. The main issue is doing something, whether you decide to the leave the beach with ten pieces of trash every time you leave or get involved with front line direct action, it's about solidarity and working as a whole to help protect the sea for the next generation.

Photo Todd Glaser

A surfer, artist, lifeguard and environmental activist and spokesperson for Surfers for Cetaceans, *Chris del Moro* spent his childhood growing up between Los Angeles, California, Florence/Sardinia, Italy and the North Island of New Zealand. Through his experiences he has learned how small the world is and how we are all connected in some way. His passion for life and the environment has been harnessed through his love for ocean sports and creating art.

www.s4cglobal.org

Photo Sam Olson

James Pribram

Q. What is the significance of having legalized surfing in the Great Lakes and Chicago, and how did that come about?...

A. When I was in Grand Haven Michigan, filming a documentary show for Fuel TV that was about my project The ECO-Warrior project and some of the local surfers told me of a story about a surfer named Jack Flynn who had been arrested for surfing in Chicago because it was illegal. Right away I had to get involved and try and help the Chicago surfers get surfing legalized there. I was astonished that something like surfing could be illegal in a great country like the United Staes. After all I believed it should be within peoples rights to go surfing if they so choose to. Within six months of our first meeting with the Chicago Parks District along with the likes of Todd Haugh and Vince Duer, we got surfing legalized there. Which in turn has created a brand new industry there, the surfing industry. Along with surf shops, surfing schools and stand up paddling is absolutely the biggest craze happening on the Great Lakes today. It's always exciting to be apart of history and more importantly giving back to the sport of surfing which has given me so much.

Q. As a surfer you have stated how it bothers you to see so many cigarette butts in the ocean, and Great Lakes, and all waterways for that matter., what are the harms to the environment of theses butts?...

A. To me there is nothing worse then sitting down on the beach and sticking my hand on top of a cigarette butt, the smell along makes me sick and sadly there are the most littered debris found on out beaches. It is estimated that world wide smokers toss 4.5 TRILLION butts each year that harmful for our environment in many different ways!!! The average cigarette butt contains numerous chemicals which are diluted in the ocean water and may be considered health hazards when swallowed

The cigarette filter was designed to trap the toxic chemicals in the cigarette smoke from entering the smoker's body. When submerged in water, the toxic chemicals trapped in the filter leak out into aquatic ecosystems, threatening the quality of the water and many forms of aquatic life;

Cigarette filters (the butts) are made of cellulose acetate (plastic) and are NOT biodegradable, while the paper and tobacco in the cigarette are. The filters contain small plastic pieces that can interfere with the digestion of food, casing marine life to starve; and in my opinion the nastiest habit one can have next to chewing tobacco.

James Pribram is a Laguna Beach native, professional surfer and John Kelly Environmental Award winner. Known as the -ECO-Warrior' his written work has appeared in the LA Times, Surfer's Path, Surfing, Surfer, Water and numerous additional publications worldwide. He is an active environmental leader in his community where he has served on the Laguna Beach Water Quality and Environmental Committees. He co-founded Eco Warrior, a grass roots organization which is dedicated to protecting oceans, beaches and sea life worldwide. Pribram's Surfing Soapbox column appears weekly in the Coastline Pilot, Daily Pilot, Huntington Beach Independent and La Times and has readership of over 50,000.

www.ecowarriorsurf.com

Photo Sam Olson

Photo Ryan Roelen

Holly Beck

Q. Having swam with the amazing Whale Sharks yourself, can you please tell us a few things about these creatures that most ordinary people probably don't already know?

A. Whale sharks are incredibly beautiful peaceful creatures. They are usually anywhere between 20 and 40ft long which might sound intimidating, but since they only eat plankton, swimming alongside such an enormous creature is completely safe and also exhilarating. Each whale shark is covered in a unique pattern of white spots like a fingerprint that can be used to identify individual sharks. They swim at a leisurely pace of only 3mph, which sounds slow but can be quite a challenge to keep up with them. Unfortunately, they are in danger and are being fished for meat and fins. I was lucky to be a part of a tagging expedition by a shark conservation organization called IEMANYA. We tagged five whale sharks in the Bahia De Los Angeles in Baja California, Mexico with tags that will measure depth and length of the dives as well as their migratory paths so that researchers can use that information to help better protect the sharks.

Q. You spend a lot of your time in Nicaragua, what is so special about Nicaragua to you in general and about the ocean there, what is the difference between the ocean there, and your home in California?

A. The biggest difference between the Pacific Ocean bordering Nicaragua and the Pacific that washes the coast of California is temperature. The water in Nicaragua is incredibly warm, which is really nice, but the reason I love it there so much has a lot more to do with the differences on land. It's a much slower pace of living. I was able to buy an acre of land and build a little house, plant a bunch of fruit trees, and adopt a pack of dogs. I'm living totally off the grid. I pump a well for water, use a solar shower for hot water, and the solar panel on the roof powers my laptop and internet. I pretty much live exclusively in boardshorts and bare feet. I walk to surf. There are no parking meters and gridlock consists of a herd of cows in the road. The people are beautiful and friendly and real. There are snakes, toads, bats, and spiders everywhere, but to me it's paradise.

Q. If you could send one message to the people of the world about the ocean what would you say to them?

A. Sharks are not trying to eat people. I actually had the chance to dive with great whites at Isla Guadalupe. We were aboard the Nautilus Explorer which drops cages to 40ft and uses a minimum amount of bait in order to see the sharks in a more natural environment. There's a trap door at the top of the cage which actually allows you to stand on top of the cage, totally unprotected. I had a 16ft long female great white pass within 3 feet of me and it was one of the most awesome experiences I've ever had. I felt an incredible amount of respect but not one ounce of fear. So many people think sharks, particularly great whites, are hungry to eat people. If that were the case, I'd be dead. I believe that shark attacks are due to cases of mistaken identity or desperation. A sick, hungry shark may bite a shore break splashing human, confusing it for an injured animal. A young curious shark may bite a human in the same way a puppy will chew on something just to see what it is. They almost always let go immediately. Sharks aren't trying to eat us. They are beautiful majestic creatures that keep the entire oceanic food chain in check. We need them. We must protect them for the health of the ocean and the planet.

Holly Beck is a professional surfer who spends half her time in California and half of her time in Nicaragua. She enjoys organic cooking, hiking, reading, gardening, scuba diving, and traveling. She is also an avid shark advocate and believes in connecting with the good energy of the world.

www.hollybecksurfs.blogspot.com

Photo Duffy Healey

Griff Alker

Q. As a commercial fisherman, living in the Azores, you have mentioned you like some of the sustainable fishing techniques that are law there, can you elaborate on this?

A. Their techniques are more old-world; even though they know there are technological advances and a more modern way to fish, they stick with tradition. I respect that and see many benefits. An example would be their tuna fleet. They're still using the "live bait," jack pole method, and it's very much man against fish. You have 80-foot boats with15 to 20 guys all catching fish one at a time, as opposed to the 200-foot purse seine boat with giant nets, a helicopter, satellite images, massive hydraulics, etc., that holds thousands of tons of fish. In one set they could destroy the whole school. With the traditional Azorean way of fishing it keeps the playing field at an even keel and doesn't decimate a whole school of tuna in one season. Another benefit with the traditional way of fishing is the number of fishermen employed. The "bait boats" employ 15-20 guys and there are many vessels among the seven islands. They fish four to six months of the year. That's a lot of jobs compared to a big purse seine boat that maybe employs 12 guys and catches 10 -15 bait boats' worth of fish. The Azorean way spreads the income around and provides a livelihood for many, as opposed to few. It's really a way of life, a part of the culture. And it has greater longevity; most of the guys' fathers and grandfathers fished before them, and hopefully their sons will be able to follow in their path and fish as well.

Q. Can you briefly explain the damage done by large commercial fishing vessels and the kind of practices these vessels use?

A. First of all, not all large commercial fishing operations damage the world's fisheries. Many are well-regulated with controlled by-catch and set quotas. I want to focus on the tuna purse seiners because that industry is global and has NO regulations or effective boundaries. All major nations have a tuna fleet, and what they do on the high seas is damaging every in-shore fishery in the world. There is a 200 mile EZZ zone off each country's coast as a boundary for the purse seiners (i.e. one country cannot fish in another country's EZZ zone.) However, these big vessels are following and catching the tuna outside the zone. They're wiping out the small fish so there are going to be none left to breed or grow big for the local fisherman. These boats are huge, and technology is a massive component in their technique. The fish don't stand a chance. They hold thousands of tons of fish, they target big schools of tuna and they want the whole school. I'm sure no purse seine captain has ever said "Let's set on only half of the school and leave the rest for next time." Also, the purse seiners are having a major impact on the schools of tuna. Fish typically swim with other same-sized fish (i.e. 300 lb. fish with other 300 lb. fish, 200 lb. with 200 lb. etc, all the way down to 10 or 20 lbs.) hence the name "schools." These seiners are cutting up the schools so badly that 20 lb. tuna are now swimming with 150 lb. and 300 lb. tuna. And we are even seeing other fish in these schools as well: Mahi, Wahoo and a few other species. This wasn't happening 20 years ago. With that said, now they're setting the giant nets on anything that looks like a school of fish. Sometimes they make a set and if it doesn't meet the criteria of what they need (i.e. a certain size or species of tuna for them to qualify for chunk light tuna at the cannery dock),

Photo Duffy Healey   Photo Griff Alker

Griff Alker has spent most of his life trolling the seas fishing, or chartering surfers throughout exotic locations like Indonesia. Currently, Alker practices sustainable crab fishing in the Azores where he resides with his family.

www.pelagic-charters.com

they open up the bottom of the net and kill 50-100 tons of pelagic fish. These fish don't survive, they sink to the bottom of the ocean floor. Then the big purse seiner just drives away and keeps hunting.

Q. In your opinion as a fisherman, if you could pass on one idea to the people around the world in regard to fishing specifically, what would you say?

A. Fishing is the livelihood for many people around the world and that's important to remember. However, management and regulations do need to be put in place in order to protect both the fishermen and the fish. I feel this should be done by the fishermen themselves, not by someone in an office, far-removed. It really needs to involve the people it directly affects. As far as the tuna goes, it has to be a global, joint effort. I'm not optimistic, but because it's such a complex issue, that's the only way.

John John Florence

Q. What suggestions can you offer to people who would like to help the ocean?

A. My generation needs to step it up and learn more about the environment. More of us need to ask more questions about ocean issues to become aware. It is so important that kids respect nature and take care of it. Our ocean is not only our playground but it is our source of food. It sounds really simple but it's super important: I think people should be responsible for their own trash. That might mean picking up your trash when you leave the beach, recycling plastic water bottles or taking care of any trash or pollution that you create. Also, If you own a business that creates trash, you need to be responsible for taking care of it.

Q. What does the ocean mean to you?

A. The ocean means everything to me, which is true for all surfers. We live in the ocean. I'm in the water, every day, surfing, bodysurfing, fishing, you name it. The ocean is my source for energy and happiness.

Photo Jen Johnson

Q. Are there any laws that we should make regarding the ocean?

A. I think that there should be laws that say if you pollute the ocean in any way there should be fines. It seems that people think about money more than they do a clean environment.

Before reaching voting age, John Florence has graced the cover of Surfer *and* Surfing *magazine, won a national surfing title, and has become the youngest surfer ever to compete in the* Vans Triple Crown of Surfing, *which many consider the ultimate surfing competition.*

www.bikepathstory.com

Zoltán "Zoli" Téglás

Ignite

Photo E. Laul Healey

Q. You have been doing pelican rescue for nearly twenty years now. Can you please explain what it is that you do for them?

A. Pelicans are faced with many daily difficulties. They are considered pests to some fishermen who dislike their presence because opportunistic pelicans steal their fish. A great danger to the pelican is the accidental hooking of the bird by a person fishing. The hook is not the most dangerous to the bird but the monofilment fishing line is. The excess trailing line that could be many feet long can causes the bird to become entangled. If the line gets wrapped around the leg it will cause a slow strangulation of the leg, intense pain, infection, and death of the foot. Line wraps around the wings of the bird resulting in cut tendons which hampers them from flying and inevitably causes starvation. Brown pelicans received severe exposure to DDT and other contaminants through consumption of contaminated fish. As was the case with many birds, this exposure resulted in the production of eggs with thin eggshells that were unable to withstand the weight of the parent during incubation, resulting in crushed eggs instead of healthy chicks. As a consequence, the number of chicks produced each year declined dramatically, and the population was reduced severely.

Other major factors contributing to the decline of the species include habitat loss, local food shortages and human disturbance. Pelicans require undisturbed habitat and abundant supplies of fish, particularly during the breeding season. If nesting pelicans are startled while on the nest, their abrupt departure often crushes their eggs. If sufficient food supplies are not readily available, pelicans will abandon breeding colonies. Factors contributing to decreased food availability include commercial fishing and naturally occurring increases in ocean water temperature.

I have been the head volunteer for Pacific Wildlife for the past 20 years. I usually take a small skiff out to local southern California harbors to look for injured and entangled birds. If I see a pelican injured or hooked, I will bait them close to my boat, net them and bring them on board to untangle the line, remove the hooks (if the hook is superficial and not set too deep into the animal's body), and examine them for any other injuries. In most instances, I will be able to return them back into the water soon after I de-hook and de-line them. If a call comes into Pacific Wildlife from animal control, lifeguards, or a volunteer concerned about sick or injured pelicans or sea birds, I will rescue the bird and transport them back to Pacific Wildlife to receive medical attention and rehabilitation. Since we are a non-profit medical center, volunteers can work off court ordered fines or community service.

Q. Do you have any advice to give people who see pelicans or other marine birds or animals that are in need of help?

A. There are many organizations that rescue birds and marine mammals, the best thing to do if someone sees an animal in distress is to call your local rescue organization, harbor patrol, or animal control. If you are witness to someone intentionally injuring the birds, the local police should be called as these animals are Federally protected. Take the initiative and place the call, do not hope that someone else will take the responsibility.

Most organizations are continually seeking dedicated volunteers and are almost always struggling for the necessary funds. If you are someone that has the time to volunteer, please contact your local rescue organization. If you don't have time on your hands, please donate to your local organization.

Q. Do you have any last thoughts you would like to share?

A. Pelican friendly fishing tips:
- Never feed pelicans - The birds should not get used to human contact.

Photo E. Laul Heale

- Reel in your line if pelicans/shorebirds are near.
- Do not leave your lines unattended when pelicans are near.
- Change location if pelicans show interest in bait or catch.
- Release catch quietly away from pelicans.
- Use circle hooks, barbless hooks, or crimp barbs to avoid injury to wildlife.
- Never cast toward wildlife.
- Recycle fishing line and stash your trash.
- If a pelican get hooked, cut the line as close to the bird as possible. In most cases the hook does not injure the bird or create lasting health risks. The fishing line is the killer.
- Long fishing line that is connected to the hook will wrap around the wings and legs, cutting tendons, entangling the bird so they can't fly or swim. Many birds are found dead on rocks and jeddies due to entangled fishing line that tied them to the rocks.
- Pelicans are a federally protected animal and if you see anyone abusing them or recklessly fishing around them, please contact the local authorities. In most cases it will be the Harbor Patrol.
- Pelicans are not pests' they are majestic, magnificent animals that should be respected and protected. We as humans are fishing in their area. Respect the wildlife around you.
- "Education without action does nothing" - Ignite "In Defense."

Photo Sebi Hartung

> *Zoltán "Zoli" Téglás is the lead singer for* Ignite *and* Pennywise. *He lives in Los Angeles but also has a house in Hungary where his parents imigrated. He spends most of his time rescuing pelicans and other sea birds to rehabilitation hospitals for the Pacific Wildlife Project.*
>
> www.igniteband.com • www.pacificwildlife.ca

Nick Hernandez

Common Sense Band

Q. If you could sum up your thoughts on the ocean, what would you say?

Photo E. Lau Healey

A. We are all made from ocean water, in order to love ourselves we must love the ocean. For us to be completely healthy, the ocean must be pollution free. The ocean has kept us healthy, providing food and activities like surfing, swimming, diving and boating to name a few, each for strength, each for sustenance, now it's time to give back. Would you feed a piece of plastic to your child? Of course not. So why do we feel it's ok to dump our waste into the ocean? We are all ocean. Our litter contaminates marine animals which are eaten by other animals, our children and ourselves.

Currently, out in the Pacific Ocean there is a swirling vortex of plastics floating just below the water's surface that is larger than the size of Texas, perhaps twice the size. It is called the Great Garbage Patch! So what can we do? We can help by picking up any plastic we see. PLASTIC is ALWAYS available for you to pick up. Unfortunately, it's in the water and on every beach. Plastics travel great distances, riding wind and ocean currents to every shore in the world. So next time you visit the ocean, don't leave empty handed. Pick up your trash or die trying!

> *Nick Hernandez is a lifelong sea lover and a natural ocean advocate supporting many charities. He's been singing songs about the ocean for over 20 years, as the lead singer for* Common Sense Band *and as a soloist a.k.a. Nick-I. Most his youth was spent skim boarding, surfing, diving, fishing, and enjoying the coastlines from Mexico to the Central Coast of California.*
>
> www.commonsenseband.com

Wang Niandong

Q. As an artist you have a lot of paintings that represent the ocean, can you explain the message you wish to convey in these paintings?

A. For me, the subject of many of my paintings shows the relationships between the ocean and people, their expressions are a major focal point while being amerced in the beauty of the ocean. The sea for me is a symbol of beauty and I truly enjoy beautiful things and do not want to see its destruction. The ocean is such a beautiful thing that may slowly disappear from the earth . . . every citizen has the inescapable obligation to protect the oceans. From the artist's point of view, it's to protect the hearts of the people in the position of their incarnation, is also to protect us in this beautiful dream. On the perspective of human society it's also to protect ourselves, protect our homeland and to protect this beautiful blue planet.

对我来说，我的很多作品的题材来自于海洋，人和海洋的关系是我的作品表达的一主要内容，海洋对我来说是美的象征，我赞美海洋的美丽，也不想让这种美丽因为人类社会活动的破坏而成为正在慢慢消失景物...每个地球上的公民都有不可推卸的保护海洋的义务，从艺术家的角度，是去保护人们心中的美丽境地的化身，是去保护我们大家美丽的梦；从人类社会的角度出发，是去保护我们自己，保护我们的家园，保护这颗蓝色的星球。

Q. What role do you see China having in regards to the ocean and the environment?

A. As we all know, China has an extremely long coastline, including the mainland and the islands, the county's coastline is more than 32,000 kilometers. China is also a rapidly developing nation, so the balance between development and ocean protection, keeping that balance is very important, it is also key to whether China will contribute even more to the protection of the world's oceans . I'm very pleased that China has issued a number strict laws as well as public advocacy and initiatives to strengthen the protection of the oceans, although there are still a number of problems, but generally speaking, everything is gradually improving and will get even better.

众所周知，中国是海岸线很长的国家，陆地和岛屿的海岸线长度超过了32,000公里，中国同时也是一个发展中的国家，在国家发展和保护海洋面前，保持一种平衡很重要，这也是对世界海洋的保护能否做出贡献的关键。很欣慰的是中国在这些年也颁发了一系列的法律以及对大众的宣传和倡议，对海洋的保护正在加强，虽然也出现有一些的问题，但总的看来，一切正在逐渐完善和慢慢变好...

Artist, Wang Niandong, was born in Zigong, Sichuan Province, China in 1978. He studied at Central Academy of Fine Art in Beijing and finished his graduate study from Sichuan Fine Art Institute in 2002 where he is an associate professor. His grandfather was a doctor, as well as a scholar and artist. This reflects in his bearing and his approach to life and art. His work appears to be meticulously executed realism, but the meaning and message go far beyond. His underwater series depicted the conflict between dream and reality; butterfly series contemplated transformation. Under those breathtakingly beautiful canvases, there is almost always a hint of darkness and sentiment, but the same time plenty hope and life's strongest desire too.

www.mandarinfineart.com

Izzy & Danielle Paskowitz

Q. Can you explain what *Surfers Healing* is, and how, and why it got started?

A. *Surfers Healing* is a non-for-profit organization started by Izzy and myself in 1999. We saw the positive effects the ocean had on our son when Izzy would take him out surfing and started taking out other kids with Autism. We had a fundraiser to raise money to start a charity and the rest is history. We now take out over 3,000 autistic children a year, using surfing as an alternative form of therapy and recreation.

Q. You guys have a new show that will be airing on the Oprah Winfrey Network when it begins called *The Swell Life*. Can you explain the premise of the show, and tell us what message you would most like people to take away from the show after seeing it?

A. We have been filming since last May for our show on OWN. The show is based on the struggles of raising an autistic teen, running a foundation for autistic kids and the challenges of running the Paskowitz Surf Camp. I'd like for the show to further promote Autism awareness and help people understand what other parents and siblings of autistic people go through. It also shows the therapeutic effect the ocean has on the kids.

Q. Izzy, you had a particularly notable life growing up, as was highlighted in the movie *Surfwise*, growing up with many siblings in a camper, and traveling anywhere there was surf. Tell us, what were some of the good environmental lessons you learned about respect for the ocean because of the way you grew up? And what was the best thing your father taught you that sticks with you?

A. We grew up with a great respect for the ocean—the ocean was our playground and classroom for that matter. Everyday we had to walk up and down the beach and pick up trash before surfing.

Q. You guys are both now running the famous Paskowitz Surf Camp, do you have any inspirational ocean stories you would like to share from your years of running the surf camp?

Photo E. Laul Healey

A. Folks from all walks of life go to the Paskowitz Surf Camp. People you would never think would put on a wet suit and go in the water, get bit by the surfing bug. We love to share our knowledge of the ocean.

Q. Do you have any last thoughts, or words of wisdom you would like to pass on about the ocean?

A. In order to share our experience of surfing with others, we all need to have respect for the ocean.

Surfers Healing seeks to enrich the lives of children with Autism and the lives of their families by exposing them to the unique experience of surfing. Surfers Healing *camps are held in California, Hawaii, Virginia, North Carolina, Rhode Island, New York, New Jersey, Cabo San Lucas, Mexico and Jobos Beach, Puerto Rico. Says Izzy, "The impact of the ocean on kids with Autism lasts for a long time, the positive reaction the kids have is amazing!"*

www.paskowitz.com • www.surfershealing.org

Christopher Gavigan
Heathy Child Healthy World

Q. What are the impacts of sunscreen on the health of our children and that of the ocean's?

A. Sunscreen is an invaluable outdoor necessity for protecting skin from the sun's damaging UV rays, but like any other product you want one that actually works and isn't loaded with potentially dangerous chemicals. Recent reports have emphasized the need to be savvy sunscreen consumers. The Environmental Working Group's comprehensive scientific review http://www.ewg.org/whichsunscreensarebest/2009report indicates that two of five brand-name sunscreens either don't protect skin from sun damage or contain hazardous chemicals — or both.

A new study from the Centers for Disease Control http://www.ehponline.org/members/2008/11269/11269.pdf. (CDC) found that nearly all Americans are contaminated with oxybenzone, a sunscreen chemical that has been linked to allergies, hormone disruption, cell damage, and low birth weight.

Here are some common ingredients to AVOID in sunscreens: PABA, Benzophenone (benzophenone-3), homosalate, and octy-methoxycinnamate (octinoxate), Oxybenzone, Parabens (butyl-, ethyl-, methyl-, and propyl-), Padimate-O, and Phthalates (often hiding in "fragrance").

Roughly 4,000 to 6,000 metric tons of toxic sunscreens are estimated to wash off swimmers into the oceans every year. By some estimates, this has led to sunscreen-induced bleaching of up to 10 percent of the world's coral reefs. Reef Safe sunscreens were subjected to a comprehensive series of independent laboratory tests to support and authenticate the biodegradability of the lotions. The research found that 99 percent of the material biodegraded in seawater within 60-80 days, while no evidence of toxicity to micro-organisms and other sea life was detected. source: http://www.pr.com/press-release/212154

Q. What specific tips and advice would you offer to parents who wish to bring their children to a safe day at the beach and swim in the ocean?

Christopher Gavigan is the author of the best-selling parenting guide: Healthy Child Healthy World: Creating a Cleaner, Greener, Safer Home, *and is the CEO / Executive Director of the national non-profit* Healthy Child Healthy World. *Gavigan has become a leading voice in the children's environmental health arena as he presses for stronger regulation and chemical policy reform and continues to help design safer, price competitive, non-toxic products for families to create healthier homes and lifestyles.*

www.healthychild.org/book

A.

- Pick a beach that is tested regularly for cleanliness, and that notifies you when it is unsafe to go in the water. Contact your local or state environmental protection office or public health agency. Oftentimes you can do an on-line search of your favorite beach's name with the words "water quality" to find information.
- Wait at least 24 hours after a heavy rainfall before swimming. Heavy rains can stir up polluted sediment and cause sewage systems to overflow into storm drains.
- If possible, choose beaches that are away from urban areas or that have good water circulation.
- Avoid swimming in beach water that is cloudy or smells bad.
- Avoid swimming near storm drains.
- Look for trash and other forms of pollution like oil slicks.
- Check out the surrounding environment. What's adjacent to the water? Farmland or golf courses could mean high levels of pesticides are running off into the water. If there's an industrial facility upstream, you could be swimming in their effluent.
- Avoid getting water in your mouth.
- The Natural Resources Defense Council rates the top 100 beaches http://oceans.nrdc.org/beachgoers/map, but for smaller beaches you'll need to do some hunting.

Q. In your opinion, what is the most critical issue(s) facing the world's oceans today, and what are the direct effects on the health of our children?

A. We are witnessing major and irreversible changes in ocean chemistry that can have extensive direct and indirect effects on ocean organisms and the ocean our children inherit.   Ocean acidification could lead to a disastrous future for all living things in the ocean.
The Monaco Declaration http://ioc3.unesco.org/oanet/Symposium2008/MonacoDeclaration.pdf, in which 155 scientists from 26 countries declared in January 2009 that:

- Ocean acidification is accelerating and severe damages are imminent;
- Ocean acidification will have broad socioeconomic impacts, affecting marine food webs, causing substantial changes in commercial fish stocks and threatening food security for millions of people;
- Ocean acidification is rapid, but recovery is slow;
- Ocean acidification can be controlled only by limiting future atmospheric carbon dioxide levels.

Needless to say, there needs to be intense global efforts and collaboration to understand the scientific implications of the problem, evaluate its impacts, and diminish emissions drastically to help curb this tremendous problem.

Christopher with his son off the coast of the Grenadines

Jo Ruxton

Q. Can you please explain a little bit about the premise of the next documentary film you are working on about the plastics in the ocean?

A. Our film, *Plastic Oceans*, is a global, environmental disaster story but with a big difference because this one looks at the tangible solution to the problem. It has the ability to change the way we think about plastics, their role in our world, where we have gone wrong and how we can not only clean up the mess we have made but put it to good use.

Plastic pieces never break down completely and they wash into, or are directly discarded into, our watercourses and end up in the coastal seas, where the massive circular currents drive them into the centre of the oceans. The combination of wind and wave action, along with sun exposure, eventually breaks them down into plankton-sized particles. Plankton forms the base of the food chain and so they enter at the bottom and in as little as three steps, they can become part of the human diet.

In concentrated areas, including the middle of the Pacific Ocean where we filmed in summer 2009, plastic particles could out-number plankton by as much as 24:1. To make matters worse, plastic particles this size have the ability to attract toxins in the water and become magnets for them including DDT and PCBs. That's the sad fact we are addressing and with 150 million tons of new plastic being manufactured every year and only a small percentage being recycled, things can only become worse if we don't do something about it.

But – there is good and very hopeful news! A new recently patented process, can convert plastics into raw diesel fuel and gas with minimum energy required and negligible waste returning to the environment. One kg. of plastic can be converted into one liter of unrefined fuel – with this knowledge, why would we want to discard it so readily? People will have incentive to collect plastic for recycling, not into more plastic but actually into a resource that is scarce and very much in demand. Plastic-clogged river mouths, landfill sites, beaches, anywhere plastic waste collects can actually be targeted. There are so many other positive things that the film has to share as well; I feel that this is the most important documentary I have ever worked on.

Q. Since you have been diving for well over 20 years now, and you do it frequently, especially in Asia, what are some of the changes you have seen?

A. Without doubt there are changes and it saddens me that they are visible enough for me to see in the mere 24 years that I have been diving. The seas remained in balance for millennia but we have managed to destroy so much just in the last 50 years. I have returned to many of the reefs I have been lucky enough to dive and witnessed so much damage to the corals as well as a decline in numbers of fish. There are dive sites named after the marine life once guaranteed to be seen there, Whitetip Alley, Barracuda Point, Manta Ridge, Coral Gardens, and the list goes on. These days returning to these wonderfully named sites is so often disappointing. The corals themselves are so vulnerable and the evidence of dynamite and cyanide fishing is all over Asia. On top of that, rising sea temperatures are disastrous for such fragile ecosystems and now we know that higher carbon levels are making the seas more acidic, their survival is seriously in question.

Q. Can you share some facts about coral reefs that people in general may not be aware of, including can you explain what coral bleaching is?

A. Coral reefs comprise less than 0.5% of the ocean floor and yet it is estimated that more than 90% of marine fish are directly or indirectly dependent on them. Think about that, that's nine out of every ten fish in the sea! There are about 4,000 coral reef fish species and they make up a quarter of all the marine fish worldwide. More than 3.5 billion people depend on the ocean for their primary source of food, in just 20 years, this number could double to 7 billion. The survival of our coral reefs is vitally important.

Corals are animals that live together in colonies, living symbiotically within their tissues, they have tiny plants, zooxanthellae, that provide them with nourishment as they go through photosynthesis. It is these little plants that give corals their wonderful colors. When corals are stressed, by pollution or rising sea temperatures, for example, they eject these minute plants and with them goes the color, giving them a 'bleached' appearance. If the conditions return to normal, the corals will take up their zooxanthellae again and survive. If not they remain bleached and will die. New coral larvae need clean surfaces to settle on so that they can grow into new colonies. When the coral reefs bleach and die, they are often quickly covered with algae which forms a mat over the surface, preventing the new coral larvae from settling securely and the new generation is lost.

Q. Do you have any inspirational stories you would like to share in regard to the ocean?

A. You don't need to look far to find people who are working to save the oceans and coastlines, but sometimes these are the last people you would imagine. I went to a small island in the Philippines a while ago working with *Project Seahorse*. The community I stayed in was very poor and all around the island, the coral reefs had been blasted by dynamite fishing. These people depended on the reef fish as their primary source of protein. Many of them had large families to feed and it is easy to understand the desperation that leads them to use dynamite to catch fish. Conservation is really a 'luxury item,' when there are hungry mouths to feed right now, who can wait for reefs to recover and fish to populate them, reproduce and for the young to mature?

And yet a group of these dynamite fishermen joined forces with the people from the project and started to protect areas of the reef. They stopped fishing within certain boundaries and soon realized the value of allowing areas to recover. These boundaries were soon rich with fish moving out from the protected area, where they were allowed to grow and reproduce. The ex-dynamite fishermen became wardens, keeping others away and trying to stop them from dynamiting the reef.

The story doesn't yet have a happy ending; other fishermen who live a hand-to-mouth existence, are still damaging parts of the reef with dynamite and cyanide. Now that they are being prevented from accessing sections of it, some are retaliating by threatening the families of the reformed fishermen.

Marine Protected Areas are very simple solutions that could be applied throughout the world in a network. However, they need to be policed and backed up by a comprehensive educational program but of course, this needs funding.

Q. Are there any other facts, or stories, or things you would like to share?

A. As a race, we tend to react to adverse situations when we see concrete evidence that something is wrong, and that's usually at the last minute. For some reason, concerns about the environment come way down government priority lists and conservationists are still regarded as the 'bearded, sandal-wearing brigade' who shouldn't be taken too seriously. It amazes me now that we have so much scientific evidence of the damage we are doing and now the ever-growing diving community can witness the degradation all over the world. Our once-beautiful beaches are covered in plastic, fishing catches are ever-decreasing and we all know how to reduce our carbon use. In years to come, our children and grandchildren and their families will ask how could we let this happen when we had so many warnings. And I ask it now. How can we continue to turn a blind eye when we know it is happening? Mother Nature is resilient; it's up to us to give her a chance.

Jo Ruxton is an underwater, wildlife producer and has been a key member of the BBC's world famous Natural History Unit diving team. She has been organizing and directing underwater shoots since the first days of filming on the award winning Blue Planet *series in 1997.*

www.mediadivecrews.com

Ross Thomas

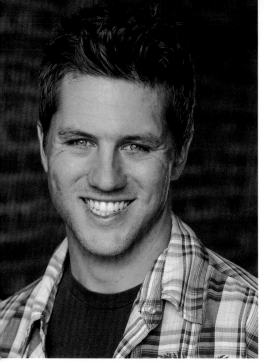

Q. Can you please explain what the ocean means to you and why it is so important to you to protect it?

A. To me, the global ocean represents the vast underworlds of our beginning, middle and question mark. It is the source with which provides infinite levels to a humanity beckoning. The ocean feeds us, it breeds us, it gives pleasure deep in its salty lairs of wisdom. The ocean makes waves for us to smile and wail and test our core, it shares its warmth, its cold, its kin, its bravado for life. The ocean gives clarity to distance. It sheds life and death and mystery within. To me the ocean is the greatest world still uncovered. The depths yet to be reached contain answers to the mystique of a global, universal, galactic existence. For our sustenance, our survival, our strength, we must stand up and honor, preserve and praise and a body of H2O who gives and never strays. The ocean brings me great splendor and joy, and without it in my life . . . forever a void. For the sake of our own survival, we must protect the ocean and its inhabitants. For without this blessing in our life . . . there would be no life.

Q. Do you have an "hotspot" that concerns you the most, and if so what you think people can do to help the problem?

A. I think one of the most urgent crisis currently facing our global ocean is the issue of long lining and over-fishing. Right now in the Gulf of Mexico, blue fin tuna, one of our most important species of fish, is being all but wiped out due to the incredibly irresponsible practice of long lining and illicit commercial fishing. Scientists estimate that the number of mature bluefin tuna has dropped more than 80% since 1970 and fewer than 20,000 adults may remain in our ocean. Our ocean is being pillaged of the fish species we admire and value so much in our global society. Lack of care and the constant influx of competing fishing companies has waged destruction and annihilation on our fish species. The fish we love; that are so crucial to human kind are disappearing right in front of our eyes.

If we do not confront this issue head on with the voracity and international communal strength necessary, fish such as the blue fin tuna will only be seen gracing the pages of picture books. The over fishing of sharks for the use of their fins bobbing in soup bowls, threatens the upset of the entire marine ecosystem. We must fight the ignorance and global lack of management and stand up for the fish species who cannot stand up for themselves. We must be smart consumers and inform ourselves. If we eat fish products, it is our responsibility to eat fish with the lowest impact.

Fisheries need to be managed by the following effective ground rules world wide: 1) We must have a limit on the total number of fish caught and landed by a fishery. 2) We must instill rules to prevent the unintentional killing and disposal of fish and other oceanic life not part of the target catch. 3)It is essential that we protect the significant habitats crucial to the spawning and nursing grounds of fish, as well as the delicate sea floor and corals. 4) We must have global monitoring and enforcement to make sure fishermen are not landing more than they are allowed and using illicit forms of cruel and unusual catching methods to do so. Those who break these rules should be punished and banned from commercial fishing indefinitely. By exposing our world community of all ages to the urgency of halting over fishing and long lining, we may still have a chance to replenish our oceans so that both its life and ours may continue to thrive.

Q. Do you have a favorite quote you would like to share with people, or a recommendation of a book you think people should read?

A. One of my favorite quotes is from the naturalist, John Muir: "Everything is flowing, going somewhere, animals and so-called lifeless rocks as well as water. Thus the snow flows fast or slow in grand beauty, making glaciers and avalanches; the air in majestic floods carrying minerals, plant leaves, seeds, spores, with streams of music and fragrance; water streams carrying rocks . . . While the stars go streaming through space pulsed on and on forever like blood . . . in Nature's warm heart."

One of my favorite books that I'd like to recommend is called, The World Is As You Dream It, by John Perkins. This book is not directly about ocean conservation, but contains ancient wisdom and elements instrumental to the world's sustainability.

Ross Thomas is an actor and enjoys surfing, snowboarding and horseback riding. Ross plans on putting more of his energy and time to learn and teach more about ocean conservation.

www.survivalinternational.org

Photo Jon Nash

Conrad Humphreys

Q. Having sailed around the world three times, and having only a limited amount of stuff you can bring with you, how did you manage your resources on board, and how can that translate to the broader scope of things?

A. As a professional yacht racer, it is important to keep weight onboard to a minimum to maximise race performance. Everything I need has to be carried onboard and therefore there is a finite amount of resource. This has to be managed very carefully with minimum wastage and minimum weight. Freshwater is a precious commodity, which is made by desalinating seawater onboard. In addition to electricity made by solar panels, fuel is required to run the generator, which in turn generates electricity to run the desalinator, the autopilot, computers, lights etc. So I cannot afford to waste a drop of freshwater or leave lights or computers switched on when not needed. Any non-biodegradable waste has to be carried onboard until I complete the race to be disposed of properly, so I need to limit the amount of packaging and keep waste to a minimum. Our planet should be treated the same – it has a finite amount of resources, and we should use only what we need and not waste energy, water and minimize the amount of waste that is produced.

Q. Whether or not people believe in global climate change, sea temperature rise can have significant consequences, can you detail how just a two degree temperature change can make a difference?

A. As an oceanographer, I know that the oceans uptake of CO_2 is vital to our ecosystems and water temperature is critical to regulating the amount of CO_2 the oceans can hold. The consequences of sea temperature rise by a few degrees could mean that the oceans capacity to be a carbon sink may be severely limited and this could have enormous implications for global climate change. As a sailor, I closely monitor the sea temperature, particularly in races like Newport-Bermuda, or the Sydney Hobart where there is a huge advantage to seek out warmer currents or eddies that can lead to increased wind and favourable current. A couple of degrees of sea temperature rise, might be the difference between winning and losing; a couple of degrees can also make the difference for coral reefs to live or die.

Q. What kinds of things are you doing with *The Blue Project* in regard to public outreach, and what message are you trying to convey?

A. Sport is intimately connected to nature and for some athletes it is the relationship with the environment that inspires and motivates them. As Jacques Cousteau once said, "People protect what they love" and it is a love for the environment that we need to engender throughout our communities. The challenge is to move beyond awareness and find the mechanisms to engage with people. People are passionate about sport and some athletes are very effective role-models who can connect with a wide fan-base. *The Blue Project* (www.theblueproject.org) helps sports people to communicate more effectively and encourages fans to participate. This medium is proving effective as a public engagement tool where we are making the emotional connection with the natural environment.

Conrad Humphreys' professional career in sailing began at 17 when he was spotted at the Junior World Cadet Championships *and was asked to join the* Youth Challenge *campaign for the 1993-94 Whitbread Round the World Race. He won the 1989 junior world championships and was a member of the winning British Team in 1990. Conrad has sailed around the world an impressive three times. With a natural passion for the sea, Conrad launched* The BLUE™ Climate and Oceans Project *in February 2007.*

www.conradhumphreys.com • www.theblueproject.org

Dr. Stephen Leatherman

Q. You are best known as "Dr. Beach", having stated that, how would you best rate the beaches of the United States today as opposed to 30-40 years ago, and what changes have you noticed if any?

A. Coastal development has continued and accelerated in the past 30-40 years along much of the U.S. coasts. Fortunately, large areas are protected by virtue of being National Seashores, state and local parks and other conservation areas. Over development has, indeed, been a problem, but many coastal areas are now starting to understand this and also not everyone wants to go to a high-rise beach development like Daytona Beach or Ocean City, MD. The most important contributions of "Dr. Beach" and the annual Top 10 Beaches List (which began in 1991) are the following: Beach communities are rewarded for their environmental stewardship, which goes beyond what regulations can do. In some cases, plans for higher-density development have been canceled because it would affect their ratings. Pollution problems have been dealt with because my rankings and analysis have generated considerable media attention so that local governments can no longer hide or ignore the problems. Do a Google search on Dr. Beach and see how many media hits that you get. Dr. Beach has also given me access to a large range of media, including the nightly news programs, in order to give voice to many other coastal issues of importance.

Q. Having a strong background in climate change, what are your thoughts, or concerns about how climate change will affect our oceans?

A. My research has focused on sea-level rise impacts, which are already happening in response to a relatively small, steady rise in the ocean levels. I have produced a large number of journal articles, several books and an award-winning documentary entitled *Vanishing Lands* on this subject. Global warming will cause sea levels to rise at any accelerated rate, which will greatly compound problems for coastal development and squeeze out some ecosystems, such as salt marshes, that are not allowed to migrate landward due to flanking development. There are millions of people who live on low-lying deltaic areas, which are subject to submergence and loss so that these inhabitants will be flushed out of their homelands. Certainly this will be a catastrophe.

Q. What do you think needs to be done in order to help protect our beaches and oceans?

A. This is a huge question that cannot be answered in a few short statements. There are so many dimensions to this question as well. Perhaps we should talk.

Q. You have done extensive research on sea level rise, and beach erosion. What is the number one thing people should be aware of regarding these subjects?

A. People are naturally drawn and want to live on the coast. There is a rush of the population and attendant development at the coastal edge. At the same time, sea level is rising and beaches are eroding. This is the classic definition of a collision course! It seems that few people take this issue seriously or else assume that government will bail them out of any problems that they have with beach erosion and storm damage, especially from hurricanes.

Stephen Leatherman (a.k.a Dr. Beach) is an internationally recognized beach and coastal scientist. He has written 16 books and hundreds of reports and articles on such issues as beach erosion, beach quality, coastal ecosystems plus more. His annual list of America's Top 10 Beaches *is to the travel and tourism board what the Oscar is to the movie industry.*

www.nhbc.fiu.edu • www.drbeach.org

Frank Scura

Q. Is there one particular ocean issue that speaks to you the most that motivates you to want to help, and if so what is it?

A. I am a lifelong surfer and lover of our great mother ocean and my health is intertwined with hers because I spend a lot of time in the ocean, and therefore, her health effects my health. I wish I could say that there was one ocean issue that resonated with me and motivated me more than another, but unfortunately the over all heath of our oceans is in a state of critical illness. We have walked too far for too long down a wrong road and it is time to turn back. Take your pick of poisons: Nuclear waste dumping is a time bomb that is on slow release and will one day equate to full-scale nuclear assault on our oceans and our ability to sustain ourselves. Clothing dyes and other processes that are contributing heavy metals such as mercury and other toxic metals have made their way into our food and our lives. Almost every piece of poly fabric has antimony (a poisonous heavy metal rich chemical used in poly fabric production) much of which is ending up in our oceans. Modern agricultural practices are producing run off from pesticides, defoliants and chemical fertilizer which are destroying oceanic eco systems by producing out of control algae blooms, dead zones, toxicity, and a myriad of other devastations. Over-fishing as a result of ineffective and non-existing international legislation and enforcement and a complete lapse of common sense practices has put our ocean and our ability to sustain life for any prolonged period in jeopardy. The eradication of sharks for their fins is destroying the food chain protocol. Sonar testing is causing mass beaching of whales and dolphins by scrambling their internal sonar navigation capabilities and blinding them. The Gyres (Plastic Ocean) are the accumulation of human filth coming back to haunt us and has implications far beyond what I believe anyone has imagined to date. If it is all gathering there it must be some kind of a essential flow area vortex that is being blocked. Storm drain and river run off pollutes coastlines. Basically what all of this means is that we are reaching into the wombs of the unborn, robbing them of their rite to livelihood, placing them in indentured servitude. You could sum it up by saying "we are killing our grandchildren to feed our children."

Q. What suggestions can you offer to people that would like to help the situation, or the ocean in general?

A. Buy organic naturally produced food and clothing, always recycle plastics, only purchase antimony free poly fabrics or no synthetics at all; only purchase chromium free tanned leather goods, never throw your cigarette buts on the ground, oppose off shore and coastal oil drilling, support groups and legislation that oppose sonar testing, either dramatically reduce your consumption on seafood or stop eating it all together. You really have no idea how poisonous it really is, our oceans are sick and when you eat from them you are becoming sick too, only wear truly organic sun screens, support groups like *Greenpeace* and the work of the *Sea Shepherd*. They are not trouble making terrorists, they are super heroes fighting for your life; honor them, support them. Whenever you go to the beach, clean up a little, and always leave a place better than when you found it.

Photo Dan Solomon

Q. What does the ocean mean to you?

A. Fun, love, strength, romance, power, change, fluidity, adaptability, surrender! It is the foundation and birthplace of life, it is the undiscovered mystery. We have gone to the moon, but we have yet to touch the bottom of the sea, and that does not make sense to me.

Frank Scura is an entrepreneur, environmentalist and activist. He runs the non-profit Action Sports Environmental Coalition (ASEC) *and he has been advocating that the sports industry be the leaders in the "green" movement for many years. He is currently working on a "Green Room" project to get eco products in centralized locations.*

www.asecaction.ning.com

Atossa Soltani

Q. The Amazon has often been called the lungs of the planet, the ocean the heart. Is there, in fact, an inter-connectivity between the two and if so can you please explain that relationship?

A. The Amazon River Basin contributes 20 percent of all the fresh water on the planet. During the wet season, 300,000 cubic meters pour from the Amazon River into the Atlantic Ocean every second. To put that number in perspective, every hour the Amazon River delivers to the ocean more fresh water than is used in the entire Los Angeles metropolitan area in one year. And most of that water is first lifted off of the ocean before condensing into drops and falling as rain over the Andes and the vast Amazonian watershed. Many indigenous cultures in South America refer to the Amazon rainforest as the "heart of the world," while forest experts have called it the lungs of the planet given its capacity to absorb carbon dioxide and generate oxygen. After the oceans, the Amazon is the Earth's largest conveyor of weather systems. That is because more vapor and heat is generated over the Amazon rainforest than any landmass on the planet. The Amazon rainforest functions like a massive heart pumping columns of heat and vapor up to the atmosphere and driving weather systems around the globe. The connection between the Amazon and the ocean is so direct and so profound that it is much easier to think of them as parts of the same organism than as separate entities.

Q. Furthermore, do you see a direct co-dependency between the overall health of the rainforest and that of the ocean?

A. There is a direct connection between the health of the rainforest and the health of the ocean. Annually deforestation from existing industrial activities in the tropics accounts for 20 percent of global carbon emissions. It is the increase in CO_2 that is causing acidification of the ocean, killing off species and further leading to global climate chaos, which in turn leads to a positive feed back loop. Warmer global temperatures, bring on more droughts and contribute to the death of trees in the Amazon as well as increasing the risk of large-scale forest fires. Scientists predict that the Amazon could loose one-third of its trees in the event of even modest temperature rises which, in turn, would have catastrophic impact on the Amazon's weather generating and climate regulating functions further destabilizing our global climate.

Q. How can we learn from indigenous cultures to live in harmony with nature? To this end, is there any specific native wisdom or lessons that have offered you guidance or provided words to live by that you would like to share with others?

A. Indigenous peoples have maintained their culture and protected their forests for thousands of years precisely because one of their principle values is honoring the earth. Many indigenous cultures view the Earth as their Mother. The U'wa of Columbia, for example, see their collective purpose as guardians of the forest and believe that through their songs and rituals, they are maintaining the balance of the entire world. Another common principle is that current generations must consider the implications of their actions on future generations. In North America, indigenous peoples say at least for seven generations. Respect for all of nature's creation and the concept of reciprocity, always giving back more than you receive are other common ethos among indigenous peoples.

Industrial 'development' in only a few decades has so harmed the Amazon rainforest that its—and our—survival is now in question. Where does the difference lie? Could it be in the prevailing world view? From the origins of the so-called "Conquest of the New World" to the front lines of contemporary deforestation, outsiders have viewed the wealth, diversity, and abundance of nature's resources in the Amazon—and throughout the world's tropical forests—as bounties to be extracted, shipped, and sold, and as a wilderness to be conquered.

California's great Central Valley was a vast seasonal wetlands and home to the second largest inland lake in North America and a vibrant and diverse indigenous population. Only 150 years after the wave of colonizers, miners, and industrial agriculturalists reached the valley, the indigenous peoples were killed or forced to relocate. Tulare Lake no longer exists and the valley has become the largest swath of land on Earth to have its ecosystem so completely altered by human activities. In a few decades, if industrial expansion and global warming continue at their current pace, the same thing could happen to the Amazon. Learning from the indigenous cultures in the Amazon and beyond would require an urgent and quite uncomfortable cultural self-criticism of our value systems. The wisdom and values we could draw from them are in no way esoteric or mystical, and yet would provoke intense social change if followed: Do not destroy that which gives life and consider the future generations.

Q. What does "Respect" for the ocean (or the Earth if you so prefer) signify to you?

A. Respect means giving someone or something their place, their due, acknowledging their autonomy, their right to exist, acknowledging them for who or what they are beyond one's own needs or desires. Respect thus means thinking of the ocean and of the Earth beyond the ways in which they may be useful for human needs and desires. Respect for the ocean is about making an effort to ensure that human actions do not violate the ocean's health and ecological integrity and do not threaten with extinction the life forms that live within it. It is safe to assume that dumping constant streams of toxic chemicals and trash, combined with over-fishing, are causing key species to die off. The current floating vortex of trash twice the size of Texas is an obvious sign of this disrespect.

Q. How do everyday choices affect the way that individuals play a role, directly or indirectly, in the environmental conservation movement? Do you have specific examples and/or any suggestions to offer to people who wish to become more pro-active?

A. While everyday individual decisions about what you consume, what you recycle or throw in the trash, and how you travel directly impact the environmental conservation movement and the environment itself, attention to individual action is only the very beginning. It does not go far enough in stopping the destruction of the Amazon, our oceans, or our planet. For such actions to have a sufficient impact on halting planetary ecological collapse, not only do millions of people in the industrialized world need to subscribe to them, but millions must organize to bring about systemic transformations to address the root causes of these problems. Thus precisely to make everyday individual choices into everyday collective and systemic change means we must organize ourselves into mass movements and become a force for transforming our economic system, our political system, and ultimately our value system. We must organize and challenge our governments, our corporations, and our society at large to find pathways of livelihood that honor and value biological and cultural diversity, social justice, ecological balance and future generations.

Dedicated to defending the rights and the territories of indigenous peoples of the Amazon basin, Atossa Soltani leads successful campaigns challenging oil companies to adopt stronger environmental and social standards globally, first at Rainforest Action Network and now at Amazon Watch, which she founded in 1996. She is fluent in Spanish and Farsi, a skilled media strategist, photographer and filmmaker.

www.amazonwatch.org

Captain Paul Watson

Q. You were only 18 years old and the eighth founding member of *Greenpeace*, so you obviously got started environmentalism at a very young age. What was your first major accomplishment that made you realize you wanted to be an activist for life?

A. I began rescuing wildlife when I was ten. I would free animals especially beavers from trap lines and then I would destroy the traps. I began doing this because I had spent the previous summer swimming and playing with a young beaver in a pond near my home in rural eastern Canada. The next summer, I could not find that little beaver or any of the beavers. A trapper had taken them all. I became very angry and a fervent opponent to hunting and trapping ever since. When I was 18, I attended a demonstration on the British Columbian and Washington State border against nuclear testing at Amchitka Island in the Aleutians. There were people from the *Sierra Club* and the Quakers. I was a *Sierra Club* member. My concern was that Amchitka Island was a wildlife preserve and a previous test had killed over a thousand sea otters.

Q. We've heard there are some strange laws with regard to photography and protecting animals in Canada. Can you explain?

A. In Canada it is illegal to approach, witness or document the killing of a harp seal without a permit from the government of Canada. The regulations are called, strangely enough - the Seal Protection Regulations. It's a very Orwellian way of describing what in reality is the seal hunt protection regulations. Two of my crew were convicted this year after being prohibited entry into Canada to defend themselves. For two counts each of documenting the killing of a seal, they received fines totaling $45,000 and 360 days in jail each should they not pay the fines. They will not pay the fines and there is no danger of them going to jail because Alex Cornelissen of the Netherlands and Peter Hammarstadt of Sweden are not allowed into Canada because they were deported before the trial for disrupting the slaughter of the seals.

Q. The *International Whaling Commission* (IWC) seems also to have some oxymoronic rules. First of all, of the name itself is suggestive that the *IWC* is for whalers, not people who want to save the whales, and then the Japanese are known to be buying off seats or "votes" from other countries. Can you explain that?

A. The *International Whaling Commission* is a toothless and useless organization. It was established in 1946 by the whaling nations to bring some sort of control into the intense slaughter of whales that was driving many species toward extinction. The *IWC* passes rules that the members ignore without penalty. Other member nations like the USA are obligated to embargo offending nations like Japan but they do not do so because of the pressure to not damage trade relations with Japan and Norway. In the early eighties, however, many non-whaling nations joined the *IWC* in an effort to transform the *IWC* into a whale conservation organization. As a result the *IWC* in 1982 passed a resolution to establish a global moratorium on commercial whaling. Norway has ignored this moratorium completely and Japan is abusing the so called "scientific research" loophole to continue commercial whaling. Over the last 15 years, Japan has brought in numerous nations to the *IWC* to vote in favor of ending the moratorium. To do so they need a two-thirds majority vote. To date they have not achieved that but every year they become stronger.

Q. You are internationally known for protecting dolphins, whales, tuna, seals, and wolves, but you even have campaigns to help protect sea cucumbers, etc. Some people claim you are the best animal activist but you say you don't do it for animal rights, but more for ecological reasons. Can you explain?

Photo Sea Shepherd Society

A. The *Sea Shepherd Conservation Society* is not an animal rights or animal welfare organization. We are a marine wildlife and habitat conservation organization and more specifically we are an anti-poaching organization specializing in targeting illegal activities that exploit marine wildlife and habitats.

Q. You have been known to take some unorthodox approaches at *Sea Shepherd* to help protect the whales, etc., including sinking whalers boats to prevent them from killing whales although, no one has ever died as a result of your efforts, you have been labeled by competing organizations as an "eco terrorist" (without naming the organizations), some may think that is actually a compliment but can you explain your thoughts?

A. We get called many things by many people but the fact remains that we have never injured anyone nor have we ever been convicted of a felony crime in the 32 year history of the *Sea Shepherd Conservation Society*. When our critics began calling us pirates, I decided to implement a little aikido and I took the accusation and made it work for us. So we designed our own version of the Jolly Roger keeping in mind that history shows us that it was not the British Navy that ended piracy in the 17th Century in the Caribbean. Most of the British politicians, military and merchants were taking bribes from the pirates. Piracy in the Caribbean was ended by the pirate Henry Morgan. Sometimes it takes pirates to stop pirates and we are pirates of compassion in pursuit of pirates of greed.

Q. Although you have been protecting whales for over 30 years, the success of *Whale Wars* is really bringing this issue to the mainstream, and it is your hope to end the massive killing of whales within a few years. What are the next couple main concerns you have for the ocean, and how can people help?

A. *The Sea Shepherd Conservation Society* is trying to address illegal exploitation ranging from plankton to the great whales. *Whale Wars* has given our Antarctic whale campaign global attention, but we are also active in Taiji, Japan to protect dolphins, in the Galapagos to protect sharks and other species, in the Mediterranean to protect bluefin tuna and in Canada to protect seals. Our bell weather project is our mission in the Galapagos. We have been there for ten years, working with the police and the rangers to stop poaching. If we can't save a place as profoundly beautiful and unique as the Galapagos Islands, then I don't think we will be able to save anything.

Q. Do you have one last thought you would like to share?

A. Captain Paul Watson: I don't think that people realize just how important the oceans are to our own survival nor do they realize just how damaged marine eco-systems have become. All coral reef eco-systems will be gone in 20 years. Ninety percent of the fish have been removed from the sea and all commercial fishing operations will crash by 2020. Mitsubishi is stockpiling tuna and investing in diminishment and extinction. Soon the only bluefin tuna left on the planet will be found only in frozen form in one of their vast refrigerated warehouses. Now Japanese and Norwegian interests are beginning to exploit plankton to make into a cheap protein paste for animal feed. Humanity has done nothing but take, take and take from our oceans and we contribute nothing back. Politicians are afraid of fishermen, and commercial fishermen get what they want, ignoring quotas and contributing to further diminishment.

The bottom line is that if the oceans die, we die. If we can not save biodiversity in the sea, we will ultimately doom our own civilizations and ourselves. I see my duty as simply trying to stop my own species from committing collective suicide.

Photo Sea Shepherd Society

Founder of the Sea Shepherd Conservation Society. *Paul Watson grew up in St. Andrews, New Brunswick, and joined the Canadian Coast Guard. In 1969, he became a* Greenpeace *founding member. Watson exhibits remarkable dedication and has been defending marine wildlife for over 30 years. Currently, the* Whale Wars *reality TV show is viewed in over 20 countries worldwide.*

www.seashepherd.org

Steve Roest

Q. Being the CEO of *Sea Shepherd Conservation Society*, and running as a Green Party parliamentary candidate in UK, if you could pass three worldwide oceanic laws, what would they be?

A. 1. The creation of permanent no-take marine reserves covering at least 50% of the world's oceans and marine habitats. 2. A permanent ban on the fishing and destruction of all endangered marine life and habitats. 3. A permanent ban on the dumping of heavy metals, PCB's and toxins into our oceans. Most importantly, we need nations to do what they have so far failed to do and take swift and severe legal action against anyone who breaks these laws.

Q. What is the most important thing to keep in mind as CEO of an environmental organization that you think could help benefit other environmental companies or organizations?

A. To remember that your responsibility is to protect the natural world, and that all actions should ultimately lead to that goal.

Q. Do you have a favorite quote that you would like to share, or any last thoughts?

A. "I think that God in creating man somewhat overestimated his ability," Oscar Wilde.

Steve Roest is the UK Director and CEO at Sea Shepherd Conservation Society. He's a Green Party Parliamentary candidate in the United Kingdom.

www.seashepherd.org

Laurens de Groot

Q. What made you decide to quit your job as a police officer in Netherlands and join *Sea Shepherd Conservation* to go fight for whales in Antarctica?

A. In my last three years working for the police, I worked as a crime investigator for the organized environmental crime department. The more and more I found out about the atrocities are that committed against our environment the more and more I wanted to do. I started looking for an organization that is really willing to uphold conservation law without comprising what it stands for. That's when I found *Sea Shepherd* and that's when I decided to do whatever I could do to help this organization.

Q. *Sea Shepherd* is now famous for its *Whale Wars* television show, but you are also fighting to protect the bluefin tuna. Can you tell us why you decided to work on this campaign as well, and what is next for you?

A. I like to work on every campaign if I can. The critical situation in our oceans is so severe and so urgent. We need to fight for life in the oceans wherever we can, whenever we can. For *Operation Blue Rage* I had more of a coordinating role in order to get the campaign going. I'm not sure what's next for me. There are so many campaigns *Sea Shepherd* likes to do. Wherever *Sea Shepherd* needs me, that's where I will go.

As a former Dutch policeman, Laurens de Groot, realized there was an area of the world where no authority was upholding international conservation laws: our oceans. He navigated the trimaran, Ady Gil, that was rammed and sunk during the latest Antarctic campaign.

www.seashepherd.org

Photo Adam Lau - Sea Shepherd Society

Anna Cummins & Marcus Eriksen
Five Gyres

Q. Can you explain what a gyre is, and where the five main gyres are?

A. An oceanic gyre is a slow rotating current system created by opposing wind patterns and the earth's rotational forces. Imagine a massive marine eddy, spanning an entire ocean. Many have now heard of the North Pacific Gyre, due to an increase in media attention about the "Great Pacific Garbage Patch". Few, however, realize that there are in fact five subtropical gyres in the world - the North and South Pacific, North and South Atlantic, and the Indian Ocean gyres. Our project Five Gyres works in partnership with the Algalita Marine Research Foundation and Pangaea Explorations, to research the accumulation of plastic pollution in the world's oceans. Pangaea Explorations provides the boat – a 72 foot steel hulled racing sloop called the *Sea Dragon*. This year, we completed two research expeditions across the North Atlantic and Indian Ocean gyres, collecting samples of the oceans surface. Our research partner Algalita analyzes our samples in a lab, measuring the weight and the type of plastic collected, as well as dissecting small fish to study potential plastic ingestion. We have expeditions planned for 2010/2011 to the South Atlantic and South Pacific Gyres. We will collect surface samples to study plastic accumulation, and fish to study potential biochemical impacts. The question being asked by the public now. Are fish that eat plastic particles also absorbing chemicals from this plastic into their tissue? If so, are these chemicals working their way up the food chain? We hope to explore this question further.

Q. What is the main problem, and how large is it, and is there a solution?

A. It makes no sense that we've created plastic to last forever, yet we design products from it to be thrown away. But where is away? Plastics at sea attract many persistent pollutants, like DDT, PCBs and floating fossil fuels. Millions of organisms, representing hundreds of species, are entangled in or swallow plastic pollution. Scientists are currently trying to figure out to what extent animals absorb toxins from plastic, how much plastic is in the world, and what the ultimate fate of plastic waste is. We know that cleaning up the gyre will not happen by going to the gyre. Going to the ocean to clean plastic is like going to the clouds to clean smog. In the case of air pollution, the solution came from shutting off the tap, by making a cleaner engine with a better muffler. The only realistic post-consumer solution is to allow islands in the gyres, like Hawaii and Bermuda, to capture plastic on their beaches as gyres spit it out. The best solutions happen far upstream. First, we must change the material. There are marine-degradable plastics, like PHA, which will not contribute to oceanic garbage patches. We must redesign the products. We can employ the Cradle-to-Cradle philosophy to plastic–improving recovery and reuse. This means that a product is designed with an afterlife, a plan for recovery, or ease of dismantling and recycling. Second, citizens and legislators can work together to lay down the law, banning single use disposables, and adopting "Extended Producer Responsibility" so companies take care of the complete lifecycle of what they make. Finally, it's up to us to change our habits – avoiding single use disposable plastics and being mindful of the things we purchase.

Q. Can you tell us about the mission of JUNK raft and what your hopes were for that project?

A. The mission of JUNK, a raft made from 15,000 plastic bottles and a Cessna 310 aircraft fuselage, was to bring attention to plastic waste accumulating in the five oceanic gyres in the world, and start the conversation about solutions. JUNKraft was part of a three-phased project called "Message In A Bottle" – first, we collected 100 small samples of the ocean's surface full of plastic and plankton during an earlier research expedition. Then, we built JUNKraft, which Joel Paschal and Marcus Eriksen sailed during 88 long days, drifting from Los Angeles to Hawaii at 1.5 knots. They could have walked faster. In that time they steered clear of three hurricanes, met Roz Savage rowing in the middle of the ocean, and sadly caught fish with plastic in their stomachs. The final phase was the JUNK ride, a 2,000-mile cycling/

5 GYRES

speaking tour from Vancouver to Mexico with Marcus and Anna Cummins. Along the way, they gave 40 presentations, and put those 100 gyre samples collected at sea in the hands of legislators – including the mayors of San Francisco, Edmonds, and Portland – as well as educators and students. Once people see the problem, literally holding it in their hands, it's difficult to ignore it. The JUNKraft is not the last expedition. On a much larger research vessel, Pangaea's *Sea Dragon*, we're traveling to the five subtropical gyres in the world to study the global impact of plastic waste. We'll follow this up with another cycling tour to spread the word – from Los Angeles to Paris. We've also got another plastic trash boat in the works: in 2012 we'll build STRAW, from 5 million used plastic straws, to raft the Seine River and cross the English Channel and perhaps beyond. You can visit www.5gyres.org to follow our research, upcoming expeditions and STRAW's construction.

Q. If you could offer words to live by what would they be?

A. Take responsibility for the stuff that passes through your hands, knowing where it comes from, where it goes, and who suffers along the way. This awareness will change your life, and add wisdom to your compassion.

Anna and her husband Marcus Eriksen recently co-founded the 5 Gyres Project, *a collaboration with Algalita and Pangaea Explorations to research and communicate plastic pollution in the world's oceans. Five Gyres Expeditions consists of eight expeditions sailing over 12,000 miles throughout the Southern Hemisphere.*

www.5gyres.org

Stephanie Soechtig

Q. What inspired you to make the movie *Tapped*, and what are you most proud of about the movie?

A. The initial seed for *Tapped* came after our executive producer, Michelle Walrath, sent me a link to a video about the North Pacific Garbage Patch. At that time there was ten times as much plastic as plankton (now there's 46x more plastic). I remember watching this video with utter disbelief. I just kept thinking, "How did I not know about this?" As I started talking about it with friends and colleagues I quickly learned NO ONE knew about this. When I spoke to Captain Charles Moore, the man responsible for discovering this plastic soup, he told me, "If you eliminate the scourge of bottled water, you'll be eliminating one of the biggest contaminants to our environment." The plastic contamination and the global water crisis led us to see bottled water as this double threat to our environment that needed exposing.

Q. If you could leave people with one message about the plastic bottle industry, and also relate it to the ocean, what would you say to people?

A. One of the most important things in making *Tapped* was that we didn't want it to seem like a doomsday scenario. I'm really proud of how many quick and easy to implement ideas we give people in the film to do their part for the environment. So if I could leave people with one message it would be: DO SOMETHING! DO ANYTHING! It's important to realize that any action, no matter how small, is better than not doing anything. Often times I think many of us are so intimidated by the scope of a problem that we do nothing because we think we can't make a difference. I hope people watch *Tapped* and walk away with a renewed sense of just how powerful one person can truly be.

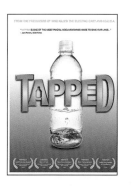

Stephanie Soechtig began her career producing documentaries for 20/20, Primetime Live, *produced for* Good Morning America *covering the 2000 presidential elections and worked with ABC's long-form unit to produce* Planet Earth *hosted by Leonardo DiCaprio.*

www.tappedthemovie.com

Gary Petersen

Q. You are known in the U.S. as a recycling pioneer, and as the "Recycling Guru." Can you please explain a few of the top most important things people should know about recycling?

A. It's important for people to understand that recycling isn't something new. We've been recycling in the U.S. for 200 years: things like paper, metals and rags. We didn't waste anything during the depression and were the best recyclers in the world during World War II. So, our parents and grandparents recycled because it was part of our culture. Unfortunately, our post-war economy was built on consumerism and convenience; as a nation we became affluent and indulgent. The invention of "disposables" really fueled an out-of-sight, out-of-mind mentality about trash. I grew up in Los Angeles, where Sam Yorty got elected mayor nearly 50 years ago when he promised residents they'd no longer have to separate tin cans from the rest of their garbage. So, we really lost our way and it's been my passion to reinvigorate the recycling ethic.

We began in the 1970s by creating community recycling programs that were mostly run by nonprofit organizations. Now, recycling is big business in California, comparable to the State's movie and video industry. It accounts for 85,000 jobs, generates $4 billion in salaries and wages, and produces $10 billion worth of goods and services annually. Californians recycle at home and at the office and are keeping 60% of what used to be "trash" from going to the landfill. Recycling doesn't just save resources; it also saves water and energy, conserves habitat, improves air quality, and lowers greenhouse gas emissions. And, as we've shown in California, recycling isn't just good for the environment. It's healthy for the economy as well.

Q. As opposed to treating just the symptom, you have suggested we need to start at the source. Can you explain what Product Stewardship is?

A. It means taking responsibility for the end-of-life management of products that we manufacture and consume. Our recycling systems for products made with paper, glass and plastic are robust because you can take those materials and reprocess them to be used over again. It's pretty straightforward and, as I said earlier, we've been doing that for a long time.

More recently though, products contain materials like heavy metals—cadmium, lead, mercury, and others—that are toxic, so these products need to be handled differently when they are discarded. Electronic products are a good example. Concern about these products began over older televisions and computer monitors that contained five to seven pounds of lead on average. Generally, anything with a circuit board in it has some small amount of heavy metals. California and other states are banning these products from landfills and establishing programs to collect and recycle them safely. More and more, they are turning to the manufacturers of these products and saying: You need to accept responsibility for this product at the end of its life.

There are a lot of products that present special problems and higher costs when we're done with them: fluorescent bulbs, batteries, paint, and other hazardous household wastes, even carpet. Municipal waste collection and recycling programs can't absorb these costs, so local officials are putting pressure on their State legislatures and on Congress to enact laws making those who make, distribute, sell, and use these products responsible for their post-consumer recycling. In a product stewardship system, collection and processing of discarded

Gary Petersen is currently the President of Environmental Problem Solving Enterprises, Chairman of the Board of Green Seal, Co-Chair of the Industry Advisory Council for the Environmental Media Association and formerly Governor Schwarzenegger's environmental appointee to CalRecycle and Chair of its Sustainability and Market Development Committee. He was also a Vice President for Waste Management Inc. and Director of Environmental Affairs for Recycle America. He guided the design and implementation of municipal and industrial recycling programs throughout the U.S. His expertise in processing, manufacturing and creating new products and markets for post-consumer materials positioned them to become the largest recycling company in the United States. Mr. Petersen served as a Task Force member for the "Greening of the White House" project in Washington, D.C., and the "Greening of the United Nations" project in New York City.

www.environmentalproblemsolving.com

products is done by organizations that are funded by the manufacturers and their partners. Ultimately, the user pays for the service through a fee on the goods they purchase. Isn't that more fair than the government charging everyone for a service whether or not they use it?

Q. Marine debris is a real threat to our oceans. What can we do to stem the tide of plastics that are the major source of this problem?

A. The first thing each and every one of us can do is to look at our own consumption of single use plastic products, the kinds of things that are finding their way into the ocean and contributing in a big way to the marine debris problem. Plastic bottles and bags for example, are things we can do without. A stainless steel bottle for your water or a reusable cloth bag for your groceries simply eliminates the need for the disposable plastic option.

When plastic gets into the environment it persists. It doesn't go away; it hangs

Photo E. Laul Healey

around for centuries. The plastic industry always says that litter is a people problem and that people just need to be educated. But the reality is that no amount of education will make everyone stop littering. And it's litter—intentional or not—that winds up in the storm drains, flows into the ocean and adds to the marine debris. Governor Schwarzenegger appointed me to the California Recycling Board, where we looked at and helped fund some very simple but efficient solutions to remove litter from the storm drains. They're mechanical devices that separate the debris from the storm flow by slowing the water current with baffles or a vortex. Installed in storm drains, they can be effective tools for reducing the flow of plastics and other debris into the ocean. So, we've figured out how to prevent most of the debris from getting into the ocean; but, how do we pay to install these systems everywhere they're needed? My idea is to conduct a study to see what products are most prevalent in the storm drains, and then to put a user fee on those products to fund installation of these mechanical separation systems. We conduct periodic follow-up surveys to see if the makeup of the debris stream has changed and adjust the fees correspondingly. That creates an incentive for the manufacturers of those products to be part of the solution instead of pointing the finger at someone else.

Q. As a surfer, and an ocean lover all your life, if you could send out one important message to people around the world, in regard to our oceans, what would it be?

A. Everybody needs to get the message that our oceans are vital to a sustainable future. The garbage patch in the Northern Pacific Gyre is alarming and all behavior that's contributing to its growth is criminal. It's a good thing that plastic floats because it's a stark reminder that we're choking the planet. The ocean isn't our trash can. David Brower is credited with the mantra "Think globally and act locally." When it comes to our oceans, it's very clear that our individual actions have large-scale consequences. No one dumped all that plastic in the ocean; it has accumulated through the careless acts of many. We need to stop that behavior or face the future consequences of our actions that are killing the oceans.

We need to think. Make conscious decisions about our resources, only use what we need, reuse what we can, and recycle the rest. If people get this in their brains then just maybe they'll be more responsible with their discards.

Louie Psihoyos

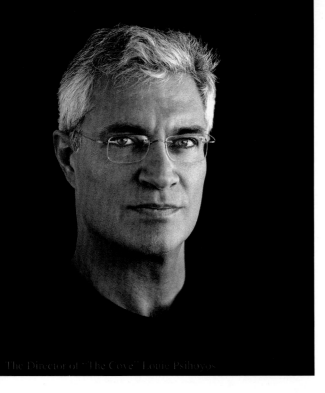

The Director of "The Cove" Louie Psihoyos

Q. Being a scuba diver, and an internationally renown still photographer with contributions to such publications as *National Geographic*, et cetera, what has been the the most noticeable change you have seen diving over the last few decades, and what do you attribute it to?

A. There is so much change happening, but it is hard to quantify. Fish are transient, and are always moving but there are obvious signs. Everywhere I go, there are less fish to see, there is less living coral, and pretty much less of everything which is attributed to several things but mostly, it has to do with humanity. Currently, we are going through a mass extinction which the geologist call the Holstein Extinction (meaning it was caused by human beings). This has been going on for thousands of years. When you look back at Africa years ago, there used to be living animals everywhere, now there are hardly any left. Every generation is adapting to this diminishment of generations before. When you see pictures of the Keyes of the 1960s, 1970s, and 1980s the difference can be shocking through the eyes of a lense. You see less birds and creatures on the land and in the sea. It is like a time capsule of the Holstein Extinction going on before your very eyes.

Much of these things you cannot see with the eye very easily like ocean acidification and coral reef destruction. We do know there is quite less plankton than there was during the Industrial era which is quite shocking because nearly two out of every three breaths you take you owe to plankton. There is approximately 30% less since the Industrial Age. So the question comes, what do you do to reverse it? We need to look at what the problems are like pollution, the fertilizer and pesticides that run off, which affect the reefs. One needs to understand these are very sensitive small animals. They are affected by changes of acidity, pollution and temperature changes. And when all these factors come together it is like we are developing the perfect storm in the ocean, making it extremely difficult for these creatures to survive. An animal or plankton may be able to survive with slight changes of temperature, but when there is change in acidification and/or there is added pollution also, the chance of it surviving go way down.

Q. You are also an Academy Award winning filmmaker now for the movie documentary *The Cove*. What prompted you to take on such a huge, and potentially dangerous project?

A. Part of it was that we didn't really know of the perimeters, or the details of what we were doing. So that allowed us to take chances, and try new things because it was all new to us, so we risked things that we had not really planned out, and we went for it. It did occur to me that it may be a little bit dangerous, and there was an unconventional band of people doing the movie. The joke on the set was that we are all professionals, but we were not professionals at doing a film like this. I think that is what allowed us to make a film that did not feel like other documentaries. We were not coming from any school, we weren't really thinking outside the box, because we did not know there was a box.

Q. Are there any other ocean related issues that you would like to make into a documentaries or movies? And if so, what topics would they cover if you were to do something like that?

A. The other day, we met with IMAX to do a movie in 3D. Although I haven't scuba dived in years, one needs to understand when you are under the sea for long periods of time it is anything but a silent world. When you dive everything is talking, fish are talking, the shrimp are talking, and whales and dolphins are talking, too! The truth of the matter is we have not been listening. So that is kind of what the next film is going to be about. Everything in the ocean is singing and talking, and communicating, and we are extinguishing these voices before even realizing that they are there. We are a small group of professional filmmakers making movies in my backyard in Colorado, land-locked in the middle of the State, to now having an ocean of opportunity available to us. We want to be cautiously optimistic to choose which movies we do to give the ocean a voice because it's a big job.

Q. Do you have any additional thoughts you would like to share?

A. I guess the question that I ponder is, If we are supposedly the smartest creatures on the earth, and we are also supposedly supposed to be the ones taking care of the planet, then why are we also the ones doing the most damage to it? No wild animal would ever be capable of doing the kinds of damage we are causing. We need to be much better stewards of our planet and not forget the smallest things can be the most important things. The food web models of the 1950s seem to look like a primitive model or a kid's drawing of how people eat fish, and fish eat smaller fish and so on. When you look at the food web today, you realize that everything is connected. Like plankton, life is totally dependant on this microscopic organism we can't even see with our own eyes. And we, as humans have this arrogance that we are this big range species. But if that is the fact, then why are we causing the Holistein Extinction? This extinction is being caused by this big brain, this arrogant species we call humans. And if we think we are so removed by the environment by our big brain, then we are heading toward this enormous crash that I think only a few people really, really understand. Our life is connected to the smallest creatures of the planet.

It's arrogant to consider ourselves custodians of the planet when we are in the middle of ruining things. We should take a look at every action that we are doing. We are so destructive. From the simplest things like turning on a light, which we are harvesting from coal or natural gas and the consequences are affecting the ocean from the great whales to the plankton. Plankton has a hard time developing a thin carbon shell with an acidic environment. We have to realize our day to day actions from turning on a light, to flying in an airplane, or driving to a meeting, every action has a consequence. We simply need to try harder and consider what we are doing before we do it.

Lastly, we should educate ourselves, and make the necessary changes. One can watch movies like *End of the Line*, *Food Inc.*, and of course *The Cove* and hopefully want to in turn make the necessary changes our big brains are capable of.

Louie Psihoyos is a Greek American filmmaker that resides in Colorado and heads the Oceanic Preservation Society. He directed the Oscar award winning documentary film The Cove *which brilliantly documents the annual Taiji dolphin hunting drive in Japan's whaling industry that has been claimed to kill 23,000 dolphins annually.*

www.opsociety.org

Left to Right: Director Louie Psihoyos, Production Manager Joe Chisholm, Associate Producer Charles Hambleton

Jean Beasley

Q. What made you decide to get so involved in sea turtle conservation?

A. Neither I nor our daughter, Karen, who founded the beach monitoring project in the mid-80s and managed it until her death at the age of 29, envisioned a hospital for sea turtles. We saw turtles who were sick or injured and washed up on our beaches. We called the wildlife authorities and took the turtles to them. We never knew much about the outcome. After Karen's death from leukemia, I picked up the reins of her work. In the mid 90s a juvenile loggerhead washed ashore with some serious boat propeller injuries. I had recently met Dr. Greg Lewbart from the College of Veterinary Medicine at NC State University who told me that if we had any injured turtles that he would be happy to help. Serendipity! I and several of our beach volunteers loaded up the turtle and off we went to the vet school. Lucky, as the turtle came to be called, did well through the treatment process, but when the time came to leave and I asked if we could come back to see the turtle, we got a shock! The answer was "We don't have any place to keep a sea turtle. It has to go home with you!" Well, we didn't have any place either but we brought Lucky back to Topsail Island where he stayed in my garage for several days with me hovering over him constantly, until we could locate a tank and a pump to pump sea water. Before we knew what was happening we were in the sea turtle rehab business. We had no money so I began recruiting volunteers to help take care of Lucky. Soon other turtles began arriving and more volunteers were needed.

I can't say enough about the dedication and commitment of these folks who are willing to do whatever it takes to help the turtles. Our common interest has bound us into family. We support each other through whatever life brings, just as we support the turtles. We all feel privileged to have the opportunity to help these ancient and mysterious creatures we have come to love. Over the years we have learned so much and about so many things. Of course a big part of it has been in the field of sea turtle medicine. We have helped to develop better treatment protocols and published papers on our findings, but more importantly we have also recognized the lessons the turtles have brought to us. The message of the degradation of their habitat was hard to ignore. We saw it in their injuries and illnesses. We began to hear their greater message, the message that without positive change we were at risk of losing the species and the very future of the oceans themselves. The challenge to bring our voice and the voice of the sea turtles to the cause of conservation was one we embraced. Our work is based on the belief that even one person can make a difference, and that together we can change the world!

Q. How many species of sea turtles are there and what is the status of them?

A. There are seven species of sea turtles worldwide, and sadly they are all endangered or threatened. One of these, the Flatback (Natator depressus) is found only in the waters of the northern coast of Australia. Of the remaining six species their distribution and status is as follows: E = Endangered T = Threatened: Green (Chelonia mydas): distributed globally status under US Endangered Species Act (ESA) = breeding colonies in Mexico's Pacific coast and in Florida = E. Elsewhere = T Loggerhead (Caretta caretta): distributed globally status under ESA = T Kemp's Ridley (Lepidochelys kempii): Gulf of Mexico and US Atlantic coastal waters status under ESA = E Leatherback (Dermochelys coriacea): all tropical and sub tropical oceans with evidence range extends into Artic Circle status under ESA = E Hawksbill (Eretmochelys imbricata): tropical waters of Atlantic, Pacific and Indian oceans status under ESA = E Olive Ridley (Lepidochelys olivacea): eastern Pacific, eastern Atlantic (Africa) and northern Indian Ocean status under ESA = Mexico's Pacific Coast = E, all other areas = T

Jean Beasley is the founder & director of Sea Turtle & Rehabilitation Center, Topsail Island, North Carolina. Awarded Animal Planet's Hero of the Year. They rescue, rehabilitate & release sick & injured sea turtles. The center also strives to inform & educate the public regarding the plight of all sea turtles and the threat of their extinction.

www.seaturtlehospital.org

Carl Safina

Q. Can you please explain the premise of your award winning book *Eye of the Albatross*, and talk about your concerns for those large magnificent birds?

A. Albatrosses live for decades and in that time fly millions of miles. Everything we are doing to the ocean, from pollution to over fishing to climate change, these birds feel. That's what I wanted to portray, the ocean as seen through the eye of an albatross.

Q. Can you further explain to people about what Midway Island is, and also what your concerns are for it?

A. Midway is the second farthest Island west of the Northwest Hawaiian Islands. It has the largest remaining colony of nesting albatrosses in the world. But those birds also forage in the vast area that has a lot of floating plastic. They eat this plastic and feed it to their chicks. Many die. This is not the relationship humans should have with the other creatures of the world.

Q. Can you name a few imperative things that need to happen in order for us to have a healthier ocean?

A. We need biodegradable plastics, not eternal plastics made for one-time use. We also need to get fishing much better under control so unintended animals are not killed, and also so that seabirds and others have enough to eat.

Q. You also wrote a book called *Voyage of the Turtle*, what would you like to share with people about turtles?

A. Turtles have been on earth since before dinosaurs. Sea turtles must come ashore to lay eggs. That has been their downfall, but in many places they are recovering due to better protections. In the Pacific, though, they are doing badly. In the Atlantic, better protection is resulting in their recovery.

Q. If you could offer words to live by for all people, what would they be?

A. Very few things, each simple, are needed. We shouldn't hate people for the group they were born into, or because we hold conflicting beliefs about things that cannot be seen or measured. We can't take infinitely more from, or indefinitely add people to, a finite planet. We can't run civilization on energy that diminishes the world, while living in a world endowed with self-renewing energy. If we can get these simple things under control, I think we could be ok. Simple does not mean easy. Yet more than ever in history, we can now understand what's needed. But nations need to act with unprecedented boldness soon. Time runs short at an accelerating pace.

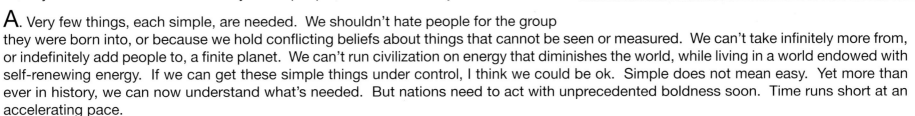

With a Ph.D. in Ecology from Rutgers University, *Carl Safina is a world leader and speaker in Marine Ecology, has authored an award winning book,* Eye of the Albatross. *His first book,* Song for the Blue Ocean *was chosen a New York Times Notable Book of the Year. Mr. Safina is a MacArthur Fellow, Lannon Prize winner and has received numerous distinction awards.*

www.blueocean.org

Jackie Savitz

Q. What are your largest concerns regarding climate change?

A. Well, mass extinctions of corals and the loss of reefs are major concerns and this is what we can expect as a result of ocean acidification, unless we make a major shift in our energy strategy. All the life that depends on the reefs may also be affected which will lead to major disruptions in ocean ecosystems. We will likely see shifts in species, as plants and animals attempt to adapt to changing conditions, and even fish may have difficulty adapting to physiological changes in their ability to get needed oxygen out of the water. So my concerns for the ocean are tremendous. The idea that our kids and grandchildren won't get to enjoy the wonders of the ocean that we all appreciate, is a very sad thought. There is little debate that ocean acidification is occurring, and the solutions are available but they will take a major change in the way we do business, with regard to our use of fossil fuels. Ultimately we need to completely shift off of fossil fuels, and into non-carbon based fuels like solar and wind. To make it happen, we need to start now; otherwise, ocean-life as we know it will be a thing of the past.

Q. In regards to ocean acidification, you mentioned there will be species shifts, and potential sea life will be extending their range. Can you elaborate on this and explain it, and also talk about the chain reaction that could happen because of it?

A. I actually think species shifts are a secondary issue. The main concern is the loss of species, the extinctions of many corals and other species that depend on calcium carbonate, or on another species that does. So we're talking about corals; mollusks like clams, oysters, and mussels; crustaceans like lobsters, crabs, shrimp, and that's just to name the ones we enjoy on menus. Many forms of plankton also will be affected, so that's the food for a whole other segment of the ocean community–the fish! So the fish will be affected through their food chains. If that wasn't enough, the change in acidity can also affect the physiology of some species, such as the ability of fish to get needed oxygen from the water which is likely to be impaired as well. So they are getting hit from all sides: the food web, their reliance on reefs for nursery, feeding, breeding, structure, and spawning areas, and their own physiological demands.

Q. If you could make four or five recommendations as to what needs to be done to help save our world oceans, what would they be?

A. Stop expanding our offshore drilling for oil and gas. The resources and efforts that go into this compromise our ability to develop offshore wind which will be a necessary component of our energy portfolio. We can't stop drilling entirely but we can agree not to drill in areas that were previously protected. That would give us a good start on a new energy economy. Invest in the development of carbon-free energy options such as solar and wind, including offshore wind. This includes developing the manufacturing base and workforce necessary to support these industries. Doing so will create jobs. In fact, renewable energy creates three times more jobs than oil and gas development. Convert the automobile fleet to run on plug-in electric power. This is important because as we begin to shift to these carbon free sources, the auto fleet will be ready to take advantage and will then automatically be running on alternative energy sources. First they will be using a small percentage of alternative fuel, but ultimately, as we complete the transition, they too will be off of oil.

Note: These don't sound like ocean solutions but because climate change is killing our oceans, we need to fix climate change to save the oceans and that means getting off of fossil fuels. Devise and put in place sensible and sustainable fishing practices. All of the stressors on the oceans are connected. Currently, bottom trawling and other destructive fishing practices are decimating fisheries and threatening other species like sea turtles. These species have a better chance at surviving climate change if their populations are healthy and resilient. We need to take steps to preserve their resilience.

Since I have one left, I'll share a pet peeve. Let's kill all the leaf blowers and outdoor space heaters. It's one thing to work hard and develop new clean energy, but at the same time we shouldn't be doing things that are just plain wasteful and pumping carbon into the atmosphere unnecessarily. If we just stopped using those outdoor heaters and went back to raking the leaves, or using a broom, that would be a good step in the right direction. These activities symbolize our lack of understanding of the problem, I'd like to see us symbolize instead that we get it. One way to do that would be to put away these two items and others like them for good.

Q. Having a Masters degree with a focus on environmental toxicology, you stated that persistent organic pollutants really worried you a lot. Can you explain what persistent organic pollutants are, and what the long term effects of them are?

A. We call them POPs for short and the name can be a little misleading. Persistent is pretty obvious, they stick around for a long time. But the term organic in this case, may throw people off. In chemistry terms, organic means that something is based on the element carbon. These chemicals are carbon-based. So when we say 'organic' we don't mean that you get them at Whole Foods, rather that they are carbon based. These are chemicals that were either manufactured for some industrial use, or they may be by-products of other processes like incineration. They generally sound like alphabet soup with names like PCBs, PBDE's, DDT, or dioxin. PCBs, or polychlorinated biphenyls were made to be used as electrical insulators, in transformers and other electrical equipment. Their production was discontinued in the 70s but they are still in use and their release to the environment continues. PBDE's or polybrominated diphenyl ethers are still made and used as flame retardants. Dioxins, on the other hand were not made intentionally, they are a by-product released when something is burned, especially during combustion of paper and plastics.

POPs have two very disturbing qualities. First they are, as the name suggests, persistent. Once they are produced and released to the environment, they will be extremely slow to break down and so they tend to stay in the environment for decades or longer. What's worse is their second quality: they build up in the food chain. So they may be found in very low concentrations in soil, or in the ocean, but the food chain magnifies their levels. They can be taken up by plankton, for example, at low levels, and then whatever eats those plankton eats A LOT of plankton, so the concentration at that step in the food chain can be magnified 100 or 1000 times. Same for the next step in the food chain, say it's a small fish that eats plankton, it eats so many that it builds up an even higher concentration. So by the time you get to the high food chain animals, like the big fish, marine mammals, and even us, we are talking about millions of times more of the chemical than what was in the water.

Most of us already have built up some level of persistent chemicals in our bodies. These chemicals have a broad and diverse set of effects, including, in some cases, causing cancer or affecting our reproductive systems. Some have even been tied to lower sperm counts and infertility. Generally these types of problems are difficult to trace back to a definitive cause. Most people don't know what gave them cancer or caused their infertility, but we all know people who have struggled with these devastating ailments, it's all too common, and our exposure to persistent organic chemicals may be the cause in some cases.

Jackie Savitz is senior campaign director for Oceana's pollution campaigns and senior scientist, based in Washington, D.C. She has shaped and led campaigns and projects dealing with global warming pollution from ships, mercury contamination of fish and cruise ship pollution.

www.oceana.org

James Balog

Q. Why do glaciers matter and what difference does it make if they melt? Or melt too fast?

A. People think that glaciers are these big, dead, static objects where nothing happens. But they're alive, and they're reacting to climate all the time. The smaller the glacier, the faster it reacts to the local climate, sometimes in months or even weeks. The ice is really the canary in the global coalmine. Because it's where you can see climate change in the most immediate, understandable fashion, and it's going on right now. The ice is reacting to climate change faster and more obviously than almost anything else. So much about climate change, down in the latitudes where we all live, tends to be a little abstract. It's based on statistical patterns: Are there more or fewer hurricanes now than there were before? Did the butterflies migrate here or there? It's hard to grasp. Or we think: "Maybe it's just a short-term variation," or "Maybe it isn't such a big deal after all." But people get it when ice melts. These things that we feel, in our gut, in our bones, are not quite right, and are encapsulated in the immediate visual experience of that ice. Ninety-five percent of the glaciers in the world outside of Antarctica are retreating or shrinking because precipitation and temperature patterns are changing. There is no significant scientific dispute about that. It is a great irony, and tragedy, that a large percentage of the general public thinks that science is still arguing about that. Science is not.

Q. What is EIS (Extreme Ice Survey) and what have you learned from doing it?

A. In 2005 and 2006 I was commissioned by the *New Yorker* and then by *National Geographic* to create photo-essays about fast-changing glacial landscapes. I was stunned by what I saw. All around the world, glaciers were retreating rapidly. Ice that had taken centuries to form was being destroyed in just a few years or even a matter of months. This was not geologic-scale change happening in the dim past or distant future, but right here, right now, in our own time.

These observations in the field became the catalyst for the Extreme Ice Survey (EIS), the most wide-ranging glacier study ever conducted using ground-based, real-time photography. In EIS, art meets science. The project is an adventurous, sometimes dangerous, collaboration between imagemakers and scientists devoted to documenting the changes that are transforming our alpine and arctic landscapes. EIS uses time-lapse photography, conventional photography and live-action video to illustrate the effects of climate change on the earth's glacial ice. Twenty-seven time-lapse cameras at 18 sites in Greenland, Iceland, Alaska and the Rockies will shoot an image every hour of daylight until fall 2009. The 300,000-plus photographs will be compiled into video sequences that will help the public understand the reality of climate change.

I believe that the immediacy of the photographic evidence can break down barriers of mental resistance in a way that nothing else can. The photographic act is an act of love, forcing the imagemaker to stop, look, and look again, to feel whatever it is he or she has seen, and perhaps even to assimilate some aspect of the scene into the core of his or her being. It is a way of saying: Wait, let's pay attention—I saw this thing, this moment, had this experience, and it was important to me, and it just might be important to you, the viewer, if you were to see it, too.

Seeing is believing. Because of my scientific training, I was a climate change skeptic until I saw the evidence in the ice. Now I spend most of my time trying to persuade people that climate change is real, and the time to act is now. So that has been a revelation for me, to realize I'm in the midst of monumental geologic change that's going to change the face of the earth forever, and I've got this tool, this camera, with which to witness the change and to bring the story back home. I feel activated and motivated in a way I never have before. Like, you've got to see this. We have to start dealing with it.

Q. What can people do to reduce their global footprint?

A. Even small changes, like reducing how many miles you drive, or switching to energy-efficient appliances, can have a large effect if enough people commit to them. It's also important, especially now, to let your elected representatives know where you stand on global warming. The two places where you can reduce your carbon footprint the fastest? Your personal household energy consumption is 27% of your total carbon footprint; your transportation habits are 19%. Some changes are small, some large.

Do the best you can. Consider the possibility that you don't need to eat strawberries from Chile and kiwi from New Zealand year-round. Eat fruit more suited to the seasons of your home continent.

Q. Do you have any other thoughts or words to live by that you would like to share?

A. When my daughters are grown and look back at this pivotal time in human history, I want to be able to say I did my best with the tools and knowledge that I had. It's tough to avoid despairing. It's overwhelmingly crushing at times. But really, despair is not an option. Failure is simply not an option for us as a society. We owe it to the image we want to have of ourselves, as a successful, intelligent society. We don't want to have a self-image as idiots. More importantly, we owe it to the future to leave them a decent world—a damaged earth is not a good legacy.

I just can't stand the thought that it could be our generation that leaves this planet in disastrously damaged condition. I believe we can do better than that. The voice of the glaciers needs to be heard. We're the vehicle for telling it. It's great to be able to give the landscape a voice.

Photo James Balog/Extreme Ice Survey

Retreat of Columbia Glacier, Alaska
June 2006 to October 2009 = 2.3 miles

June 2006
June 2008
Sept 2008
May 2009

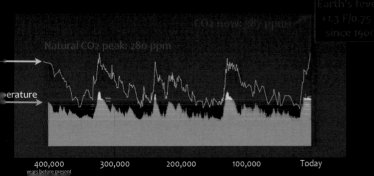

EARTH'S CLIMATE RHYTHM

Earth's fever: +1.3 F/0.75 C since 1900

CO2 now: 387 ppm

Natural CO2 peak: 280 ppm

Temperature

400,000   300,000   200,000   100,000   Today
years before present

Nature Isn't Natural Anymore

1. Natural variation during the last million years produced an atmospheric CO_2 concentration of no more than 280 ppm.

2. CO_2 is now at 387 ppm, increasing 2.5-3 ppm annually.

3. Our earth is now far beyond its natural range of variation.

For nearly 30 years, James Balog consistently has broken new ground in the art of photographing nature. James is the author of Extreme Ice Now: Vanishing Glaciers and Changing Climate: A Progress Report, *released by National Geographic Books.*

www.extremeicesurvey.org

Sources: National Geographic, U.S. Department of Energy, NASA Goddard Institute for Space Studies, Oak Ridge National Laboratory, Scripps Institution of Oceanography

Frances Beinecke

Photo © Matt Greenslade/photo-nyc.com

Q. What does the *Natural Resources Defense Council (NRDC)* do, and how can people help make a difference in the ocean by joining *NRDC*?

A. *NRDC* is the nation's most effective environmental action organization. Our purpose is to safeguard the earth, its people, its plants and animals and the natural systems on which all life depends. With the support of our 1.3 million members and online activists, *NRDC* works to solve the most pressing environmental issues we face today. Reviving and protecting the world's oceans is one of *NRDC's* top institutional priorities. By joining *NRDC*, you support our use of the best science, policy and law to keep our oceans and marine life healthy and thriving. Our proven record of success shows we can make it happen: we have already led successful efforts to restrict destructive bottom trawling, rebuild fish populations and block the worldwide deployment of military sonar.

Q. What are the top priorities in regard to the ocean for *NRDC*?

A. Our oceans are facing pressure from all angles and have fallen into a state of silent collapse. We drill them for oil, pollute them with waste, and deplete fish populations beyond recovery. One of the biggest emerging threats to our seas is excess carbon dioxide in the atmosphere, which not only causes warming water temperatures, it is making the water acidic in a process called ocean acidification that threatens significant impacts up and down the ocean food chain. That's why *NRDC* is working to reduce carbon dioxide emissions, and to make the seas as healthy, and therefore as resilient as possible to these impacts. To do this, we're working to address a wide range of ocean issues: We're working to curb sewage pollution in America's beachwater. We're advocating for the creation of more marine protected areas, like national parks on land, where marine life can thrive safe from industrial harm. We're working for a national ocean protection policy, like a Clean Air or Water Act for our seas, and we're fighting to end destructive fishing practices.

Q. What are your personal favorite things about the ocean, and why does it mean so much to you to protect it?

A. Protecting coastal communities was one of the first things I worked on as an environmentalist, and for 30 years I have fought for sound ocean policies. Our oceans are critical to all life on earth, no matter where we live. They not only give us the beaches and waves – they feed the world, regulate our climate, produce oxygen, provide jobs and transportation. And they are economic engines. Protecting our oceans not only preserves an essential element of our natural heritage for future generations – it protects thousands of American jobs and billions of dollars in revenue.

Q. Do you have any last thoughts you would like to share?

A. In the wake of one of the greatest environmental catastrophes in recent history – the Gulf oil rig disaster – I took a trip to the region to assess the damage from air, land and water shortly after the explosion. From a helicopter, I looked down in horror and sadness at blue waters streaked with rivers of crude oil flowing toward the open sea. As we flew back toward shore over miles of essential habitat for shrimp, oysters, fish and birds, I recalled the voices of fishermen who took me out on a boat out on the bayou below – terrified of the risks to their very livelihoods. The extent of the calamity unfolding in the Gulf took my breath away. No matter how hard we struggled to contain it, we couldn't put it back in the well. The oil was there and the pollution with it was in the ocean, in the air, and headed, inevitably, toward the shallow coastal waters, fertile wetlands and shore. This kind of tragedy provides an all-too-real and painful illustration of the urgency and widespread need to decrease our dependence on dirty fossil fuels, and transition to clean energy that can't spill or run out. At *NRDC* – we know this day in and day out – but even after 30 years of advocacy it reminded me of why we fight.

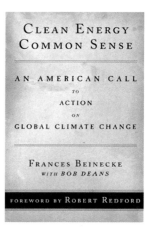

Frances Beinecke is the President of the Natural Resources Defense Council (NRDC). *Under Frances's leadership, the organization focuses on curbing global warming, developing a clean energy future, reviving the world's oceans, saving endangered wild places, stemming the tide of toxic chemicals and accelerating the greening of China. Frances has worked with* NRDC *for 30 years.*

www.nrdc.org

Wyland

Wyland painting blue whales - New Orleans 1998

Q. What is the message you are trying to portray by painting all of your whale murals around the world?

A. Years ago, I embarked on a career of showing the beauty of whales through the world of fine art, but it wasn't long before I realized that to portray the size and majesty of these great creatures I would need great canvases. At the time, no one I knew was making canvases big enough to fit a life-size humpback whale. So I began to consider the possibility of painting my favorite subjects on the sides of buildings. After about two years of deliberation with the city of Laguna Beach, I found a location, rented scaffolding for thirty days and exhausted my small bank account to pay for the paint. Slowly, a life-size portrait of a thirty-five-foot gray whale and her newborn calf began to take shape.

Then something really strange happened.

About halfway into the mural, I noticed that it seemed to be having an impact on the thousands of people who drove past it each day. Traffic backed up along the highway. Crowds formed. Suddenly, I was barraged with questions about the whales: What do they eat? How much do they weigh? Where could they be seen? Clearly, this wasn't just another painting. It was a message that people were responding to. I decided then that the best thing I could do for raising environmental awareness was to paint one hundred life-size portraits of all the great whales and other marine life in public places. Now, my team and I have focused on teaching people about the health of watersheds miles away that are impacting our oceans. I've said it over and over: Art is a very powerful medium, and history has shown that art can have a profound impact on civilization. The Whaling Walls, as people began to call them, have been living proof of this.

Marine Life Artist Wyland has earned the distinction as one of America's most unique creative influences and a leading advocate for marine resource conservation. An accomplished painter, sculptor, photographer, writer, and scuba diver, he has traveled the farthest reaches of the globe for more than 25 years, capturing the raw power and beauty of the undersea universe.

www.wylandfoundation.org

Photo Gary Firstenberg © Wyland Worldwide LLC

Photo Marc Evan

Fabien Cousteau

Q. Can you explain a little bit about your new organization *Plant A Fish*?

A. My grandfather often said that 'People protect what they love.' The mission of *Plant A Fish* is to help people learn more, and ultimately care more, by 'getting wet' and getting directly involved in restoring and protecting distressed water bodies and marine life. Sadly, entire species of marine life are disappearing at an alarming rate. In the past 50 years, almost 60% of our world's fish stocks have been consumed, and less than 10% of the big fish species are left in the world. *Plant A Fish* will seek to restore key species in targeted, local areas that will make a global impact – initial targeted projects in 2010-2011 will include responsible re-planting of oysters in the New York Harbor, sea turtles in El Salvador, mangroves in South Florida and corals in the Maldives.

Q. What is the importance of the Beluga Whale, some say they are a bit like the canary in the coal mine, can you explain that?

A. Beluga whales, the mystic, beautiful and intelligent white creatures that populate much of the Arctic Ocean (and some subarctic areas), are known as the canaries of the sea for their remarkable song and wide-ranging vocal repertoire. In addition, the beluga acts as a barometer for the health of the Arctic waters as it sits atop the food chain with few predators, enjoys a relatively long lifespan, and bears large percentages of fat and blubber (which more readily capture pollutants and carcinogens). It has also been more thoroughly studied than its other whale counterparts. The Arctic has been dubbed "the ground zero for climate change," as it is where we have seen global warming's most pronounced effects to date. It is effectively a "coal mine" – due to climate change, pollution and commercial whaling, the beluga whales' numbers have dwindled. As of 2008, beluga whales have been classified as "near threatened," a decline from "vulnerable," and certain population sub-segments such as the Cook Inlet's beluga whale have been all but wiped out, adversely affecting local Inuit communities. What's more, pollutants found in beluga corpses that shore up in river estuaries such as the St. Lawrence are at such toxic levels that they are considered health safety hazards and need to be disposed of accordingly.

As my father Jean-Michel Cousteau perhaps best said while we and the Ocean Adventures team filmed *Sea Ghosts*, a documentary that surveyed the increasingly precarious conditions that beluga whales are facing, "I've always said that if you protect the ocean you protect yourself and it's never been more true, especially when you think about belugas and contaminants and the implications for human health. But maybe it is worth protecting the beluga just for its own sake, for the beauty of its songs, and for the warmth of its social groups, and for their lifelong bonds to each other in the cold Arctic Ocean. Maybe protecting the beluga for its own sake improves us and helps us to define who we are. Protecting the beauty and wonder of these creatures and the natural world may be as essential to our spirit as food is to our bodies. I believe it's important after all, that the sea continues to be filled with these songs."

Photo Carrie Vonderhaar, Ocean Futures Soc

Q. The Hudson River used to be the world's largest oyster bay, what has happened? . . . and can you explain your initiative to help the oysters with *Plant A Fish*?

A. In the 16th and 17th centuries, Governors Island in the New York Harbor was rife with oysters, with an estimated population of nine billion that spanned across more than 350 square miles, effectively making it one of the largest known oyster rookeries in the world. As settlers came to develop the land into what would eventually become New York City, years of pollution and overfishing would leave the New York Harbor largely bereft of oysters.

Oysters, like mussels and clams, act as a natural filtration system for our oceans. They remove pollutants and improve oxygen levels and water flow. Given the special role that they play in our delicate marine ecosystems, we felt it was instrumental to reestablish a thriving oyster population in the Hudson and surrounding areas.

We are currently working closely with students and teachers of the Urban Assembly New York Harbor School to begin an oyster restoration program in the New York Harbor. On June 7th, we officially launched *Plant A Fish* and conducted our first survey dive of the Bay Ridge Flats south of Governors Island with the Harbor School, with plans to 're-plant' oysters in August. *Plant A Fish's* goal is to eventually increase the oyster population by upwards of one billion in the New York City area and water bodies around the world.

This is a fantastic, mutually beneficial partnership, as students will not only participate in a robust scientific program that will boost their confidence and afford them greater post-secondary opportunities . . . but they will also learn 'to protect what they love,' become impassioned about our oceans, and lead the next generation to steward and safeguard our planet.

Q. What are your programs for coral reefs, and why are coral reefs vital?

A. Coral reefs, created through a delicate symbiotic relationship between coral polyps and tiny algae called zooxanthellae, are the tropical forests of our oceans. While they may occupy little more than a fifth of 1% of the undersea world, coral reefs are inhabited by over 25% of all known marine species (and sustain an even greater percentage of species at some point in their lives); the economic impact of which is significant to the more than 450 million individuals who live in their proximity. Boat strikes, storms and especially coral bleaching (caused by fertilizers and climate change) have posed serious threats to our world's corals. If nothing is done to protect the reefs, it is estimated that we will lose up to 60% of worldwide corals in the next few decades.

Plant A Fish will work with local schools, people and organizations such as *Six Senses* to develop coral restoration programs and 're-plant' one million corals in several hot spots worldwide, like the Maldives and the Florida Keys.

Q. Do you have a special message that you would like to share?

A. For far too long, we've been using our ocean planet as both an infinite resource and a garbage can. The recent Gulf oil spill vividly demonstrates the devastating impact our careless actions are causing. The potential upside that we can hope for, however, is that the tragedy is gaining public awareness and compassion. Perhaps now, we will begin to comprehend the fragility of the ocean world and the severe impact our carelessness is having on our one and only life support system. With regard to the invaluable resources our oceans provide, we must see our natural world as a bank account and start living on the interest instead of eating away at the capital. Despite the current challenges we face as a species, we must go forward and strike a delicate balance with the oceans if we are to survive well into the future. By ending our wasteful practices, weaning ourselves off of our 100-year-addiction to fossil fuels and shifting to and embracing renewable energy sources, we can reach this critical balance. There is no 'Planet B' – as challenging as it may be, let's do everything we can to properly clean up this disaster, focus on how we can prevent such a tragedy from reoccurring and start nursing our planet back to health.

Growing up on the salt-stained decks of his grandfather Jacques Cousteau's ships, Calypso *and* Alcyone*, Fabien Cousteau, third-generation ocean explorer, documentary filmmaker and environmental ambassador, was destined to further his family's legacy by exploring and protecting our water planet's wondrous and endangered marine habitats. Fabien most recently launched* Plant A Fish, *a new non-profit organization whose mission is to empower communities to become involved with responsible 're-planting' of key marine species in distressed bodies of water around the world. For more information, please visit www.plantafish.org.*

www.fabiencousteau.org • www.plantafish.org

Debbie Levin

Q. Who is the *Environmental Media Association (EMA*, and what are the *EMA's* goals for supporting the environment?

A. We were founded in 1989, and this is our 20th anniversary of the Environmental Media Awards (the originator of the Green Carpet.) We were founded by Norman and Lynn Lear, and Alan and Cindy Horn. Norman, the seminal producer of such shows like All In The Family, Maude and Good Times, really changed the way we look at television by putting social messaging into television for the first time through. Alan is currently the COO of Warner Brothers and he and Rob Reiner started Castle Rock Entertainment together.

So these two very influential families came together and decided since they were already politically and environmentally active, that they could do more for the industry and the environment collectively. They realized they could do for the environment what Norman Lear did for social messaging; they could create a platform for environmental messaging. The EMA core mission is to integrate positive environmental messaging into the entertainment through feature film, media and television, and to engage celebrities to act as role models to drive behavioral change. We have expanded the messaging to include major programs including the EMA Green Seal for productions and have greened over 200 productions and award shows in the last few years.

Hand in hand with celebrities, we collectively created an organic gardens program to support low-income schools in how to build their own edible gardens. We are presently working with cities and mayors on developing Green Communities. Our mission is to shine the light on creating sustainable behaviors and engaging celebrities to push those trends and to make it sexy and cool to be green.

Q. What are your feelings about today's generation as compared to our previous generations and their focus on the environment?

A. When I took over EMA ten years ago, I realized that everyone attending most of the events were over 40 years old. I had teenage kids at home, and I knew they were more influenced by people their own age so we created the Young Hollywood Board which is targeted for the under 35 crowd. We have accomplished so much with Amy Smart such as making a Public Service Announcement (PSA) about commitment to lowering ocean pollution. She actually wore Daryl Hannah's old mermaid suit from the movie Splash.

We have worked with Gwyneth Paltrow, Cameron Diaz and Nicole Richie for many years. They are also part of the EMA family.

We are focusing on the next generation. We present the EMA awards to assist in global awareness for the future. At the EMA awards we include presenters such as Harrison Ford, Jason Mraz, Amy Smart, and many other recognizable celebrities mostly highlighted in People magazine at that time. Some other young celebrities who attend the EMA Awards and participate in our many campaigns are Olivia Wilde, Emmanuelle Chriqui, Jake Gyllenhaal, plus many more . . . These people are able to leverage the media via blogs and websites that follow their lifestyles and monitor trends. We know the youth is motivated by the actions of young celebrities.

The Young Hollywood Board is a group of amazing young actors who want to keep driving our message, and assist EMA with other projects. As mentioned, our project "Organic Gardens for the Schools" assigns each school a celebrity mentor who will become their green guide adopting that school. We got monster press from our launch event with Amy Smart and Nicole Ritchie for the garden project. We even received tons of emails from kids from around the country explaining how they want to have an organic garden at their school or home. We are very proud to be known for the organization that drives this young generation to think "green." Look how Cameron Diaz has influenced many people to drive hybrid cars. I know my own daughter drives a hybrid car because of Cameron Diaz, not because of me. The power of celebrity influencing the youth is an amazing thing!

Q. What has motivated you to focus on the environment and the ocean?

A. I would think that anyone alive wants to make sure the ocean is healthy. It's devastating to see the amount of pollution in our oceans, and the mercury in the fish. It really hurts to know the fish and other sea creatures are not healthy because of what we are doing. This is another reason we promote the organic gardens because all of the chemicals and pesticides are toxic to the oceans. It's only common sense to me to help the ocean and be proactive for change. Everything good and healthy we do on land ultimately helps the ocean.

Q. Do you have any last thoughts, for example: if you could send out one message to everyone out there, what would it be?

A. think that everyone has their own responsibility to live a sustainable and environmental lifestyle. Each day everyone can wake up and be an environmentalist that day. It's not something that you have to go to school for, or that you have to travel for, you can make choices every day that are going to effect change for generations to come. You can choose to always recycle, reduce your energy consumption, buy local and organic foods, buy fish that is sustainable simply by looking at the Monterey Bay Fish Guide.

You can make choices, and you can do it without spending extra money, by simply pre-planning. This is something you can be proud of! For example, you can go to the supermarket, bring your own bags and hope that people watch you and think that is what should be done. I cringe when I see people walking out of the market with paper and plastic bags. It drives me crazy! It's so easy to bring your own bags. These are simple changes that I believe within the next generation will become natural and logical so that all people will hold more respect toward the earth. The future of the environment relies on humans making the proper choices today. Yesterday doesn't matter, you can make the choice today!

Debbie Levin is the President of Environmental Media Association (EMA) *and is on a Board of Directors that include some of the most influential names in the entertainment business. She has moved* EMA *in a new direction with strong emphasis on Young Hollywood to role model and influence globally on essential environmental issues.*

www.ema-online.org

Kathleen Frith

Q. What made you decide to executively produce the award winning *Once Upon a Tide*?

A. My work is to try to help people understand how our health, and that of our children, depends on a healthy ocean. That we need to take care of the ocean in order for it to continue to take care of us. From the air we breathe, to the water that feeds our crops, to the discovery of medicines inspired by marine organisms, to the role seafood plays in our diet and livelihood, we simply cannot continue to degrade the ocean environment without it having a profound effect on our health and well-being. We've worked to get this message out in a number of ways, including exhibits, websites, lectures and publications. In 2006, we produced a short web-movie narrated by Meryl Streep and it received a very positive response, so we decided that the short film could be an incredibly powerful way to reach a large number of people. I then met Mark Shelley of *Sea Studios Foundation* and his creativity and enthusiasm enabled us to take the idea to the next level. We partnered with aquariums, museums and schools across the country and around the world. We just produced a Spanish version and other language editions are in the works.

Q. You mentioned the importance of engaging kids and young people in a creative manor. Can you expand on that?

A. Our front-end research told us that the children in family groups that watch movies at institutions like aquariums weren't connecting with the documentary style of the presentations. We felt like we needed to showcase a child's perspective of these issues and tell a story about how one girl learned about the importance of the ocean. The production team we enlisted were incredibly creative and I feel, really captured a child's sense of imagination, magic and fantasy while, at the same time, demonstrating how one girl grappled with and eventually became inspired by ocean conservation issues.

Q. What do you think needs to be done in order to protect our oceans, and how can the typical person help?

A. I think talking and sharing concerns about this issue is critical to help people understand why we need to conserve the ocean environment. Understandably, for many, the ocean seems far away and disconnected from our daily lives – so helping people understand that we depend on the ocean is critical. I've been so pleased to see more programs that encourage people to share their own voice about the need to protect the marine environment. We are now working on media projects that enable teachers and students to make short films about why the ocean is important to them and share those messages with their communities and their political representatives. Of course, other actions, such as only buying sustainable seafood, supporting Marine Protected Areas, cutting down on greenhouse gas emissions, not using plastic – these are all important personal actions we can take to help heal the ocean.

Q. If you could have on last thing to say, what would it be?

A. All of us have a role in protecting our environment, I would say just find it. Whether it is helping to green your school, creating ocean-inspired artwork, running for office, changing your family's diet, whatever it is, find your way to help preserve the natural world upon which all of us depend.

Kathleen Frith directs the Healthy Ocean, Healthy Humans *program that aims to increase awareness about the human health connections to the ocean environment by developing media and exhibitry for educational institutions such as aquariums and museums. This is one of many programs she leads at* Harvard Medical Schools Center for Health and the Global Environment.

www.chge.med.harvard.edu/about/staff/frith.html
www.chge.med.harvard.edu/programs/healthyoceans/once_upon_a_tide/

Michael Muller

Q. How did you get into underwater photography, and once you did, how did it change your perspective on the ocean, or did it?

A. My first camera was a Minolta Weathermatic, a waterproof camera which I received at the age of eight living in Saudi Arabia. I got seriously into underwater photography at the turn of the century and have pushed the boundaries ever since. I recently was issued a Patent Pending status on the world's most powerful underwater strobes which I have been using the last year and a half everywhere from the Galapagos to up close and personal with great whites. The only thing shooting pictures in the ocean has done to change my perception of it is to have a deeper love for it. The ocean and everything in it just draws me to it, calls me to it, and I feel at home when I am surrounded by it.

Q. You have been a great advocate for sharks. What is your main concern for them, and what would you like people to know about them?

A. My main concern is the numbers by which they are being slaughtered daily. We are killing them to the tune of 90 million-a-year for their fins and fins only. These creatures strike a chord of fear inside us, a primal scream we hear from thousands of years of ignorance. Yes, they are capable of killing us, but we are more likely to die from a soda machine falling on us than a shark attack. These creatures should fear us much more then we fear them. I want my daughters and their children to have the ability to see these animals in the wild if they choose, but the way our world is going, not only the sharks but much of what is in the ocean, I worry will be gone. We MUST change our habits and our treatment of our fragile environment quickly and drastically if we are to have any hope for the future generations to enjoy the wildlife that still roam our oceans today.

Q. You were involved also in a campaign to help preserve the Galapagos Islands. What is so special about those islands to you?

\A. I was honored to be involved with *The Charles Darwin Foundation, UNESCO*, and *IWC* for the anniversary of Charles Darwin documenting and photographing the Islands above and below the water. The Galapagos are magical, they truly make one feel the sense one's going back in time. The animals are neither fearful nor aggressive as Charles said, and it still holds true today. Of all the places I have been, for me there is no better place to dive than the Galapagos.

Q. You must have tons of great stories surrounding the ocean, is there one in particular that you would like to share?

A. Yes, I have many stories, but none that come to mind as being colorful enough to hold your attention. What I will say is that I simply love the water and if I could I would live aboard a boat, set sail, and finish my days atop the sea. That is a nice vision right!

Photo Michael Muller

Q. If you could give people a list of things they can do to help save our precious oceans and their creatures, focus on the issues that are closest to your heart. What advice would you give?

A. To put your trash where it belongs. Pick up trash when at the beach, and try to pick up someone else's as well. Do not order blue fin tuna anymore. Get involved with an organization that is doing something to help save our oceans. Everyone can do something, even if it's picking up the phone and calling your local congressman, sending a letter, whatever you can do, JUST DO SOMETHING and stop waiting for someone else to do it for you.

Michael Muller is a world renowned celebrity photographer. He recently climbed Mount Kilimanjaro for a clean water campaign and has been on numerous ocean expeditions.

www.mullerphoto.com

Tristan Bayer

Q. As an activist, do you have any specific stories you would like to share that made you feel like becoming more of an ocean protector yourself, or was it simply the more you learned, the more you wanted to help?

A. The ocean conjures up stories of great adventure. Flying alongside giant manta rays with 20 foot wingspan; searching for days for schooling hammerheads off the magical and remote realm of the undersea mountains around Cocos Island; diving 680 feet down in a mini-sub to touch the bottom of the sea like a space craft landing on the moon; finding bizarre alien looking life-forms that live in the perpetual darkness of the deep; exploring sunken ships that have been completely transformed into colorful communities of corals and fish; night diving with feeding sharks; swimming with turtles during massive arribadas; swimming among clouds of friendly jellyfish; cold water diving in backlit kelp forests with curious sea lions tugging at my flippers . . . such memories are permanently ingrained in my psyche.

I grew up traveling the world making wildlife films with my father. I was a certified scuba diver by age 12 and discovered that I am happiest swimming through a foreign underwater realm, pondering the beauty and complexity of our planet. During one adventure we'd spent weeks tracking a pod of sperm whales in Dominica. In one moment, I remember being positioned perfectly in front of the pod after they had surfaced from their feeding cycle. I took a big breath and dove down to meet them 40 feet below. I decided to dive deeper yet to put the passing whales in between my camera and the sun for a silhouette shot, light rays dancing around the fifty foot bull, close enough to notice the white scars on his head case, earned from battles with other males and from fights with giant squid. So there I was, out of my element, pushing my human limits, face to face with the largest toothed predator in the world. I felt at peace. Another whale in the pod swam by. His unusual silhouette caught my eye. What looked like a cancerous tumor, I realized, was a big rubber buoy that was entangled with rope from a fishing net around his jaw. It was then that I came to understand that nothing is safe from humankind. Even the most powerful creatures in the sea are sometimes the most vulnerable and need protection. I have never felt afraid or in danger of anything I've encountered underwater. No matter what is happening on the surface, it is calm and peaceful underneath, a world away. Or so I thought.

Q. You were hired to produce and direct the short movie documentary *Acid Test* for the *Natural Resource Defense Council*. Can you describe the filmmaking process and explain the message of the movie for those who have not yet seen it?

A. When the NRDC asked me to direct a documentary about ocean acidification, I quickly came to realize the gravity of the task at hand. This was an opportunity to use power of the camera lens, one of the world's most influential tools, to raise awareness and to hopefully elicit a much needed change.

To begin the project, we assembled an "Ocean Alliance" of top ocean scientists, policy makers, fishermen, underwater cinematographers and film production professionals. This multifaceted team worked meticulously to get it right: The creation of a ground breaking documentary that would convey the profound effects of ocean acidification to policy makers on Capitol Hill without excluding the attention of general audiences. It was a daunting task. Soon we had ocean advocate and actress Sigourney Weaver interested in contributing her efforts. She would later prove to have an integral role, not only as the narrator, but as someone giving the ocean a voice, from the news, to broadcast television and to aquarium theaters.

The result of our hard work is *Acid Test: The Global Challenge of Ocean Acidification*, which can be viewed free of cost in HD online at www.acidtestmovie.com. I hope you can take 22 minutes to watch it. To get more insight, check out the extended interviews and links to articles on the site.

Q. What is ocean acidification?

A. Some refer to ocean acidification as the "other carbon problem" or "global warming's evil twin." I think of it as a ticking time bomb, a real and frightening threat to the fabric of life in the ocean as we know it. Ocean acidification is the name given to describe the acidification of the world's oceans caused by increased quantities of anthropogenic (or man-made) carbon dioxide in the atmosphere.

Scientists have only recently discovered that when carbon dioxide comes into contact with the ocean, it doesn't just disappear, but is absorbed instead as carbonic acid. The increased quantities of carbon dioxide in our atmosphere since pre-Industrial times have measurably changed the chemistry of the ocean. It is more difficult for life forms at the base of the oceanic food web to build their protective shells in acidic water, compromising their ability to compete ecologically and putting them at risk of extinction. Combined with the effects of global warming, the deterioration of these basic lifeforms will place the balance of ocean systems, and the billions of people who depend on it for sustenance, in serious jeopardy.

Based on current projections, scientists believe we have very little time to turn our energy economy around and find a sustainable solution to this carbon dioxide threat, or we will approach a tipping point that the vast majority of the public, and much of the policy making and scientific community have yet to even understand, let alone stand up against.

Q. What are your feelings in regards to ocean acidification, and what needs to be done to help the situation?

A. Ocean acidification is one of the largest threats to human health we've ever confronted. But we still have a chance to do something about it by drastically reducing carbon dioxide emissions and quickly transitioning to a renewable energy economy worldwide. Most of us, I believe, would make the right choice if we actually understood the gravity of the situation we face. We have to cry out, ramp up our goals for climate protection and alter our economic trajectory in order to stop this runaway train from powering us straight over the edge.

As Sigourney Weaver contends in the documentary's final sequence, "we can go on as we have, forcing future generations to survive, somehow, without the vast ocean resources that have sustained us, or, we can move beyond fossil fuels, securing a future that works for all of us, for all living things. What will we choose?" We need leaders. We need action. We need you and everyone you know. We still have time. I still have hope!

"The difference between what we do and what we are capable of doing would suffice to solve most of the world's problems." -Gandhi

At two weeks old Tristan Bayer traveled around the world with his parents who were making documentaries. His deep exposure to the world made him a leading wildlife filmmaker. He has worked with many TV networks and won numerous awards. Recently, produced Acid Test : The Global Challenge of Ocean Acidification *which was hosted by Sigourney Weaver.*

www.earthnative.com

Boris Worm, Ph.D.

Q. What concerns you the most about the loss of biodiversity in our oceans, and what are the implications?

A. Biodiversity is the very thread that weaves the fabric of life. It provides nature's building blocks, its fuel, and its insurance against catastrophic change. Scientists all over the world have been busy over the last decade studying the precise implications of species loss for the functioning of the whole ecosystem. With every species that has been lost they saw the productivity of the ecosystem declining and its robustness to environmental changes diminishing. Conversely, where biodiversity is restored, for example, in marine protected areas, we see productivity and stability increasing. This means that the harmful effects of biodiversity loss are in principle reversible, if, and only if the species themselves are still around. Extinctions in the sea have been many on local scales, but most species still occur in some parts of the ocean. My biggest worry is that the combined effects of global warming, acidification, and over fishing among other human impacts will trigger a tidal wave of extinctions that will undermine our ocean ecosystems. Above all, we must ensure that we protect all species that remain, and avoid further extinctions at all cost.

Q. In your opinion, what is the plight of sharks?

A. As top predators sharks have played a supreme ecological role for millions of years, yet today they are among the fastest declining species on the planet. One in three sharks is estimated to be threatened with extinction, mostly from over fishing, this is much worse than birds or mammals, for example. Sharks are simply not equipped to withstand much fishing pressure; with their slow growth, late maturity, and few young, their life history is much closer to humans than fish. Decades of intense fishing have depleted most large sharks, such as the iconic great white and hammerhead sharks, or the plankton-feeding whale and basking sharks. Many sharks have been targeted directly, and many more are caught incidentally in fisheries for other species such as tuna or swordfish. Another major threat comes from the luxury shark fin trade, whereas the fins are sliced off the shark and sold for soup in Asia, while the animal is discarded dead or dying. Many divers in the Caribbean, for example, have experienced the complete disappearance of sharks from reefs within their lifetime. Some tropical countries such as Palau and French Polynesia have recently moved to protect sharks from fishing and the fin trade – these efforts must quickly spread to other regions in order to help sharks survive.

Q. If you could make 2-3 suggestions that all world leaders should do regarding protecting the ocean, what would they be?

A. #1: Reduce fishing pressure globally and make the rebuilding of depleted stocks a top priority for fisheries' management. These changes would not only protect the stocks and ecosystems that the fisheries depend on; they have also been shown to be much more economically profitable than over fishing. In many cases, too many boats race to catch too few fish, often supported by tax-payers' money in the form of subsidies. This needs to change. You must also pay particular attention to vulnerable species such as sharks, and make sure they are not going extinct. This is not a pipe dream. People in countries as different as California and Kenya have begun to make these changes, but much more needs to happen to stem the threat of over fishing globally.
#2: Transition to a carbon-neutral economy as quickly as possible. Carbon dioxide from fossil fuels not only warms the planet, but also acidifies the ocean, both of which can have dramatic effects on ocean life. Coral reefs, for example, will likely disappear entirely if we remain

---

Dr. Boris Worm is a global leader in spreading public awareness regarding marine conservation. His research focuses on the causes and consequences of changes in the marine life, and its conservation on a global scale. Dr. Worm works as a marine research ecologist at Dalhousie University which is located in Nova Scotia, Canada.

www.wormlab.biology.dal.ca

on the emission trajectory we are on. Fossil fuels are a finite resource, so we will have to transition to renewable energies anyway. If we do this sooner rather than later, we can help save the ocean in the process.

#3: Help people in developing countries to not repeat the mistakes made by others, both in terms of destructive over fishing and carbon-intensive development. We need to provide people with alternatives that help to heal the oceans, rather than harm them further. This often comes down to individual people making a difference. I recently talked to a *Peace Corps* Volunteer who had worked for years in the Philippines to help end illegal dynamite fishing there. This seemed impossible at first but was achieved in that region after only two years, thanks to her personal commitment. One key is to provide people with alternatives and incentives that help guide positive change.

Q. Do you have any last thoughts you would like to share?

A. We truly live on a blue planet. Our oceans have spawned life on earth, and we know of no other planet where this has happened. In a very real sense the ocean is our cradle, our mother, and our life support system (are you aware that every second breath of oxygen you take was produced by the ocean?). We must do everything we can to protect this vital ecosystem. In doing so, we are protecting ourselves.

Photo Aquarium Of The Pacific

Jerry Schubel
Aquarium of the Pacific

Q. As the President and CEO of the Aquarium of the Pacific in Long Beach, California, can you explain first of all what the distinguishing characteristics of the Aquarium of the Pacific are, and what your objectives are as an organization?

A. The Aquarium of the Pacific combines the qualities of a great traditional, classical aquarium with outstanding live animal exhibits and a rich array of programs that connect it to the major ocean issues of the region, the state, the nation and the world and that connect the nation's most diverse population with each other and with their environment. It uses media and technology extensively in making these connections. The Aquarium is a community gathering place where diverse cultures and the arts are celebrated and a place where important topics facing humans and our relationships with our planet and our ocean are explored by scientists, policy-makers, and stakeholders in the search for sustainable solutions. Our mission is to instill a sense of wonder, respect, and stewardship for the Pacific Ocean, its inhabitants, and ecosystems. More importantly, our vision is to create an aquarium dedicated to conserving and building natural capital (nature and nature's services) by building social capital (the interactions between and among peoples.)

Q. We believe good aquariums can play a vital role worldwide; however, there are people who oppose animals in captivity in general. Why do you think aquariums are so important, and what is your rational for having animals in captivity?

A. Aquariums are the only opportunity many millions of people in the U.S. and around the world have to observe live marine life in natural looking habitats and to make connections with it, both intellectually and emotionally. Aquariums serve to make the ocean and its complexity and diversity real and tangible for the public. People care for and protect what they value and understand and the best way to value and understand something is through personal experience. Aquariums convey important messages about what is happening to animals in the ocean and to the ocean habitats and ecosystems they depend upon for their survival, and that we ultimately depend upon for our survival.

All of our marine mammals, our sea lions, seals and otters, were either born in captivity or rescued and rehabilitated and were deemed by the U.S. Fish and Wildlife Service to be unable to survive in the wild. Under these conditions and when proper accommodations are provided—those mandated by law—animals in aquariums can be ambassadors for telling important ocean stories.

Q. Can you briefly explain in your opinion what the major problems are that we face in our world oceans, and what can be done to alleviate these issues?

Jerry Schubel's emphasis is to distinguish the Aquarium of the Pacific as a free-choice learning institution in addition to its status as a world-class aquarium. He is an author and has an extensive background with marine institutes and ocean affairs around the world from the New England Aquarium to the National Institute of Oceanography in Pakistan.

www.aquariumofpacific.org

A. Over the decades we have seen a steady decline in many ocean qualities, and an improvement in only a few. Pollution, habitat destruction, and over-fishing remain serious problems in much of the world ocean although some improvements have been made in the U.S. and in many developed countries. Many commercial fish stocks are still over-fished and fisheries sometimes employ destructive fishing practices such as bottom trawling that can destroy habitat. By-catch remains a serious problem. The control of non-point source pollution remains a challenge worldwide.

We now have an emerging set of problems driven by emissions of CO_2 and other greenhouse gases to the atmosphere primarily from the burning of fossil fuels. These include the warming of the upper ocean, sea level rise and inundation and ocean acidification. Warming has contributed to stressing coral reefs and other marine life and to coral bleaching. It also has contributed to sea level rise and coastal flooding that will be the most immediate, direct and dramatic effects of global climate change on human societies.

Ocean acidification is perhaps the most insidious threat to ocean ecosystems. When CO_2 is added to the atmosphere it remains for about a century and then much of it is transferred to the ocean where it remains for a thousand years, or longer. Increases in CO_2 levels in the ocean have increased the acidity of the ocean making it more difficult for animals—from plankton to coral reefs—to form calcium carbonate shells and skeletons. Collapses of planktonic populations have effects that cascade through entire ecosystems.

Q. Do you have any last thoughts you would like to share?

A. Humans have put earth on a trajectory that may well put its ability to sustain human life at risk unless fundamental shifts are made soon, particularly in the kinds and amounts of energy we use and the ways we produce our food. We must reduce significantly our use of fossil fuels in the short term, grow more food to feed a growing population, and do it on less land with a smaller environmental footprint. We have strategies to accomplish these. Aquariums can and should play leading roles in engaging the public in the exploration of these and other important goals; issues that are critical to our ocean, our planet, and to our descendants. We see this as one of our responsibilities. We pursue this role through exhibits, lectures, our Aquatic Academy, and a new series of Coastal Conversations.

Manuel Maqueda

Q. You were one of the founders of *Plastic Pollution Coalition*; what are some of the most important things you think people should know about plastic etc.?

A. *Plastic Pollution Coalition* was created with the vision of a world free of plastic pollution and of the toxic impacts of plastic on humans, the environment, wildlife and marine life. We want to create a collaborative space for community, synergy, strategy and support for all the individuals and organizations interested in the study and remediation of this problem. Plastic pollution is a new environmental challenge that is now starting to emerge into our consciousness, sort of like global warming 25 years ago. Nowadays, Internet and new media provide fantastic tools for collaboration and citizen activism. In the spirit of this new era, *Plastic Pollution Coalition* does not seek to replace the actions of any particular organization, but to help the entire movement grow, spread virally and incubate new ideas and solutions. Plastics in the ocean are just the tip of a very complex and serious problem, and there is a great need for urgent action. In the marine environment, plastic breaks down into smaller and smaller particles that become powerful chemical attractors for really nasty pollutants such as PCBs and DDEs that are present in our ocean water. Almost all species of sea life are ingesting these toxic bits of plastic, either directly or indirectly, starting with plankton and filtering invertebrates which are eating tiny microplastics, and culminating with sea birds, whales, sea turtles. Not surprisingly, harmful chemicals leached by plastics are already present in the bloodstream and tissues of almost every human baby. In fact, I like to say that the real garbage patch is not in the Pacific, but here on land: in our stores, homes, and refrigerators . . . and increasingly inside of our own bodies.

Plastic pollution is the result of a problem of design, not merely improper disposal, or lack of recycling. It is absolutely absurd and obscene to use a toxic material that takes 700 years to biodegrade to make objects that are designed to be thrown away after a few seconds, minutes, or days. That's the root of the problem. Single use plastics, such as plastic bags, plastic bottles and plastic packaging, are so pervasive, and being produced and discarded at such a gigantic scale, that our planet is drowning in a waste that the earth cannot digest. We will not solve this problem unless we pledge to change this throwaway mentality and shift away from these disposable habits. Businesses, not tax payers, should take responsibility for the end life of their products. When that happens, single use plastics and over packaging will stop spiraling out of control. We need to incorporate producer responsibility into our economies and demand transparency in the ways plastics are manufactured and disposed of. At the same time, we need to start holding businesses and governments accountable for the toxic effects of plastics on human health, and establish the precautionary principle as a general and compulsory principle of the law. It is unbelievable that Bisphenol A and other toxic chemicals present in plastic are still legal, when scientific research has already established a risk to human health. The famous "three R's" of Reduce, Reuse and Recycle, are not the only "R's" we need. When I see a disposable object, such as a bag, or a bottle made out of a material that I know is so pervasive and toxic as plastic, the only R-word that comes to my mind is "Refuse!" That is the R that nobody is talking about, and I believe that it is the most important. Bring your own bag, carry your own bottle and reusable mugs, and refuse to participate in this disposable madness. Together we can effect huge change and become a part of the solution. Visit www.plasticpollutioncoalition.org to learn more.

Q. You spent a year of your life aboard a tall ship; how was that, and what did you learn from that experience?

A. I served aboard the training ship for the navy of Spain, a gorgeous four-masted schooner called *Juan Sebastián de Elcano*. The *Juan Sebastián de Elcano*, also known as the *Elcano* for short, was built in Cádiz in 1927, and has been in continuous service sailing the world's oceans since then. In fact, she is the ship that has logged the most miles in history. I joined the crew of the *Elcano* when I was young as a lowly second class seaman, the very

Born and educated in Spain, Manuel Maqueda has sailed around the Americas for nine months on four-masted, top-sail schooner Juan Sebastián de Elcano, *where he introduced recycling. He is the VP of Community and Strategy of BlooSee.com, a social atlas of the oceans, and a co-founder of the* Plastic Pollution Coalition.

www.bloosee.org • www.plasticpollutioncoalition.org

bottom of the rank in the Spanish navy. The unofficial motto among my peers was "If it moves, you salute; if it doesn't move, you paint it." Sailing aboard the *Elcano* satisfied my childhood dreams, only the discovery that I embarked on was not that of a foreign land but that of myself. The ever changing nature of the ocean, its mystery, its complexity, and its boundless beauty, became a gateway through in which I started to delve deeper into the great questions that to this day, continue to fascinate me. The contemplation of the ocean instantly conjures up anew these complex feelings, and awakens in me a deep and moving sense of wonder. The same sense of wonder and amazement that prevailed over my childhood, that accompanied me as a sailor aboard the *Elcano* in my 20s, are what I seek to preserve and nurture as I grow old.

Q. Having been to Midway Island with Chris Jordan, what does Midway signify to you?

A. Midway is a tiny island, only two miles long, located right in the middle of the North Pacific Ocean. A speck in the map surrounded by thousands of miles of open ocean. For the Hawaiians, however, Midway is a place of ancient power and significance, a revered elder in a long dynasty of volcanic islands that once stretched from Kure Atoll to Kaua'i. Flowers of molten lava bloomed and decayed with the long seasons of geology, and left a marine landscape strewn with exquisite petals of azure. In the Hawaiian tradition, the rosary of atolls that form the Northwestern Hawaiian Islands represents a long lineage of Kupuna, ancestors, who live a solitary life, in the heart of Papahanaumokuakea, the place where the union of Papa, the Mother Earth, and Wakea, the paternal sky, "gives birth to islands in the vast expanses."

Midway is a sacred place, so sequestered and remote as Midway should be absolutely pristine. And yet the entire island is polluted with millions of disposable plastic objects such as cigarette lighters, toothbrushes, disposable razors and bottle caps. All this junk gets here inside of the bodies of the albatrosses that come to nest on Midway. Albatrosses are large seabirds that forage all over the Central Pacific Ocean, can fly 300 miles a day, live to be 60 years old, and mate for life. Today, these majestic creatures find toxic junk of bright colors floating on the surface of the ocean, mistake it for food, and feed it lovingly to their nesting chicks. What a powerful metaphor. I went to Midway with four artists to witness and document this strange and profound phenomenon. However, there were many layers of depth to our endeavor. In a sense I saw Midway as a symbol of where we are as a culture. Our society has not yet figured out ways to deal with the planetary problems that we create. We are starting to realize that our present economic model, built around permanent growth, is not going to take us to a sustainable future. However, we don't know yet what the new model is going to be, or how we will get there. As for the albatross, to me it is a heroic messenger. An animal that is giving up its life to bring us a powerful message. A message that speaks of interconnection of all living systems, and also of our increasing disconnection with who we really are. Ultimately, plastic pollution originates inside of our hearts, and the prophecy of the albatross is that it shall return from where it came. Only then, maybe, the pain will make us leave this midway place and leap forward into the future.

Keith Malloy

Q. What is your #1 pet peeve about the ocean, and what do you think needs to be done about it?

A. The saddest thing I have ever seen pertaining to the ocean, is being in the middle of nowhere and seeing beaches covered with trash and plastic. I think people need to be more aware about using plastic and where it ultimately ends up. In most cases, we use a plastic product once and it stays on our planet for an unknown amount of time. We need to fix that.

Q. Do you have any thoughts you would like to share about the ocean?

A. The ocean is the life blood of our planet and since we are just beginning to understand how polluted our oceans really are, we should take immediate action. Whether it is picking up trash on the beach, using less plastic or being conscious of what we let go down our storm drain, there is something we can all do.

Dan Malloy

Q. If you could give three suggestions to all people about protecting the ocean, what would they be aside from, do not litter?

A. One is start a kitchen garden. That's advice from Wendell Berry that has affected me much more than petitions and bumper stickers. Two is go find your creeks, your water source and your river mouth. Find your old creeks that are now culverts, find your storm drains that connect to your water shed. Most of these things start to surface the second you start walking and riding your bike around town and walking around in the hills. And three, join your local community supported agriculture. By doing this you will ultimately help the ocean.

Chris Malloy

Q. On the Patagonia website you make mention you like small grass-roots groups to help educate people on environmental matters the best. Can you expand on that?

A. From my experience I have noticed a disconnect between peoples philanthropic energies and their final outcomes when it comes to the sea. We all live in places that need our time and energy in terms of the natural world, but somehow we get caught up in sending money to places we have never been, places we will most likely never go. By putting energy into the places we live we become so much more passionate and knowledgeable about what's going on, and in that, much more effective. so many big multinational environmental groups burn time and money while the small grass-roots groups use everything they have to make change. The biomass connected to our watersheds and oceans here at home need help as much as anywhere on earth. The places we have grown up surfing have made us who we are, they are ours, why not start there?

Q. If you could offer people words to live by, regarding the ocean, what would that be?

A. Never turn your back on the sea.

Emmett Malloy

Q. As the co-founder of Brushfire Records, and Jack Johnson's manager, you have made it a goal to reduce your environmental footprint as much as possible, including using solar panels on your building, etc. and made your music tours as "green" as possible. What is the main message you are trying to spread, and why is it so important to you to take such measure?

A. About a decade ago my brother, my cousins, my friend Jack and I all got inspired to start making films and put out records. At the beginning everything felt so simple and homemade, and there was no thought of business or business practices. But now over a decade later, we have a fully functioning record label, a film company, and Jack has sold a lot of records around the world and has become a big touring act. Although we are still a family and friends operation, we have become a brand and business. So with this natural evolution, we have had to monitor our growth and do it as responsibly as we know how. We have continued to keep things small and simple, certainly compared to most record labels and production companies, but we do make our impact. There are realities to making records, shooting films, and touring in front of big audiences, so we just started paying attention, and tried our best to push an old-school industry. We looked to some of our mentors, like Neil Young and Willie Nelson, and saw that they were using things like bio-diesel for their tour busses and using recycled materials for their CDs and albums. We looked to the clothing company Patagonia and found good alternatives for our merchandise items and saw that they had installed solar panels in their headquarters. They also turned us on to *1% for the Planet*, which is an organization that we have been a part of in all our business for over five years now. These things were eye-openers for us, and with a partner like Jack, these were things that really resonated with him. So from there we began down our own road of finding our own way that would work best for us. Now we have renovated our own office building, and learned a lot about alternative materials to use that would be better for the environment. We now have a solar powered studio, our CDs are made of 100% recycled goods, and Jacks world tour had set a new environmental precedent in the business. Now, things that seemed overwhelming at the beginning are just the way we do business.

Q. Have you considered taking your whole "green"message that you spread while on tour and talking to people about also being more "blue"?

A. For us, most of what we have been hipped to as far as environmental improvements are inspired from a lifetime of being in the ocean. The ocean is very dear to all of us, and it is something we all spend a lot of time and resources toward protecting. Jack and his family have been a huge leader in this movement. Jack has had an amazing run as a musician and has some great successes, and with each new level of success he gives that much more back to causes he believes in. Jack has created the *Kokua Hawaii Foundation* and the *All At Once* organization as ways for people to be exposed to things that are important to him. They are both focused on the environment and environmental education. We have become a bit of a lifestyle brand, so we want to continue to make good records and films, but also tip people off to things we believe in and help keep the planet in good shape.

Emmett Malloy is the co founder of Brushfire Records*, a filmmaker and renowned photographer. He encourages "greening" the entertainment industry from recording in their solar powered studios to promoting grass root, environmental groups when on tour.*

www.brushfirerecords.com

Q. If you could send one message to all people regardless of if they live near the beach, what would it be?

A. I saw a T-shirt the other day that says "the more you know . . . the less you need." I feel that is a good message to live by heading into this new decade.

Doug Tompkins

Q. As one of the top known clothing moguls from the end of the last century with an environmental message, what would your message be for the clothing and textile companies, and designers of today, regarding their environmentalism?

A. Of course there are all kinds of clothing companies and I would say that most all of them, even the industrial clothing companies making work clothes could reduce their output by four to five times. A survey I read in the 1980s showed that in the closets of each American, since the end of the WWII, there were now five items of clothing where there was once only one item. That is to say, in 40 or so years clothing consumption or purchase went up five times. No one was shirtless in the post WWII era either. So, what we have is a population in the (over) developed world at least that is vastly over-clothed. What does that say to the managers, owners and designers of apparel companies today? The needs need to be evaluated since we are producing five times more items of clothing than people really need. This overconsumption is perhaps the main driving force of the eco-social crisis we are all ensnared worldwide. The conclusions are easy to draw from there.

Q. As a business owner you had surprising views on over consumerism and had an ad campaign that said, "Only Buy What You Need." Can you explain your feelings on that issue today?

A. Well, as I answered above, I came (slowly as it were) to the conclusion that we had to rethink what we are buying and buy for legitimate needs and not just to have more stuff. I knew at the time that it was contradictory to have an anti-consumer campaign for a marketing and producing company, but I thought perhaps we could set an example and draw attention to the idea of overconsumption. It was laughed at of course by many, although I have a sense that they also knew in their heart of hearts that they were over-consuming themselves and locked into a system which fostered and fomented that kind of behavior. The point is that we have developed and enveloped ourselves in a system that is hell bent on self destructing. Where can we break the vicious circle, that is the question? Where do you cycle out of the pathological process of constant consumption and an ever and ever materialist society that in turn is chewing through the Earth's resource base as if there were no tomorrow and thus creating the extinction crisis, the mother of all crises. Extinction is forever. It is the death of birth if you will, and the end of evolution. Monstrous crisis.

Q. What are your largest concerns for our oceans, and what do you think can be done about it?

Doug Tompkins co-founded The North Face and Espirit clothing companies 'selling people countless things they didn't need.' Now, Doug Tompkins is spending his earned money and time saving the planet. Doug and his wife, Kristine conserved over 2 million acres of wilderness in Chile and Argentina, more than any other private individual. The Tomkins' are opposing the construction of five dams on two of Patagonia's largest and wildest rivers. The Tomkins' are co-founders of Deep Ecology Foundation *which believes that If we are to achieve ecological sustainability, nature can no longer be viewed only as a commodity; it must be seen as a partner and model in all human enterprise.*

www.deepecology.com

A. The health and integrity of the marine ecology is and should be of concern to everyone. If the ocean goes, so does the world. It will not be like sitting on the shore and looking out at a dead sea. The marine systems are intimately interwoven with terrestrial systems and with weather patterns and with carbon sequestration, although their role now as a carbon sink is greatly diminished. The "fix" for the ocean's health is not something that can be done either technically nor in isolation. It is going to require a massive paradigm shift and a systemic change in the way civilization is conducted. That is a long answer, too, but I would list a few things to give one an idea that would have to be eliminated or severely reformed. Among them: capitalism, anthropocentrism, industrial agriculture and industrialism itself to a great extent, mega-technology (nuclear, computers, global trade agreements, nanotechnology, bio-technology, large dams, combustion engines), land concentrations in the ownership of large corporations or individuals, specialized fields of knowledge (experts), mega-urban concentrations, straight lines, applied science, the education industry, industrialized medicine . . . I could go on for a long time, but that gives one the gist of things.

Q. Do you have any ocean related stories that really affected you, or any last thoughts you would like to share in regard to the ocean?

A. I am mostly a landlubber although we just came back from a ten day junket on a tall ship, a Dutch Clipper ship sailing from the tip of South America to our place in southern Chile. I was six weeks on the *Sea Shepherd Conservation Society's* anti-Japanese Whaler Pirate campaign in the Southern Oceans a year ago. When I was younger I sailed some delivering sail boats down in the Caribbean so I have some ocean sensibility. Plus in southern Chile we live on the ocean, too. I think that the work of the *Sea Shepherd* is really compelling and they are really the activists

that I admire most, as they get out there and put their heart and soul plus risk their lives to protect whales and the world oceans. They don't just talk about it as some organizations do, but they are right there on the front lines. If people admire those that stick by their values and are committed, then they should at least support the *Sea Shepherd Conservation Society* which as I say, really does something and is not just out there spouting words and making photo op campaigns. There is nothing like it in marine protection activism in the whole world.

Photo Agustin Muñoz

Photo Agustin Muñoz

Ahmed Pérez

Q. Being one of Latin America's top environmental surfers, you have become an important influence and a role model to a lot of kids; do you have a message about the ocean and its preservation that you would like to share with them in particular?

A. The participation of young people is important for the conservation of the sea and the marine species. But considering that education is the most important tool to make a difference in the future of the sea, my first message is for the adults. According to psychology, people can usually love what they know . . . and come to feel affection through a learning process. The more you learn, the better. We need a commitment to children to teach them and develop ongoing activism for the environment in all levels: kinder, primary, secondary, university, and institutional.

My message to the kids is a conservation strategy thought in three groups of kids, to develop in each of their communities: Gray group, which includes children living in the reality of a city where you mostly see streets and buildings that is different to the life near the oceans or the mountains. You can help save the planet by promoting campaigns to create awareness about pollution and its affects on the ocean, promoting recycling plastic and organizing ecologic activities. Blue group, which represents children in coastal communities that live in a city closely related to the ocean environment. You can create art competitions developed with marine motives in conservation and messages to be displayed to the public. Another idea is to organize beach cleanups with classmates and friends. Sending letters to local authorities about environmental conservation, as a priority in your city, can also have tremendous effects. Green Group, that shows children who live in rural or mountain areas. You can promote local ecological fairs to provide information on the conservation of nature, benefits of eating natural foods and fun in outdoor spaces. Many of you can be the leaders of your communities! All you have to do is try!

Q. Can you tell us about your own environmental heroes, who they are, and how they have influenced you?

A. I think it is necessary to start living in an era of new kinds of heroes and idols, ordinary people who make positive and constructive things are all heroes. My own heroes are the people I see who stop to pick up a trash from the ground, and put it in the right place to begin with, and also people who carry their own cloth bag, or reusable bag, to the store to avoid accumulating plastic bags that cause big damage to the planet. Other heroes are the persons who greet you with warmth but do not know you, who arrive at a place and say "good morning," the person using the daily water with responsibility, even when he know that millions of people are wasting it in that same moment. Actions like these are heroic!

A great inspiration for me has also been the work of the surfer Dave Rastovich, and having the opportunity of working with him on some environmental activities throughout South America . . . Thanks Rasta! And the passion and dedication of Captain Paul Watson, and his years spent fighting for a better world for all of us . . . Thanks also Paul!!

Q. Is there anything you would like to point out from the stand point of being Latin American?

A. Yes, there is a global problem of pollution and conservation associated mainly with two factors: ignorance or negligence, and in both cases these are behaviors that know no borders. As a Latino I have something to say . . . the regions hosting the world's largest energy reserves are the least to benefit from them, by a disproportionate distribution. Africa and Latin America together consume just 8%, and yet we are the largest producers of energy. Canada, USA and Europe consume 55% of global energy and if we keep pace with current consumption, the natural reserves will perish.

The sources of clean renewable energy (solar, hydro, wind, geothermal and biomass) are emerging as viable alternatives, despite requiring an initial investment. And the character of local renewable energy allows the South to reduce its dependence on imported fuel and will increase energy security, while releasing the dependency imposed by energy multinationals - BP, Shell, Standard Oil - (to name a few) not only acquire the "rights of exploitation" of our natural heritage for decades, but they use cheap labor to work from sunrise to sunset who live in poverty.

Q. Do you have any words to live by or special quotes you would like to share with others?

A. Yes - one word - Believe! Phrases: "In the end we preserve only what we love, we will love only what we understand, we will understand only what we learn." Baba Dioum, conservationist of Senegal. Then there is a saying I have "When we understand that the nature with all its species is our true home . . . conservation will be a reality."

Q. What kinds of changes have you witnessed in regards to the nature around you since you were a kid?

A. In my community many things have changed because of the changes in nature. For example, when I was a child learning how to surf, I remember going often to a beach which was very close to a fishermen pier. It always was full of small boats (one or two people boats) that colored the landscape to the enjoyment of the people, but all that changed over the years because of the lack of fish. Now there are a few boats from the same people, but they now pull inflatables for the fun of bathers.

Nevertheless, I must admit that recently the president of Venezuela's decree banning the commercial trawling fishing, was incredible news that probably (in a long-term) will help to create new marine ecosystems, corals and optimal habitat for the creatures of the ocean system. Also in Chile, after conservation activities we did with Rasta and Sea Shepherd, I could see how after many years of brutal mammal and cetacean fishing . . . to the point of contempt of the marine species, the President of Chile presented an initiative to the Congress in order to declare its waters as a Sanctuary for Cetaceans and issued a ban on such hunting. Earlier that same year, Costa Rica had done the same, for the same reason, to create peace with the planet.

Venezuelan environmentalist, pro surfer, Ahmed Pérez has gone on campaigns with Dave Rastovish along with the Sea Sheperd Society *advocating the rights of whales and sanctuaries of cetaceans. The best music I know is the ocean and its waves - La major musica que conozco es el sonido del oceano y sus olas.*

Photo Agustin Munoz

Bob McKnight

Q. What is your favorite thing about the ocean other than surfing?

A. The key thing for me about the ocean is the serenity and the whole vibe of it all really brings me to peace whether it is putting my toes in the ocean or simply being near it. Living near the sea allows me to feel balanced, the ocean is peaceful, it is zen like, it is always moving, the sounds are wonderful, the visuals are colorful, and the lighting is constantly changing. Whether you are cruising in a boat, flying above it, under the ocean diving, or sitting there on your surfboard, the ocean is a very tranquil place even though it can get wild and vicious. Most of my thoughts of the ocean are a state of relaxation and one of my favorite places to be.

Q. Do you have any meaningful stories of people helping the ocean that stand out in your mind?

A. There are certainly many pioneers of ocean conservation that I pay my respects to. Especially some of the founders of the non-profit ocean conservation groups like Surfrider Foundation, Reef Check, Mi Ocean, and others. Because they're the ones who have put their money, time and passion to the cause of keeping the ocean clean for the benefit of us. I really admire Greg MacGillivry because he has done wonderful IMAX movies which speak to millions of people. He is able to entertain people yet sneak in the scientific or environmental message. That kind of approach is profound because most people hear about ocean problems but don't ever get to see them.

I understand the perspective most people may have that do not live near the ocean or never get to see the ocean, too. People say, "You shouldn't flick your cigarette butts in the street, or wash your car in the driveway." And those people may say "who are you to preach to me, what I should do or not do, living here in the mountains, or living inland, while you guys on the coast go play in the ocean, we do not even get a sniff of the ocean." I understand the kind of conflict there may be out there, but we have to message this in a way so it is more entertaining and educational. Perhaps with a sense of humor so that every one is on the same page whether you live in Cleveland Ohio, on the coast, Moscow, or Shanghai. Everyone needs to know that we have to respect our ocean and our planet, because it is a resource, it is not infinite. Most importantly, the ocean is at risk, so what are we going to do about it?

The people who impress me are the ones that are doing something, rather than talking about it. Those who spend their money and time, and truly push the envelope on doing what is right.

Q. What worries you the most about the ocean?

A. The pollution factor worries me the most. I remember days when I could not get in the water due to sewage spills which can make you really sick, and that is really frustrating. These are very real issues. I remember in the 90s people were stepping on syringes on the beach in New Jersey, then getting AIDS. We soon began measuring urban run off and realizing how high the levels of bacteria were going into the ocean, which indicated that people could get hepatitis and other sicknesses. This is when we really began watching the outflow of sewage treatment plants. We need to remember this is only a 20-year-old type of science. What concerns me is urban run off along with population growth is scarring our oceans. We need more people educating and learning about these issues. More of us need to change our normal tendencies and to start thinking about all this stuff in our daily lives.

Q. If you can offer a few suggestions to help the ocean, what would they be?

A. Educate yourself. Use the Internet and read more books, we all need to get more educated to understand how it all works. Dive into a problem you care about and be open to learning more about how everything is connected. And I think the more we teach our kids the better, they are natural sponges, and they are the future.

> *Bob McKnight is the co-founder of Quiksilver since 1976 which is a global surf apparel company responsible for revenues over $2 billion a year. He recognizes the concept of corporate responsibility and benevolence. Their foundation wants philanthropic work to have impact beyond what they do as a company.*
>
> www.quiksilverfoundation.org

Q. Any last thoughts you would like to share or favorite quotes to pass on?

A. The ocean is such a beautiful body of water that we all share. Half the world's population lives near the beach, and the other half can't wait to get there. All around the world eyes light up when the word "beach" is mentioned. People will always tell you of a nice experience they have had near the ocean or even near a lake. The whole water world is so amazing and special. We need to respect our oceans and waterways by working locally first, then really spreading the word globally.

Mark Cunningham, Bob and George Downing   Photo Duffy Healey

Photo E. Laul Healey

Joey Santley

Q. How and why did you come up with Resurf.org, and Green Foam Blanks. Can you please expand on this a little for us?

A. When my son was diagnosed with Autism, it really woke me up to the disaster that we are facing regarding the environment. I realized that I had the moral obligation to do something positive to be part of the solution. As a surfer, and coming from a family history of large scale surfboard production, I had a pretty good idea of how much waste is created on a daily basis. After some discussion, some friends and I got together and started Resurf.org to raise awareness of the amount of waste that the surf industry creates, and to try to find alternative homes for the waste trying to extend the life of the material as far as possible. During our exploration and R&D efforts, my partner Steve and I figured that the next logical step was to create a cradle to cradle recycling system for surfboard foam, since it makes up the majority of the waste pile we create. After some R&D we had finally done it; we had the world's first Recycled Polyurethane Surfboard Blank. Green Foam Blanks was created. We have since made thousands of blanks and have some of the best surfers in the world riding them and spreading the news message.

Q. Because of your son's diagnosis, and knowing it changed your entire life, can you share your new found philosophies on life, and tell people about what you did, and how it changed your life for the better. Share your feelings on what others can do to help make a difference themselves.

A. My wife and I had to stay away from acting as victims and keep focused on our son's needs, which were many. Then we had to make adjustments in our daily lives, be happy with the fact that we are together as a family, and move on. I have learned more on this journey than any other in life and have found great joy and peace knowing that I am working on solutions rather than being part of the problem. I think it takes passion and heart to affect change, and I am inspired daily by what some of the younger generation is doing to affect change in the world. I have also learned to appreciate how healing the ocean is for the whole family.

Joey Santley markets recycled surfboards to the hands of celebrities, respected surfboard builders and pro surfers. He is determined to be a green leader in the $7 billion surf industry. Polyurethane surfboards are made with a carcinogenic chemical compound, this waste has been going straight to the landfill for 50 years and is still today.

www.greenfoamblanks.blogspot.com • www.kidnaturalhero.com

Photo E. Laul Healey

Dianna Cohen

Q. Can you please explain how your work as a visual artist led you to ultimately form the *Plastic Pollution Coalition*?

A. Working with recycled plastic bags as the primary medium of my artwork for the last 20 years (www.diannacohen.com), has led me to contemplate the chemical makeup of these plastic bags, which are primarily petroleum based, and on to the discovery of thousands of tons of plastic in the oceans. The idea arose to create an art project to bring attention/raise awareness, which led me to self edification along the way. As I became more aware of the issues and far reaching repercussions of our societies single use plastic throw away habits and its environmental and human health consequences, my perspective shifted to the bigger picture; plastic used in this way is toxic and not sustainable. While I enjoy talking about these issues more abstractly through my artwork, this larger perspective dictates that we join together to change this disastrous course and so, along with other concerned scientists, artists, surfers and citizens, the coalition was created: www.plasticpollutioncoalition.org

Q. Can you explain exactly what *Plastic Pollution Coalition* is and does?

A. The mission of *Plastic Pollution Coalition* is to stop plastic pollution and its toxic impacts on humans, the environment and wildlife worldwide. Plastic Pollution Coalition provides a platform for strategic planning and coherent communications; increases awareness and understanding of the problem and sustainable solutions; and it empowers action to eliminate the negative impacts of plastics on the environment, wildlife, marine life and human health.

Q. What are the *Plastic Pollution Coalition's* three main goals?

A. 1. Awareness: To bring the issue of plastic pollution to the forefront of the social, scientific, economic, and political debates, educating citizens about the threats posed by plastic to their own health and the wellbeing of the planet and its inhabitants.
2. Community Building: To provide a platform for individuals and institutions to share resources and coordinate efforts to reduce plastic pollution, with an emphasis on eliminating single-use disposables. 3. Empowerment: To empower citizens to shift our societies away from the disposable habits that poison our oceans and land, eliminate our consumption of throwaway plastics, and begin embracing a culture of sustainability. People need to understand that plastic is a material that the earth cannot digest. It makes no sense whatsoever to use a material meant to last forever in the environment to manufacture disposable products and packaging that we use for a few seconds, minutes or days. This has to stop and we need to urgently rethink the way plastics are used in our society. The plastics that are the most damaging to the environment are precisely those that are the easiest to give up: single-use disposables, such as bags and bottles, straws, cups, plates, silverware, etc. A great departure point is to follow the rule of the 4 Rs, in the following order of preference: Refuse, Reduce, Reuse, & Recycle. Ultimately, the solutions are going to involve legislative measures and an international dialogue of all parts involved: citizens, scientists, governments and businesses. Being informed and politically and socially active in your community is also essential.

Please make a commitment toward sustainability and sign the S.U.P.E.R. Hero pledge at: www.plasticpollutioncoalition.org

> *Dianna Cohen is co-founder of the* Plastic Pollution Coalition, *which has a mission to stop plastic pollution and its toxic impacts on humans, the environment, and wildlife worldwide. She is also an artist and has been very successful using plastic as her primary medium. Dianna strives to empower citizens to shift our societies away from the disposable habits that poison our oceans and land, to eliminate our consumption of throwaway plastics to begin embracing a culture of sustainability. Recyling plastic is a bandaid.*
>
> www.plasticpollutioncoalition.org

Captain Charles Moore

Q. You are famous for accidentally discovering what they call "The Great Pacific Garbage Patch" in 1997, how did that come about?

A. Well I don't know if I discovered it, but I have been given that credit, but I didn't name it that. None the less I have studied it ever since. We discovered it when we were on our way back from the Los Angeles to Hawaii Transpac sailing race, and we took a non-typical way home and sailed straight through the trash in a place sailors call the doldrums.

Q. What is the Pacific Garbage Patch?

Photo E. Laul Healey

A. It is a plastic wasteland in the middle of the North Pacific Central Gyre, an extremely large convergence zone that stretches from China to just off the coast of California. It is a circulating current that has a tendency to pull all of our trash from the Pacific Rim into a main central zone that is referred to as the Great Pacific Garbage Patch, which I think is a misleading name. It is a sea of plastic as far as the eye can see, all caused from human waste. It is a disgusting plastic cesspool. The problem is that plastic is very slow to biodegrade and the plastic does not drive off oily contaminants and therefore becomes a sponge for our pollutants absorbing all the toxins floating around in the ocean and transmitting them back up the food web back to us. It is an enormous problem that we as a race need to contend with. Only humans make the waste that nature cannot digest. Plastics are also very hard to recycle, and only a tiny fraction of them are actually recycled. We are finding more combined plastic in the ocean than zooplankton by a ratio of about six to one! It is killing our fish, the marine mammals, and tens of thousands of marine birds including the albatross. The birds and animals mistake the plastic as food and they can't digest it. Then their stomaches fill will plastic which gives them the illusion that they are full, and they actually starve to death with bellies filled with plastic pieces. Their stomachs are filled with micro pieces of plastic up to entire cigarette lighters, but mostly there bellies are filled with bottle caps.

Q. Do you have any thoughts you would like to share?

A. We must consider the legacy that we are handing off to our children and future generations. We are the throw away generation. Did you know that we use two million plastic bottles in the United States alone every FIVE MINUTES? This is astounding. And it is a problem that is global. The throw away society cannot be contained, we simply cannot store and maintain or recycle all of our stuff, we have to throw it away. We need to stop the plastic at its source. We must stop it on land before it goes into the ocean because there is no possible way to clean up all of the plastic that we have littered. Before plastic we did not have this issue. We need to reconsider all that we are doing.

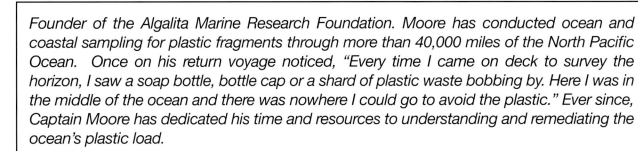

Photo E. Laul Healey

Founder of the Algalita Marine Research Foundation. Moore has conducted ocean and coastal sampling for plastic fragments through more than 40,000 miles of the North Pacific Ocean. Once on his return voyage noticed, "Every time I came on deck to survey the horizon, I saw a soap bottle, bottle cap or a shard of plastic waste bobbing by. Here I was in the middle of the ocean and there was nowhere I could go to avoid the plastic." Ever since, Captain Moore has dedicated his time and resources to understanding and remediating the ocean's plastic load.

www.algalita.org

Adam Gardner

Q. What is your personal connection to the ocean?

A. II grew up spending my summers on Cape Cod in Massachusetts and the ocean has always been a very important part of my life. I now live in Portland, Maine on the ocean and I spend as much time as I can at the beach or on the water. I try to make it a part of my everyday life whether I go out kayaking or I simply take my two-year-old daughter to the beach to play in the sand. I love to experience the ocean through her eyes as she lights up picking up sea shells, and sea glass, and as she looks at the different sea creatures. The beach is a wonderful multi-sensory experience from the sound of the ocean, to the feel of the sand, to the smell of the salt air. The ocean represents everything good to me: nature, summer, good family times, water sports and good memories.

Q. How did you end up starting Reverb, and what is it all about?

A. Well, I am a musician and I have been in a band for many years, and my wife has always been an environmentalist. So at home we were really used to being as eco minded as possible, yet when I was on the road touring with my band it felt like a contradiction to the environmental habits we practiced at home. There is typically a large environmental footprint involved in touring with a band and putting on concerts, from the busses, to lighting, to all of the garbage left behind by fans at the end of the night. As I toured the country sharing the stage with dozens of other bands, I realized that other musicians also lamented the fact that their tours damaged the environment. So when my wife came up with the idea of starting Reverb, I knew it would be well received.

Reverb helps bands to lessen their negative impact of putting on musical tours, from switching to biodiesel for their tour busses, to reducing waste, to neutralizing carbon emissions from the power used at shows, to using local and organic catering and much more. We also engage millions of concertgoers face to face at shows in our Eco-Villages that travel with the tours we help make green. At concerts we already have a built-in audience that generally is interested in making positive changes and are given additional incentives from the bands themselves, so it has worked out really well. We've partnered with thousands of local non-profit environmental groups in the Eco-Villages, and we organize local projects like beach clean-ups with organizations like Surfrider and Ocean Conservancy.

Q. You have been really interested in climate change for a number of years now, what are your thoughts on climate change as it relates to the ocean?

A. As I'm sure the readers of this book know, we are all playing a role in accelerating climate change beyond how the earth would typically react without humans. It's interesting if you look at other species like ants for instance, they outweigh humans pound for pound on this planet yet they enhance and nurture the planet. To put it mildly, we are not doing the same thing. And why not? We all have a role to play in nurturing our world from individuals, to governments, to corporations, we all have a duty to protect our home which we all share.

Q. Do you have any last thought you would like to share?

A. Despite the problems we are currently facing, I remain incredibly hopeful and optimistic. I have seen such positive changes in the education and drive and determination of people to want to make a difference since 2006, it's truly incredible. I think even the perception of environmentalism and activism itself has changed from sandal-wearing hippies, to the average person, despite political lines. I think young people especially care, and they are making a huge change for the better. We can and will change our ways to heal the wounds we have caused to our ecosystem.

Adam Gardner is the Co-Director of Reverb, a non-profit environmental organization which he co-founded with his wife Lauren Sullivan in 2004. Reverb "greens" musicians' tours for Dave Matthews Band, Coldplay, Maroon 5, Jack Johnson, Sheryl Crow, John Legend, John Mayer and many more. Also a musician in the band Guster, Adam has been outspoken on environmental issues from testifying in front of congress on sustainable biodoesel, to being a keynote speaker to over 10,000 students at Powershift '09 in D.C.

www.reverb.org • www.guster.com

Photo Duffy Healey

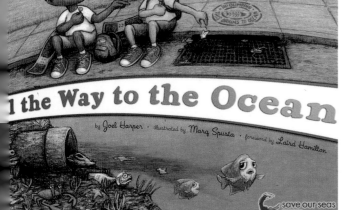

1 the Way to the Ocean

by Joel Harper · illustrated by Marq Spusta · foreword by Laird Hamilton

save our seas FOUNDATION

Joel Harper

Q. Why did you decide to write *All the Way to the Ocean*? Why did you write a children's book?

A. The first thing that comes to mind in answering this question is my childhood. I have wonderful memories as a child enjoying the ocean. My family would rent a beach house in Laguna Beach, California every summer. I wrote *All the Way to the Ocean* back in 1998. I was driving along in my car, it was pouring rain and I noticed a storm drain so full of garbage the rain could not even enter the storm drain. That sparked an incredible rage in me. I live in one of the most beautiful towns in California, I remember thinking to myself: "how can this be."? As I was driving home the story line for the book played out in my head. When I got home I immediately wrote the story down. That was the easy part. However, it would take eight years before the book would make its way into the world. Why did I write a children's book? I don't know exactly . . . maybe because I like to think that I still have my 'children's soul'. I think children are so much smarter than we adults give them credit for. I think it is more crucial than ever, that we reach out to children and help educate and inspire them to want to make a difference. I never had big dreams of writing children's books. It was more like one of those things where one thing led to another.

Q. When a child reads *All the Way to the Ocean*, what lesson or idea do you hope they take from the book, and what makes it so special?

A. I hope that children and adults absorb the message that little things add up and when we all pitch in and work together, we have the potential to make a huge difference for the better. Just picking up a piece of trash from the ground before it enters into a storm drain, is making a critical impact toward a cleaner, safer ocean planet!

Joel Harper is a writer, musician, music teacher, and author of All the Way to the Ocean. *The children's book delivers a strong message to adults about protecting the ocean, keeping our sewers free from garbage and also about friendship and teamwork.*

www.freedomthree.com

Photo Oceana.org

Andrew Sharpless

Q. Krill is very important to the overall food chain of the ocean. Can you briefly explain what krill is, why it's so important, and what *Oceana* and others are doing to help protect krill?

A. Krill are small, shrimp-like crustaceans. There are 85 species of krill, and they are present in all of the world's oceans, and are particularly abundant in the Southern Ocean. Krill have light emitting organs called 'photophores' that make them glow in the dark; swarms of krill at night or in the dark ocean depths make impressive swirling light displays. The largest krill, the Antarctic krill, is thought to live up to 11 years old. Ocean wildlife eats between 150 and 300 million metric tons of krill each year. Many seabirds, whales and fish rely on krill as an integral part of their diets. Wild salmon eat krill; it is what makes their meat healthy and pink. The blue whale, the largest animal that has ever lived, feeds exclusively on tiny krill. Remember the *March of the Penguins*? Those emperor penguins march hundreds of miles every year . . . to eat krill. Their survival, as with the survival of many marine species, is directly linked to the abundance of krill. Fish farms also use krill for food. In particular, salmon farms want to use krill to avoid injecting red dyes into farmed salmon to mimic the color of wild salmon meat. Harvesting krill to feed farmed fish takes away krill to feed wild fish, seabirds, and whales. The results could be catastrophic for the marine food web. Krill are a key component of the ocean ecosystem. If krill are suddenly removed, the marine food web is severely disrupted. A few summers ago, unusual weather resulted in low krill populations in the Pacific, and thousands of starved, dead seabirds washed up on Oregon, Washington and California beaches. This tragic event underscores the delicate balance between krill and the health of our oceans. We can't change the weather but we can prevent the commercial use of krill at the expense of fish, birds and whales.

In 2009, federal policy makers banned all fishing for krill in U.S. Pacific waters of California, Oregon and Washington after campaigning led by *Oceana* and others with strong support from scientists, conservationists, fishermen, coastal businesses and local communities. But we still have more work to do. Over fishing of krill and other prey species is now causing food shortages in the ocean, further devastating ocean ecosystems. *Oceana* believes the following critical steps need to be taken immediately to protect krill and other prey fish:

A.) No new fisheries for prey. A moratorium on the establishment of new fisheries for prey fish is an important first step to protecting prey. The banning of new prey fisheries, like krill, safeguards against potential ecosystem collapses that could arise through over fishing.

B.) Set conservative limits for prey fisheries in cases where fisheries already exist, setting conservative catch limits is an important component of ecosystem-based management. Conservative catch limits allow populations to recover to healthy levels and can be used to plan for potential losses due to climate change and other threats.

C.) Prioritize uses for prey. When setting conservative catch levels, managers should specifically keep the needs of the entire ecosystem in mind. This includes allocating a portion of prey resources to predators prior to setting catch limits for fisheries. Fish caught should also be prioritized for direct human consumption rather than as a fuel for aquaculture or other industrial uses.

Q. Preventing mercury from entering into our environment is also a vital ocean issue, especially to *Oceana*. Can you elaborate on this?

A. Mercury released to the environment from industrial sources ends up in our oceans, contaminating seafood. Because it builds up in wildlife through a process called bioaccumulation, animals high on the food chain carry the most mercury. Many of the fish we eat, such as tuna and swordfish, are close to the top of the marine food chain and thus contain higher levels of mercury. People exposed to high levels of mercury in fish can experience health effects, such as delayed neurological development in children. Both the Food and Drug Administration and the Environmental Protection Agency have advised women of childbearing age and children not to eat certain types of fish due to high levels of mercury. Elevated mercury levels are also being found in wildlife, like polar bears, whales and sharks. Most people remain unaware that a small subset of the chlorine industry makes a major – and completely preventable – contribution to the global mercury crisis. A handful of chlorine plants still use mercury in the chlorine manufacturing process. Not only has newer, mercury-free technology been around for decades, but over 100 factories globally have switched to the modern technology because of environmental reasons as well as increased energy savings. *Oceana's* campaign to stop seafood contamination is working to convince grocery stores to post the FDA's mercury advice and to convince the remaining chlorine plants who use mercury to convert to mercury-free technology. Since the campaign began, hundreds of grocery stores have started posting the advice and several chlorine factories have closed or converted.

Q. The dumping of inadequately treated waste water from cruise ships is another threat to our world oceans. Can you explain why this is a big issue, and briefly explain *Oceana's* accomplishments in this area, and state what still needs to be done?

A. Cruise ships generate an astonishing amount of pollution: up to 25,000 gallons of sewage from toilets and 143,000 gallons of sewage from sinks, galleys and showers each day. Currently, lax state and federal laws allow cruise ships to dump untreated sewage from toilets once the ships are three miles from shore. Within three miles, cruise ships can dump sewage from toilets that has been treated by marine sanitation devices, which have been shown to be inadequate. In addition, sewage from sinks and showers can be dumped without treatment. Our coastal environment and marine life are at risk from the threats of bacteria, pathogens and heavy metals generated in these waste streams. In June 2003, *Oceana's Stop Cruise Pollution* campaign set out to convince Royal Caribbean Cruise Lines, the world's second largest cruise company, to improve its waste treatment practices. Eleven months later in May 2004, Royal Caribbean agreed to install advanced wastewater treatment technology on all of its ships (then 29, plus any new ones). With the first cruise company committed to upgrading sewage and wastewater treatment fleet-wide, *Oceana* declared victory and concluded the campaign.

Q. Although there are many serious issues we are facing in our world oceans, *Oceana* is an organization with a lot of hope for the future in regards to what can be done. What is the good news?

A. The good news is that we have answers, and experts believe there is still enough time to bring back our oceans. This is a major global problem that we can solve because most of the life found in the oceans is found on the continental shelf, and is therefore mostly under national and not international jurisdictions. This means we can implement policy changes to save the oceans country by country without creating a new international mandate or body. Studies have shown that when the right policies are put in place, the ocean and fisheries can and do recover. Many of the most serious threats to the oceans can be addressed with solutions that already exist. New technology has made many kinds of pollution preventable; mercury-cell chlorine plants eliminate mercury releases entirely by shifting to newer membrane-cell technology.

Gear modifications allow commercial fishermen to avoid catching untargeted species; thousands of endangered sea turtles are saved each year when fishermen equip their nets with turtle excluder devices. Changes in fishing practices can protect coral gardens; restricting bottom trawling in small areas of dense coral growth can preserve invaluable marine life without compromising the fishing industry's profits. We can also think of our oceans as part of the solution to energy problems. Clean, carbon-free ocean energy such as wind, tidal, wave and current power can be a part of our sustainable energy future.

CEO of Oceana*, graduate of* Harvard Law School*, and the* London School of Economics*. "All we can do right now is slow down the pace of destruction of the ocean, but once we build the constituency, we can win the changes that will keep the ocean and its wildlife alive forever."*

www.oceana.org

Photo Bentley Cavazzi

Dan Stetson
The Ocean Institute

Q. What role does the *Ocean Institute* play in ocean conservation?

A. Located adjacent to the ocean, with a marine protected area and a harbor, and with a dedicated staff of highly-trained educators, the *Ocean Institute* is in a unique and perfect position in southern California to introduce the importance of the ocean to thousands of K-12 students each year. Our mission statement is to inspire all generations, through education, to become responsible stewards of the oceans. Our motto is, "Experience is the teacher." With these ideas in mind, we play a direct role in ocean conservation by educating students of all ages each year about the importance of preserving and protecting the ocean environment. Woven into every aspect of our marine science and maritime history programs is the crucial message of responsibility and ocean conservation. All *Ocean Institute* programs are designed to maximize immersion, inspire deep commitment to learning and spark curiosity, questions and future discovery. The programs have received the inaugural Walter Cronkite Award for Excellence in Maritime Education from the *National Maritime Historical Society* and the Sea Education Program of the Year from the *American Sail Training Association*. In addition, the Weather and Water fifth grade program was recognized by the *National Science Teacher Association* as an exemplary science program in an informal education setting.

Q. What is the reach of the Ocean Institute?

A. Imagine a sellout crowd at the Rose Bowl stadium and then half again. Our reach is very broad and annually includes over 115,000 students, 6,000 teachers, and 25,000 general public visitors from throughout the country with a concentration on the western United States. Many teachers tell us that this is their first time that their students see and experience the ocean. We are often surprised by their reactions. One little boy got off the bus and glanced out upon the vast Pacific for the first time in his life. He paused for a long moment and then matter-of-factly remarked, "Gosh, I thought it would have been bigger."

Q. What do you hope mostly to teach the children who come through *Ocean Institute*?

A. We hope to inspire learning, literacy and a lifelong love of our ocean planet. Using the allure and intrigue of the ocean, we provide programs that are motivating and challenging while stimulating curiosity and critical thinking.

Here is one success story! For a full semester, some 2,000 fifth grade students in our Watershed Education Program had been preparing for this particular presentation day, having first come to the *Ocean Institute* the previous September to learn about the relationships of watersheds and the ocean. Each group of students had developed a scientific and environmental hypothesis using scientific methods the *Ocean Institute* instructors had taught them. The students had spent months testing these hypotheses by collecting and analyzing data. At the culmination of this project, each student group returned to the *Ocean Institute* to formally present its findings in front of hundreds of their peers, community leaders and scientists. Following the presentations, the students were having lunch together. One precocious young boy asked to make a toast and after getting permission, he stood up and said, "Talking about our project in front of everybody was kind of hard, and I was pretty nervous. I want to toast all my team mates for helping me." Everyone cheered and clinked their juice cartons. Soon, a young girl asked if she could make a toast. "I'd like to toast all of you who will be making your presentations after lunch. Good Luck! You can do it! You will be great!" Everyone cheered again. After a few minutes, another fifth grader got up and said, "Well, I've really learned a lot and I want to make a toast to science!" All the fifth graders spontaneously stood, raised their juice boxes and cheered. At that moment, the adults all realized that the *Ocean Institute*

Photo Ocean Institute

programs had just made a lasting difference in the lives of these children.

Q. You are an avid scuba diver and you made mention of the changing baselines from when you were young, to how they are for the kids of today, and you had some thoughts for the future kids, too. Can you expand on those thoughts?

A. My mother used to tell me that whenever we borrow anything, we should always return it in better shape than when we got it. Over time I've come to learn that this is more than just borrowing a cup of sugar or a friend's car. "We," the global community, have borrowed and almost emptied the earth's cup and gas tank without even a thought of refilling them. Now we must be careful that we don't also crash the car. There is an old Native American saying that goes something like, "We have not inherited the oceans from our ancestors, but rather borrowed them from our children." Unfortunately, for generations, "we" have abused this sacred trust. We have contributed to and accepted declining baselines as the "New Normal." Science tells us we may be quickly approaching the tipping, or crashing point. No one knows for sure. What we do know is that we must start today to stop this decline and reverse direction. Otherwise, ecosystems will crash and our children's children will have nothing . . . nothing to lend, nothing to borrow.

Q. If you personally had one message to deliver to kids living everywhere, what would it be?

A. May your dreams point your inner compass to future horizons. May you chart a life long course of learning and understanding. Never, never give up on your dreams, and let experience be your teacher.

Dan Stetson is president and CEO of Ocean Institute which offers state-of-the-art educational facilities, three ships and a dedicated, professional staff to achieve the Institute's goal, ocean preservation through education. More than 110,000 K-12 students and 6,000 teachers annually participate in the Institute's 61 award-winning, immersion style programs.

www.ocean-institute.org

Monika Steinberg

Q. What has been the biggest factor in making you want to help the ocean now more than ever?

A. The biggest factor would have to be my own mortality. What am I doing today that will supersede my lifetime? As I've come into my thirties, I start questioning everything, from love to faith, and the human condition. There has always been one place that I can go in peace to think of such things, one place that has always inspired me and electrically charged my soul, that place is the ocean. Whether I'm walking on the beach in Bridgehampton, NY burying my toes in the sand of the North Shore, Oahu or just home in Newport, CA, I feel a great attachment to mother Earth, and it's by the water's edge where I feel my purest. So, when I see cigarette butts, candy wrappers or water bottles lining my path, and along the same line I see children running, laughing, building in the sand, I think of what will my future children be encountering when they take off their sandals to dig their precious feet in the beach. This is why I make a point to pick up trash, every time and in every place I travel to as a deep and honest respect for what the beautiful sea has given to me. I believe that every little bit helps . . . Think globally, act locally.

Q. If you could motivate people into making three new habits to help the ocean, what would they be?

A. 1. Reduce 2. Reuse 3. Recycle

Born in Peru, Monika has worked in the surf publishing industry for many years connecting with leaders and athletes throughout the world.

www.monivine.com

Photo Tony Vera

María Celeste Arrarás

Q. You were given the "Hero to the Environment Award" by Monterey Bay Aquarium, that is a pretty big deal, do you mind describing what it was for?

A. I received the award because of my dedication to create awareness for the need to protect the well being of the oceans through the media. I'm honored but I believe it's a duty as a human being.

Q. White sharks seem to be of particular importance to you, can you tell us a few important facts about these creatures, and also what is the plight of white sharks?

A. Throughout the years, sharks have had an undeserved reputation as "sea monsters." But the reality is that white sharks are not "hungry man-killers." The risk of death from lightning is 30 times greater than death from a shark attack. Actually, it is humans that hunt sharks, driving them to the brink of extinction. White sharks have an essential role in the balance and health of the ecosystem.

Q. What is it that you love the most about the ocean, and what worries you the most about it?

A. I love everything about the ocean, especially the magnificent creatures that call it home. I grew up watching the documentaries of Jacques Cousteau travelling in his beloved *Calypso* and they instilled in me a deep appreciation for the wonders of the ocean. Today, I worry about the many species on the brink of extinction and I worry about the indifference of mankind.

Q. If you could send one message about anything regarding the ocean to all the people of the world, what would it be?

A. We probably know more about outer space than we know about the ocean even though it's one of the world's greatest resources and a vital part of life on the planet. The ocean holds so many mysteries, yet we are destroying it inch by inch, turning it into a massive dump site. We need to educate ourselves and realize that the health of the ocean is essential to our survival.

Petting whale in Laguna San Ignacio, Baja California

Television host María Celeste Arrarás from Al Rojo Vivo *was honored as "Hero of the Environment" from the* Monterey Bay Aquarium *for her work in producing and airing segments on ocean conservation on her popular TV show. She is also an Emmy* award *winning journalist from Puerto Rico for the* Telemundo Network.

www.costasalvaje.com • www.wildcoast.net

Gregory Harrison

Q. Was there a particular incident that has happened that has driven you to want to help protect the ocean, or was it more of an accumulation of things that all added up?

A. Well, I suppose it was an accumulation of things. A little background history . . . I was born and raised on a lovely little island off the California coast called Santa Catalina. I'm a third generation islander . . . my grandfather was one of the first people who operated the Glass Bottom Boat over there in the early 1900s, and my father captained the boat for 55 years. I was destined to be the third generation of Harrison men running the tour and would have been but for the filming of the movie *The Glass Bottom Boat* in 1965, which totally turned my head around about what I'd do with my life. Anyway, I spent the first 18 years of my life in the sea over there, diving for coins from tourists, swimming in amazingly lush bays and surfing off the pristine beaches and rocky coastline that surrounded the island. It was the most beautiful place. The water was crystal clear and the fish and ocean creatures were everywhere. Truly unbelievable beauty. Heck, my family's daily survival depended on the clarity and lushness of those "undersea gardens" that the tourists saw through the glass. But it's changed. As much as folks today like to say how beautiful the ocean is over there, it's not even a third as amazing as it was back in the 50s and 60s. I've been an active witness for nearly 60 years now to the decay and degeneration of the ocean, Catalina waters particularly, but around the rest of the globe as well. I still love to surf and swim daily, often the same places I have since my childhood, but it's bittersweet for me because I grieve for the loss of the ocean of my memories, and I hate realizing that my children can't experience the pure joys of the sea as I did.

Q. What is your ocean "hotspot," or ocean issue that bothers you the most, and what do you suggest people do to help alleviate the situation?

A. The thing that irks me the most is plastic. I find loads of it everywhere I surf around the world. I was just surfing in Los Cabos, Mexico and there were lots of plastic grocery bags floating in the surfline. Beaches are littered with bits of plastic on every continent I've visited. My suggestion is hard core; that we all just refuse to use plastic anymore . . . for anything. Let's back up to what it was like when I was a kid, when glass, wood, metal and cloth were used and reused for holding and containing things. And stop using individual packaging! It's so insanely ridiculous to do that. Let's use our brains as we fill our stomachs.

Q. Do you have any fascinating facts or stories about the ocean, or any thoughts about the ocean that you would like to share in closing?

A. We've always been told that the rain forests are the lungs of planet Earth, and I believe that's true. But if the rain forests are the lungs, then the oceans are the heart. They are responsible for the circulation of everything that makes life possible . . . including the temperatures, the winds, the nutrients of life. We've ignored the importance of the seas for too long, taking for granted that it would always be there for us, ever-forgiving and nurturing. But like every human heart, a lifetime of abuse and disrespect will destroy its ability to function, and like the human body, the earth will die. We must start taking care of the oceans now before it's too late.

Born in Avalon, Santa Catalina Island, California, Gregory Harrison became the unofficial poster boy of Catalina Island chamber of commerce. Accomplished actor, Harrison is probably best known for cult favorite North Shore, *and on the CBS series* Trapper John, M.D. *As a native of that offshore isle, Harrison developed a strong connection to the marine wildlife and is an advocate for ocean conservation.*

www.gregoryharrison.com

John Picard

Q. Can you explain why and how building "Green" is so important not only to our environment, but also to how it affects the ocean as well?

A. Our next buildings will be designed and engineered with standards and respect for all the world's oceans. Today we are building green, on site, with local concerns. Tomorrow we will build with full awareness of global impact. We can, and we will. The most attuned leaders see the clear strategic advantage of building to not just protect, not only to be carbon neutral, but to harness returns. Half the people in the world are living near their country's water source. With careful building, that water can be healthy. And that water must be healthy to fulfill its role in the elegant natural systems the earth gives us.

Q. You were one of the people involved in the "greening" of The White House, can you explain briefly what that meant, and why symbolically it is so important?

A. If ever an address should be a showcase for sustainability, it is 1600 Pennsylvania Avenue. Greening The White House was the ultimate retrofit prototype. It was a puzzle, a genuine challenge and incredible fun. The visibility was a huge bonus; we were saying, do try this at home. In the process, our team realized we were creating the how-to guide for every property owner tasked with transforming obsolete energy systems in a still functioning building—whether 40 years old or 200 years old. The lessons learned in greening The White House fueled the founding of the U.S. Green Building Council which is having enormous impact changing the world's built environments, and by extension, changing the whole world.

Q. Is there a message you would like to convey to the people of the world stemming from your own relationship with the ocean?

A. I'm a water man. I surf, I dive, I run along the beach. I wasn't aware of it at the time, but my initiation into my life's work began at the ocean. I went from surfing to saving dolphins from net capture and from there to being more thoughtful about my projects. How was I building what I built? How was I honoring or affecting the ocean I loved, where I played, where I now take my kids to play? I look at the ocean when I come over the hill on the way home from the office at the end each a day and ask myself: How are we doing? The ocean is an honest gauge of how we are treating the planet.

John Picard is one of the preeminent environmental consultants in North America. He has pioneered a philosophy of natural systems and sustainable design in his work as a green building engineer. John is a founding member of U.S. Green Building Council and was honored for greening The White House.

www.johnpicard.com

Kama Dean

Q. You play an important role in Pro Peninsula, especially with regards to the sea turtles, can you please explain what Pro Peninsula does, and what it does for the sea turtles?

A. Pro Peninsula is dedicated to strengthening individual and community efforts to protect the natural environment throughout the Baja California peninsula. Our programs span sea turtle conservation, environmental education, advocacy and more, but one thing is the same throughout all of our work: It is carried out at the community level, by community members, with the fundamental goal of involving communities in long-term conservation of their natural resources. As far as sea turtle conservation goes, Pro Peninsula is home to various sea turtle research and conservation programs including working with *Grupo Tortuguero, Proyecto Caguama* loggerhead conservation program, and Carey! Hawksbill recovery program.

Q. Can you explain a little bit about the types of sea turtles you deal with and where they are from?

A. Five species of sea turtle are found in the waters surrounding the Baja California peninsula. Black sea turtles migrate from southern Mexico to grow and feed in the bays and lagoons around the peninsula. The loggerhead sea turtles migrate from Japan to feed off of the Pacific Coast of the peninsula until they reach maturity and return to Japan to nest. Hawksbill turtles are found throughout the Sea of Cortez; however, their origins (where they nest, where they are migrating from) are still a mystery. Olive Ridley turtles feed and nest around the peninsula and the Sea of Cortez, with their main nesting areas in southern Mexico. And the leatherback turtle nests along the southern tip of the peninsula, migrating from areas off Alaska and California.

Q. The sea turtles are in danger right now, can you explain their current threats?

A. Currently, the greatest threats to sea turtles around the peninsula are accidental capture in fishing gear (bycatch) and direct capture, or poaching, for consumption and illegal trade. Habitat destruction and pollution are also major threats to turtles, to a lesser degree in Baja, but a major problem in other areas of the world.

Q. How is Pro Peninsula helping the turtles?

A. Our work focuses on involving communities to ensure the survival of sea turtle species. This includes working with coastal fishermen to identify and mitigate bycatch, especially through our Proyecto Caguama project. This also includes engaging communities to study sea turtles, as with the Carey! Project, which allow us to learn more about these species and engage local communities in their protection at the same time. And, working through environmental education and the buiding of a conservation network, as in the case of the Grupo Tortuguero, to change perceptions of sea turtle conservation and consumption habits (Do Not Eat Sea Turtle)!

Q. What can ordinary people do to help the sea turtles?

A. Through our Adopt a Sea Turtle program everyone can learn more about the turtles, what they can do to save them and our work. Through this program you are directly supporting the conservation work taking place throughout the Baja peninsula. Individuals can help sea turtles by not polluting, using canvas bags and reducing consumption.

Kama Dean has worked extensively on community conservation issues, with a focus on the Baja California peninsula. She managed the Grupo Tortuguero de las Californias, or Sea Turtle Conservation Network of the Californias, overseeing their monitoring, education and network building programs.

www.oceanfdn.org • www.propeninsula.org

Photo Sea Shepherd Society

Shannon Mann

Q. What advice can you offer to people that would like to make a major serious difference like you have for our oceans and ocean creatures?

A. Know that every choice we make has an impact on the environment. A change in simple everyday choices . . . bike when you can, consume less, eating locally, reducing plastic consumption, use environmentally friendly products . . . will contribute to the greater well-being of the planet. After that, I can say that there are so many ocean and environmental groups to get involved with and they are almost certainly underfunded and understaffed. There is nothing more soul satisfying to me than chasing the whaling fleet, pulling in illegal long lines, or being involved in a rescue situation! It becomes addictive.

Q. What are your hopes for *Sea Shepherd* in regard to its hit series *Whale Wars*?

A. We are a volunteer crew sailing down through treacherous seas to one of the most remote and unforgiving environments on the planet - to save the lives of whales. We put our lives on the line for a cause. And, we are just ordinary people with passion for the cause. *Whale Wars* reaches a lot of households in many different countries and my greatest hope is that it inspires people to get active and fight for what they believe in.

Born and raised in the prairies of Canada, Shannon Mann developed an affinity for all living creatures and their interaction with the environment. As the Quartermaster to Captain Paul Watson of the Sea Shepherd Conservation Society *her most passionate goal is to put an end to whaling in the Antarctic Sanctuary forever.*

www.seashepherd.org

Charles Hambleton

Q. How did you get involved in the making of the movie *The Cove*?

A. I was working in the Marine department on the *Pirates of the Caribbean* movie. I was on the Black Pearl in the Bahamas, and my good friend, photographer Louie Psihoyos, called me during a break and told me about the situation in Tiaji, Japan. After working with Louie for many years with still photos I knew this was going to be one of the more interesting shoots (he usually calls me when it's difficult and dangerous). I instantly said I would do it and he said "good, we leave tomorrow - I already bought you a ticket." I then had to explain to my bosses that I had to leave for Japan in the morning (and ask, did I have a job when I returned in two weeks?) The timing was good as the Black Pearl was tied to the dock for a few weeks and my bosses both loved the idea of using film to expose something horrible going on in the world and being able to "make a difference." That was the first of many trips to Japan and around the world to film *The Cove*. I have always been an environmentalist, sailor, diver and water person so it was a great way to help create change.

Q. What compels you the most to risk potential arrest to help the dolphins in Taiji, Japan?

A. Although a consideration, arrest was never a deterrent. "Filming wildlife in a National Park" is a charge of dubious legality (no matter what is happening to the wildlife). The more serious charge, and what they have tried to arrest several environmental groups on, is "Conspiracy to Disrupt Commerce." Dolphins are whales, large amounts of money are changing hands and commercial whaling has been illegal since the IWC moratorium in 1986. This is commercial whaling. This would have been great in court and I almost looked forward to it. Our team planned meticulously to "eliminate the variables" for arrest, of which there where many. Being in the woods for long periods of times, I personally took my own precautions. Being arrested for a noble cause seems trivial compared to be able to be part of making the world a better place - historically you are in good company.

Q. What other aspects of the ocean concern you the most?

A. Ocean acidification, complete disregard for global fisheries management (although there is much positive work done on this), pollution (not just mercury, but plastics, and a wide assortment of Persistent Organic Compounds.) The plastic in the Pacific Gyre is insane. Generally it's the "Tragedy of the Commons" and the "Myth of Plenty" working together. You don't have to live by the sea to notice the effects. Tuna consumed in the Midwest is just as toxic as tuna caught off the coast (oh yeah, without the carbon footprint to fly it around the world to market and back). Reef degradation is alarming, they are the gauge of our ocean, and in turn, our planet's health. Every two out of three breaths every human takes, they owe to O_2 production from marine algae. Other concerns include oil exploration from off shore drilling, and naval sonar testing.

Q. If you had three wishes for the ocean regarding people helping it, what would they be?

A. Enjoy and have respect for our oceans in every regard, you will be leaving them for your children and for the future. Spread the word. Get involved with any ocean/ water-keeper organization wherever you live. Every person makes a difference. Examine your energy usage and household waste. Everything runs to the sea.

Charles Hambleton worked on the Clandestine Operations for Oscar awarding winning movie The Cove. Hambleton studied environmental microbiology at University of Vermont, yet he grew up all over the world from Colorado to London, then to Antigua, West Indies. As a diver he has discovered numerous wrecks around the Caribbean. He is an advocate on whaling and Japanese dolphin slaughtering.

www.thecovemovie.com/the_team/the-team.htm

Photo Anna Webber

Daniela Sea

Photo Eden Batki

Q. You had kind of an extraordinary life growing up in Malibu and learning to surf at age six. Were you ever fearful of the ocean? How did it make you feel?

A. My learning about the ocean came about by living near it all of my life. My parents were ocean babies, lucky enough to grow up next to her. I remember when my mom taught me to body surf at age five, how to swim under the waves, hold onto the sand and feel for the subtle movement of the wave washing over to know it was safe to come up again. Being in the water with my mom and seeing her so strong and alive is one of my favorite memories. Another was when my step-father, a surfer since the early 50s, would take me out on his surfboard on the North Shore and ride waves in while I sat in front of his feet. At that moment, I knew it was something that I would do all of my life. As for if I'm fearful of the ocean? Yes. This goes without saying. She is an immense force. I feel alive and insignificant when I enter the water, and I think this is a healthy respect. That said, there is nowhere I'd rather be than tossed around in her embrace. Everything comes to the forefront then, things like what life is worth and the unending cycle of life and death. Spreading my stepfather's ashes at sea was a moment of deep understanding along these lines. I surfed wave after wave as his ashes mixed in and became the water all around me. She is where we will all return to, if we are lucky. And in her we live on, in a fish's belly or a perfect wave.

Q. Do you believe you have a different perspective on our global environment, and on our oceans, due to the extensive traveling you have done? (for example, are there things we may take for granted as Americans, or vice versa compared to other cultures you have experienced?)

A.What I learned most from living with different cultures, especially ones that are more self sustaining and less destructive to the natural environment, is the importance of thinking far ahead to future generations with every decision big and small, considering what they will need to live a good life, or to live at all. This way of thinking inevitably leads to a less destructive way of living on this earth. I also learned about the importance of thinking of others as well as yourself, and the power of living a life that balances the individual and the communal more equally. Thinking beyond the self leaves room for understanding the value of the life forms around us, for their own right to a good life and for our survival.

Q. It is hard to protect what you have not experienced, having said that, what message would you like to express to those people who have not had the fortune to experience the sea, and why should they make an effort to do so?

A. There are so many reasons to protect the sea. She is a vital organ to the living organism that is our planet. The ocean is also a place to experience the essence of what it is to be alive. She is energy moving constantly, full of life, ancient and simply magical. So many cultures live out of her generous bounty, some could argue that we all do. It is important to learn the laws of balance from some of these communities so that we do not destroy the lifeblood of the earth.

Daniela Sea is an artist, an actor and a musician. Daniela plays the groundbreaking role of Max of The L Word. *She can also be seen in John Cameron Mitchell's* Hedwig and the Angry Inch *feature film,* Shortbus, *as well as Jamie Babbitt's* But I'm a Cheerleader, Itty Bitty Titty Committee, *and in Fruit Chan's* Don't Look Up. *She publishes her own books of poetry, speaks Polish, and plays accordion, guitar and penny whistle.*

www.danielasea.com

William J. Cooper, Ph.D.

Q. In your opinion what is the largest concern for the oceans?

A. Sustainability of biodiversity. Clearly the biggest issue regarding the sustainability of our oceans is the uncontrolled human population growth. However, it is the one thing that people rarely talk about because it is extremely contentious. If people understood the benefits, to the earth, of having less children, and the ramifications of too many people having too many kids, we would be taking one more step in a sea of change.

Q. What role does technology play in regard to our oceans?

A. Technological solutions can both benefit and spell the demise of the oceans, but the pivot point is simply greed. By technology what I mean are ships that have a world-wide capability. In the open ocean, there is little if any enforcement, and as long as there are large profits to be made, the oceans are likely to be over fished, and the collapse of the world fisheries inevitable.

These technological advances also can be seen in increase in the strength and agility of fishing gear, plastic netting, monofilament, fish traps that, once lost, fish on, totally unregulated and out of sight. Whereas, the fishing gear of generations past was made from natural materials such as hemp and wood we now rely almost exclusively on plastics, polymers of lasting strength and a life time that far exceeds us. The plastics in our oceans continue to build up and it is estimated that millions of sea birds, fish, sea turtles, and marine mammals die each year. A very subtle point is that when people go to the beach, or fly over the oceans, they see oceans that appear peaceful and infinite. Many people feel disconnected from the oceans, and feel that changes in their own behavior would not significantly result in a difference in the oceanic environment. That is false. With 6.7 billion people, even one act per day per person to save the oceans could have a dramatic and lasting effect! Another technological advance that has actually set the ocean back tremendously is commercial bottom trawling. We have created the ability to scrape unthinkable swaths of the ocean floor where we literally have hundreds of miles at a time completely wiped out, and millions more fish and animals are killed in by-catch alone. It is similar to the clear cutting of our forests without regard for the future sustainability. It is also another example of out of sight, out of mind.

Q. What might be some solutions?

A. I believe the most important of all potential solutions is the education of everyone! If one wants to think of this as a business proposition, think return on investment (ROI), clearly reaching out to young students is at the top of the list. Education, outreach, mentoring, can also involve a cascading of educational levels starting with life long learners mentoring college and university students, and those students teaching younger students, and younger students teaching yet younger students, this would result in a downward age stair step amplification of this investment.

Professor of Civil & Environmental Engineering, and Director of the Urban Water Research Center *at the* University of California, Irvine. *Cooper received his Ph. D. from the* University of Miami's, Rosensteil School of Marine and Atmospheric Sciences*, in Marine & Atmospheric Chemistry. He directed the Drinking Water Research Center at* Florida International University *while obtaining his Ph.D. Cooper's research focuses on carbon cycling in oceanic systems, the application of free radical chemistry in advanced oxidation processes to control pharmaceuticals in natural waters, the use of ozone for the control of invasive species in ships ballast water, and recently has conducted three cruises in the North Atlantic and North Pacific examining plastic pollution.*

www.uwrc.uci.edu/about/Cooper-Intro.php

Photo Edwin Morales

Coco Nogales www.carloscoconogales.com/dat/bioe.html

Q. Was there any certain event or things that made you want to be more of an ocean advocate and speak up for the ocean?

A. Right now my home town does not have the best sewage treatment plant because of poor planning, rapid development and population growth. This worries me that my favorite beach break may be adversely affected. It motivates me to speak out for the people and help educate them about the future effects of greedy developers that do not care about the ocean, the people's views, the environment, proper set backs or ruining the surf breaks. I want to protect future generations of Puerto chargers so they have unpolluted beaches, too. Remember, once a pristine location is lost, it may never come back - ever.

Timmy Curran www.timmycurran.com

Q. In your experience from traveling the world, what is your main concern for our global oceans?

A. My concern is about the whole ocean and teaming up with organizations like *Surfrider Foundation* to support their projects that help clean and protect the beaches from pollution. I believe that travelling the world has helped me see first hand how terrible pollution can be, especially where people are not taught about proper ways of dumping their trash. Some of the most beautiful beaches in the world are littered with trash, and that is sad.

Photo De

Raimana Van Bastolaer

www.ultimatewavetahiti.com

Photo The Ultimate Wave Tahiti 3D

Q. What does the ocean mean to you and for your community?

A. We are very lucky we don't have the big environmental problems that other coastal cities and larger countries have. There are some spots of the reefs that have turned white (coral bleaching) but it is not very extreme. Most the damaged reefs are near the larger cities of Tahiti. There are organizations that educate the farmers in the villages that what we put in the river directly affects our reefs near the river mouths. We are trying very hard to become more organic in our farming practices, too. In the next three years we want the entire country to be organic and the farmers are being educated on the negative effects of pesticides. We are also lucky we don't have the big hotels like Waikiki and other major tourist cities around the world.

Tom Servais

Photo Duffy Healey

Q. As an experienced photographer around the world, what is the most significant change regarding the ocean you have noticed in the last few decades?

A. I've noticed the depletion of coastal water quality especially in our coastlines of Southern California. Some of my concerns are for the new generation of surfers who will never know how clear and clean our waters use to be. The key is educating the youth about the significance of understanding coastal issues. It's easy to get involved and now is time for this generation to push the envelope about ocean awareness. The ocean is resilient and we owe it to the future. Let's quit looking the other way, and lead by example. Even with the little things like bringing your own bags to the grocery store, leaving extra bags in the car, and picking up someone else's plastic on the beach. It all matters, it makes a difference.

> Tom Servais is a master surf photographer. Since the mid 1970's, Tom has captured some of the pinnacle moments of the sport, and has earned one of the best wave action portfolios of Fiji and Tahiti in the industry. www.tomservais.com

Peter "PT" Townend

Q. If you could sum up your thoughts on the ocean what would you say?

A. The ocean has been a part of my life since infancy in the fifties. Growing up in a town like Coolangatta, Australia where you have these great white-sand beaches, year round tropical water and great waves, you can't help but end up at the beach. My parents were beach people, my dad was a "Clubbie" (volunteer lifeguard) and my grandparents owned the Coolangatta Hotel dead center on Coolangatta Beach, so it was just natural I ended loving the ocean which ultimately lead to my career in surfing.

Learning to catch a wave and getting a great ride, get's you hooked, that feeling or thrill never goes away. You always believe you will get a better wave and better ride tomorrow. That's what's so great about surfing, no two rides can ever be the same, it's like being a musician in the ocean, you just try to hit the right notes and your instrument is your surfboard or like an artist where every wave is a blank canvas to paint on.

Because the ocean has given so much to me, I feel the motivation to speak up on its behalf. There are many things that ail the ocean and we need to take better care of the ocean that takes care of us. Don't take the ocean for granted, it's one of our greatest resources, it provides us with pleasure and feeds us too.

> Peter "PT" Townend is an Australian. He was the first world champion pro surfer in 1976. He is a consultant, coach, event announcer, publisher and is an outstanding promoter for the sport of surfing. He was inducted into the international surfing hall of fame.
>
> www.theactivempire.com

Fernando Aguerre

Q. You are such a busy person yet you give so much of your time to environmental causes, clearly you don't need the money or publicity, so what is the driving force behind why you do what you do?

A. I'm a firm believer that a better world is achievable if we all become involved in making it happen. Even if at times we feel alone, I'm convinced it's a battle worth fighting. It gives meaning to one's life. Once my grandmother Lucia told me: "It's better to give than to receive" and toward the end of her life, "If you want to bring me flowers, do it while I'm alive, I won't be able to smell them after I die." Unless you give, you are really poor, regardless of your wealth, and the time to do it is always now. I can assure you without doubt, that doing the right thing is positively addictive and life enhancing.

Q. What does the ocean mean to you and what is the largest area of concern for you regarding the ocean?

A. The ocean is the place where life in this world originated. The ocean gives balance to our earth. It's very clear that we are increasingly destroying the oceans and the lives that they contain. We are turning the oceans into lifeless sewers. We can do much better, if we want to. Everyone can help from the amount of times you flush your toilet, to what you throw down your sinks. Most importantly, become a spokesperson for the voiceless oceans every day of your life.

I believe that most inhabitants of the world are blind to the environment. A very small but growing group understands the matter and is changing in an inspiring way. However, the forces of destruction, greatly added by the corrupting power of business, aided by the easily corruptible political establishment and the quiet denial of most of the media scare the life out of me for the future world we are going to deliver to our children.

Q. You also love books. Are there any books in particular that you would like to recommend to people in general and specifically any environmental ones, or movies, or informative websites you can share?

A. I highly recommend two movies I recently saw: "Food Inc" and "The World According to Monsanto". They are wake up calls to how our lives really are. Books are a great piece to add on to what you learn in the real world. I love books about history, politics, philosophy, most importantly, books that inspire me to continue to believe in the hope of a better world. I love to read what was said and done by the people that made a difference, be that Mandela or Biko, Ghandi, King, Guevara or Buddha. I don't believe in wars of aggression or invasions to impose one's lifestyle on others. I'm working on my own book, wrapping up my first 50 years of life, and what I learned by living in the USA after spending the first half of my life in Argentina. The tentative title: "Surf, Girls and Sandals, The Latin art of mixing business and pleasure." The world needs more understanding, more reaching out, more hugs, and certainly less "owners" of the truth. Everyone of us are able to be part of the solution.understanding, more reaching out, more hugs, and certainly less "owners" of the truth.

Born and raised in the coastal city of Mar del Plata, Argentina, Fernando Aguerre and brother Santiago founded surf brand Reef, which later sold. He has been very active in promoting the sport of surfing. He is the President of the IOC recognized International Surfing Association (ISA), the President of the SIMA Humanitarian Fund, board member of Save the Waves, founder of Surfrider Foundation Argentina, and a member of the Senior Advisory board for the Surf Industry Manufacturers Association (SIMA). He is a true pioneer in the surf industry.

www.savethewaves.org

Karina Petroni

Q. What is it about sharks that makes you want to protect them so much, and how did you get involved with the sharks to begin with?

A. Since as long as we can remember sharks have always been viewed as such fierce creatures, and being a surfer and having your office as the ocean, you are constantly thinking you could be potential lunch to a shark, but in all actuality, sharks aren't all that into munching on humans. Sharks are some of the most incredibly interesting creatures in the ocean. And after becoming aware on the brutality that was going on especially with "shark fin soup," I became involved with a group of fascinating people that were putting together a movie called *Shark Water* and was invited to do some free diving with sharks and was completely humbled and in awe of how amazing these creatures really are.

Q. What are your "pet peeves" about the ocean and its flaws, and what can people do to help?

A. It's baffling on how much we rely on the ocean for all its amazing resources it is constantly offering us. It's the largest creation on the planet and to think that the earth is nearly 75% water very similar to our own bodies we live in every day, we must do everything in our power to conserve it as well as the amazing creatures in it, with the simplest things. Whenever you spot something that doesn't belong in the ocean think about what you could do to prevent it from going into the ocean, pick it up and throw it away.

Q. A lot of people look up to you as a professional surfer, activist and model. Who are your environmental heroes? And why?

A. My environmental hero is anybody who applies themself to make a conscious effort to keep the earth as beautiful as we can, whether your making monumental changes or picking up garbage off your hometown beach, it's all about the heart. Somebody that I really admire, that I'm so fortunate to call a friend, is Dave Rastovich. I have had the pleasure to work alongside him on amazing projects; he is a wonderful person inside and out and one day I hope I can be a female version of him.

Karina Petroni is a professional female surfer, model, and a spokesperson for Oceana. *She was featured in* The Fear, Shark Week *and supports and promotes the importance of sharks.*

www.karinapetroni.com

Greg MacGillivray

Q. You have produced so many films starting with surfing films four decades ago and have produced dozens of other IMAX films, including films nominated for Academy Awards such as The *Living Sea* and other ocean related films like *Dolphins and Coral Reef Adventure*; what is the most profound thing you have learned about the ocean as a direct result of your filmmaking on the ocean?

A. I've learned that even though oceans can seem like these gigantic bodies of water with an infinite amount of life and abundance, they are actually a series of fragile ecosystems—from the shallow and deep water coral reefs to the open blue water where the larger animals live—that are being profoundly impacted by human behavior. In fact, we are changing the very make-up of our oceans. I have personally seen the ocean change over time at the beach right outside my home in Laguna Beach. I've grown more and more alarmed over the years to see how much the oceans are being depleted without any real public understanding or outcry over what is happening, or what is at stake. For some fisheries, we are on the brink of reaching a point of no return, where we might wipe out entire fisheries simply for short-term economic gain. Fortunately, there are positive signs of changes being made in our laws that give greater protection to the ocean environments that need it most. So I have hope that before it's too late we'll take the necessary action and save our ocean environments and allow them to flourish once again. My films are about trying to increase public awareness of our oceans and what we stand to lose if we don't take more action now.

Q. Most of your films seem to have an underlying environmental message of both need and hope. Can you please simplify the message you are trying to relay to the audience in the following films?

A. *The Living Sea*—The film uses a series of unique and stunningly beautiful images to show the beauty of unspoiled, healthy oceans and celebrate ocean life and its diversity. The film isn't overtly critical of humankind's use of the ocean. I felt the message would be more powerfully felt if the audience was allowed to draw its own conclusions about how fragile the global ocean system is, and why we must protect it.

Dolphins—This film is about the joy of ocean science and about the dedication of researchers who spend their whole lives studying specific ocean life—in this case dolphins and their communication—to give us a better understanding of our world oceans as a whole.

Coral Reef Adventure—This film celebrates the amazing panoply of life found in the coral reefs of the world and the symbiotic behaviors of its many creatures. At the same time, the film more overtly shows the adverse effects of human behavior on these fragile ecosystems. In the film you see dying reefs as well as healthy ones. We're trying to raise awareness about the realities of our actions and how they are impacting life in the oceans.

To The Arctic—This film will explore the extreme ocean environments of the Arctic, and the effects of climate change which is rapidly changing the environment there. There is such an abundance of life in the Arctic, even in such harsh conditions. As with *The Living Sea*, we want to let the beauty and diversity of the Arctic oceans speak for themselves, hopefully impressing on viewers all that we have at stake if we don't address global climate change now.

Q. Are there any other topics of concern regarding the ocean that you would eventually like to produce a film on, and if so what concerns you the most, and what message would you like to deliver to the audience?

A. I'm interested in exploring the idea of "one world ocean"—the idea that all our world oceans are interconnected and in fact part of the same thing. I think we need to raise the public profile of the oceans, not only their importance to the survival of all life that lives within them, but their importance to our survival and health as humans. We depend on the ocean in so many ways, for producing most of our planet's oxygen, for absorbing carbon dioxide, for much of the food we eat. I want to make a film that imparts this to the audience in a new and powerful way.

Q. Do you have any words to live by, or any final quotes you would like to share?

A. I have found success, I believe, because I set goals, work very hard to achieve those goals, and always try to do the right thing for everyone concerned—a long term strategy—when faced with a problem and decision. Honesty plays a big part in this strategy—you have to be honest with yourself as well as with others.

Greg MacGillivray is a legendary filmmaker and the largest film producer/distributor of IMAX films. Two time Academy Award *nominee for Best Director with 40 years of filmmaking experience, MacGillivry is able to deliver key environmental messages to people of all ages. Films include: The* Living Sea, Coral Reef Adventure, Dolphins, Everest *and many more.*

www.macfreefilms.com

"nakiphoto 2009
EL SALVADOR"

Donovan Frankenreiter

Q. Is there one particular ocean issue that speaks to you the most that motivates you to want to help, and if so what is it?

A. Everything about the ocean speaks loud and clear to me but one thing in particular is "keeping the oceans blue," keeping them clean inside and out and trying to educate people on the dangers in the water that we need to start cleaning up. One good example of that is the "pacific gyre." A huge "garbage patch" of plastics and debris that have been collecting in this one spot in the north pacific that is causing some serious harm to the marine life in that area.

Q. What does the ocean mean to you?

A. The ocean means everything to me. It is the planet's main life line, without a clean ocean all living creatures would die. Being around the ocean has taught me so much about life and how we are all connected as one, no matter where you are in the world, the ocean connects us all.

Q. What is the largest problem affecting the ocean, and what do you think can be done about it?

A. The largest problem I see is the lack of education. It is really important that all people are educated about their impact on the ocean whether they live on the beach or in the middle of the country. They must know that all water makes its way to the beach one way or another, so what is dumped in rivers and streams and all the waterways is a huge factor of what ends up in the oceans and on the beaches of the world.

Q. Do you have any favorite quotes you would like to share?

A. "When the power of love overcomes the love of power, the world will know peace" - Jimi Hendrix

Donovan Frankenreiter, musician and pro surfer supports many ocean charities.

www.donavonf.com

Slater Jewell-Kemker

Q. You participated in the Youth Environmental Summit in Kobe Japan, and you stated there were kids from many countries and what was shocking to you was the fact that so many of these kids were worried about the garbage their respective countries are creating in our consumerist societies. Can you elaborate on this?

A. In May 2008, I was one of several representatives of Canada at the *Youth Environmental G8 Summit*, in Kobe, Japan. Obviously, when you have delegates from around the world, you are bound to have varying problems: rising sea levels, deforestation, pollution, etc. But one of the similarities most of us shared was trash. Not very exciting, but the truth. Our societies are becoming increasingly reliant on the magic land of "away" to hold our garbage; "away" allows us to continue our consumerist lifestyles and not worry about the after effects. The environmental the movement is making it clear that our lifestyle must change quickly. Even though we're aware of the harm to people and our ecosystems that garbage is having, we continue to get that new car, that new computer, more and more plastic items, and we just "throw away" the excess. One delegate from Italy was telling me of the piles and piles of garbage stacked several feet high lining the streets of Naples because all the landfills were full. Even in my local community, the landfill is closing this year. Our beaches are filled with plastic pollution. Some of this waste ends up on beaches thousands of miles away or just floating in the ocean where birds and marine life proceed to eat or give their young plastic bags, small toys and bits of garbage mistaken for food. Seeing as the plastic can't break down, it eventually fills up or lines their stomachs, starving them to death. Other times marine life will mistake plastic bags for jellyfish, lighters for small fish, etc. Our garbage also ends up in the world's largest landfill, the Great Pacific Garbage Patch, a mass of garbage estimated to be twice the size of Texas. This embarrassment is a disgrace, but it's hardly spoken of, because it, too, inhabits that magical land of away. Too many times humans will not address problems because they can't see them. Just because we can't see our floating landfill estimated to contain 3.5 million tons of trash, doesn't mean it isn't there, It's growing every day. We need to start breaking our habit of buying without thinking, of throwing away without thinking, of our lifestyle of non thinking. Our actions, however small, led us into this very large problem of over-consumerism, which is killing our co-habitants of the planet.

Q. What is the biggest environmental issue you're facing in Canada in your opinion?

A. Canada is experiencing deforestation, mining, pollution and a warming Arctic. But the issue I want to talk about is dirty oil. Canada is harboring the largest industrial project on earth, and one of the biggest crimes against the environment: the highly profitable Tar Sands. The oil sands underlie 140,800 km2 of Alberta (roughly the size of Florida). Thousands of acres of boreal forest have been cut down and the soil ripped apart to access bitumen; sand and clay mixed with oil. The refining process for this thick, almost molasses like sand requires four barrels of fresh water for every barrel of oil. The toxic sludge that is the product of this refining is then dumped into the tailing ponds, the only other thing visible from space apart from the Great Wall of China. Measuring 130 km2, with 200 million litres produced every day, the toxic water will lie there, poisoning water tables and any unfortunate creature that happens to fly into it, for thousands of years. The reclamation of tailings lakes has never been demonstrated. (Information from the Pembina Institute) When I moved up to Canada from the States seven years ago, I had never heard of the Tar Sands, never heard of the indigenous families being taken advantage of, how living by the Athabasca River, which is being fouled by the oil sands industry, was causing indigenous communities living downstream of the oil sands to experience

Slater and Jean-Michel Cousteau off Catalina Island   Photo Wendy Milette

unusually high levels of cancer and rare diseases. When I first heard of the oil sands, I was thinking they couldn't be as bad as that. Then again, the reassuring information I was getting from my relatives that worked for the oil sands was covering up some major injustices going on, to people and to the land. My first uncensored look at the Tar Sands took place a few years ago. At the time I was working on a short film about the environment and our need to act now. I contacted the Pembina Institute in Alberta and Greenpeace, and they graciously sent me footage of the Tar Sands, deforestation and other environmental calamities. I couldn't believe what I saw. I couldn't believe that Albertans would approve of such utter destruction, such devastation. It looked like the moon, an oozing, death soaked image of the moon. I freaked out when I learned that they weren't being shut down immediately. But being the No.2 producer of bitumen has its advantages . . . and padding. Our current Prime Minister is a strong supporter of the Tar Sands, and it was revealed at the Copenhagen Climate Change Conference that he intends to expand, not shut down, or even cut back, oil production in Alberta. It's very easy to point the finger at other countries and proclaim them environmental monsters. But in our own backyard, we're destroying our home, we're destroying any hope of a green home for our children when we continue to practice such horrific and devastating practices.

In Copenhagen alongside one of many globes showing two possible paths   Photo Wendy Jewell

Q. As a teenage filmmaker, you have already interviewed some very prominent people, who have you interviewed, and what is the most important thing you have learned so far in doing so?

A. I first interviewed peace activist Ron Kovic when I was only five. Most of the interviews I've conducted would not have been possible without the help of the *My Hero Project*, that I've worked for all my life. I've also interviewed the likes of Jean-Michel Cousteau, Congresswoman Jackie Speier, Robert F. Kennedy Jr., Louie Psihoyos, Peter Jackson, Alexandra and Philippe Cousteau, Leonardo DiCaprio, United Nations Ambassador Chowdhury, Environment Minister John Baird, Mayor David Miller of Toronto, and numerous youth environmentalists such as Emily Hunter, a fantastic young environmental journalist. Interviewing celebrities, activists and politicians at such a young age, has given me the confidence to not be afraid to speak out and contact the leaders that are making a difference. I'm proud I can then take their message and distribute it among the youth, to inform and inspire them. I think the impact on my life has been huge. It's given me the feeling of being part of a large community, and that I have the right to contact and talk with even the higher ups making decisions. I think it's important for kids to realize they can contact the people who inspire them and the leaders of our world. Sometimes we forget we have that great power to question.

Q. Do you have any last thoughts to share?

A. We live in a world of awesome creatures, amazing landscapes and brilliantly diverse ecosystems, a world of breathtaking beauty. Now, more than ever, we have to fight to keep our blue planet safe from ourselves. We hear every day of animals going extinct, of humans driven from their homes from freak weather, of another scar created on our planet's surface. We know the time to act is now, we know we have to drastically change our individual lifestyles and societies to move forward into a green, sustainable world. There are many out there against this change, who would take profit over the welfare of future generations and their right to a beautiful earth, to a legacy we would be proud to leave them. We, as a species, as children, need to remember that we have the power to create change. We have so much potential. We are standing at a crossroads, one road is the path well worn, the business as usual way of thinking which just isn't going to cut it. The other path is new, scary even, but this path will lead us to a new society that embraces our planet and recognizes that we must live in harmony with it.

Chris Jordan

Q. How did you get involved in your art?

A. The art came to me when I left my corporate lawyer career. I was always interested in photography although I really had no interest in the environment. I just love taking good pictures with composition, which is called formalism. So one day, during my "formalist" project, I took a big picture of a giant pile of garbage I found down in the industrial part of Seattle. After I photographed it, I thought it was the best photography I had ever done, not because I had any interest in consumerism, just because it was beautiful. It was very complex and made up of very small colors which fit with the color series I was working with at the time. So I made a big print of it, and hung it in my studio. Then all my friends would come over and start talking about consumerism. But that was annoying to me because they were misinterpreting my work. Eventually my friends and I would end up in conversations about mass over-consumption. They said I made a relevant photograph, even if it was by good luck. So I went back to these industrial places and began making photographs of these piles of our detritus of mass consumption, while at the same time I was researching and reading about consumerism. I learned with astonishment that this a massive, incredibly, frightening and pervasive issue that has been sitting right in front of my nose my entire adult life. It now was having a profound effect on my own life. It's the over consumption that is typical of Americans who focus on the accumulation of material things as a way to find happiness.

Q. What is the main goal you are trying to convey through your art and your speeches?

A. Well, that process has evolved a lot. For awhile I became more of an advocate for the environment. In some ways, I was appropriated by the green movement as a green artist. Then I started making this argument about how everyone matters, and every vote counts, and every plastic bottle we serve isn't a good thing, and I realized after awhile that there is a lot of irony and possible hypocracy in that view point. I also began to realize that I really didn't buy it myself.

The cause of action behind my work is not really so much an environmentalist, like "we must recycle every bottle, and save every sheet of paper," kind of thing. I'm more interested in facing these issues and making people just stop for a second. I'm trying to raise some questions which I have no idea what the answers are, but I look at the issue of whether each one of us matters; do I matter in this huge and complex world I live in? Do I really matter? And if I believe I don't matter, then what about my responsibility as a citizen? Because in my own view, and probably millions of other people too, I'm too small to matter, and why bother making a big sacrifice in my lifestyle because it is not going to make a difference. For example, we all get defensive, which is the fundamental philosophical conundrum which the green movement faces. Each of us have a feeling that we don't actually matter, but we also each have the knowledge that if we all act as if we do matter, and we all can get our act together, then it will all make an enormous difference.

Everybody is waiting for everyone else to do it, and we all already know what to do. We all have our top ten lists which are being printed up everywhere now. Like pump up your car tires, but all these things that are fundamental, meaningless gestures, are all good things to do, and the world is a better place if we all do them. What needs to happen are huge policy changes in our government and our corporations. And so, individuals, can't solve this problem even if we want too. The problems arose collectively but the collective actions of hundreds of millions of people, that's how the problems will be solved, if they can be. But how we go about orchestrating collective actions of hundreds of millions of people remains to be unseen, but I have a feeling that mass communication devices: Internet, Twittter, Facebook, and all those tools will be instrumental in this process.

Chris Jordan was once a corporate lawyer, now a Seattle based artist who photographs garbage bringing awareness of the world's problem of consumerism. Jordan exhibits arresting views of what Western culture looks like via his supersized images portraying unimaginable statistics-like the number of paper cups, cell phones and objects we discard or use every day. Jordan exhibits his art worldwide and is a renowned speaker.

www.chrisjordan.com

Q'orianka Kilcher

Q. Is there any particular ocean issue that speaks to you the most, and if so what is it and how are you involved in creating solutions?

A. A dear friend of mine Dixie Belcher from Turning The Tides, a small grassroots organization in Juneau, Alaska, recently told me about oceans of plastics, and how hundreds of thousands of birds, fish, and marine reptiles and mammals die each year from eating plastic bags mistaken for food. Alaska is thousands of miles away from plastic bags made in China, thousands of miles away from chemical ocean dumps somewhere, who knows where, and thousands of miles away from a million other devastating environmental issues. But this is one planet, we are connected by oceans, air and foreign trade. Migrating birds and fish do not care about borders, rain clouds, rivers and oceans do not know boundaries. There is an absolute beautiful interdependence and connection between the oceans, the earth, the air, the plants, the animals, forests and all living things, including us. What happens thousands of miles away, while we comfortably indulge in cheap, disposable products, made by somebody else's cheap labor? It will ultimately be affecting all of us in some way, regardless where we live.

There are many causes of ocean pollution, from toxic chemical and nuclear storage dumps to the seemingly harmless plastic shopping bag. The problem is huge! And this problem runs deep! All the way to the depths of the ocean, and all the way up the food chain. This problem is not confined within borders! The ocean covers 71% of the Earth's surface and supplies up to 85% of the world's oxygen and nitrogen.

While reading through TTT's website I learned some shocking facts and figures: The world consumes almost 1 million plastic bags per minute. The U.S. consumes 100 billion plastic shopping bags annually, and is throwing them away at an estimated 8 billion pounds every year. Only 5% of all plastics are recycled; 40% end up in landfills; 55% are unaccounted for which means that the majority of plastics end up in unknown locations, unknown locations like the ocean.

Plastic bags layer huge parts of the ocean floor, choking all ocean life. They are mistaken as food by hundreds of thousands of birds, fish and marine reptiles and mammals who ingest plastic bags and microscopic plastic bits and die, only to be eaten themselves by yet another animal, passing the toxins up the food chain. Some of these marine animals contain so much of these plastic toxins that they can legally be classified as toxic dumps. This problem clearly is not confined within regions or species. Sooner or later poisoned water and soil affects the entire food chain. Toxic molecules from plastics are now found in human breast milk, as well as the blood of babies, children and adults.

There is no quick fix. The challenge with plastic waste found littered and dumped all over the world is that this problem will not just go away. Plastic does not biodegrade. It breaks down into smaller but persistent particles. So recycling or cleaning it up will only do so much. The problem runs deeper than landfills, contaminated oceans and beaches or even recycling. It is rooted so deep that we have to take an honest look at our culture, our habits, our laws, and our lifestyle.

The key is to stop the problem at the source, right at the production level with the irresponsible over-use of these toxic plastic materials. We can't continue to indulge ourselves in the extravagant and irresponsible use of plastic bottles, plastic bags, Tupperware, or the millions of other disposable plastic products, and then expect a simple solution like a mad diet-pill we can swallow, while continuing our over consumption and negligence. With great privilege, comes great responsibility, and we have been negligent.

Q. You have done a lot of work in the rainforest conservation movement; do you see a direct connection between the state of the world's oceans and that of the rainforest? And if so please explain.

A. I do see a clear connection. Pressing environmental issues facing our world today are directly connected to our disconnectedness to nature itself. In the name of development, profit and greed, we have not only become the leaders of environmental destruction but have come to see our relationship with nature as an obstacle rather than a necessity. To me, this is one of the main problems, and a sign of the fact that somehow we have chosen to disregard that there is an absolute beautiful interdependence and connection between the oceans, the earth, the air, the plants, the animals, the forests and all living things, including us. Also, I see a clear connection between globalization and pressing environmental issues, and I believe that it is up to us to ensure that the environment and all living things don't suffer because of politics and greed. We cannot eat, drink or breath money or profits. We have to realize that we are all interconnected and what happens thousands of miles away . . . while we comfortably indulge in our consumer attitude, will ultimately be affecting all of us in some way, regardless of where we live . . . because, environmental issues are NOT confined within borders!

In these times of information and technology, we have the power of knowledge and should be able to look back in history and really see what's worked and what hasn't worked. We need to learn from our past so we don't repeat the same mistakes. We all have one common need as inhabitants of this beautiful planet. A clean healthy environment. The abundant fragile biodiversity of our world's oceans and rainforest are quickly being exploited to the point of extinction of certain plants and animals, and, because our world has such a fragile balance, the loss or extinction leads to another and it becomes quickly like a game of dominoes. We must rise up to the challenges of not only today but tomorrow and ensure a future for all unborn generations. It's not too late yet, but we need to start having a shift in our human consciousness.

Q. What can we learn from Indigenous cultures and ways of life in this struggle to protect and preserve the natural world?

A. We all are here today as the result of our ancestor's prayers offered for the survival of our nations. Taking care and respecting our earth, our oceans and the air we breathe is of global importance to all of humanity. Traditionally indigenous peoples around the world live in harmony with mother earth and their lifestyles are based on environmentally sustainable principles and practices, without exploiting and destroying their children's future. Therefore, indigenous people's wisdom, knowledge and way of life has absolute contemporary relevance to modern society.

Q. How would you inspire and/or suggest other members of your generation to become involved in protecting the earth?

A. As a young person I feel it is my gift and blessing to be able to use my youth rebellion in a positive way. We need to be rebellious against failure!!! Getting involved and defending our environment can be super fun and inspiring. We can't expect the people who caused the problems to fix them. Sure, sometimes it is easy to feel overwhelmed by the seemingly endless assortments of environmental and social injustice in this world. Many times we can feel unsure what exactly it is we as individuals can really do to contribute. But there are so many incredible every day heroes within our communities who we can learn from and we can follow in their footsteps and support their legacy through our own actions. There are so many amazing organizations we can join and last but not least there are so many initiatives all of us can take. Positive change starts inside ourselves, our hearts and minds as well as in our own actions.

We all need to contribute to a climate change and shift in human consciousness and be part of the global warming of hearts.

Born in Schweigmatt, Germany, Quorianka Kilcher emerged into the front ranks of young actors best known for her role in Pocahontas *and* The New World *with Colin Farrell. She launched her own youth driven human rights and environmental organization on-Q initiative, heading off campaigns to connect young Hollywood with youth activist leaders and projects from around the world, in support of environmental sustainability, corporate accountability, basic human rights and universal dignity and compassion in all its forms.*

www.QonQ.org

Ric O'Barry

Q. You were once famous for training the dolphins used for the popular TV series, Flipper in the 1960s. Over the past 40 years, you have since become most well known for freeing dolphins from captivity and for continually risking your life to speak out and take action against dolphinariums and aquariums that 'showcase' dolphins. When did this shift occur, and why it is cruel to keep these animals in captivity?

A. The shift occurred in 1970 when Flipper died in my arms at the Miami Seaquarium. For a long time before she died, I knew that dolphins did not belong in captivity, but I didn't do anything about it. The entire dolphin captivity industry is based on deception and, as a dolphin trainer, one must go along with it. You lie to the public, to the media and you lie to yourself everyday. Captivity is extremely stressful for animals that are free-ranging, whose primary sense is sound. We are talking about a sonic creature confined to life in a concrete box! This grim reality has been covered up by this industry for so long. Watching dolphins doing silly tricks does not translate into education. Most dolphins born into captivity have never even seen a live fish! They do not know the natural rhythms of the ocean, the tides and currents, their natural environment, nor can they ever be released into the wild and that is sad.

Q. Can you explain why this practice occurs, and the impact that it has had on the local community of Taiji, Japan?

A. Dolphin captures are the economic underpinning of the slaughter in Taiji. One dolphin sold into captivity can generate as much as $154,000. A dead dolphin is only worth $500 which is sold to be eaten. However, the people of Japan really do not know what is going on there, and therefore are not guilty; it is the government that needs to be held accountable for its actions. The Japanese people simply do not have the information that we take for granted, but one can not argue the facts about mercury poisoning. Once the public knows that the dolphin meat is contaminated with mercury, it is a human rights issue and the Japanese people have the right to know, which has been denied by the media up until now. Dolphin meat has higher levels of mercury than the fish that caused the Minamata poisoning!

Q. You have recently been involved in the award winning documentary film, The Cove, which exposes the annual slaughter of dolphins and cetaceans, do you see this issue coming to an end in your lifetime, and how can the average person help?

A. Yes, it takes films like The Cove and the international media getting behind it. The Cove will do what the Japanese media failed to do: inform the Japanese public. The world association of zoos and aquariums also have to get involved and start policing their own industry and get their dolphin trainers out of places like Japan, Cuba, and the Solomon Islands if this industry is to be shut down once and for all. These Japanese dolphins are currently being exported to China, Mexico, Turkey, and Philippines. The United States is no longer importing dolphins that were not caught in a humane way. This is a step in the right direction; however, we have much more work to do on the worldwide front.

If you really love dolphins do not buy a ticket to a performing dolphin show where they have to perform just to be fed. It's simple, it is based on supply and demand and If consumers will stop buying tickets then the problem will go away. The zoo and aquarium and dolphin industry is a 2 billion dollar a year industry in the U.S. alone. It is all profit however. Consumers can in fact make a difference by voting with their wallets. Also, sign petitions, and go to the website to learn more.

Rick O'Barry is best known from the 1960s TV series Flipper. *After years of training dolphins in captivity, Mr. O'Barry realized it was cruel to take dolphins out of their natural environment for entertainment and financial purposes. In 1970, Mr. O'Barry founded* Dolphin Project *which is dedicated to abolishing the billion-dollar dolphin slave trade. He is also the Director of* Save Japan Dolphins *coalition. He is the lead character in the Oscar award winning movie* The Cove.

www.savejapandolphins.com • www.dolphinproject.org

Lincoln O'Barry

Q. Your Dad, Ric O'Barry, is perhaps the single most effective and renown dolphin activist in the world. How has his example lead you to become directly involved in this work and mission? At what point did you make the conscious decision to "follow in his footsteps" or was this path something that has been innately ingrained in you and/or a part of your life since day one?

A. For the first couple years of my life, we actually had dolphins right at our house. Liberty and Florida were two dolphins that my dad bought from a roadside dolphin attraction in the Florida Everglades. We had a couple of trailers next to a fenced-in lagoon. President Nixon was our next door neighbor. This is where dad first started developing a method for the re-adaption and release of dolphins back into the wild. At age four is when I first went to Taiji, Japan. Working with my dad on the dolphin trail is just something that has always been in my blood. I think dolphins have a greater capacity to understand and process information than humans do. They have a sonar that is dramatically better than anything humans have. They are perfectly adapted for their environment, more so than any other animal. They are also self aware. When dolphins look in a mirror, they understand what they are seeing. There are many places in the world where wild pods and lone dolphins actually seek out interactionswith people. This is the most pure form of inter species communication.

Ramon Cardena and Judith Pascual

Q. What are the largest concerns for the oceans in regard to Spain specifically, and what solutions can you offer to possibly help alleviate the problem?

A. Over-fishing by the Spanish fleet around the world is one of the most serious problems for the oceans today. Reducing the fleets overcapacity and the immediate conversion are essential to address this serious problem. It should discourage the sector and promote immediate conversion to bring the true economic value that is the wealth of a healthy ecosystem. It would be a more courageous policy by the creation of more and larger marine protected areas in Spanish territorial waters to regenerate the deteriorating marine environment. This is not a precautionary measure we can consider or not, but the only option left to avoid global collapse of the entire ecosystem. Spanish territory produces coastal degradation due to excessive urban development, growth of fish farms that degrade and pollute the environment in which they are installed, and aggressive fishing gear for local fishermen who have destroyed the rich sea life of the Mediterranean coast.

Q. Could individuals do something to help?

A. The marine ecosystem deserves the same protection as the terrestrial ecosystem. Not eating fish, or reducing the amount of fish you eat can be a small action, but overall is a great relief to one of the most fragile and vulnerable environments that are essential to life on this planet.

Q. If you could send a message to the people of the world about our shared world oceans, what would you say?

A. We believe in raising awareness worldwide that the problems in the oceans are not local, there is only one ocean that we all share. An oil spill from a foreign company off the Spanish or U.S. coastlines can affect migrating species that in a few months would be off of the Australian or South African coast. The sea is a large interconnected system and thus its protection is a global responsibility for each and every one of us.

Judith Pascual and Ramon Cardena were born and still live near the Mediterranean coast in Spain. They have realized the existing lack of awareness on marine ecosystems and their inhabitants with respect to terrestrial ecosystems. This led them to found the Ocean Sentry organization in order to publicize the plight of the oceans in two of the most spoken languages in the world, English and Spanish. The latest actions of Ocean Sentry are in its contribution to the call for comments in the Fisheries Policy Reform in the EU, its presence in the IWC preparatory meetings, and at the annual meeting as observers, and also to address over-fishing from Spanish fleets.

www.oceansentry.org

Photo Jim Lieber

Captain Kurt Lieber

Q. Can you explain what you do at Ocean Defenders Alliance (ODA), and the damage this ghost gear causes?

A. We remove abandoned fishing gear, otherwise known as "ghost gear." This is a significant problem throughout the world's oceans as this gear continues to kill animals long after it is discarded. Researchers estimate that 10-15% of marine life mortality is caused by this gear every year. The primary way fishing gear becomes abandoned is by the net becoming tangled on a reef, wreck, or rock, and the fisherman has no way of untangling it, so they cut it loose. In California, as long as it does not cause a hazard to navigation, it is completely legal to leave the gear in the water. This needs to be changed by legislation. ODA is in the process of working with other non-profits and state legislators to write a law that addresses this issue. Nets in particular can be devastating. There was an abandoned gill net off of San Pedro, CA that was over two miles long, lying in 100 feet of water. It was still suspended in the water column, rising up about 30 feet from the bottom. There were 21 sea lions, 12 cormorants and 12 pelicans, all dead in that one net alone! This net was over 11,000 feet long. With 90% of the large animals in the ocean gone, that is, killed by man, there is little time left for us to do something to stop this destruction of life.

Q. You have spoke of the dangers and ramifications of using fishing nets, especially monofilament fishing nets. Can you please explain what type of net would be better to use and why if a person is going to use a net? And can you please explain the alternative to nets and why it's better to use hooks and lines?

A. Monofilament nets are made of almost indestructible plastic; they are designed to last for decades. In fact, plastics have only been around for about 100 years, so we really don't know how long these nets and traps will last. Even if the net breaks down into smaller pieces, the small stuff is very toxic to all forms of marine life. Toxins adhere to it and smaller animals ingest it, thinking the plastics are pieces are food. Albatross chicks have been found dead in their nests with their stomachs stuffed with indigestible plastic that their parents had fed to them. Far less destructive is cloth, or better yet, hemp nets. They will degrade over time and not pose a risk to wildlife forever like monofilament nets do. But any net is hazardous to marine life. The netting technique is indiscriminate; it kills anything that swims into it, including whales, dolphins, seals and sharks. Nets have a very significant by-catch rate. Depending on what type of fish is being targeted, the by-catch rate can be as high as 40%, or in the case of netting shrimp, it can be over 80%! By-catch is defined as the amount of fish that are tossed back overboard, dead, because they weren't profitable enough to keep. So that means, for instance, for every two pounds of shrimp that you eat results in eight pounds of dead fish. The responsible way to catch fish is by hook and line. This technique catches just one animal at a time and the fisherman can usually target a particular species of fish by the type of line and tackle he uses. In my opinion though, the best way to treat fish is, don't eat them. I stopped eating fish around 1988. The oceans cannot support humanity's insatiable demand for seafood. At least if everyone cut way back, we'd be better off.

Q. Is there any last thought you would like to share about the ocean that you would like people to know?

A. We need to look at the oceans differently than past generations have. They saw marine life as nothing but a commodity, something to be killed and sold. Many fortunes were made through the destruction of the oceans. The result is a lot of extinct species. There used to be manatees up and down the coast from Mexico to Alaska. They were hunted to extinction. Then walruses were next. If it wasn't for a small population in central California, the sea otters would be gone as well. Otters have a very significant ecological role to play. They eat urchins and abalone. Where the otters have been eliminated, the urchin population has exploded, with disastrous results for the kelp forests. Urchins eat kelp with such ferocity that we have vast expanses of coastline that are devoid of kelp, now known as urchin barrens. When the kelp is gone there is no habitat for the fish that use these forests for protection from predators and to raise their young. It has a domino effect when you eliminate one animal from an intact ecosystem, especially predators.

Ocean Defenders Alliance
www.oceandefenders Photo E. Laul He

If we are to leave a healthy environment for future generations, we have to act now. Jacques Cousteau once lamented that "the oceans are dying." but is not too late to act if we act now. California is in the process of establishing Marine Protected Areas (MPAs). Some of these areas will be "no take zones." There will be no fishing whatsoever in these no take zones. It has been proven that fish populations rebound quickly when given such protections. For example, a no take area that was created off of Scotland had a 700% increase in the lobster population within five years.

Photo Elaine Jobin

I urge everyone that wants to see a brighter future to get involved in doing whatever they can do to save the oceans. Whatever you are good at put it to good use by promoting the oceans. Artists, musicians, writers, scuba divers, boat mechanics and people with fund-raising skills are just some examples of professions that can make a difference by painting, singing, publishing articles, helping out with computer issues, working on non-profit boats and raising money. There are lots of ways to help out - be creative. Humans cannot exist for very long without an intact marine environment.   If the oceans die, so do we.   Let's make a difference, and have fun at the same time!

> *Kurt Lieber operates the* Ocean Defenders Alliance *which strives to make southern California's coastal waters safer for marine wildlife by reducing dangerous man-made objects from vital habitat, focusing on abandoned commercial fishing gear that poses serious threats to numerous species.*
> www.oceandefenders.org

Captain Brett McBride

Photo Mark Frapwell

Q. What is the disposition of the black sea bass and the black sea bass in Mexico?

A. I once saw a black sea bass when I was ten years old in Southern Baja where a 143 big black sea bass were landed in one night through the following morning. Although that sounds exceptional, sights like that were not uncommon. Today, I rarely hear any mention of black sea bass from boats traveling between San Diego and Cabo San Lucas. When they are mentioned, it is usually from a stray diver who sees an individual fish or two. I do see them in certain areas where I know colonies are making a comeback which is encouraging. I think most fishermen and divers are now aware of their plight and do their best to release them unharmed. But they are slow growing and vulnerable, and it wouldńt take too many poachers to do a lot of damage. Southern California has the advantage over Baja in that it is more protected. The black sea bass are becoming a more common sight in Southern California kelp beds.

Q. You once said that the ocean has given you so much all of your life, and it is time for you to give back. Can you elaborate on these feelings?

A. The ocean really has been my entire life. It has been my calling since I was less than 4 years old. There have been very few days in my life where I was not either fishing, diving or surfing. It was a strong enough calling that I knew early on that I was not going to follow the normal path of finishing high school, going to college then getting a job. I started working on boats the summer after sixth grade and knew then that that was what I would always do. I followed my passion and had faith that that would be enough. Íve obviously been very lucky as well. Now that I am older, I see things from a different perspective. I have been able to see the difference in the state of the world's oceans first hand over almost four decades. Coming from a lifestyle that allowed me to see both above and below the surface, I realize my perspective is unique. Now, I notice the things that are not there anymore, are less abundant, or are unhealthy. I feel a sense of obligation to give back. To take care of what has always taken care of me.

> *Brett McBride is the captain of the* MV Ocean. *He began working on fishing boats at age 12 and went on to work on day-charter boats, long-range charter boats, and long-range private yachts. Over the past 14 years, he has fished from Alaska to Central America as a leading member of ESPN's* Offshore Adventures. *Currently, McBride is working with Dr. Michael Domeier, the Executive Director of* The Marine Conservation Science Institute. *Their show* Great White Expedition *is on* National Geographic.
> www.ocearch.org • www.fischerproductions.com

Greg McCormack

Q. Salmon Management seems to be a rather complex subject with various issues that not everyone is aware of. Can you explain several salmon issues that you feel are critical issues of concern?

A. Seeing a salmon complete the final stages of its life cycle will leave an indelible impression on you. Their lives epitomize going against all odds, overcoming major obstacles while attaining super-athlete strength in order to attain the ultimate measure of biological success: Passing genes to progeny. Indeed, watching salmon furiously swim upstream against currents and leaping over cascades, perhaps out of the reach of bear claws or eagle talons, may inspire you to cheer. What makes wild Pacific salmon so fascinating and so difficult to protect is that they inhabit millions of square miles in the North Pacific Ocean between California and the Korean Peninsula. Their pelagic wanderings in search of a shifting prey base bring them to countries with different management strategies. Juveniles and adults frequent estuarine, coastal, river and stream ecosystems from California to Alaska, Beringia and much of East Asia. Salmon are a keystone species, a significant part of the oceanic food web and their nutrient-rich carcasses are valuable to over 100 kinds of vertebrates, including charismatic megafauna such as bears, wolves and eagles. Streamside vegetation also benefits from this marine nutrient subsidy along with invertebrates that feed developing salmon fry. Salmon have been a mainstay of native cultures for thousands of years, are a part of Native American and First Nation cultural and spiritual identity and are an icon for the North Pacific bioregion.

Threats to salmon include habitat destruction or fragmentation, and degradation of the environment, such as agricultural run-off and land development. Over 90% of the original lowland old-growth forests have been cut in the Pacific Northwest. Most of the forestry practices on federal, state, private and tribal lands in the past were abysmal in regards to road building and preserving salmon spawning habitat. Stripped of riparian vegetation, stream temperatures increase, an environmental stressor for wild salmon. Winter storms lead to erosion and the resultant sediment asphyxiates fertilized salmon eggs and developing alevin. Clear-cut timberlands means a reduction in the number of snags, branches and windthrow (trees uprooted or broken by wind) or "course woody debris" in streams. This important structural component disperses stream energy and leads to the creation of gravel bars, oxygenated plunge pools, hiding spots and acts as a nutrient source for aquatic insects (salmon food).

Hatcheries have played a vitally important role in cultivating and breeding a large number of salmon, increasing landings by recreational and commercial fisherman and helping many tribal, and regional economies. There is concern that hatchery fish may compete with their wild ancestors for food resources, transmit disease, and affect the gene pool of the wild stocks.

Q. How have dams impacted Pacific salmon, and will dam removal help restore ecosystem health?

A. Years ago I worked as a ship naturalist onboard a 49-passenger vessel going up and down the Columbia and Snake Rivers. We transited 8 locks and dams to the furthest navigable spot in Lewiston, Idaho, 500 river miles above the Pacific Ocean. The most interesting shore excursion on this week-long voyage is the McNary Dam. Here a series of diversion screens re-direct ocean-bound juvenile salmon or "smolts" through a series of elaborate pipes to a holding tank area. Smolts are injected with PIT tags, tiny identification chips used to monitor returning adults. After hundreds of thousands of fish are collected, they are pumped into a truck or barge. The latter has a water circulation system to help the smolt imprint the olfactory signature of the river, part of their homing instinct. After "hitching" downriver, they are released below the Bonneville Dam, the lowest on the mighty Columbia near Portland, Oregon. The barge delivers 20 million smolts a year, but hasn't proven effective for all fish stocks. There is significant mortality for the smolts that take a dive down a spillway or penstock and spin 90 times a second in electricity generating turbines. Obviously, this leaves them dead, discombobulated, or injured and easy prey for the gulls, terns, northern pikeminnow and pinnipeds lurking in the outflow area. Despite the predators, survival rates increase once smolt are below the dam. Above the dam, the river is a series of current-less reservoirs that slows the out-migration to the ocean where a more consistent and improved diet awaits.

During the 2000s I was employed as a NOAA education specialist. My job led me to an orca whale science symposium. Researchers presented papers on the most-studied whales on Earth, the Southern Resident Killer Whales (SRKW), recently listed as "endangered." The biggest "buzz" came from a presentation on the preferred diet of the 3 family groups (J, K, and L pods) of whales: Chinook salmon are selected more often than other salmonids in the Salish Sea. With low returns in the NW, this preference has SRKW singing "San Francisco Here I Come" where they've been spotted echo-locating on Chinook returning to the Sacramento River. Perhaps a temporary rendezvous since the plummeting chinook fishery there has led to historic closures.

Good news: The largest dam removal and restoration project in U.S. history will begin in 2011 on the Elwha River in Olympic National Park, Washington. Seventy miles of pristine fish habitat will open up for the first time in about 100 years and all 5 species of salmon are expected to return after two dams are removed. Restoration will take many years, but the SRKW sightings should increase! Now if the Obama Administration would look at the removal of the four lower Snake River dams . . .

such as the piscivorous or fish-eating birds and marine mammals.

I've interviewed hundreds of old-timer fisherman at dozens of remote archipelagos while island-hopping from Hawaii to Easter Island, Fiji to Guam, Papua New Guinea to Palau, among other itineraries while working as ship Divemaster. My sub-surface forays leading divers has led me to conclude that our worlds fisheries are in severe decline.

MARINE RESERVES are a type of management tool that helps protect entire marine ecosystems. An analogy will help: Farmers have an agricultural practice that leaves 25% of their fields fallow each year, a deliberate method in which they avoid the intensive use of industrial chemicals and allow the soils to be replenished with nitrogen, the key to fertility in lands. This practice is an investment into the future of the land. We need a new ocean ethic that keeps in mind the investment into the future of marine habitats . . . leaving areas of the ocean untouched for periods of time to allow the possibility for recovery of diminishing commercial fish and shellfish stocks.

A professional naturalist and marine educator, Greg McCormack has explored 69 countries and all seven continents. Fascinated by coastal ecosystems, Greg McCormack has bicycled the entire length of the Americas - 18,350 rugged, adventurous miles from Prudhoe Bay, Alaska to Ushuaia, Argentina. Greg McCormack trained forty marine protected area managers from the Galapagos in Ecuador, and parks in Colombia, Panama, and Costa Rica on sustainable tourism. Some of his favorite dive sites include Caroline Island, Truk Lagoon, Palau, Ras Mohammed, Komodo Island and cold water diving off of the Alaska, British Colombia, and California coasts.

www.gregmccormack.com

Thomas P. Peschak

Q. Why are sharks important?

A. Sharks are one of Mother Nature's great evolutionary success stories. Their blueprint is so near perfect that it has remained almost unchanged for at least 100 million years. Today, more than 440 species of shark roam the world's seas, inhabiting every realm from the shallowest coral reefs to the deepest ocean trenches. Sharks are the lions and tigers of the sea; they throne on the apex of the marine food chain and are crucial to maintain a healthy balance in the ocean. Sharks are the glue that holds many of our marine ecosystems together and their removal sends fishing ripples throughout the ecosystem. We are only beginning to understand the effects of our actions, but we do know that healthy shark populations are vital for the survival of coral reefs in the Caribbean. Sharks regulate reef fish populations, which in turn keep algae-grazing fish populations in check. Too few sharks equals too many reef fish and therefore not enough herbivores to control the algae and seaweed growth on the reef. In the words of Walt Whitman, "When you pull on any string, you find that it is connected to everything else in the universe." By keeping predators of commercially important species in check, sharks can also be essential for healthy fisheries. The reduction of sharks in Chesapeake Bay in the U.S., for example, was a key factor leading to the collapse of the scallop fishery as ray numbers increased in the absence of their principal predators.

Q. How are sharks faring in your home country of South Africa?

A. South Africa manages its shark stocks better than most nations and in 1991 became the first country in the world to protect the Great White Shark. Shark diving is very popular in South Africa and shark tourism brings in more than 30 million U.S. dollars annually. Despite this economic incentive, South Africa has still not banned shark fishing like the island nations of Palau and the Maldives who realize that sharks are worth significantly more alive than dead. South Africa also continues to systemically exterminate sharks under the guise of protecting bathers. A 27-mile-long installation of gill nets that entangle, suffocate and kill sharks has been positioned off the east coast since the early 1960s. In addition to catching so called dangerous sharks, most of the catch is, in fact, made up of harmless species and other marine animals such as rays, dolphins and turtles. A credible alternative to shark nets is the use of shark spotters employed to scan the ocean from high vantage points for any approaching sharks. The system has been successfully used in Cape Town since 2004 and whenever a shark is spotted, a white flag with a shark motive is hoisted and a siren sounded to get people out of the water. For sharks to survive in South Africa's seas in the long term, far more people will need to know and care about the role that they play in the ocean. Who, though, is going to have the drive, commitment and desire to protect an animal that they are convinced is going to eat them the moment they venture into the sea? It is therefore essential to first transform fear into fascination and hate into awe.

Q. What has resulted from our fear of sharks?

A. The fear of sharks unfortunately permeates all levels of society, from young to old and from rich to poor, yet less than 99.99% of interactions between sharks and people result in bites. In 2008, with the world population soaring to 6.7 billion people, there were only 58 shark bites, of which four were fatal. In comparison, approximately 1 million people die in car accidents and 791 are killed by their toasters every year, but we toast our bread and drive our cars without thinking twice about it. Sharks, in fact, have much more to fear from people. Everyday, vast fleets from major shark fishing nations such as Japan, China, Taiwan and Spain comb the world's oceans. There are frighteningly few places left on our planet where sharks are not being overexploited. It is estimated that up to 73 million sharks are killed annually around the world. As a result, 50 species are now listed as vulnerable or in danger of extinction. Sharks are primarily caught for their fins, a sought after commodity for use in shark fin soup. Fins can fetch up to 300 U.S. dollars per pound and are often sliced off while the shark is still alive and the rest of the body is then wastefully dumped at sea.

Q. Why are mangroves important?

A. When many people think of mangroves, they unfortunately envisage malaria-infested swamps full of dangerous and deadly beasts. The mangrove's bad reputation, which dates back to the age of Victorian explorers is tragic because these tidal forests, which effortlessly straddle the realm between land and sea are one of the most important ecosystems to grace our planet. They act as nurseries and are the ocean's kindergarten for many species of fish, mollusks and crustaceans. Without mangroves coral reefs would be shadows of their riotous diverse selves. Mangroves protect against coastal erosion and are our first line of defense against sea level rise as the world witnessed during the

2004 Asian Tsunami. Coastlines with intact and healthy mangroves experienced less natural damage and a lower death toll than areas where they had been cleared. Despite these glaringly vital roles that mangroves play, they are vigorously exploited. Their formidable wood, largely resistant to wet rot and termites is a desirable building material for boats and houses, but the greatest danger to mangroves is coastal development. Their prime sea front location is often a death sentence as large-scale clearing goes hand in hand with the development of tourist infrastructure, shrimp farming ponds and commercial agriculture projects.

Thomas P. Peschak lives in Cape Town, South Africa and is the Chief Photographer of the Save our Seas Foundation. *A former marine biologist, he left science to pursue a life in environmental photojournalism. He has photographed and written three books,* Currents of Contrast, Great White Shark *and* Wild Seas Secret Shores of Africa.

www.saveourseas.com • www.thomaspeschak.com

Tony Hawk

Q. Growing up in San Diego, California, and being surrounded by the ocean, what are some of your favorite things about the ocean? Also what are your least favorite things about it? (ie: is there a particular ocean issue that bothers you the most)?

A. My favorite thing is that it is a massive playground, especially on the shore. I grew up surfing, skim boarding and bodysurfing, so I have always had an appreciation for the waves and how much fun they can be. I also like that the beach can be a great family outing.

My least favorite thing is litter on the sand left behind by irresponsible visitors, and pollution in the water that can actually make you sick. The ocean should be pure, not something toxic.

Q. You have taken a stance on global warming for over five years now. What are some of the simple things people can do to help curb it, and why should they do so?

A. Recycle, drive less and choose greener products whenever possible. We are providing for our kids' kids so we have to be more concerned.

Q. You are a hero to many, but who are your favorite ocean heroes, or organizations, and why?

A. *Surfrider* is the most progressive and effective champion of keeping the ocean clean. I also think Kelly Slater does a good job in using his celebrity status to help raise awareness of ocean issues.

Q. Do you have any favorite relevant quote you would like to share, or words to live by?

A. My dad always told me: "You can enjoy the ocean but you have to respect it"

Tony Hawk was born and raised in San Diego California. By age 16 he became the best skateboarder the world and by far he holds the best record in skateboarding's history. With the creation of the Tony Hawk Foundation*, Hawk also has made an effort to give something back to the sport that has given him so much. Being a skateboarder and surfer, it was ingrained in him to desire to be an advocate for the ocean.*

www.tonyhawk.com

Ken Jordan
The Crystal Method

Q. What is it about Costa Rica that attracts you to the sea there, and what are your favorite things about the ocean in general?

A. I really love the ocean! I scuba dive, snorkel, and have recently started surfing. The ocean has such a calming influence over me, even when I'm just driving up the coast of California, as soon as I see the water I feel better. I was drawn to our spot in Costa Rica (the Mal Pais area) because of its undeveloped beauty. There is amazing surf all the time in our front yard and there's nearby tide pools just meters away. My fiancé and I get down to Costa Rica several times a year, and we never miss a sunset.

Q. Having the opportunity to share your environmental message with so many fans all the time, what are the things you do in regard to that kind of responsibility? (for instance your solar panels etc.).

A. I try to tweet every green event I attend and also share all my eco-experiences online. Working closely with *Green Wave*, I try to be a good "living example." One small thing I do is to try to never drink out of plastic cups or plastic bottles, always using glass or my Klean Kanteen. I think that provides a positive example onstage or on camera without having to preach.

Q. Is there a particular ocean issue that bothers you the most, and if so, what is it, and what can you suggest people do in order to help alleviate the situation?

A. Aside from the obvious global problem of plastics, one of the things I'm helping with is sea turtle conservation awareness in Costa Rica with *Green Wave*. It's an education and protection program. Working with *Rainsong Wildlife Sanctuary* (www.rainsongsanctuary.com), we're helping kids go to school through an eco-scholarship program, in turn they do sea turtle patrols and receive free tutoring. It's a cultural challenge because of the tradition and myths surrounding the eating of turtle eggs, but we are making progress.

Q. Do you have any other thoughts that you would like to share?

A. Rethink first. Then Refuse all possible single use plastics you can, over consumption of these items is preventable. Reuse all goods you can before throwing them out, and always Recycle anything that you cannot Reuse whenever possible!

The Crystal Method *is an American electronic music duo that was created in Los Angeles, California by Ken Jordan and Scott Kirkland in the early 1990s.* The Crystal Method's *music has appeared in numerous TV shows, films, video games, and advertisements. Their best-selling album,* Vegas, *was certified Platinum in 2007. In addition to being one of the best selling electronic bands in the world,* The Crystal Method *is also a dedicated force for environmental good.*

www.thecrystalmethod.com

Jeff Pantukhoff
Whaleman Foundation

Q. Why do you choose to focus most of your efforts on dolphins and whales as opposed to other other issues?

A. The reason why I choose to focus my efforts on saving the dolphins and whales is two-fold. First is that people seem to care much more about saving dolphins and whales than let's say they care about saving tunas, swordfish, krill, sharks, and shrimp . . . you get the picture. The second is that dolphins and whales are the barometer to the overall health of our oceans, so as go the dolphins and whales, so go our oceans, and as go the oceans, so goes all life on earth, so you see, it's really quite simple. If we can save the dolphins and whales, ultimately, we will save the planet and ourselves! So the time to act is now. It's time to save the whales again!

Q. With all that is going on in the ocean what do you think needs to be done, and do you have hope?

A. There is hope because our oceans and the life it contains are very resilient and, believe it or not, I'm optimistic, because we still have time to do this. I believe we have a 10 to 15 year window to make some very necessary changes, but we can do it. As I look out at our oceans today though, and visit some of my favorite places I've been diving over the past 40 years, I can't help but feel a very deep sadness. Many of my favorite coral reefs that were so colorful and full of life just ten years ago are now seemingly devoid of fish and are colorless and covered in silt and thick algae blooms which are virtually choking the very life out of them. Just in my lifetime, over the last 50 years, we have over-fished our oceans to the point that over 90% of the world's large fish are gone. Global warming, which is real, and its devastating effects, which we are now just beginning to understand, has had enormous negative impacts on the ocean. Over 80% of the krill, which forms the basis of the oceans food chain, are gone as a result of warming sea temperatures and loss of the polar icepacks. As our oceans absorb more carbon dioxide and warm up, it's causing a chemical imbalance to the composition of saltwater itself which is called ocean acidification, which is also causing coral reefs to die.

But the problem that to me is the most insidious is that we have poisoned our ocean's food chain from the bottom up with mercury, DDT, Dioxin, fire retardants, and other toxins that do not break down in nature, and they exponentially increase as we move up the food chain so that by the time you reach the level where many species of dolphins and whales feed, they are carrying over one million times the amount of contaminants that are found at the base of the food chain and become the most contaminated animals on the planet. And guess what, we, human beings, eat at this same level in the sea, so ultimately, we are poisoning ourselves and we have to end this vicious cycle.

Pierce Brosnan & Jeff Pantukhoff

First, we need to set up true marine protected areas all around the world that will not allow any commercial exploitation of any kind within their boundaries. Second, we need to create a global whale sanctuary. Third, we have to outlaw the manufacture, sale and and use of certain chemicals including mercury, DTT, Dioxin, PCBs, PDBEs and other toxic chemicals.

Q. Who are your ocean heroes?

A. No one has had a more profound impact on my life than award winning filmmakers and photographers Howard and Michele Hall, not even Jacques Cousteau. Howard and Michele gave me sound, honest and direct advice telling me how to get into the underwater photography business, and what camera, lens and film to use, how to use it, and they told me to just go start shooting. I asked Howard if I could volunteer and he said they didn't take volunteers but only hired dive instructors. I enrolled in dive instructor training the next day, and they changed my life.

I got to work as a member of their camera team on their IMAX 3D film *Into the Deep*. I couldn't believe it. Here I was, getting to work with and learn filmmaking from one of the greatest underwater filmmaking teams in the world. I later found out while working on that shoot, that out of our eight-member dive team, the only other dive instructor on the team was Howard. While filming *Into the Deep* I asked Howard which of the gray whale breeding grounds he thought would be the best one to visit. He replied "For a whale hugger like you, that's easy, go to San Ignacio Lagoon because that is where all the friendly whales are." That was another story that changed my life.

Jeff Pantukhoff & Hayden Panettiere   Photo Lisa Denning

Q. How did it change your life?

A. To make a long story short, it all started in March 1995 when I drove down to San Ignacio Lagoon in Baja, Mexico. I spent five magical days there among the friendly gray whales and the local people who make this place where mountains and desert meet the sea, their home. This trip was life changing on so many levels, from being eye to eye and getting to touch these magnificent gentle giants and their newborn calves, to experiencing one of the most beautiful and virtually untouched places I had ever been. But on my last night there, I was told by one of the local people running the camp that Mitsubishi Corporation and the Mexican government were planning to build the world's largest salt plant right there in the heart of San Ignacio Lagoon. I had an epiphany right there and then and remember saying to myself, "Over my dead body!" and that is where my non-profit organization *The Whaleman Foundation*, was born, right there among the friendly gray whales of San Ignacio Lagoon: Bringing whales and mankind together to preserve and protect our world. Whaleman's mission is to forever protect and preserve dolphins, whales and their ocean habitat.

In thinking of what it was that I could actually do to make the most impact, the thing I remembered most about Jacques Cousteau was how passionate he was about raising awareness to the plight of our oceans and marine life and how he used his films as the vehicle to get that message out. So in March of 1996, I began production of my first film with the intent to help save San Ignacio Lagoon, which was a Whale Sanctuary and a United Nations (UN) World Heritage Site. Not long after that, I was introduced to Pierce Brosnan and his wife Keely Shaye Smith and told them about my film and what I hoped to accomplish. I asked if they would help me. They said yes so in 1997, Pierce and his son Sean traveled to San Ignacio Lagoon to join us in a gathering that included several environmental organizations working on this issue including *The Whaleman Foundation*, the *International Fund for Animal Welfare* (*IFAW*), the *Natural Resources Defense Council* (*NRDC*), and *Mexico's Group of 100*.

In the summer of '98, I sent my completed film *Gray Magic: The Plight of San Ignacio Lagoon* to Dr. Rossler, who shared the film with her colleagues at the UN and the *World Conservation Union* (*IUCN*) and later that year presented and distributed the film to a meeting of the UN in Kyoto, Japan. As a direct result, in 1999, the UN sent an investigative team to San Ignacio and Scammon's Lagoons and met with then Mexican President Ernesto Zedillo. The following year, President Zedillo and his family traveled to the lagoon and nearly five years later to the day that I first found out about the proposed salt plant, President Zedillo announced his government was withdrawing its support for the salt plant and signed an executive order to forever protect San Ignacio Lagoon.

I feel one of the main reasons we were ultimately successful in stopping Mitsubishi from building the world's largest salt plant in San Ignacio Lagoon was because Pierce went to the lagoon with us and personally witnessed its beauty and the amazing encounters with the friendly gray whales there first hand.

Currently, my main focus is on the "Save the Whales Again!" campaign (www.savehtewhalesagain.org), a global media conservation campaign that was officially launched in Hollywood in February 2007

Hayden Panettiere & whales   Photo Juan "Tito" Baldwin

by campaign spokesperson Hayden Panettiere along with several of her Heroe's cast-mates. Joining Hayden as our campaign spokespersons are Pierce and Keely Brosnan, Isabel Lucas, Leonor Varela, Alexandra Paul, Dave Rastovich, and others.

Hayden Panettiere & dolphin   Photo Gene Flipse

Jeff Pantukhoff is not only an award winning underwater photographer and filmmaker, but the founder of The Whaleman Foundation *dedicated to the preservation and protection of cetaceans (dolphins, porpoises and whales) and their habitats. Pantukhoff helped, along with others, to save San Ignacio Lagoon, Baja Mexico's last pristine whale sanctuary from being turned into the world's largest salt plant by Mitsubishi Corporation.*

www.whaleman.org • www.savethewhalesagain.com

Garry Brown

Q. What is Liquefied Natural Gas (LNG) and its potential effects on the ocean?

A. Liquefied Natural Gas, or LNG, is natural gas in its liquid form.   When natural gas is cooled to minus 259° Fahrenheit it becomes a clear, colorless, odorless liquid. Liquefied Natural Gas is neither corrosive nor toxic. When liquefied vastly greater quantities of the gas can be transported more easily than in its natural gaseous form in specially designed insulated ships. Liquefied Natural Gas is imported from countries with large natural gas reserves to many European countries, Japan, South Korea, and the United States. The U.S. has numerous LNG terminals located on the East Coast and in the Gulf of Mexico. Though transporting LNG has experienced an unusually good record of safety throughout the world, a major concern is that these ships and terminals can be targets of terrorism, especially near dense populations. Liquefied Natural Gas when exposed through a spill and a rapid transition in temperature has a great deal of energy generated and a physical explosion can occur impacting humans and buildings for significant distances from the actual point of source. As there have been numerous proposals to locate LNG terminals on the West Coast of the United States, the concern has been does the need for more natural gas balance the added exposure to possible catastrophic consequence of an accident or terrorist attack. It is the opinion of the collective environmental community that it does not. The United States has large natural reserves and LNG is not worth the risk.

Q. What are your thoughts on the ocean?

A. Not only are we polluting and degrading the water quality but also we are causing fish and marine animals population to crash on a worldwide scale. This damage has been caused by the collective activities of mankind. WE are the cause of the problem. We must learn to be the solution in order to reverse this critical course. Our disregard for the health of the oceans must come to an end. Urban runoff from the coastlines of the world is one of the largest sources of pollution. In California alone we allow over 5 billion gallons per day of polluted water to discharge into the Pacific Ocean. With the advent of technological advances in our ability to commercially fish, we are over-fishing the ocean's ability to re-populate. We destroy complete habitats by bottom trawling. We continue to disseminate certain species, such as whales, tuna, swordfish and sharks, for our short-term gain with total disregard for the sustainability of these populations. We have the ability and the knowledge to turn this degradation of our oceans around, but we have to have the collective will to do it. Through education, international agreements, better practices and methods at all levels, and the desire to enforce our agreements, we can change this devastating course of degrading our oceans. The real solution is a worldwide understanding and acknowledgment that we as a people must change our ways to preserve and protect our greatest natural resource—our oceans.

Garry Brown is the Founder, President and Chief Executive Officer of the Orange County Coastkeeper (OCCK). *Garry has in-depth knowledge of marine and water runoff issues as well as water supply issues.*

www.coastkeeper.org

Bonnie Monteleone

Q. When and how did you first come across the topic of plastic in the sea, and how did you get the idea to write your master's thesis about this topic?

A. I started reading Plastic Ocean by Susan Casey and I sincerely lost sleep over it. I read it three times! In the article, she described a snapping turtle that got a plastic milk jug ring stuck around its body mid-shell and it grew around it making its shell the shape of a figure eight. I woke up one night with this image in my head and had to see if I could find a picture of it online. And sure enough, I did. Her name is May West. She is nine years old and lives in Atlanta, Georgia. A week later I found the Algalita Marine Research Foundation online and filled out their volunteer application. Working with chemists in the University of North Carolina, Wilmington, we offered to start an East Coast/West Coast collaboration with Algalita. It was then that I decided to make this the topic for my master's thesis. Currently, we are looking at the plastic samples from both the North Atlantic and the North Pacific gyres and attempting to type the plastics. I continue researching marine animals that suffer from entanglement or plastic ingestion and found hundreds of sites and reports dealing with these issues.

Q. Before travelling to the North Atlantic and the Pacific garbage patch did you have preconceived ideas of what they would be like, and can you describe what you saw?

Photo Dino Ferris

A. I know that when I first read about the North Pacific Garbage Patch, I visualized a smooth ocean like glass and plastic floating on the surface like ducks on a pond. I envisioned we could look out over the ocean and see this plastic debris stretched across the surface for miles. Some people even have told me that they have heard it's like an island twice the size of Texas. Sadly, it is not like that because if it were, we could take pictures of it and send them to every form of mass media there is. But like an iceberg, the bulk of it is mostly below the surface with only a small part of it breaking the surface. For example we found a couple of 55 gallon drums. These plastic drums are about 4' tall and nearly 3' wide. When we saw them in the ocean only a few inches broke the surface making them visible. The visible items were things like bottles with caps still on them, and lots of Styrofoam, many ghost nets, and even toilet seats. So it didn't look like anything I imagined. Not being able to see it until you're on top of it is hard because it impedes any clean up initiative Also, many items out there are navigational hazards.

So the combination of wave action, sun reflection, and only a small portion of the debris breaking the surface makes it difficult to see let alone photograph or video. One person would be driving the boat and the rest of us would be out on the bow shouting out sightings and it always amazed me how much there was.

Q. Would you know of any promising ideas, how this plastic problem could be solved or at least diminished?

A. I like to compare the problem to an overflowing bathtub that has the faucets running. What would you do first? Would you clean up the water on the floor or would you shut off the faucets first and then clean up the mess? That is what we are faced with. Sure we can go out and get it. But the fact of the matter is that it keeps going out there because we haven't figure out a way to educate people on proper disposal and that there is value to much of our plastic. The other thing is to do ocean cleanups closer to shore. For example, the Sargassum in the Atlantic often times forms in windrows. A lot of plastic is found in these windrows. There are websites that can show fisherman where these windrows are (because it's a great place to fish as well). Boats could go out and clean up these windrows that have a lot of plastic debris in them. Sargassum has its own ecosystem where sea life live and feed, so removing plastic may help prevent ingestion and entanglement. New technologies are turning plastic into energy, electricity and fuel. Giving plastic waste value is the resolution to this major environmental problem.

Bonnie Monteleone is a graduate student at University of North Carolina, Wilmington, studying the impact of marine debris in particular PLASTICS in the North Atlantic and North Pacific Gyres. Monteleone's The Plastic Ocean blog covers her two ocean voyages, the North Atlantic & North Pacific Gyre.

www.theplasticocean.blogspot.com

Acknowledgments

Mary Sponholtz
Spontaneous Design
Graphics-Production Director
www.TheSpontaneousGroup.com

Mary, we are so privileged to have you in our lives for so many years. You're very talented and very patient. We love you so much!

Lee Sponholtz
Spontaneous Design
Graphic Designer-Photo Editor
www.TheSpontaneousGroup.com

Lee, you are so wonderful to work with and you are great with color. It has been an honor to work with you.

Andrew M. Barbolla
Author and Creative Arts Instructor
Senior Editor
www.AndrewMBarbolla.com

Andrew, grammarian in chief, thanks for having such a great attitude and for giving all of us the lessons.
You rock! You are also a great author!

Teresa London
Creative Design & Graphics
www.TeresaLondon.com

Teresa, all the marketing and promotional materials you designed were a huge help during our campaign.
Well done!

We would also like to thank our contributing editors who helped introduce us to wonderful people for the book and gave us lots of support along our journey.

William J. Cooper, Ph.D.
Professor of Civil & Environmental Engineering,
Director of the Urban Water Research Center
at University of California, Irvine

We love your energy!

Nancy Christiano
Development Manager, Oceana

A beautiful writer and kind soul. Thanks for the encouragement and your keen ocean mind.

Pierre André Senizergues
Founder / CEO of Sole Technology

Continue to lead, inspire and promote "green equals green" to the business world.

Deborah Bassett
Consultant for Non Profit Organizations

Thanks for your contribution and the ten very important people you worked on.
You are a very talented writer and activist.

Timmy Donnelly
Writer / Producer / Activist

Thanks for the introductions and all your efforts. Keep surfing, and don't loose the positive attitude.

Special Thanks

This book was compiled with the help, love, and support of many people. We could not have done it alone. First of all, we would like to thank Valarie Whiting for introducing us to *Oceana* and involving us in her *SeaChange* committee to help raise funds and awareness for our oceans. Without that as a starting point, we may not have done this book at all.

There are tons of others who were also instrumental as well. We would like to thank Mary Massot a.k.a. Grama Mary (Duffy's mother), for all of her love and support, and of course for babysitting while we have spent the last year and a half compiling this book. We would like to remember Dr. Karen Lundegaard (Elizabeth's mother) also for her inspiration and activism. Karen was an activist all of her life. She paved the way for Duffy and me to follow in her footsteps. We would like to thank Virgil Laul (Elizabeth's father) who passed away from cancer during the making of this book. I enjoyed telling my father about all of the new people we were getting in the book, and some of my best conversations were with him in the hospital listening to his reactions and advice. We would also like to acknowledge Robert Healey Sr. (Duffy's father) for teaching him a good work ethic. We need to say "Muchas Gracias" to Herbert Bedolfe a.k.a. Sr. Beto: You are a true inspiration!!! Thanks for leading the way and giving us your valuable time to meet and give us advice during this whole process.

We would also like to thank Uncle Dick, Richard McCormack Sr. and Aunt Grace, and Aunt Anne a.k.a. Auntie Guy, for their love and support throughout our lives. Other important people that helped us are Brian Merkin, a fabulous friend and true believer in us, and Eric Laul a.k.a. Tio Eric, and Uncle D.J. Thanks also to Parivash Mirsoltani and Wendy Whiting for help with our little ones! We send special prayers out to Joanne Tawfilis, who is currently suffering from stage four cancer and yet is still a giver through and through. We love you Joanne!!! Bonny Schumaker, you are a wonderful person, thanks for flying us around the Gulf of Mexico! Bonnie Monteleone thanks for the introduction to Jean Beasley, and Jean thanks for the introduction to Dr. Supraja Dharini! This book has been a wonderful chain of events of meeting one great ocean loving person after another! Captain Philip Renaud, you were a joy to speak with, and many thanks for helping us with HRH Prince Khaled bin Sultan and for making some other introductions as well. You really deserve to be in the book too!

Thanks also to Kathy Almon, you are the best! Thank you to Michael Berns for contributing your beautiful photos, and Tricia, you are great too! Greg Butler, many many thanks to you also for the beautiful photos, and for your love and support! To Captain Kurt Lieber, our thank you list is long and the ocean is much better off because of you! Merci beaucoup to you Shannon Mann, John Binaski, Ted Parker, James Lynch, Joey Santley, Nick-I Hernandez, Jerry Schubel, Keith Addis, Greg Carr, Pete and Jen Johnson, Thom Olson, Sylvia Mizokami, Diana Dehm, Dan Stetson, Bentley Cavazzi and Shelby Meade. Beverly Factor, your photos are fantastic, thank you! Matt Littlejohn, we owe you big!

And six more incredible ocean warriors: Bob Sulnick, Terry Tamminen, Ted Danson, Wallace J. Nichols, Serge Dedina and Gary Petersen. Thanks for all you do for our oceans, what an inspiration you have all been!

In Closing . . .

We would like to thank you for taking the time to read this book,
and we would like to leave you with a few of our favorite quotes.

"Never doubt that a small group of thoughtful, committed citizens can change the world.
Indeed, it is the only thing that ever has." Margaret Mead

"You must be the change you want to see in the world." Mahatma Gandhi

"Commit random acts of kindness daily." Unknown

"Our lives begin to end the day we become silent about things that matter." Martin Luther King, Jr.

and

"Love the earth as if you will revisit it someday!" Elizabeth & Duffy Healey

Healey
Publishing,
Inc.

ENVIRONMENTAL BENEFITS STATEMENT
Healey Publishing saved the following resources by printing the pages of this book on chlorine free paper made partially from post-consumer waste.

TREES	WATER	SOLID WASTE	GREENHOUSE GASES
10	**4,389**	**266**	**911**
FULLY GROWN	GALLONS	POUNDS	POUNDS

Calculations based on research by Environmental Defense and the Paper Task Force.

Working toward a sea change